Annie Burrows has been  amusement since she first w... ...t the hang of using a pencil ...... Her love of books meant sh...... ...h literature. And her love of writing mean...... ...er take on a job where she didn't have time to jot down notes when inspiration for a new plot struck her. She still wants the heroines of her stories to wear beautiful floaty dresses, and triumph over all that life can throw at them. But when she got married she discovered that finding a hero is an essential ingredient to arriving at "happily ever after".

Don't miss these other Regency delights from Mills & Boon® Historical romance's bestselling authors!

REGENCY
Innocents

Annie Burrows

MILLS &
BOON

Mills & Boon, an imprint of Harlequin (UK) Limited,
Eton House, 18-24 Paradise Road, Richmond, Surrey TW9 1SR

REGENCY INNOCENTS © Harlequin Books S.A. 2011

The publisher acknowledges the copyright holder of the individual works
as follows:

The Earl's Untouched Bride © Annie Burrows 2008
Captain Fawley's Innocent Bride © Annie Burrows 2008

ISBN: 978 0 263 88741 9

052-1211

Harlequin (UK) policy is to use papers that are natural, renewable
and recyclable products and made from wood grown in sustainable
forests. The logging and manufacturing processes conform to the legal
environmental regulations of the country of origin.

Printed and bound by CPI Group
(UK) Ltd, Croydon, CR0 4YY

The Earl's
Untouched Bride

Chapter One

Giddings opened the door to find His Lordship standing upon the step, his face set in such rigid lines a shiver went down his spine. It was a relief when the Earl of Walton looked straight through him as he handed over his hat and coat, turning immediately towards the door to the salon. Thank God young Conningsby had taken it into his head to pass out on one of the sofas in there, instead of staggering back to his own lodgings the previous night. It was far better that it should be a man who could answer back, rather than a hapless member of staff, who became the butt of His Lordship's present mood.

But Charles Algernon Fawley, the ninth Earl of Walton, ignored Conningsby too. Striding across the room to the sideboard, he merely unstoppered a crystal decanter, pouring its entire contents into the last clean tumbler upon the tray.

Conningsby opened one eye warily, and rolled it in the Earl's direction. 'Breakfast at Tortoni's?' he grated hoarsely.

Charles tossed the glass of brandy back in one go, and reached for the decanter again.

'Don't look as though you enjoyed it much,' Conningsby observed, wincing as he struggled to sit up.

'No.' As the Earl realised the decanter was empty, his fingers curled round its neck as though he wished he could strangle it. 'And if you dare say I told you so…'

'Wouldn't dream of it, my lord. But what I will say is—'

'No. I listened to all you had to say last night, and, while I am grateful for your concern, my decision remains the same. I am not going to slink out of Paris with my tail between my legs like some whipped cur. I will not have it said that some false, painted jilt has made the slightest impact on my heart. I am staying until the lease on this apartment expires, not one hour sooner. Do you hear me?'

Conningsby raised a feeble hand to his brow. 'Only too clearly.' He eyed the empty decanter ruefully. 'And while you're proving to the whole world that you don't care a rap about your betrothed running off with some penniless artist, I don't suppose you could get your man to rustle up some coffee, could you?'

'Engraver,' snapped the Earl as he tugged viciously on the bell-pull.

Conningsby sank back into the sofa cushions, waving a languid hand to dismiss the profession of the Earl's betrothed's lover as the irrelevance it was. 'Judging by the expression on your face, the gossip-mongers have already been at work. It's not going to get any easier for you…'

'My mood now has nothing whatever to do with the fickle Mademoiselle Bergeron,' he snarled. 'It is her countrymen's actions which could almost induce me to leave this vile charnel house that calls itself a civilised city and return to London, where the most violent emotion I am likely to suffer is acute boredom.'

'But it was boredom you came to Paris to escape from!'

He let the inaccuracy of that remark pass. Staying in London, with his crippled half-brother, had simply become intolerable. Seeking refuge down at Wycke had not been a viable alternative, either. There was no respite from what ailed him there. The very opulence of the vast estate only served as a painful reminder of the injustice that had been perpetrated so that he could inherit it all.

Paris had seemed like the perfect solution. Since Bonaparte had abdicated, it had become extremely fashionable to hop across the Channel to see the sights.

Leaning one arm on the mantelpiece, he remarked, with an eloquent shudder, 'I will never complain of that particular malady again, I do assure you.'

'What is it?' Conningsby asked. 'What else has happened?'

'Another murder.'

'Du Mauriac again, I take it?' Conningsby's face was grim. The French officer was gaining a reputation for provoking hot-headed young Englishmen to duel with him, and dispatching them with a ruthless efficiency gleaned from his years of active service. And then celebrating his kill by breakfasting on broiled kidneys at Tortoni's. 'Who was it this morning? Not anybody we know, I hope?'

'On the contrary. The poor fellow he slaughtered before breakfast today was a subaltern by the name of Lennox.' At Conningsby's frown, Charles explained, 'Oh, there is no reason why you should know him. He was typical of all the others who have fallen by that butcher's sword. An obscure young man with no powerful connections.'

'Then how…?'

'He served in the same regiment as my unfortunate half-brother. He was one of those young men who constantly paraded through my London house, attempting to rouse him to some semblance of normality.' Sometimes it seemed as if an entire regiment must have marched through his hall at one time or another, to visit the poor wreck of a man who had once been a valiant soldier. Though few of them paid a second visit after encountering his blistering rejection. Captain Fawley did not want to be an object of pity.

Pity! If only he knew! If he, the ninth Earl, had been injured so badly, there would be not one well-wisher hastening to his bedside in an attempt to cheer him. On the contrary, it would be vultures who would begin to hover, eager to see who among them would gain his title, his wealth…

'At least he was a soldier, then.'

'He never stood a chance against a man of Du Mauriac's stamp, and the blackguard knew it! He sat there laughing about the fact that the boy did not look as though he needed to shave more than once a week! And sneered at his milk-white countenance as he faced him… God, the boy must have been sick with fright.'

Charles smote one fist into his palm. 'If only Lennox had asked me to be his second, I would have found a way to stop it!'

Conningsby eyed him with surprise. The only thing he had known about the Earl before his arrival in Paris was that, upon coming of age, he had caused a ripple through society by ousting his guardians from his ancestral home and subsequently severing all connections with that branch of his family. He had not known of a single man who dared claim friendship with the chillingly insular young lord. In Conningsby's capacity as a junior aide at the English embassy, he had dutifully helped him to find these lodgings in the Rue de Richelieu, and generally smoothed his entry into the social scene. It had been quite a surprise, the previous night, when the Earl had reacted as any man might on discovering the beautiful Parisienne to whom he had just proposed had run off with her lover. He had gone straight home to drown his sorrows. Though his head had proved stronger than Conningsby's.

'Couldn't have backed down, though, could he?' he ventured sympathetically. 'Wouldn't have wanted to live with an accusation of cowardice hanging round his neck.'

'Somebody should have found some way to save Lennox,' the Earl persisted. 'If only…'

He was prevented from saying anything further when the butler opened the door. 'There is a visitor for you, my lord.'

'I am not receiving,' Charles growled.

Giddings cleared his throat, and eyed Conningsby warily, before saying diffidently, 'The young person insists you would wish to see her.' He stepped forward and, in a voice intended only for his master, said, 'She says her name is Mademoiselle Bergeron.'

Charles felt as though he had been punched in the stomach.

While he struggled to draw breath, Conningsby, who had remarkably acute hearing, rose gingerly to his feet. 'She has in all probability come to beg your forgiveness…'

'She shall not have it!' Charles turned to grasp the mantelpiece with both hands, his shoulders hunched. 'I shall not take her back. If she prefers some artist to me, then she may go to him and welcome!'

'But there may have been some dreadful mistake. Let's face it, my lord, the Bergeron household last night was in such a state of turmoil, who knows what may have been going on?'

They had gone to escort Felice to a ball, where the engagement was to have been announced. They had found Monsieur Bergeron slumped in his chair, as though all the stuffing had been knocked out of him, and Madame Bergeron suffering from a noisy bout of hysterics upon the sofa. The only clear piece of information either of them had been able to glean was that she had turned off the wicked maidservant who had aided and abetted her ungrateful daughter to elope with a nobody when she could have married an English earl.

The Earl was breathing rather rapidly. 'I am not safe to see her.' He turned back to face the room, his entire face leached of colour. 'I may well attempt to strangle her.'

'Not you,' Conningsby assured him.

The Earl looked at him sharply, then straightened up. 'No,' he said, his face freezing into a chillingly aloof mask. 'Not I.' He went to one of the fireside chairs, sat down, and crossed one leg nonchalantly over the other. 'You may show Mademoiselle Bergeron in, Giddings,' he said, keeping his eyes fixed on the door.

Conningsby got the peculiar impression he had just become invisible. And, though he could tell the Earl would not care one way or another, he had no intention of becoming a witness to the impending confrontation. It was one thing helping a man to drown his sorrows in a companionable way. Hell, what man hadn't been in a similar predicament at one time or another? But becoming embroiled with some hysterical Frenchwoman, with his head in its present delicate state, was asking too much! He looked wildly round the room for some other means of escape than the door through which Mademoiselle Bergeron would shortly appear. The only other exit appeared to be through the windows.

It took but a second to vault over the sofa on which he'd spent the night and dive through the heavy velvet curtains.

'Mademoiselle Bergeron,' he heard Giddings intone, as he fumbled open the shutter bolts.

Charles experienced a spurt of satisfaction when she paused on the threshold, her gloved hand fluttering to the heavy veil draped from her bonnet.

Instead of rising to his feet, he deliberately leaned back in his chair and crossed his arms, eyeing her with unremitting coldness. She squared her shoulders, taking one faltering step forward. Then, to his complete astonishment, she broke into a run, flying across the room and landing upon her knees at his feet. Seizing his hand, she pulled it to her face, kissing it through the veil.

Impatiently, he snatched it back. Whatever she had been up to last night, he was not prepared to unbend towards her without a really good explanation. And probably not even then. To feel such strong emotions that they could reduce you to the state of mind where not even copious quantities of alcohol could anaesthetise them was something he did not care to experience again. He was just about to tell her so when she knelt back, lifting the veil from her face.

'Oh, thank you, milord! Thank you for letting me in. I was so afraid! You have no idea how unpleasant it is to walk the streets unescorted with feelings running so high…'

Charles reeled back in his seat. 'You are not…not…'

'Felice? No.' The young woman who knelt before him returned his look rather defiantly. 'I regret the deception, but I did not think you would agree to see anyone but her today. And so I led your butler to believe I was she. And, indeed, the deception was not so very great. You were expecting Mademoiselle Bergeron, and I am Mademoiselle Bergeron…'

'You are entirely the wrong Mademoiselle Bergeron,'

he snapped. How could he have mistaken the much shorter and utterly plain Heloise for her beautiful, glamorous, and entirely captivating younger sister? He couldn't blame the bonnet, though the peak of it did protrude from her face by over a foot, nor the heavy veil that was suspended from it, though it had concealed her features. He had wanted to see Felice, he acknowledged painfully. He had clung to the faint hope that there had been some dreadful mistake, and that she had come to tell him that she wanted no other man but him. And so he had seen what he wanted to see. What kind of fool did that make him?

Heloise swallowed nervously. She had been expecting a little antagonism, but the reality of facing a man whose heart had been broken was altogether more daunting than she had supposed it would be.

'No,' she persisted. 'I do not think you will find that I am when you hear what I have to propose…'

'I cannot imagine what you hope to accomplish by coming here and prostrating yourself in this manner,' he began angrily.

'Oh, no—how could you, when I have not yet explained? But you only need to listen for a very few minutes and I will tell you!' Suddenly very conscious that she was still kneeling like a supplicant at his feet, she glanced about the room.

'May I sit upon one of these so comfortable-looking chairs, my lord? This floor it is most hard, and really I do not see that you can take me at all seriously if I do not make some effort to look more rational. Only I did not know what was to become of me if you did not let me in. I was followed all the way from the Tuileries gardens by a contingent of the National Guard of the most vile manners. They refused to believe at all that I am a respectable female, merely visiting a friend of the family who also happens to be an English milord, and that they would be entirely sorry for accusing me of the things they did—for why should I not be entirely innocent? Just because you are English, that does not make me a bad person, or unpatriotic at all, even if I am not wearing either the white lily or the violet. If they are going to arrest anyone, it should have been the crowd who were brawling in the gardens, not someone who does not care at all that the emperor has gone, and that a Bourbon sits on the throne. Not but that they got the chance, because your so kind butler permitted me to enter the hall the moment he saw how things were, and even if you would not see me, he said there was a door to the back through the kitchens from which I could return home, after I had drunk a little something to restore my nerves…'

The Earl found he had no defence against the torrent of words that washed over him. She didn't even seem to pause for breath until Giddings returned, bearing a tray upon which was a bottle of Madeira and two glasses.

She'd risen to her feet, removed her bonnet and gloves, and perched on the edge of the chair facing him, twittering all the while like some little brown bird, hopping about and fluffing its plumage before finally roosting for the night.

She smiled and thanked Giddings as she took the proffered drink, but her hand shook so much that she spilled several drops down the front of her coat.

'I am sorry that you have been offered insults,' he heard himself saying as she dabbed ineffectually at the droplets soaking into the cloth. 'But you should have known better than to come to my house alone.' Far from being the haven for tourists that he had been led to believe, many Parisians were showing a marked hostility to the English. It had started, so he had been reliably informed, when trade embargoes had been lifted and cheap English goods had come on sale again. But tensions were rising between die-hard Bonapartists and supporters of the new Bourbon regime as well. If factions were now brawling in the Tuileries gardens, then Mademoiselle Bergeron might well not be safe to venture out alone. 'I will have you escorted home…'

'Oh, not yet!' she exclaimed, a look of dismay on her face. 'For you have not heard what I came to say!'

'I am waiting to hear it,' he replied dryly. 'I have been waiting since you walked through the door.'

Heloise drained the contents of her glass and set it down smartly upon the table that Giddings had placed thoughtfully at her elbow.

'Forgive me. I am so nervous, you see. I tend to babble when I am nervous. Well, I was only nervous when I set out. But then, after the incident in the Tuileries, I became quite scared, and then—'

'Mademoiselle Bergeron!' He slapped the arm of his chair with decided irritation. 'Will you please come to the point?'

'Oh.' She gulped, her face growing hot. It was not at all easy to come to the point with a man as icily furious as the Earl of Walton. In fact, if she wasn't quite so desperate, she would wish she hadn't come here at all. Looking into those chips of ice that he had for eyes, and feeling their contempt for her chilling her to the marrow, Heloise felt what little courage she had left ebb away. Sitting on a chair instead of staying prostrate at his feet had not redressed their positions at all. She still had to look up to meet his forbidding features, for the Earl was quite a tall man. And she had nothing with which to combat his hostility but strength of will. Not beauty, or grace, or cleverness. She had the misfortune to have taken after her mother in looks. While Felice had inherited her father's even features and long-limbed grace, she had got the Corbiere nose, diminutive size, and nondescript colouring. Her only weapon was an idea. But what an idea! If he would only hear her out, it would solve all their difficulties at a stroke!

'It is quite simple, after all,' she declared. 'It is that I think you should marry me instead of Felice.'

She cocked her head to one side as she waited for his response, reminding him of a street sparrow begging for crumbs. Before he could gather his wits, she had taken another breath and set off again.

'I know you must think that this is preposterous just at first. But only think of the advantages!'

'Advantages for whom?' he sneered. He had never thought of little Heloise as a scheming gold-digger before. But then nor had he thought her capable of such fluent speech. Whenever she had played chaperon for himself and her sister she had been so quiet he had tended to forget she was there at all. He had been quite unguarded, he now recalled with mounting irritation, assuming, after a few half-hearted attempts to draw her out, that she could not speak English very well.

Though the look he sent her was one that had frozen the blood in the veins of full-grown men, Heloise was determined to have her say.

'Why, for you, of course! Unless… Your engagement to Felice has not been announced in England yet, has it? She told me you had not sent any notice to the London papers. And of course in Paris, though everyone thinks they know that you wished to marry Felice, you have only to say, when they see me on your arm instead of my sister,

"You will find you are mistaken," in that tone you use for giving an encroaching person a set-down, if anyone should dare to question you, and that will be that!'

'But why, pray, should I wish to say any such thing?'

'So that nobody will know she broke your heart, of course!' Her words, coupled with her look of genuine sympathy, touched a place buried so deep inside him that for years he had been denying its very existence.

'I know how her actions must have bruised your pride, too,' she ploughed on, astonishing him with the accuracy of her observations. Even Conningsby claimed he had not guessed how deep his feelings ran until the night before, when, in his cups, he'd poured out the whole sorry tale. But this girl, of whom he had never taken much notice, had read him like an open book.

'But this way nobody will ever guess! You are so good at keeping your face frozen, so that nobody can tell what you are truly feeling. You can easily convince everyone that it was my family that wished for the match, and that they put Felice forward, but all the time it was me in whom you were interested, for I am the eldest, or—oh, I am sure you can come up with some convincing reason. For of course they would not believe that you could truly be attracted to me. I know that well! And if any rumours about a Mademoiselle Bergeron have reached as far as London—well, I have already shown you how one Mademoiselle Bergeron may enter a room as another. Nobody else need know it was quite another Mademoiselle Bergeron you had set your sights on. If you marry me, you may walk round Paris with your head held high, and return home with your pride intact!'

'You are talking nonsense. Arrant nonsense!' He sprang from his chair, and paced moodily towards the sideboard. He had ridden out malicious gossip before. He could do so again. 'The connection with your family is severed,' he snapped, grasping the decanter, then slamming it back onto the tray on discovering it was still empty. He was not going to be driven from Paris because a few tattle-mongers had nothing better to talk about than a failed love affair. Nor would anything induce him to betray his hurt by so much as a flicker of an eyelid. 'I see no need to restore it!'

He turned to see her little face crumple. Her shoulders sagged. He braced himself for a further outpouring as he saw her eyes fill with tears. But she surprised him yet again. Rising to her feet with shaky dignity, she said, 'Then I apologise for intruding on you this morning. I will go now.'

She had reached the door and was fumbling her hands into her gloves when he cried out, 'Wait!' His quarrel was not with her. She had never given him a moment's trouble during the entire time he had been courting Felice. She had never voiced any protest, no matter where they had dragged her, though at times he had been able to tell she had been uncomfortable. All she had done on those occasions was withdraw into the shadows, as though she wished to efface herself from the scene completely. That was more her nature, he realised with a flash of insight. To have come here this morning and voiced that ridiculous proposition must have been the hardest thing for her to do. It had not been only the brush with the National Guard that had made her shake with fright.

He had no right to vent his anger on her. Besides, to let her out alone and unprotected onto the streets was not the act of a gentleman.

'*Mademoiselle,*' he said stiffly, 'I told you I would ensure you returned to your house safely. Please, won't you sit down again, while I get Giddings to summon a cabriolet?'

'Thank you,' she sighed, leaning back against the door. 'It was not at all pleasant getting here. I had no idea! To think I was glad Maman had turned off Joanne, so that it was an easy matter for me to sneak out without anyone noticing.' She shook her head ruefully. 'It is true what Papa says. I am a complete imbecile. When I had to pass that crowd in the Tuileries, I knew how stupid I had been. Then to walk right up to the door of an Englishman, on my own, as though I was a woman of no virtue…'

Seeing her tense white face, Charles felt impelled to check the direction of her thoughts.

'Please, sit down on the sofa while you are waiting.'

She did so, noting with a start that her bonnet still lay amongst its cushions. As she picked it up, turning it over in her hands as though it was an object she had never seen before, he continued, 'Whatever prompted you to take such drastic steps to come to my house, *mademoiselle*? I cannot believe you are so concerned about my wounded pride, or my—' He checked himself before alluding to his allegedly broken heart.

She turned crimson, suddenly becoming very busy untangling the ribbons of her bonnet. Her discomfort brought a sudden suspicion leaping to his mind.

'Never tell me you are in love with me!' The notion that this plain young woman had been harbouring a secret passion for him, while he had been making love to her sister under her very nose, gave him a very uncomfortable feeling. 'I had no idea! I did not think you even liked me!'

Her head flew up, an arrested expression on her face when she detected the tiniest grain of sympathy in the tone of his voice. 'Would you marry me, then, if I said I loved you?' she breathed, her eyes filled with hope. But as he returned her gaze steadily she began to look uncomfortable. Worrying at her lower lip with her teeth, she hung her head.

'It is no good,' she sighed. 'I cannot tell you a lie.' She sank back against the cushions, her whole attitude one of despondency. 'I'm not clever enough to make you believe it. And apart from that,' she continued, as Charles settled into his favourite fireside chair with a profound feeling of relief, 'I confess I did dislike you when you first came calling on Felice and she encouraged your attentions. Even though Maman said I was letting the family down by making my disapproval plain, and Felice insisted I was being a baby. But I couldn't help feeling as I did.' She frowned. 'Although, really, it was not you at all I did not like, so much as the idea of you. You see?'

He had just opened his mouth to reply that he did not see at all, when she continued, 'and then, when I got to know you better, and saw how much you truly felt for Felice, even though you hid it so well, I couldn't dislike you at all. Indeed, I felt most sorry for you, because I knew she never cared for you in the least.'

When she saw a flash of surprise flicker across his face, she explained.

'Well, how could she, when she had been in love with Jean-Claude for ever? Even though Maman and Papa had forbidden the match, because he has no money at all. I really hated the way you dazzled them all with your wealth and elegance and seemed to make Felice forget Jean-Claude.' Her face brightened perceptibly. 'But of course you hadn't at all. She merely used your visits as a smoke-screen to fool Maman into thinking she was obeying her orders, which gave Jean-Claude time to make plans for their escape. Which is all as it should be.' She sighed dreamily. 'She was not false to her true love.' She sat up straight suddenly, looking at him with an expression of chagrin. 'Though she was very cruel to you when you did not deserve it at all. Even if you are an Englishman.'

Charles found himself suddenly conscious of a desire to laugh. 'So, you wish to marry me to make up for your sister's cruel treatment of me? In fact because you feel sorry for me—is that it?'

She looked at him hopefully for a few seconds, before once more lowering her eyes and shaking her head.

'No, it is not that. Not only that. Although I should like to make things right for you. Of course I should. Because of my sister you have suffered a grievous hurt. I know you can never feel for me what you felt for her, but at least your pride could be restored by keeping the nature of her betrayal a secret. It is not too late. If you acted today, if you made Papa give his consent today, we could attend a function together this evening and stop the gossip before it starts.' She looked up at him with eyes blazing with intensity. 'Together, we could sort out the mess she has left behind. For it is truly terrible at home.' She shook her head mournfully. 'Maman has taken to her bed. Papa is threatening to shoot himself, because now there is not to be the connection with you he can see no other way out.' She twined one of the bonnet ribbons round her index finger as she looked at him imploringly. 'You would only have to stroll in and say, "Never mind about Felice. I will take the other one," in that off-hand way you have, as though you don't care about anything at all, and he would grovel at your feet in gratitude. Then nobody would suspect she broke your heart! Even if they really believe you wanted to marry her, when they hear of the insouciance with which you took me they will have to admit they were mistaken!'

'I see,' he said slowly. 'You wish to save your family

from some sort of disgrace which my marrying Felice would have averted. That is admirable, but—'

The look of guilt on her face stopped him in his tracks. He could see yet another denial rising to her lips.

'Not family honour?' he ventured.

She shook her head mournfully. 'No.' Her voice was barely more than a whisper. 'All I have told you is part of it. All those good things would result if only you would marry me, and I will be glad to achieve all of them, but—' She hung her head, burying her hands completely in the by now rather mangled bonnet. 'My prime reason is a completely selfish one. You see, if only I can persuade you to marry me, then Papa would be so relieved that you are still to pull him out of the suds that he will forget all about compelling me to marry the man he has chosen for me.'

'In short,' said Charles, 'I am easier to swallow than this other fellow?'

'Yes—much!' she cried, looking up at him with pleading eyes. 'You cannot imagine how much I hate him. If you will only say yes, I will be such a good wife! I shall not be in the least trouble to you, I promise! I will live in a cottage in the country and keep hens, and you need never even see me if you don't want. I shan't interfere with you, or stop you from enjoying yourself however you wish. I will never complain—no, not even if you beat me!' she declared dramatically, her eyes growing luminous with unshed tears.

'Why,' said Charles, somewhat taken aback by her vehemence, 'would you suspect me of wishing to beat you?'

'Because I am such a tiresome creature!'

If it hadn't been for the fact Heloise was clearly on the verge of tears, Charles would have found it hard not to laugh.

'Papa is always saying so. So did Gaspard.'

'Gaspard?'

'My brother. He said any man fool enough to marry me would soon be driven to beat me. But I feel sure…' her lower lip quivered ominously '…that you would only beat me when I *really* deserved it. You are not a cruel man. You are not cold, either, in spite of what they all say about you. You are a good person underneath your haughty manner. I know because I have watched you. I have had much opportunity, because you never took the least notice of me when Felice was in the same room. And I would not be afraid to go away with you, because you would not ever wish to beat a woman for sport like he would…'

'Come now,' Charles remonstrated, as the first tears began to trickle down her heated cheeks. 'I cannot believe your papa would force you to marry a man who would be as cruel as that…'

'Oh, but you English know nothing!' She leapt to her feet. 'He would very easily sacrifice me to such a man for the sake of preserving the rest of the family!' She was quivering from head to toe with quite another emotion than fear now. He could see that. Indignation had brought a decidedly militant gleam to her eye. She was incapable of standing still. Taking brisk little paces between the sofa and the fireplace, she did not notice that she was systematically trampling the bonnet, which had fallen to the floor when she had leapt to her feet. It occurred to him, when she stepped on it for the third time, that her sister would never have been so careless of her apparel. Not that she would have been seen dead in such an unflattering item in the first place.

'And, besides being so cruel, he is quite old!' She shuddered.

'I am thirty-five, you know,' he pointed out.

She paused mid-stride, running her eyes over him assessingly. The Earl's light blue eyes twinkled with amusement from a face that was devoid of lines of care. Elegant clothes covered a healthily muscled physique. His tawny hair was a little disarrayed this morning, to be sure, but it was neither receding nor showing any hint of grey. 'I did not know you were as old as that,' she eventually admitted with candour.

Once again, Charles was hard put to it not to burst out laughing at the absurdity of this little creature who had invaded the darkness of his lair like some cheeky little song bird hopping about between a lion's paws, pecking for crumbs, confident she was too insignificant to rate the energy required to swat her.

'Come, child, admit it. You are too young to marry anyone!'

'Well, yes!' she readily admitted. 'But Felice was younger, and you still wanted to marry her. And in time, of course, I will grow older. And by then you might have got used to me. You might even be able to teach me how to behave better!' she said brightly. Then, just as quickly, her face fell. 'Although I very much doubt it.'

She subsided into the chair opposite his own, leaning her elbows on her knees. 'I suppose I always knew I could not be any sort of wife to you.' She gazed up at him mournfully. 'But I know I would have been better off with you. For even if you are as old as you say, you don't…' Her forehead wrinkled, as though it was hard for her to find the words she wanted. 'You don't smell like him.'

Finding it increasingly hard to keep his face straight, he said, 'Perhaps you could encourage your suitor to bathe…'

Her eyes snapped with anger. Taking a deep breath, she flung at him, 'Oh, it is easy for you to laugh at me. You think I am a foolish little woman of no consequence. But this is no laughing matter to me. Whenever he comes close I want to run to a window and open it and breathe clean air. It is like when you go into a room that has been shut up too long, and you know something has decayed in it. And before you make the joke about bathing again, I must tell you that it is in my head that I smell this feeling. In my heart!' She smote her breast. 'He is steeped in so much blood!'

However absurdly she was behaving, however quaint her way of expressing herself, there was no doubt that she really felt repelled by the man her father thought she ought to marry. It was a shame that such a sensitive little creature should be forced into a marriage that was so distasteful to her. Though he could never contemplate marrying her himself, he did feel a pang of sympathy. And, in that spirit, he asked, 'Do I take it this man is a soldier, then?'

'A hero of France,' she replied gloomily. 'It is an honour for our family that such a man should wish for an alliance. An astonishment to my papa that any man should really want to take on a little mouse like me. You wonder how I came to his notice, perhaps?' When Charles nodded, humouring her whilst privately wondering why on earth it was taking Giddings so long to procure a cab to send her home in, she went on, 'He commanded Gaspard's regiment in Spain. He was…' An expression of anguish crossed her face. 'I was not supposed to hear. But people sometimes do talk when I am there, assuming that I am not paying attention—for I very often don't, you know. My brother sometimes talked about the Spanish campaign. The things his officers commanded him to do! Such barbarity!' She shuddered. 'I am not so stupid that I would willingly surrender to a man who has treated other women and children like cattle in a butcher's shop. And forced decent Frenchmen to descend to his level. And how is it,' she continued, her fists clenching, 'that while my brother died of hunger outside what you call the lines of Torres Vedras, Du Mauriac came home looking as fit as a flea?'

'Du Mauriac?' Charles echoed. 'The man your father wishes you to marry is Du Mauriac?'

Heloise nodded. 'As commander of Gaspard's regiment, he was often in our home when my brother was still alive. He used to insist it was I who sat beside him. From my hand that he wished to be served.' She shuddered. 'Then, after Gaspard died, he kept right on visiting. Papa says I am stupid to persist in refusing his proposals. He says I should feel honoured that a man so distinguished persists in courting me when I have not even beauty to recommend me. But he does not see that it is mainly my reluctance that Du Mauriac likes. He revels in the knowledge that, though he repels me, my parents will somehow contrive to force me to surrender to him!'

Heloise ground to a halt, her revulsion at the prospect of what marriage to Du Mauriac would entail finally overwhelming her. Bowing forward, she buried her face in her hands until she had herself under control. And then, alerted by the frozen silence which filled the room, she looked up at the Earl of Walton. Up until that moment she would have said he had been experiencing little more than mild amusement at her expense. But now his eyes had returned to that glacial state which had so intimidated her when first she had walked into the room. Except…now his anger was not directed at her. Indeed, it was as if he had frozen her out of his consciousness altogether.

'Go home, *mademoiselle*,' he said brusquely, rising to his feet and tugging at the bell pull. 'This interview is at an end.'

He meant it this time. With a sinking heart, Heloise turned and stumbled to the door. She had offended him somehow, by being so open about her feelings of revulsion for the man her father had decided she should marry. She had staked everything on being honest with the Earl of Walton.

But she had lost.

Chapter Two

It came as something of a shock, once the door had closed on Heloise's dejected little figure, when Conningsby stepped in over the windowsill.

'My God,' the man blustered. 'If I had known this room overlooked the street, and I was to have spent the entire interview wedged onto a balcony when I fully expected to be able to escape through your gardens...'

'And the curtains were no impediment to your hearing every single word, I shouldn't wonder?' The Earl sighed. 'Dare I hope you will respect the confidentiality of that conversation?'

'I work for the diplomatic service!' Conningsby bristled. 'Besides which, no man of sense would wish to repeat one word of that absurd woman's proposition!'

Although Charles himself thought Heloise absurd, for some reason he did not like hearing anyone else voice that opinion. 'I think it was remarkably brave of her to come here to try to save her family from ruin.'

'Yes, my lord. If you say so,' the other man conceded dubiously.

'I do say so,' said the Earl. 'I will not have any man disparage my fiancée.'

'You aren't really going to accept that outrageous proposal?' Conningsby gasped.

Charles studied the tips of his fingers intently.

'You cannot deny that her solution to my…uh…predicament, will certainly afford me a great deal of solace.'

'Well,' said Conningsby hesitantly, loath to offend a man of Lord Walton's reputation, 'I suppose she is quite a captivating little thing, in her way. Jolly amusing. She certainly has a gift for mimicry that almost had me giving myself away! Had to stuff a handkerchief in my mouth to choke down the laughter when she aped your voice!'

The Earl stared at him. Captivating? Until this morning he had barely looked at her. Like a little wren, she hid in the background as much as she could. And when he had looked he had seen nothing to recommend her. She had a beak of a nose, set above lips that were too thin for their width, and a sharp little chin. Her hair was a mid-brown, without a hint of a curl to render it interesting. Her eyes, though…

Before this morning she had kept them demurely lowered whenever he glanced in her direction. But today he had seen a vibrancy burning in their dark depths that had tugged a grudging response from him.

'What she may or may not be is largely irrelevant,' he said coldly. 'What just might prompt me to take her to wife is that in so doing I shall put Du Mauriac's nose out of joint.'

Conningsby laughed nervously. 'Surely you can't wish to marry a woman just so that some other fellow cannot have her?'

The Earl returned his look with a coldness of purpose that chilled him. 'She does not expect me to like her very much. You heard what she said. She will not even be surprised if I come to detest her so heartily that I beat her. All she wants is the opportunity to escape from an intolerable position. Don't you think I should oblige her?'

'Well, I…' Conningsby ran his finger round his collar, his face growing red.

'Come, now, you cannot expect me to stand by and permit her father to marry her off to that butcher, can you? She does not deserve such a fate.'

No, Conningsby thought, she does not. But then, would marriage to a man who only wanted revenge on her former suitor, a man without an ounce of fondness for her, be any less painful to her in the long run?

Heloise gripped her charcoal and bent her head over her sketchpad, blotting out the noise of her mother's sobs as she focussed on her drawing. She had achieved nothing. Nothing. She had braved the streets, and the insults of those soldiers, then endured the Earl's mockery, for nothing. Oh, why, she thought resentfully, had she ever thought she might be able to influence the intractable Earl one way or another? And how could she ever have felt sorry for him? Her fingers worked furiously, making angry slashes across the page. He had coaxed her most secret thoughts from her, let her hope he was feeling some shred of sympathy, and then spurned her. The only good thing about this morning's excursion was that nobody had noticed she had taken it, she reflected, finding some satisfaction in creating a most unflattering caricature of the Earl of Walton in the guise of a sleekly cruel tabby cat. She could not have borne it if anyone had found out where she had been. It had been bad enough when her *maman* had laid the blame for Felice's elopement at her door—as though she had ever had the least influence with her headstrong and pampered little sister!

With a few deft strokes Heloise added a timorous little mouse below the grinning mouth of the tabby cat, then set to work fashioning a pair of large paws. Folly—sheer folly! To walk into that man's lair and prostrate herself as she had!

There was a knock on the front door.

Madame Bergeron blew her nose before wailing, 'We are not receiving visitors today. I cannot endure any more. They will all come, you mark my words, to mock at us...'

Heloise rose to her feet to relay the information to their manservant before he had a chance to open the door. Since her seat was by the window, where she could get the most light for her sketching, she had a clear view of their front step.

'It is the Earl!' she gasped, her charcoal slipping from her suddenly nerveless fingers.

'It cannot be!' Her papa sprang from the chair in which he had been slumped, his head in his hands. 'What can he want with us, now?' he muttered darkly, peering through the window. 'I might have known a man of his station would not sit back and take an insult such as Felice has dealt him. He will sue us for breach of promise at the very least,' he prophesied, as Heloise sank to the floor to retrieve her pencil. 'Well, I will shoot myself first, and that will show him!' he cried wildly, while she regained her seat, bending her head over her sketchbook as much to counteract a sudden wave of faintness as to hide the hopeful expression she was sure must be showing on her face.

'*Noo!*' From the sofa, her *maman* began to weep again. 'You cannot abandon me now! How can you threaten to leave me after all we have been through?'

Instantly contrite, Monsieur Bergeron flung himself to his knees beside the sofa, seizing his wife's hand and pressing it to his lips. 'Forgive me, my precious.'

Heloise admired her parents for being so devoted to each other, but sometimes she wished they were not quite so demonstrative. Or that they didn't assume, because she had her sketchpad open, that they could behave as though she was not there.

'You know I will always worship you, my angel.' He slobbered over her hand, before clasping her briefly to his bosom. 'You are much too good for me.'

Now, that was something Heloise had long disputed. It was true that her mother should have been far beyond her father's matrimonial aspirations, since she was a younger daughter of the *seigneur* in whose district he had been a lowly but ambitious clerk. And that it might have been reprehensible of him to induce an aristocrat to elope with him. But it turned out to have been the most sensible thing her mother had ever done. Marriage to him had saved her from the fate many others of her class had suffered.

The affecting scene was cut short when the manservant announced the Earl of Walton. Raising himself tragically to his full height, Monsieur Bergeron declared, 'To spare you pain, my angel, I will receive him in my study alone.'

But before he had even reached the door Charles himself strolled in, his gloves clasped negligently in one hand. Bowing punctiliously to Madame Bergeron, who was struggling to rise from a mound of crushed cushions, he drawled, 'Good morning, *madame, monsieur.*'

Blocking his pathway further into the room, Monsieur Bergeron replied, with a somewhat martyred air, 'I suppose you wish to speak with me, my lord? Shall we retire to my study and leave the ladies in peace?'

Charles raised one eyebrow, as though astonished by this suggestion. 'Why, if you wish, of course I will wait with you while *mademoiselle* makes herself ready. Or had you forgot that I had arranged to take your daughter out driving this morning? *Mademoiselle*—' he addressed Heloise directly, his expression bland '—I hope it will not take you long to dress appropriately? I do not like to keep my horses standing.'

Until their eyes met she had hardly dared to let herself hope. But now she was sure. He was going to go through with it!

'B…but it was Felice,' Monsieur Bergeron blustered. 'You had arranged to take Felice out driving. M…my lord, she is not here! I was sure you were aware that last night she…'

'I am engaged to take your daughter out driving this morning,' he continued implacably, 'and take your daughter I shall. I see no reason to alter my schedule for the day. In the absence of Felice, Heloise must bear me company.'

For a moment the room pulsed with silence, while everyone seemed to be holding their breath.

Then Madame Bergeron sprang from the sofa, darted across the room, and seized Heloise by the wrist. 'She will not keep you waiting above ten minutes, my lord.' Then, to her husband, 'What are you thinking of, not offering his lordship a seat? And wine—he must have a glass of wine while he is waiting!' She pushed Heloise through the door, then paused to specify, 'The Chambertin!'

While Monsieur Bergeron stood gaping at him, Charles strolled over to the table at which Heloise had been sitting and began to idly flick through her sketchbook. It seemed to contain nothing but pictures of animals. Quite strange-looking animals, some of them, in most unrealistic poses. Though one, of a bird in a cage, caught his attention. The bedraggled specimen

was chained to its perch. He could feel its misery
flowing off the page. He was just wondering what
species of bird it was supposed to represent, when something about the tilt of its head, the anguish burning in its
black eyes, put him forcibly in mind of Heloise, as she
had appeared earlier that day. His eyes followed the
chain that bound the miserable-looking creature to its
perch, and saw that it culminated in what looked like a
golden wedding ring.

His blood running cold, he flicked back a page, to a
scene he had first supposed represented a fanciful scene
from a circus. He could now perceive that the creature that
was just recognisable as a lion, lying on its back with a
besotted grin on its face, was meant to represent himself.
The woman who was standing with her foot upon his chest,
smiling with smug cruelty, was definitely Felice. He
snapped the book shut and turned on Monsieur Bergeron.

'I trust you have not made the nature of my interest in
your elder daughter public?'

'Alas, my lord,' he shrugged, spreading his hands wide,
'but I did give assurances in certain quarters that a match
was imminent.'

'To your creditors, no doubt?'

'Debt? Pah—it is nothing!' Monsieur Bergeron spat. 'A
man may recover from debt!'

When Charles raised one disbelieving eyebrow, he explained, 'You English, you do not understand how one
must live in France. When power changes hands, those who
support the fallen regime must always suffer from the next.
To survive, a man must court friends in all camps. He must
be sensitive to what is in the wind, and know the precise
moment to jump...'

In short the man was, like Talleyrand, '*un homme girou-*

ette', who was prepared, like a weather vane, to swing in whichever direction the wind blew.

Somewhat red in the face, Monsieur Bergeron sank onto the sofa which his wife had recently vacated.

'So,' Charles said slowly, 'promoting an alliance with an English noble, at a time when many Parisians are openly declaring hostility to the English, was an attempt to…?' He quirked an inquisitive eyebrow at the man, encouraging him to explain.

'To get one of my daughters safely out of the country! The days are coming,' he said, pulling a handkerchief from his pocket and mopping at his brow, 'when any man or woman might go to the guillotine for the most paltry excuse. I can feel it in the air. Say what you like about Bonaparte, but during the last few years I managed to hold down a responsible government post and make steady advancements, entirely through hard work and capability. But now the Bourbons are back in power, clearly bent on taking revenge on all who have opposed them, that will count for nothing!' he finished resentfully.

Charles eyed him thoughtfully. Monsieur Bergeron feared he was teetering on the verge of ruin. So he had spread his safety net wide. He had encouraged his pretty daughter to entrap an English earl, who would provide a safe bolthole in a foreign land should things become too hot for his family in France. And he had encouraged the attentions of his plain daughter's only suitor though he was an ardent Bonapartist. Every day Du Mauriac openly drank the health of his exiled emperor in cafés such as the Tabagie de la Comete, with other ex-officers of the Grand Armée. Much as he disliked the man, there was no denying he would make both a powerful ally and a dangerous enemy.

Finding himself somewhat less out of charity with his prospective father-in-law, Charles settled himself in a chair and stretched his legs out, crossing them at the ankles.

'Let me put a proposition to you.'

Monsieur Bergeron eyed him warily.

'I have my own reasons for not wanting my…er…disappointment to be made public. I wish, in fact, to carry on as though nothing untoward has occurred.'

'But…Felice has run off. That is not news we can keep quiet indefinitely. It may take some time to find her, if you insist you still wish to marry her…'

He made an impatient gesture with his hand. 'I am finished with Felice. But nobody knows for certain that it was her I intended to marry. Do they?'

'Well, no…'

'Then the sooner I am seen about in public with your other daughter, the sooner we can begin to persuade people that they were entirely mistaken to suppose it was Felice to whom I became engaged.'

'What are you suggesting?'

'Isn't it obvious? Since Felice is out of the picture, I will marry your other daughter instead.'

'But—but…'

'You can have no objections, surely? She is not contracted to anyone else, is she?' He held his breath while he watched the cogs whirring in Monsieur Bergeron's head. Heloise had spoken of proposals to which she had not agreed, but if her father and Du Mauriac had drawn up any form of legal agreement things might be about to get complicated.

'No, my lord,' Monsieur Bergeron said, having clearly made up his mind to ditch the potential alliance with the man whose star was in the descendant. 'She is free to marry you. Only…' He slumped back against the cushions, closing his eyes and shaking his head. 'It will not be a simple matter of substituting one girl for the other. Heloise has so little sense. What if she won't agree? Ah!' he moaned, crumpling the handkerchief in his fist. 'That our fortunes should all rest in the hands of such a little fool!'

Charles found himself rather indignant on Heloise's behalf. It seemed to him that it was Felice who had plunged her family into this mess, but not a word was being said against her. And, far from being a fool, Heloise had been the one to come up with this coldly rational plan which would wipe out, at a stroke, all the unpleasantness her sister had created.

'I beg your pardon?' he said coldly.

'Of course our family owes it to you to redress the insult my younger daughter has offered you. But I pray you won't be offended if I cannot make Heloise see reason.'

His brief feelings of charity towards the older man evaporated. He had no compunction about forcing his daughter into any marriage, no matter how distasteful it might be to her, so long as he stood to gain by it. If Charles hadn't already known that Heloise was all for it, he would have turned away at that point and left the entire Bergeron family to sink in their own mire.

'I am sure she will do the right thing,' he said, in as even a tone as he could muster.

'That's because you don't know her,' her father bit out glumly. 'There is no telling what the silly creature will take it into her head to do. Or to say. She is nowhere near as clever as her sister.'

Charles eyed Monsieur Bergeron coldly. He had encouraged Felice to ensnare him when she'd never had the slightest intention of marrying him. Heloise, for being, as she put it, too stupid to tell a lie, was castigated as being useless. On the whole, he found he preferred Heloise's brand of stupidity to Felice's sort of cleverness.

'A man does not look for a great deal of intellect in his wife,' he bit out. 'I am sure we shall deal well together. Ah,' he said, as the door opened and Heloise and her mother returned to the room. 'Here she is now, and looking quite charming.' Walking to her side, he bowed over her hand.

'Pray, don't overdo it,' she whispered, her eyes sparking with alarm.

Tucking her hand under his arm, and patting her gloved hand reassuringly, he smiled at her mother, who had also hastily donned her coat and bonnet. 'I am sure you will agree there is no need for you to act as chaperon, *madame*, since the news of my engagement to Heloise will soon be common knowledge.'

Her jaw dropped open as she reeled back. 'You wish to marry Heloise?' she gasped.

'Why not?' he retorted. 'I have already settled the matter with your papa,' he turned to inform Heloise. 'He thinks your family should make recompense to me for the insult your younger sister offered me. Since I have rather got used to the idea of returning to England with a bride, it might as well be you. And, before you raise any foolish objections, let me inform you that I expect your full co-operation.' He bent a rather stern eye on her. 'I have no wish to appear as an object for vulgar gossip. I do not want anyone to know your sister jilted me. You will explain, if you please,' he said, turning once more to Madame Bergeron, 'that naturally you are upset by Felice's running off with a totally unsuitable man, but that it has no bearing on the relationship which already existed between me and her older, better-behaved sister.'

The woman plumped down onto the sofa next to her husband.

'People have grown used to seeing the three of us about together over the last few weeks. And while Felice was always the more flamboyant of the two, if we but stick to our story we can easily persuade people that it was Heloise all along who was the object of my interest. She is much better suited to becoming my countess, since her manner is modest and discreet. What man of breeding would want to take an outrageous flirt to wife?'

'Heloise,' her father now put in, rather sternly. 'I hope you are paying attention to what his lordship is saying. As a dutiful daughter you must do all you can to protect the honour of this family. I expect you to submit to me in this, young woman! You will keep your mouth shut about how far things went between Felice and his lordship, and you *will* marry him.'

Meekly bowing her head, Heloise replied, 'Whatever you say, Papa.'

Not wishing to linger any longer with that pair of opportunists, Charles ushered Heloise to the door.

She stayed silent, her head bowed to conceal her jubilant expression from her parents, until they were outside. Her eyes ran over the smart two-wheeled carrick Charles had procured for the occasion with approval. She had recognised the vehicle the moment it had drawn up outside. He had borrowed it once before, from another English noble who had brought it over to Paris for the express purpose of cutting a dash in the Bois de Boulogne. When Charles had taken Felice out in it, he had hired two liveried and mounted servants to ride behind, ensuring that everyone knew he was *someone*, even if he had picked up his passenger from a modest little dwelling on the Quai Voltaire.

Borrowing this conveyance, which he could drive himself, giving them the requisite privacy to plan their strategy whilst contriving to look as though they were merely being fashionable, was a stroke of genius.

He tossed a coin to the street urchin who was holding the horses' heads, and handed her up onto the narrow bench seat.

'You were magnificent!' she breathed, turning to him with unfeigned admiration as he urged the perfectly matched pair of bays out into the light traffic. 'Oh, if only we were not driving down a public street I could kiss you. I really could!'

'We are already attracting enough notice, *mademoiselle*, by driving about without a chaperon of any sort, without the necessity of giving way to vulgar displays of emotion.'

'Oh!' Heloise turned to face front, her back ramrod-straight, her face glowing red with chagrin. How could she have presumed to speak in such a familiar fashion? Never mind harbour such an inappropriate impulse?

'You may place one hand upon my sleeve, if you must.'

His clipped tones indicated that this was quite a concession on his part. Gingerly, she laid her hand upon his forearm.

'I have decided upon the tale we shall tell,' he said, 'and it is this. Our alliance has withstood the scandal of Felice's elopement with an unsuitable young man. I am not ashamed to continue my connection with your family. After all, your mother came from an ancient and noble house. That your sister has lamentably been infected by revolutionary tendencies and run off with a nobody has nothing to do with us.'

The feeling of happiness which his put-down had momentarily quelled swelled up all over again. She had known that if anyone could rescue her it was the Earl of Walton! He had grasped the importance of acting swiftly, then taken her rather vague plan and furnished it with convincing detail. She had always suspected he was quite intelligent, even though he had been prone to utter the most specious drivel to Felice. What was more, he would never let her down by making a slip in a moment of carelessness, like some men might. He was always fully in control of himself, regarding men who got drunk and made an exhibition of themselves in public with disdain.

Oh, yes, he was the perfect man to carry her scheme through successfully!

'I was planning to announce my engagement officially at Lady Dalrymple Hamilton's ball last evening.'

'I know,' she replied. It had been his decision to make that announcement which had finally driven Felice to take off so precipitously. She had hoped to keep him dangling for another week at the very least. Heloise worried at her lower lip. She hoped Felice had managed to reach Jean-Claude safely. Although he had gone ahead to Switzerland, and secured a job with a printing firm, he had planned to return and escort Felice across France personally.

'No need to look so crestfallen. I do not expect you to shine in society as your sister did. I will steer you through the social shoals.'

'It is not that!' she replied indignantly. She might not 'shine', as he put it, but she had mingled freely with some of the highest in the land. Why, she had once even been introduced to Wellington! Though, she admitted to herself with chagrin, he had looked right through her.

He glanced down at the rim of her bonnet, which was all he could see of her now that she had turned her head away. How shy she was. How hard she would find it to take her place in society! Well, he would do all he could to smooth her passage. It was her idea, after all, that was going to enable him to salvage his pride. He would never have thought of something so outrageous. He owed her for that. And to start with he was going to have to smarten her up. He was not going to expose her to ridicule for her lack of dress sense.

'Deuce take it,' he swore. 'I'm going to have to buy you some more flattering headgear. That bonnet is the ugliest thing I think I've ever seen.' He leant a little closer. 'Is it the same unfortunate article you trampled so ruthlessly in my drawing room this morning?'

She looked up at him then, suddenly cripplingly conscious of how far short of the Earl's standard she fell. 'It is practical,' she protested. 'It can withstand any amount of abuse and still look—'

'Disreputable,' he finished for her. 'And that reminds me. While we are shopping, I shall have to get you a ring.'

His eyes narrowed as a look of guilt flickered across her mobile little features. No wonder she did not attempt to tell lies, he reflected. Her face was so expressive every thought was written clearly there.

'What is it?' he sighed.

'First, I have to tell you that I do not wish you at all to take me shopping!' she declared defiantly.

'You are unique amongst your sex, then,' he replied dryly. 'And what is second?'

'And second,' she gulped, the expression of guilt returning in force, 'is that you do not need to buy me a ring.' Holding up her hand to prevent his retort, she hastened to explain, 'I already have a ring.'

He stiffened. 'Our engagement may not have been my idea, *mademoiselle*, but it is my place to provide the ring.'

'But you already have. That is—' She blushed. 'The ring I have is the one you gave Felice. The very one that made her run away. She gave it to me.'

'The ring…made her run away?' He had chosen it with such care. The great emerald that gleamed in its cluster of diamonds was the exact shade of Felice's bewitching eyes. He had thought he was past being hurt, but the thought that she found his taste so deficient she had run to another man…

'Yes, for until that moment it had not been at all real to her,' he heard Heloise say. 'She thought you were merely amusing yourself with a little flirtation. Though I warned her over and over again, she never believed that she could hurt you. She said that nobody could touch your heart— if you had one, which she did not believe—and so you made the perfect smokescreen.'

'Is that estimation of my character supposed to be making me feel better?' he growled.

'Perhaps not. But at least it may help you to forgive her. It was not until you gave her that ring that she understood you really had feelings for her. So then of course she had to run away, before things progressed beyond hope.'

'In short, she would have kept me dangling on a string indefinitely if I hadn't proposed marriage?'

'Well, no. For she always meant to go to Jean-Claude. But she did not mean to hurt you. Truly. She just thought—'

'That I had no heart,' he finished, in clipped tones.

Inadvertently he jerked on the reins, giving the horses the impression that he wished them to break into a trot. Since they were approaching a corner, there were a few moments where it took all his concentration to ensure they were not involved in an accident.

'Oh, dear.' Heloise was gripping onto his sleeve with both hands now, her face puckered with concern. 'Now I have made you angry again, which is precisely what I wished not to do. For I have to inform you that when we are married, if you forbid me to contact her, knowing that I must obey I will do so—but until then I fully intend to write to her. Even if she has wronged you, she is still my sister!'

The moment of danger being past, the horses having been successfully brought back to a brisk walk, she folded her arms, and turned away from him, as though she had suddenly become interested in the pair of dogs with frills round their necks which were dancing for the amusement of those strolling along the boulevard.

'Ah, yes,' he replied, reaching over to take her hand and place it back upon his own arm. 'You fully intend to bow to my every whim, don't you, once we are married?'

'Of course! For you had no thought of marrying me until I put the notion in your head, so the least I can do is be the best wife you would wish for. I will do everything I can,' she declared earnestly. 'Whatever you ask, I will do with alacrity!' Pulling herself up short, she suddenly frowned at him suspiciously. 'And, by the way, why did you suddenly change your mind about me? When you made me leave, you seemed so set against it!'

'Well, your proposal was so sudden,' he teased her. 'It took me by surprise. Naturally I had to consider…'

She shook her head. 'No, I may have surprised you, but you had made up your mind it was an absurd idea.'

'So absurd, in fact,' he countered, 'that nobody would credit it. Nobody would believe I would take one Mademoiselle Bergeron merely to save face at being embarrassed by the other Mademoiselle Bergeron. And therefore they will have to believe that you were the object of my interest all along.'

When she continued to look less than convinced by his complete about-face, he decided it was high time he regained control of the conversation.

'Now, getting back to the ring. May I enquire, although I somehow feel I am about to regret doing so, why your sister left it with you? The normal practice, I should remind you, when an engagement is terminated, is for the lady to return the ring to the man who gave it to her.'

'I had it with me when I came to visit you this morning,' she declared. 'I was going to return it to you for her if you should not agree to my suggestion.'

'Indeed?' His voice was laced with scepticism. 'And yet somehow it remains in your possession. How did that come about, I wonder?'

'Well, because you were so beastly to me, if you must know! I told you the deepest secret of my heart and you laughed at me. For the moment I quite lost my temper, and decided I should do with it exactly as Felice said I ought to do! For you are so wealthy it is not as if you *needed* to have it back, whereas for me…'

She let go of his arm again, folding her own across her chest with a mutinous little pout which, for the first time in their acquaintance, made Charles wonder what it would be like to silence one of her tirades with a kiss. It would probably be the only way to stop her once she had built up a head of steam. Something in the pit of his stomach stirred at the thought of mastering her militant spirit in such a manner. He shook his head. It was not like him to regard sexual encounters as contests of will. But then, he frowned, when had he ever had to do more than crook his finger for a woman to fall obediently in line with his every whim?

'I take it you meant to sell it, then?'

Heloise eyed his lowered brows contritely.

'Yes,' she confessed. 'Because I needed the money to get to Dieppe.'

'Dieppe?' He shook himself out of his reverie. 'What is at Dieppe?'

'Not what, but who. And that is Jeannine!'

'Jeannine?' he echoed, becoming fascinated in spite of himself. 'What part does she play in this farce, I wonder?'

'She was Maman's nurse, until she eloped with Papa.'

'There seems to have been a great deal of eloping going on in your family.'

'But in my parents' case it was a good thing, don't you think? Because even if they were terribly poor for the first few years they were married, since my grandpapa cut her off entirely, she was the only one to survive the Terror because her family were all so abominably cruel to the *menu peuple*—the common people, that is. Jeannine was cast out, but she married a *fermier*, and I know she would take me in. I would have to learn how to milk a cow, to be sure, and make butter and cheese, but how hard could that be?'

'I thought it was hens,' he reflected.

'Hens?'

'Yes, you said when you married me you would live in a cottage so that you could keep hens. Now I find that in reality you would rather milk cows and make cheese.' He sighed. 'I do wish you would make up your mind.'

Heloise blinked. Though the abstracted frown remained between his brows, she was almost sure he was teasing her. 'I do not wish to milk cows at all,' she finally admitted.

'Good. Because I warn you right now that no wife of mine will ever do anything so plebeian. You must abandon all these fantasies about living on a farm and tending to live-stock of any sort. When we return to England you will move in the first circles and behave with the decorum commensurate with your station in life. You are not to go anywhere near any livestock of any description. Is that clear?'

For a moment Heloise regarded the mock sternness of his features with her head tilted to one side. She had never been on the receiving end of one of these teasing scolds before. Whenever he had been playful like this, she had never been able to understand how Felice could remain impervious to his charm.

'Not even a horse?' she asked, taking her courage in both hands and deciding to play along, just once. 'I am quite near a horse already, sitting up here in your carriage.'

'Horses, yes,' he conceded. 'You may ride with me, or a suitable companion in the park. A horse is not a farm animal.'

'Some horses are,' she persisted.

'Not my carriage horses,' he growled, though she could tell he was not really the least bit cross.

The ride in the fresh air seemed to be doing him good. He was far less tense than he had been when they set out. Oh, it was not to be expected that he would get over Felice all at once, but if she could make him laugh now and again, or even put that twinkle in his eye that she could see when he bent his head in her direction to give her this mock scold, she would be happy.

'What about dogs, then? What if I should go into some drawing room and a lady should have a little dog. Must I not go into the room? Or should I just stay away from it? By, say, five feet? Or six?'

'Pets, yes—of course you will come across pets from time to time. That is not what I meant at all, you little minx!'

Pretending exasperation he did not feel, to disguise the fact he was on the verge of laughter, he said, 'No wonder your brother said I should end up beating you. You would drive a saint to distraction!'

'I was only,' she declared with an impish grin, 'trying to establish exactly what you expected of me. I promised to behave exactly as you would wish, so I need to know exactly what you want!'

He laughed aloud then. 'You, *mademoiselle*, were doing nothing of the kind.' Why had he never noticed her mischievous sense of humour before now? Why had he never noticed what an entertaining companion she could be when she put her mind to it? The truth was, he decided with a sinking feeling, that whenever Felice had been in the room he'd had eyes for nobody else. With her sultry beauty and her vivacious nature she had utterly bewitched him.

Flicking the reins in renewed irritation, he turned the curricle for home.

Chapter Three

His eyes, which a moment ago had been twinkling with amusement, had gone dull and lifeless. It was as though he had retreated into a dark and lonely room, slamming the shutters against her.

She was positively relieved to get home, where her *maman* greeted her with enthusiasm.

'I never thought to have secured such a brilliant match for my plain daughter!' she beamed. 'But we must do something about your attire,' she said as Heloise untied the ribbons of the one bonnet she possessed. 'He cannot want people thinking he is marrying a dowd.'

Hustling her up the newly carpeted stairs to the room she had shared with Felice, her mother grumbled, 'We do not have time to cut down one of Felice's gowns before tonight. If only I had known,' she complained, flinging open the doors to the armoire, 'that you would be the one to marry into the nobility, we could have laid out a little capital on your wardrobe.'

Nearly all the dresses hanging there belonged to Felice. From the day the allies had marched into Paris the previous summer, what money her parents had been able to spare had been spent on dressing her sister. She had, after all, been the Bergeron family's secret weapon. She had flirted and charmed her way through the ranks of the occupying forces, playing the coquette to the hilt, whilst adroitly managing to hang onto her virtue, catapulting the family to the very heart of the new society which had rapidly formed to replace Napoleon's court.

'Nobody could have foreseen such an unlikely event,' Heloise replied rather dispiritedly, hitching her hip onto her bed.

She worried at her lower lip. What was her sister going to do now? She had left carrying only a modest bundle of possessions, and her young husband would not have the means to provide either the kind of dress allowance she had enjoyed for so long, nor the stimulating company of the upper echelons of society.

Heloise sighed. 'What about the lilac muslin?' she suggested. It was quite her favourite dress. She always felt that it made her look almost girlishly attractive, though the underskirt, which went with the full, shorter overdress, was embroidered about the hem with violets. Surely she could not be taken for a supporter of Bonaparte if she appeared in public on the arm of an Englishman?

'Where is His Lordship taking you tonight?' her *maman* enquired sharply.

'To the theatre first, and then on to Tortoni's for ices.'

Her mother clicked her tongue. 'Muslin to the theatre? I should think not!' she snapped, entirely overlooking the political symbolism of the violets, Bonaparte's emblem. 'When Felice went to the theatre with him she wore the gold satin!'

'I cannot compete with Felice, Maman,' Heloise remonstrated. 'Nor do I think it would be wise to try to be like her. Do you not think he might find it in poor taste if I did?'

'I had no idea,' her mother remarked sarcastically, 'that you had such a grasp of what is in men's hearts.' Flinging a bundle of Felice's discarded gowns to the bare boards, she gripped the iron foot-rail of the wide bed the girls had shared. 'Don't, I beg of you, do anything to make him change his mind about marrying you.'

'He has only taken me to save face,' Heloise pointed out. 'I know he still loves Felice. Nothing I do will matter to him.'

Her mother regarded the bleak look that washed over her daughter's features with concern.

'But you are going to be his wife, you foolish creature!' Coming round the side of the bed, her mother took her hand, chafing it to emphasise her point. 'Listen to me! And listen well! You will be going away to live in a foreign country, amongst strangers. You will be utterly dependent on your husband's goodwill. So you must make an effort to please him. Of course he will never fall in love with you—' she made a dismissive gesture with her hand '—the sister of the woman who betrayed him. Not even if you were half so beautiful or clever as she. But at least you can try not to antagonise him. You must learn to behave in a manner worthy of the title he is going to bestow on you. He will expect you to dress well and behave well, as a reflection of his taste. You must never embarrass him by displaying any emotion in public.'

He had only just informed her that displaying emotion in public was vulgar. So her mother's next words took on a greater power.

'Above all, you must never clamour for his attention if he does not wish to give it. You must let him go to his mistresses when he is bored with you, and pretend not to notice or to mind.'

A great lump formed in her throat. He would, of course, be unfaithful. She was the one who had instigated this marriage, and though he was disposed to go through with it, she knew only too well that it was not because he found her attractive.

How could he? Even her mother, who loved her as well as she was able, referred to her as her plain daughter.

'Mistresses?' she whispered, a sickening vision of a lifetime of humiliation unfolding before her.

'Of course,' her mother replied, stroking her hand soothingly. 'You are not blind. You know that is what men do. All men,' she said grimly, her thin lips compressing until they were almost white. 'Just as soon as they can afford it.'

Heloise's stomach turned over at the implication of her mother's words. Even her papa, who behaved as though he was deeply in love with her mother, must have strayed.

'If he is very considerate of your feelings he will conduct his affairs discreetly. But I warn you, if you make any protest, or even show that you care, he will be most annoyed! If you wish him to treat you well, you must not place any restrictions on his little *divertissements*.'

'I have already informed him that I will not interfere with his pleasures,' Heloise replied dully. And when she had told him that she had meant it. But now the idea that he could hasten to the arms of some other woman, when he could barely bring himself to allow her to lay her hand upon his sleeve, was unbelievably painful. Rising to her feet swiftly, she went to the open armoire. 'What about the grey shot silk?' she said, keeping her face carefully averted from her mother. 'I have not worn that for some time. I don't think His Lordship has ever seen me in it.'

Heloise did not particularly like the dress, for it had bad

associations. The first time Du Mauriac had asked her father if he might pay his addresses to his oldest daughter, he had been so proud that she had captured the interest of a hero of France that he had sent her to the dressmaker with the instruction to buy something pretty to wear when her suitor came calling. She had been torn. Oh, how pleasant it had been, to be able to go and choose a gown with no expense spared! And yet the reason for the treat had almost robbed her of all joy in the purchase. In the end she had not been able to resist the lure of silk, but had chosen a sombre shade of grey, in a very demure style, hoping that Du Mauriac would not think she was trying to dress for his pleasure.

'It is not at all the sort of thing Felice would have worn,' her mother remarked, shaking her head. 'But it will do for you. I shall get it sponged down and pressed.' She bustled away with Heloise's best gown over her arm, leaving her to her solitary and rather depressing reflections.

He had never seen her dressed so well, Charles thought with approval, when he came to collect her that evening. The exquisitely cut silk put him in mind of moonbeams playing over water. If only her eyes did not look so haunted. He frowned, pulling up short on the verge of paying her a compliment.

For the first time it hit him that she did not really wish to marry him any more than he wished to marry her. And she looked so small and vulnerable, hovering in the doorway, gazing up at him with those darkly anxious eyes.

She needed solid reassurance, not empty flattery.

Taking her hand in his, he led her to the sofa.

'May I have a few moments alone with your daughter before we go out?' he enquired of her parents. They left the room with such alacrity he was not sure whether to feel amused at their determination to pander to his every whim, or irritated at their lack of concern for their daughter's evident discomfort.

Heloise sank onto the sofa next to him, her hand resting limply in his own, and gazed up into his handsome face. Of course he would have mistresses. He was a most virile man. She would just somehow have to deal with this crushing sense of rejection the awareness of his infidelity caused her. She must learn not to mind that he frowned when he saw her, and stifle the memories of how his eyes had lit with pleasure whenever Felice had walked into a room.

'Heloise!' he said, so sharply that she collected he must have been speaking to her for quite some time, while she had not heard one word he had said.

Blushing guiltily, she tried to pay attention.

'I said, do you have the ring?'

Now he must think she was stupid, as well as unattractive. Her shoulders drooping, she held out her left hand obediently.

'Hell and damnation!' he swore. 'It's too big!'

'Well, you bought it for Felice,' she pointed out.

'Yes, and I would have bought you one that did fit if only you'd told me this one didn't! Why in God's name didn't you tell me, when I raised the subject this afternoon, that this ring was not going to be any good?'

'Because I didn't know it wouldn't fit. Although of course I should have known,' she ended despondently. Felice had long, strong, capable fingers, unlike her own, which were too slender for anything more strenuous than plying a needle or wielding a pencil.

'Do you mean to tell me that you had an emerald of this value in your possession and you were never tempted to try it on? Not once?'

'Oh, is it very valuable, then?' She looked with renewed interest at the jewel which hung from her ring finger. In order not to lose it, she knew she was going to have to keep her hand balled into a fist throughout the evening. 'I was not at all convinced it would get me all the way to Dieppe. Even if I'd managed to find a jeweller who would not try to cheat me, I fully expected to end up stranded halfway there.'

Her reference to her alternative plan of escaping Du Mauriac turned his momentary irritation instantly to alarm. He would do well to remember that he held no personal interest for her for his own sake at all. He was only providing the means, one way or another, for her to escape from an intolerable match with another man.

'Well, you won't be running off to Dieppe now, so you can put that notion right out of your head,' he seethed. Damn, but he hoped her distress was not an indication she was seriously considering fleeing from him!

Though he could see she was scared as hell of him right now. And no wonder. She had entrusted him with her entire future, and all he could do was berate her over the trifling matter of the fit of a ring!

'Come, now,' he said in a rallying tone. 'We struck an honest bargain this morning. It is in both our interests to stick with it.' He took her hands between his own and gave them what he hoped was a reassuring squeeze. 'We are in this together.'

Yes. She sighed. And so was Felice. He would never be able to keep from comparing her, and unfavourably. Just look at the way he was coaxing her out of the sulks in that patronising tone, as though she were a petulant child.

'It is easier for you,' she began. He was used to disguising his feelings behind that glacial mask he wore in public. But she had never been any good at dissembling.

'Why do you suppose that?' he said harshly.

'Because I won't know what to say to people!' she snapped. Had he forgotten already that she had told him she was hopeless at telling lies?

'Oh, come,' he scoffed. 'You ran on like a rattle in my drawing room this morning!'

'That was entirely different,' she protested. 'It does not matter what you think.' They were co-conspirators. She had no need to convince him she was anything other than herself.

Charles swiftly repressed the sharp stab of hurt these words inflicted. Why should he be bothered if she did not care what he thought of her? It was not as if she meant anything to him, either. He must just accept that playing the role of his fiancée was not going to be easy for her.

'Very well,' he nodded, 'you need not attempt to speak. I will do all the talking for us both. Providing—' he fixed her with a stern eye '—you make an attempt to look as though you are enjoying yourself tonight.'

'Oh, I am sure I shall—in my own way,' she assured him.

She loved studying how people behaved in social situations. Their posturing and jostling both amused and inspired her with ideas that went straight into her sketchbook the minute she got home.

A vague recollection of her sitting alone at a table littered with empty glasses, a rapt expression on her face as she observed the boisterous crowd at the *guingette* that Felice had dared him to take her to, sprang to Charles' mind. He began to feel a little calmer. The theatre was the best place he could have chosen for their first outing together *à deux*. She would be content to sit quietly and watch the performance.

Then she alarmed him all over again by saying mourn-fully, 'It was a stupid idea. I wish I had never mentioned it. Nobody looking at the two of us together will ever believe you wish at all to marry me.'

'Well, they will not if you carry on like this!' It was bad enough that Felice had jilted him; now Heloise was exhibiting clear signs of wanting to hedge off. What was wrong with the Bergeron sisters? He knew of half a dozen women who would give their eye teeth to be in their position. Why, he had been fending off females who wished to become his countess since his first foray into society!

'You came up with this plan, not I. And I expect you to play your part now you have wheedled me into it!'

'Wheedled?' she gasped, desperately hurt. She had not wheedled. She had put her proposition rationally and calmly...well, perhaps not calmly, for she had been very nervous. But he was making it sound as though she had put unfair pressure on him in some way.

'If that is what you think—' she began, sliding the ring from her finger.

His hand grabbed hers, thrusting the ring back down her finger.

'No, *mademoiselle*,' he said sternly, holding her hands captive between his own, his steely fingers keeping the ring firmly in place.

She took a breath, her brow furrowing in preparation for another round of argument.

There was only one sure way to silence her. And Charles took it.

She flinched when his lips met hers, rousing Charles' anger to new heights.

What was the woman doing proposing marriage if she could not even bear the thought of kissing him? Leaving go of her hands, he grasped her by the nape of the neck, holding her still, while he demonstrated his inalienable right, as her betrothed, to kiss her as thoroughly as he pleased!

Charles had taken her completely by surprise. She didn't know what to do. No man had ever kissed her before. Du Mauriac had tried, once or twice, but she had been expecting it from him, and had always managed to take evasive action.

But she didn't want to evade Charles, she discovered after only a fleeting moment of shock. What she really wanted, she acknowledged, relaxing into his hold, was to put her arms about him and kiss him back. If only she knew how!

Well, she might not know anything about kissing, but there was nothing to stop her from putting her arms about his neck. Uttering a little whimper of pleasure, she raised shaky hands from her lap and tentatively reached out for him.

'My God,' he panted, breaking free. 'I never meant to do that!'

Leaping to his feet, he strode to the very far side of the room. Hearing her little cry of protest, feeling her hands fluttering against his chest in an attempt to push him away, had brought him to his senses.

'I can only offer my sincere apologies,' he ground out between clenched teeth. He could not think what had come over him. What kind of blackguard chose that particular way to silence a woman?

He had accepted intellectually that one day he would have to get his heirs by Heloise. But judging from her shocked recoil it had been the furthest thing from her mind.

The fierce surge of desire that even now was having a visible effect on his anatomy was an unexpected bonus. When the time was right, he was going to enjoy teaching his wife all there was to know about loving.

Until then he must exercise great restraint. He would have to get her used to the idea of him before broaching the subject of heirs. He already knew how shy she was, and had realised she would need to feel she could rely on him. How could she do that if she was worried he was going to pounce on her at any moment?

'You need not fear that I shall importune you in that way again,' he grated, his back still turned to her while he desperately fought to regain mastery over his unruly body.

Heloise pressed her hand to her bruised lips, her heart sinking as swiftly as it had soared when he had seized and kissed her so excitingly. Why had he done it if he was now adamant he would not be doing it again? Had it only been some sort of experiment? To see if he could stomach touching her as a man should want to touch his wife? If so, it was evident he regretted giving in to the impulse.

It was a while before he could bear to so much as turn round and look at her! But at least it gave her the time to wipe away the few tears that she had been unable to prevent from trickling down her cheeks. For she would never let him see how humiliated his rejection made her feel. If he did not wish to kiss her, then she would not beg for his kisses. Never!

She got to her feet, determination stiffening her carriage. She would never let him suspect—not by one lingering look, one plaintive sigh—that she… She faltered, her hand flying to her breast.

No, this was too appalling! She could not be in love with him. She *must* not be in love with him. She was certain she had not lied when she had denied being in love with him that morning. Her feelings could not have changed so swiftly during the course of one day. Just because he had strolled into the drawing room and swept all her problems away with his marvellously insouciant declaration of intent to marry her. Not because she had felt a momentary rapport with him while they had gently teased each other during their carriage ride.

And yet she could not deny that since her *maman* had broached the subject of his infidelity she had been eaten up by jealousy.

No, that was not love! It was wounded pride that made her eyes smart so. It had to be.

Her abstracted air, coupled with the Earl's barely tamped down lust, created quite a stir when they entered the theatre arm in arm.

As soon as they were seated, Charles tore off a corner of the programme and wedged it under her ring. 'That should hold it in place for now.'

'Thank you,' she murmured, keeping her face averted. It was stupid to feel resentful because he was being so practical about everything. She sighed.

'Mademoiselle,' he murmured, 'I am about to put my arm along the back of your chair, and I do not want you to flinch when I do it.'

A shiver slid all the way down her spine to her toes at the warmth of his arm behind her shoulders. With him so close, every breath she took filled her nostrils with his clean, spicy scent. Though his arm was not quite touching her, she remembered the strength of it, holding her captive while he ravaged her mouth. She felt weak, and flustered, and utterly feminine.

'I promise I shall not do anything you will not like. Only I must sometimes seem to be…how shall I put it? …lover-like when we appear in public. I shall not go beyond the bounds of what is proper, I assure you.'

No, she reflected with annoyance. For he'd found kissing her such an unpleasant experience he had vowed never to do it again! This show of being 'lover-like', as he put it, was as much of a performance as what was going on upon the stage. But then, she reflected bleakly, she had known from the outset that all he wanted from her was the means to salvage his pride.

'Y…you may do what you like,' she conceded, feeling utterly wretched. 'I understand how important this show is to you.' Turning towards him, so that their faces were only a few scant inches apart, she declared, 'It was for this reason that you agreed to marry me, was it not? So that nobody would suspect you had been hurt. I think the worst thing you could endure is to have someone mock you.' Raising one hand, she laid it against his cheek. 'I trust you,' she said, resolving that, come what may, she would never be sorry to have given him this one source of consolation. 'However you decide to behave tonight, I will go along with it.'

Charles found it hard not to display his hurt. Go along with it, indeed! She could not conceal how nervous he made her. She was drawing on every ounce of courage she possessed to conceal her disquiet at his proximity. She had shuddered when he put his arm round her, tensed up when he had whispered in her ear.

Was it possible, he wondered, his heart skipping a beat, that she found him as repellent as Du Mauriac?

Regarding her nervously averted eyes, he refused to entertain that notion. She had come to him, after all. He had not put any pressure on her. She was just shy, that was all. He doubted many men had so much as flirted with her, let alone kissed her. She was as innocent as her sister had been experienced.

His expression bland, he murmured, 'We should take advantage of our relative privacy to organise the practical details of our wedding, don't you think?'

The sooner he secured her, the sooner he could stop worrying that she might run away.

By the end of the first act, by dint of keeping their heads close together and keeping their voices low, they had managed to agree upon a simple civic wedding. Conningsby, upon whose discretion he relied, would serve as his witness, and her parents would support Heloise. It would take next to no time to arrange it.

They had also managed to create the very impression Charles had sought. The audience, agog with curiosity, spent as much time training their opera glasses upon the unchaperoned young couple who appeared so intent on each other as they did upon the stage.

Heloise ordered a lemon ice once they finally managed to secure a table at Tortoni's. But she did not appear to be enjoying it much. She was still ill at ease in his company. The truth was that much of the behaviour upon which she had to judge him might well have given her a false impression of his character.

He shuddered, recalling that excursion beyond the city boundaries to the *guingette*, where ordinary working people went to spend their wages on food, drink and dancing. Felice had made it seem like such fun, and in its way it had been. But Heloise, he suddenly realised, watching as she daintily licked the confection from her spoon, had not only refused to join in the hurly-burly, but would never have cajoled him to attend such a venue. He would have to reassure her that he would never so browbeat her again.

'Since I have been in Paris,' he began, frowning, 'I have done things I would never consider for a minute in London. Things that are breaches of good *ton*.'

Heloise tried not to display her hurt that he should regard marrying her as a breach of ton. She already knew she was not at all the sort of wife an English earl ought to marry. His infatuation with Felice would have been much easier for society to forgive, given that she was so very enchanting. But nobody would be able to understand why he had picked up a plain little bourgeoise like her, and elevated her to the position of Countess.

'Allow me to be the first to congratulate you,' a voice purred. Dropping her spoon with a clatter on the table, she looked up to see Mrs Austell hovering over their table, her beady eyes fixed on Felice's emerald ring. 'Though I had heard…' She paused to smile like a cat that had got at the cream, and Heloise braced herself to hear whatever gossip had been noised abroad concerning the Earl and her sister. 'I had heard that you were going to make an announcement at the Dalrymple Hamilton ball.'

'Circumstances made it impossible for us to attend,' Charles replied blandly.

'Ah, yes, I hear there was some unpleasantness in your family, *mademoiselle*?'

Laying his hand firmly over hers, Charles prevented her from needing to answer. 'Mademoiselle Bergeron does not wish to speak of it.'

'Oh, but I am the soul of discretion! Is there nothing to be done for your poor sister? Too late to prevent her ruination, I suppose?'

'Oh, you have the matter quite out. The affair is not of that nature. The young man fully intends to marry my fiancée's sister. Has done for some considerable time. It is only parental opposition that has forced the silly children to feel they needed to run off together in that manner.'

Heloise marvelled that he could appear so unconcerned as he related the tale. Deep down, she knew he was still smarting. But it was this very *sang-froid* she had factored as being of paramount importance to her scheme. Why should she be surprised, she chastised herself, when he played the part she had written for him so perfectly?

'A little embarrassing for me to have an escapade of that nature in the family,' he shrugged, 'to be sure. But it is of no great import in the long run.' With a smile that would have convinced the most cynical onlooker, Lord Walton carried Heloise's hand to his lips and kissed it.

'Of course I never held to the prevalent opinion that you would make the younger Mademoiselle Bergeron your wife,' Mrs Austell declared. 'A man of your station! Of course you would prefer the more refined Mademoiselle Bergeron to her flighty little sister. Though I must warn you—' she turned to Heloise, a malicious gleam in her eye '—that you ought not to make your dislike of Wellington so apparent when you get to London. They idolise him there, you know. If anyone were to catch a glimpse of that scurrilous drawing you made of him…' She went off into a peal of laughter. 'Though it was highly entertaining. And as for the one you showed me of Madame de Stael, as a pouter pigeon!'

'I collect you have had sight of my betrothed's sketch-book?'

'Felice handed it round one afternoon,' Heloise put in, in her defence. 'When a few ladies connected with the embassy paid us a visit.'

'Oh, yes! Such a delight to see us all there in her me-nagerie, in one form or another. Of course, since the one of myself was quite flattering, I suppose I had more freedom to find the thing amusing than others, to whom *mademoiselle* had clearly taken a dislike.'

At his enquiring look, Heloise, somewhat red-faced, admitted, 'I portrayed Mrs Austell as one of the birds in an aviary.'

With a completely straight face, Charles suggested, 'With beautiful plumage, no doubt, since she always dresses so well?'

'Yes, that's it,' she agreed, though she could tell he had guessed, even without seeing the picture, that all the birds portrayed on that particular page had been singing their heads off. If there was one thing Mrs Austell's set could do, it was make a lot of noise about nothing.

'And dare I ask how you portrayed Wellington?'

But it was Mrs Austell who answered, her face alight with glee. 'As a giraffe, if you please, with a great long neck, loping down the Champs-Elysées, looking down with such a supercilious air on the herd of fat little donkeys waddling along behind!'

'For I see him as being head and shoulders above his contemporaries,' Heloise pleaded.

'Oh, I see!' Mrs Austell said. 'Well, that explains it. Have you seen your own likeness among your talented little betrothed's pages, my lord?' she simpered.

'Why, yes,' he admitted, feeling Heloise tense beneath his grasp. 'I feature as a lion in a circus, if you please.'

'Oh, of course. The king of the beasts!' she trilled. 'Well, I must not take up any more of your time. I am sure you two lovebirds—' she paused to laugh at her own witticism '—would much rather be alone.'

'As soon as you have finished your ice,' Charles said, once Mrs Austell had departed, 'I shall take you home. Our "news" will be all over Paris by the morning. Mrs Austell will convince everyone how it was without us having to perjure ourselves.'

He was quiet during the short carriage ride home. But as he was handing her out onto the pavement he said, 'I trust you will destroy your sketchbook before it does any more damage?'

'Damage?' Heloise echoed, bemused. 'I think it served its purpose very well.'

'There are pictures in there that in the wrong hands could cause me acute embarrassment,' he grated. He had no wish to see himself portrayed as a besotted fool, completely under the heel of a designing female. 'Can I trust you to burn the thing yourself, or must I come into your parents' house and take it from you?'

Heloise gasped. She had only one skill of which she was proud, and that was drawing. It was unfair of him to ask her to destroy all her work! It was not as if she had made her assessment of her subjects obvious. Only someone who knew the character of her subject well would know what she was saying about them by portraying them as one type of animal or another.

It had been really careless of her to leave that sketchbook lying on the table when she had gone up to change. She had not been gone many minutes, but he had clearly found the picture she had drawn of him prostrate at her sister's feet, while she prepared to walk all over him. And been intelligent enough to recognise himself, and proud enough to resent her portrayal of him in a position of weakness.

He was not a man to forgive slights. Look how quickly he had written Felice out of his life, and he had loved her! Swallowing nervously, she acknowledged that all the power in their relationship lay with him. If she displeased him, she had no doubt he could make her future as his wife quite uncomfortable. Besides, had she not promised to obey his slightest whim? If she argued with him over this, the first real demand he had made of her, she would feel as though she were breaking the terms of their agreement.

'I will burn it,' she whispered, her eyes filling with tears. 'I promised you, did I not, that I would do my best to be a good wife, and never cause you a moment's trouble? I will do whatever you ask of me.' However it hurt her to destroy that which she had spent hours creating, the one thing in her life she felt proud to have achieved, her word of honour meant far more.

'Heloise, no—dammit!' he cried, reaching out his hand. That had been tactless of him. He should have requested to examine the book, and then decided whether to destroy the one or two sketches which might have caused him some discomfort. Or he should have been more subtle still. He should have asked if he could keep the whole thing, and then ensured it was kept locked away where nobody could see it. Not demand her obedience in that positively medieval way!

But it was too late. She had fled up the steps to her house, the sound of her sobs sending a chill down his spine.

How had the evening gone so wrong? He had decided she needed reassurance, and what had he done? Bullied and frightened her, and sent her home in floods of tears.

If he carried on like this she might still decide to run away to her farm in Dieppe. And where would that leave him?

Chapter Four

Heloise gazed wide-eyed around the mirror-lined interior of the most expensive and therefore the most exclusive restaurant in Paris.

'Most people come to Very Frères to sample the truffles,' Charles had informed her when they had taken their places at a granite-topped table in one of the brilliantly lit salons.

That seemed inordinately foolish, considering the menu contained such a staggering variety of dishes. 'I will have the *poulet à la* Marengo.' She leaned forward and confided, 'Although it is much cheaper in the Trois Frères Provencaux.'

'You do not need to consider the expense,' he pointed out. 'I am a very wealthy man.'

Heloise shifted uncomfortably as his gaze seemed to settle critically upon her rather worn lilac muslin. 'I am not marrying you for that.'

'I know,' he acknowledged. 'But you must admit having a wealthy husband will make your lot more tolerable.'

'Will it?' she replied in a forlorn little voice. She really could not see that it mattered how wealthy her husband was when he was in love with someone else. Someone he could not have. And when she would only ever be a poor second best.

'Of course,' he replied briskly. He had decided to make amends for his overbearing attitude the previous evening by spoiling her a little. And demonstrating that he was prepared to consider her feelings. 'I appreciate that you may find certain aspects of marrying me more uncomfortable than I had at first assumed.' If he didn't want her bolting to Dieppe, he would have to persuade her that marriage to him would be nothing like the picture she had painted of being chained down by Du Mauriac.

'I shall not forbid you from pursuing your own pleasures.' He did not want her worrying he would be forever breathing down her neck. 'Nor shall I expect you to hang on my arm.' He would not force her to any event that she would rather not attend. He knew that her rather retiring nature might make it hard for her to hold her own with some of the people with whom he routinely crossed swords during the course of his public life. However, he did not want her to feel he saw her shyness as a failing. 'It is not done for a man to be seen about too much with his wife,' he explained. 'And though we must live in the same house, there is no reason we may not live virtually separate lives.'

Her heart fluttered in panic. It sounded as if he meant to deposit her in some house in a foreign country, where she knew nobody, and leave her to fend for herself.

'D...don't you want people to think we have a true marriage?'

He felt touched that she could still think of his image, when she must have so many reservations about the new life she was about to embark upon.

'We must be seen about together occasionally, yes,' he acknowledged. 'Just once every se'en night or so should be sufficient.'

She bit her lip. She could hardly complain if he could not face wasting more than one evening a week on her. Hadn't she rashly declared she would go and live in a cottage and keep hens if he did not wish to be burdened with her company?

'Do you have a house in the country, my lord?' she asked. The hens were seeming increasingly attractive.

'That is far too formal a way to address me now we are to be married,' he countered, puzzled by her abrupt change of subject. He had done what he could to put her at ease. Now it was time to take things to a more intimate level. 'You had best call me Walton. Or Charles.'

'Ch…Charles,' she stammered, the familiarity of his name catching on her tongue.

'And may I call you Heloise?'

She nodded, rendered speechless at the warmth of the smile he turned on her for acceding to this small request.

'I hope you will like Wycke.'

'Wycke?'

'Although I have a house in London, where I reside whilst Parliament is in session, Wycke is my principal seat, and it is where…' Where the heirs are traditionally born, he refrained from finishing. Regarding her upturned, wary little face, he wondered with a pang if there would ever come a time when he would be able to tackle such a delicate subject with her.

Though, legally, he already had an heir.

'There is one rather serious matter I must broach with you,' he said firmly. It was no good trying to shield her from everything. There were some things she would just have to accept. 'I have someone…residing with me in Walton House—that is, my London home.'

Heloise attacked the tender breast of chicken the waiter had set before her with unnecessary savagery. She had wondered just how long it would be before he raised the topic of his mistress. Of course she would not voice any objections to him visiting such a woman. But if he expected her to let his mistress carry on living with him, then he was very much mistaken!

'Indeed?' she said frostily.

'He is not going to be easy to get along with, and on re-flection I recommend you had better not try.'

He? Oh, thank goodness—not a mistress.

Then why should she not try to get along with this guest? Heat flared in her cheeks. Of course—she was not good *ton*, and this person was clearly someone whose opinion he valued.

'Whatever you say,' she replied dully, taking a sip of the *meursault* that had somehow appeared in her glass when she had not been attending.

'And, while we are on the topic, I must inform you there are several other persons that I do not wish you to associate with.'

'Really?' she said bleakly. She was not good enough to mix with his friends. How much more humiliation did he intend to heap on her? 'Perhaps you had better provide me with a list?'

'That might be a good idea,' he replied in an abstracted manner. In marrying him, Heloise would become a target through which his enemies might try to strike at him. It would be unfair to leave her exposed when, with a little forethought, he could protect her. Some people would take great pleasure in making her as uncomfortable as possible simply because she was French. Others would be livid that she had thwarted their matrimonial ambitions towards him. 'Those you need to be wariest of are certain members of my family.'

She knew it! He was downright ashamed of her! What further proof did she need than to hear him warn her that his own family would be her bitterest enemies?

'You see, I have severed all connection with certain of them—'

Catching the appalled expression on her face, he pulled up short.

'Beware, Heloise,' he mocked. 'Your husband is a man notorious for being so lacking in familial feeling that even my closest relatives are not safe from my cold, vengeful nature.'

She was so relieved to hear that his forbidding her to mix with these people was not because he was ashamed of her that she could easily dismiss the challenge aimed at her with those bitter words. Whatever had happened in the past was nothing to do with her! It was her future conduct that mattered to him.

'Of course I would not have anything to do with people who would say such things about you,' she declared, with a vehemence that shook him.

'Your loyalty is…touching,' he said cynically.

'I will be your wife,' she pointed out with an expressive shrug, as though matrimonial loyalty went without saying. Her declaration effectively stunned him into silence.

'Shall we stroll awhile?' he eventually recovered enough to say, when they had finished their meal.

Heloise nodded. At this hour of the evening, the brightly lit central quadrangle of the Palais Royale would be crowded with Parisians and tourists looking for entertainment of all sorts. From the restaurants in the basements and the shops beneath the colonnade, to the casinos and brothels on the upper floors, there was something in the arcades to cater for all tastes. Strolling amongst the pleasure-seeking crowds would be one way of demonstrating that he was not in the least broken-hearted.

They had barely stepped outside when she heard an angry and all too familiar voice crying, 'Hey, Heloise—stop!'

Looking across the square, in the direction from which the voice hailed, she saw Du Mauriac bearing down on them like an avenging whirlwind.

To her consternation, rather than retreating into the relative safety of the restaurant, Charles continued to stroll nonchalantly towards the most dangerous man in Paris.

'Didn't you hear me calling you?' he snarled, coming to a halt directly in front of them. His black moustache bristled in a face that was mottled red from wine and anger. Heloise tried to detach her hand from Charles' arm. The waiters would not deign to help, but many of the diners in Very Frères were Englishmen, who would be bound to come to their aid if she could only get to them.

But Charles would not relax his grip.

Eyeing the lean figure of her former suitor with cool disdain, he drawled, 'My fiancée does not answer to strangers shouting in the street.'

'Fiancée!' Ignoring Lord Walton, Du Mauriac turned the full force of his fury on the slender form cringing at his side.

'Y…yes,' she stuttered.

'Do not let this fellow unsettle you, my sweet. I will deal with him.'

'Your sweet?' The Earl's endearment drew Du Mauriac's fire down upon himself. 'She is not your sweet. Everyone knows you are in love with her sister! Not her! What could a man like you want with a little mouse like her?'

'Since you speak of her in such a derogatory manner,' he replied stiffly, 'it is clear you care little for her either. So what exactly is your problem?'

'You have no notion of what I feel for Heloise. Before you came to France, with your money and your title, she was going to be my wife! Mine! And if she had an ounce of loyalty she would be mine still. But it is the same with so many of her sort. They can wear the violet on their gowns, but their heart is filled only with greed and ambition.'

The confrontation between a slender officer in his shabby uniform and an obviously wealthy Englishman, in the doorway of such an exclusive restaurant, was beginning to attract the attention of passers-by.

'I collect from your agitation,' Charles said, finally relinquishing his vice-like grip on her hand, so that he could interpose his own body between her and Du Mauriac, 'that you were once an aspirant to Mademoiselle Bergeron's hand?'

Heloise was too shocked by these words to think of running for help. Charles knew exactly how things had stood between them. So why was he pretending differently? Oh, she thought, her hands flying to her cheeks. To conceal her part in the plot! He was shielding her from Du Mauriac's wrath. Her heart thudded in her chest. It was wonderful to know Charles was intent on protecting her, but did he not know Du Mauriac would calmly put a bullet through a man on far flimsier quarrel than that of stealing his woman?

'I fully understand,' Charles said in an almost bored tone, 'if the harsh words you level at this lady stem from thwarted affection. Being aware that you French are apt to be somewhat excitable, I also forgive you your appalling lapse of manners. Though naturally were you an English-man it would be quite another matter.'

Du Mauriac laughed mockingly. 'I insult your woman and you stand there and let me do it, like the coward you are. What must I do to make you take the honourable course? Slap your face?'

The Earl looked thoughtful. 'You could do so, of course, if it would help to relieve your feelings. But then I would be obliged to have you arrested on a charge of assault.'

'In short, you are such a coward that nothing would induce you to meet me!'

Heloise gasped. No gentleman could allow another to call him a coward to his face. Especially not in such a public place.

But Charles merely looked puzzled. 'Surely you are not suggesting I would wish to fight a duel with you?' He shook his head, a pitying smile on his face. 'Quite apart from the fact I do not accept there is any reason for us to quarrel, I understand your father was a fisherman of some sort? I hate to have to be the one to break it to you, but duelling is a *gentleman's* solution to a quarrel.'

'I am an officer of the French army!' Du Mauriac shouted.

'Well, that's as may be,' Charles replied. 'Plenty of upstarts are masquerading as gentlemen in France these days. I,' he said, drawing himself up a little, 'do not share such republican ideals. A man is a gentleman by birth and manners—and frankly, sir, you have neither.'

Du Mauriac, now completely beside himself, took a step forward, his hand raised to strike the blow that would have made a duel inevitable. And met the full force of the Earl's left fist. Before he knew what had hit him, the Earl followed through with a swift right, leaving the notorious duellist lying stretched, insensible, on the gravel path.

'I am so sorry you had to witness that, Heloise,' the Earl said, flexing his knuckles with a satisfied smile. 'But it is well past time somebody knocked him down.'

Heloise was torn by a mixture of emotions. It had been quite wonderful to see Du Mauriac floored with such precision. And yet she knew he was not a man to take such a public insult lying down. At least, she thought somewhat hysterically, only while he was unconscious. As soon as he came to he would be hell-bent on revenge. If he could not take it legitimately, by murdering the Earl under the guise of duelling with him, then he would do it by stealthy means. It would be a knife in the ribs as he mounted the steps to the theatre, or a shot fired from a balcony as they rode along the boulevard in the borrowed carrick. She could see the Earl's blood soaking into the dust of some Parisian street as she held his dying body in her arms.

She burst into tears.

Putting one arm around her, Lord Walton pushed a way through the excited crowd that was milling round Du Mauriac's prone form.

It had been a tactical error, he acknowledged as he bundled her into a cab, to deal with Du Mauriac while she was watching. Gentlemen did not brawl in front of ladies. Displays of masculine aggression were abhorrent to them. But it had seemed too good an opportunity to pass up! Wellington had forbidden officers of the occupying forces to engage in fisticuffs in public places. He had stipulated that the sword was the weapon of gentlemen, and Du Mauriac had taken advantage of that order to murder one young Englishman after another. Only a man like Walton, who was exempt from Wellington's orders, was free to mete out the humiliating form of punishment that such a scoundrel deserved.

But witnessing what an aggressive brute she was about to marry had clearly devastated Heloise. By the time they reached the Quai Voltaire she had worked herself into such a pitch he had no option but to carry her into the house and hand her over to the care of her mother, while he went in search of some brandy.

'He will kill him, *Maman*,' Heloise sobbed into her mother's bosom. 'And then he will take his revenge on me. Whatever shall I do?'

'We will bring the wedding forward to tomorrow,' her mother said, comforting Heloise immensely by not decrying her fears as groundless. 'And you will leave Paris immediately after the ceremony.'

'What if he should pursue us?' Heloise hiccupped, sitting up and blowing her nose.

'You leave that to me,' her mother said with a decisive nod. 'He has plenty of enemies who want only a little push to move against him, and we can keep him tied up long enough for you to escape France.'

'But I thought you wanted me to marry him!'

'And so I did, my dear.' Her mother absently stroked a lock of hair from her daughter's heated forehead. 'When I thought you could get no other suitor, and when I thought Bonaparte's ambition would keep him away from Paris, fighting for ten months of the year. But I would never have permitted you to go on campaign with him. Besides,' she concluded pragmatically, 'Bonaparte is finished now. Of what use is a man like Du Mauriac when he has no emperor to fight for?'

The moment Charles heard Madame Bergeron suggest that, due to Heloise's state of nerves, it might be better to bring the wedding forward, he completely forgot his determination that nothing would induce him to leave Paris before the lease on his apartment had run its course. Nothing mattered except making sure of Heloise.

'I will go and order the removal of my own household,' he said, rising from his chair and pulling his gloves on over his bruised knuckles. It would take some time to pack up the house and arrange transport for his staff. But he could leave all that in Giddings' capable hands. He could most certainly leave immediately after the wedding ceremony. It only required his valet to pack an overnight case.

At first he assumed that once she had spoken her vows, and signed all the necessary documents, he would feel easier in his mind. But it was not so. Every time he glanced at the tense set of her pale face he wondered if she still considered the dairy farm at Dieppe a preferable option to being leg-shackled to a man of whom she was growing increasingly afraid. He was not being fanciful. She had admitted almost as soon as they had set out that she had left her one decent dress behind because it brought back bad memories.

It was the one she had been wearing the night he had forced that kiss on her.

Before long, he realised he was not going to be able to relax until he had her on board ship and out into the Channel. While they were in France there were innumerable ways for her to wriggle out of his grasp.

It was a great relief when, about ten miles out of Paris, her head began to droop. She couldn't have slept a wink the night before to be sleeping so soundly in the jolting carriage. She must have been scared stiff of leaving her family and her country behind, and going to live amongst strangers. She made no demur when he tucked her wilting form against his shoulder, and once he was certain she was fully asleep he took the liberty of putting his arm round her, and settling her into a more comfortable position. She was so tiny, tucked against his heart. So frail a creature.

Surely there must be some way he could get her to see he was not a monster? Just a man who wanted to be her friend and protector. But how? When so far all he had done was bully and frighten her?

She did not wake until well into the afternoon.

'Where are we?' she yawned, pushing herself upright.

'Abbeville. Since you were sleeping so soundly, I took the opportunity to press on. We have been able to cover far more ground than if we had needed to keep stopping to see to your comfort.'

His matter-of-fact tone brought her sharply to her senses. For a blissful moment, as she had come awake within the cradle of his powerful arms, she had mistaken the fact that he had allowed her to use his broad chest for her pillow as a mark of tenderness.

'You will have your own suite of rooms tonight,' he said, plunging her deeper into gloom. Of course he would not want any real intimacy with her. Their marriage was only for public show.

She was not very much surprised when a meal was brought to her own little parlour, or when she ate it alone. He had barely spoken a handful of words to her all day. On seeing the meagre amount of luggage she had packed, instead of appreciating her ability to travel light he had made a sarcastic comment about having to arrange credit at various smart outfitters once they arrived in London. After that Charles had turned from her and gazed fixedly out of the window.

The hotel was naturally first class, and the maid

provided to help her prepare for bed was both efficient and friendly. But Heloise knew she would not sleep a wink, no matter how soft the feather mattress was. She had dozed in her husband's arms nearly all day, and now she was wide awake—and as troubled as she had been the night before.

She had nobody but herself to blame for her predicament. She had approached Charles and offered to be the means by which he could salve his wounded pride. She should not feel offended that he cared so little for her that he would not even fight a duel when she was insulted in a public square. Besides, she had not wanted him to fight a duel. She could not bear to think of him being injured or, worse, killed on her account.

She would not be able to rest properly until he was safely in England, where Du Mauriac would not dare follow, she reflected, chewing at a fingernail.

Anyway, she had worked out, during the long sleepless hours of the previous night, that the quarrel in the Palais Royale had not been about her at all, no matter what words the men had used. Charles had clearly known far more about Du Mauriac than she had told him, else how would he have been able to sneer at his parentage? And another thing—it had only been when she had told him Du Mauriac was the suitor she wished to escape that he had shown any inclination to take her proposition seriously.

She shivered at the cold, calculating way Charles had behaved. He must have studied Du Mauriac closely to have taken the very course which would hurt him most. He had stolen his woman, refused to acknowledge him as a social equal, then knocked him down in a public place, rendering him an object of ridicule.

She drew the coverlet up to her chin, the cold seeping into her very soul. Felice had said he had no heart. He had warned her himself that his nature was so cold and vengeful he could sever the ties to his own family without a qualm.

No. She shook her head. Felice had been wrong. And when Charles himself had informed her of his nature there had been something in his eyes—almost as though he was taunting her with the description she had heard applied to him so often.

His treatment of Du Mauriac had been cold and vengeful, that was true. But Du Mauriac was a vile man who fully deserved all that Charles had done to him. And as for that business about cutting ties with the family who had raised him…well, yes, that did sound bad. But, knowing what she did of Charles, she would not be a bit surprised to learn that it was they who had done something dreadful, and that rather than expose them he'd let the gossip-mongers make what they would of it all.

She was startled out of her reverie when someone pushed her bedroom door open. This might be a first-class inn, but clearly some people lodging here had no manners. She was just opening her mouth to scream her objection at having her room invaded when she realised it was only Charles, entering not from the corridor but from a connecting door to another bedroom.

'I am not a monster, Heloise,' he sighed, stalking towards her. 'You do not need to clutch the sheet up to your chin as though you fear I mean to ravish you. I can assure you, nothing is further from my mind.'

Relief that it was not some stranger about to assault her had her sagging into the pillows. Though his words rankled. Did he think she was a complete fool? She knew all too well that when he wanted a woman he would go to one of his mistresses.

'I only came to inform you of the fact that I will not be making demands of that nature upon you. I said from the start that you are far too young to be married at all, leave alone face motherhood.' He bent over her and placed a perfunctory kiss on her forehead. 'Goodnight, Lady Walton,' he said.

'Goodnight, Charles,' she replied, betraying by only the very slightest quiver in her lower lip her feeling of humiliated rejection.

She would not cry until he had left the room. He detested any display of emotion. She could only imagine how disgusted her complete breakdown the night before must have made him. But it probably accounted for his distant behaviour with her today. She must not make the mistake of showing such lack of breeding again. Even if he never came to care all that much for her, she would do her utmost to be the kind of wife he wanted—compliant and undemonstrative.

To prove that she could do this, she tried a shaky smile. To tell the truth, she did feel a measure of relief. She was totally unprepared for a wedding night with a husband who regarded her as a necessary evil. Or to endure the ordeal of being deflowered by a man who would regard it as a duty to be performed in the cold-blooded way he seemed to live the rest of his life.

Lord Walton ripped off his cravat the moment he entered his room, and flung it aside to land he knew not where. He felt as though he could not breathe. God, how scared of him she had looked! And how relieved when he had told her he had no intentions of claiming his husbandly rights!

He strode to the side table and poured a measure of brandy into a tumbler. Then slumped into a chair, staring into its amber depths. He would find no solace there, he reflected, swirling the liquid round and round, warming it to release its fragrant fumes. The one time he had attempted to use alcohol as an anaesthetic it had failed him miserably. All it had done was make him feel sorry for himself. He had spouted the most maudlin nonsense to a virtual stranger, and woken with a thick head in the morning. He would need a clear head the next morning. If they could make an early enough start they would reach Calais and be sailing for home on the evening tide.

Providing Heloise did not fly from him during the night. Starting to his feet, he crossed to the chamber door. And paused with his hand on the latch.

Perhaps the gentlemanly thing to do would be to let her go.

Heloise deserved a man who could love and nurture her, not scare and bully her.

Dammit, why was it so impossible to behave rationally around her? He ran a hand over his brow.

Seeing her sitting in that bed, chewing her nails like a frightened, lonely child, had made him want to take her in his arms and comfort her. But he knew it would not have worked. He was the last person she would want to seek comfort from. He was the worst of her problems. Besides, the feel of her slight body, snuggled trustingly against his in the coach, had filled him with most unchivalrous longings. Right this moment he wanted her with a ferocity that made him disgusted with himself.

God, what had he done? What was he to do?

Determined to prove she was capable of behaving correctly, Heloise sat bolt upright in the carriage all the way to Calais. In spite of the fact she had spent most of the night crying into her pillow, she was not going to repeat the mistake of yielding to exhaustion and falling asleep on a husband who seemed to regard any form of touching as an intrusion on his personal dignity.

She had served her purpose—giving him the opportunity to take revenge on Du Mauriac and concealing the chink in his armour that was his love for Felice. And now he did not know quite what to do with her.

He was avoiding her as much as he could. When they got to Calais, he left her in the carriage while he arranged their passage, then installed her in a private parlour to await the sailing while he went off for a walk. On the few occasions when he had deigned to speak to her, he had done so with such icy civility she just knew he regretted giving in to the rash impulse to marry her.

And who could blame him? No one was more unsuitable to be the wife of such a man than she!

By the time he came to inform her it was time to embark, she was trembling so badly she had to cling to his arm for support.

Just as they reached the companionway, a messenger dashed up to them. 'Countess of Walton? Formerly Mademoiselle Bergeron?' he panted.

When she nodded, he reached into his pocket and pulled out a letter. 'Thank heaven I reached you in time.' He grinned. 'Urgent, the sender said it was, that I got this to you before you left France.' His mission complete, the man melted back into the crowd that thronged the quayside.

'You had better open it at once,' she heard Charles say, and he pulled her slightly to one side, so that they did not impede other passengers from boarding.

'It is from my mother,' she said, after swiftly scanning the few lines of hastily scrawled script. 'Du Mauriac is dead.'

Translating for Charles, she read, "'…the Royalist officials sent to arrest him employed such zeal that many Bonapartists rushed to his aid. In the ensuing brawl, somebody stabbed him. Nobody knows yet who it was…'"

She clutched the letter to her bosom, her eyes closing in relief. Charles was safe.

'What violent times we live in,' Charles remarked, wondering why it felt as though the dock had lurched beneath his feet.

Heloise had only married him to escape Du Mauriac's clutches. What a pointless gesture she had made. If only she had waited a few days, and not panicked, she would not have had to make that ultimate sacrifice.

'Dear me,' he observed. 'You need not have married me after all.'

Chapter Five

Oh, poor Charles! He was already smarting from taking on a wife he did not really want, and now he had learned that at least part of his reason for doing so had ceased to exist.

But, instead of betraying his annoyance, he held out his arm and said in an icily polite voice, 'Will you come aboard now, madam?'

Oh, dear. She gulped. How he must wish he could just leave her on the quayside and go back to England alone. But he was too honourable even to suggest such a thing. Laying her hand upon his sleeve, she followed him up the gangplank, her heart so leaden in her chest she wondered it could keep beating.

He showed her to the cabin he had procured for the voyage, then informed her that he was going on deck. His face was frozen, his posture rigid, and she ached for his misery. It hurt all the more to know she was the cause of it!

Charles hardly dared breathe until the last rope was cast off and the ship began to slide out of the harbour. She had not made a last desperate bid for freedom. Even when the coast of France was no more than a smudge on the horizon, she remained resolutely belowdecks.

Avoiding him.

He paced restlessly, heedless of the spray which repeatedly scoured the decks.

His conscience was clear. After a night spent wrestling with it, he had deliberately given her several opportunities to give him the slip during the day. Why had she not taken them? She was not staying with him because she was avaricious, nor was she all that impressed by his title.

The only thing that might explain her resolute determination to stick to their bargain was the fact she had given her word. Did it mean so much to her? He pictured her eyes, burning with zeal when she had promised to be the best wife she knew how to be, and accepted that it must.

It was a novel concept, to link a woman with integrity. But then Heloise, he was beginning to see, was not like any woman he had ever known.

Below decks, Heloise groaned, wishing she could die. Then he would be sorry. She whimpered, reaching for the conveniently positioned bucket yet again. Or would he? No, he would probably just shrug one shoulder and declare that it was a great pity, but after all he could always marry someone else. It was not as though he cared for her—no, not one jot. How could he, to leave her to endure such suffering alone?

Not that she wanted him to see her in such a demeaning state, she amended, heaving into the bucket for what seemed like the hundredth time.

Oh, when would this nightmare be over? How long before she could leave this foul-smelling cupboard and breathe fresh air again?

Never, she realised, after an eternity had rolled and pitched relentlessly past. Though she could hear the sounds of the hull grating against the dock, of officers shouting commands and sailors running to obey, she was too weak to so much as lift her head from the coarse cotton pillow.

'Come, now, my lady,' she heard her husband's voice say, none too patiently. 'We have docked. It is high time to disembark—Good God!'

The evidence of Heloise's violent seasickness finally caught his eyes.

'Go away,' she managed resentfully when he approached the bunk, stern purpose in his eyes. He was a brute to insist she get up and move. Later, once the ship had remained steady for several hours, she might regain the strength to crawl. 'Leave me here to die,' she moaned.

'Nobody has ever yet died of seasickness,' he said briskly, swinging her into his arms. It was amazing how cheerful he felt to discover it was seasickness which had kept her belowdecks, when he had been imagining her lying there weeping for her lost freedom. 'I know it must have been unpleasant for you, but you will be right as a trivet once you get upon dry land.'

'Unpleasant?' she protested. 'I have never suffered anything so horrid. How could you be so cruel as to force me to go to sea in a storm? I think—' she hiccupped down a sob '—that I hate you.'

'I am sure you don't mean that,' he reproved her mildly. Although he wasn't at all convinced. 'Besides, the sea was scarcely more than a bit choppy.' He consoled himself with the reflection that, even if she did hate him, nothing but the direst distress would ever induce her to endure another sea voyage.

He had planned to push on to London straight away, but

he could not force Heloise to travel in her weakened state. He told the coachman to stop at the first hotel that could offer a suite of rooms.

He left her to herself for as long as he could. But when night fell concern for her had him knocking on her door and marching in before she had time to deny him admittance.

She was sitting up in bed, looking much better. Indeed, the nearer he got to the bed, the rosier her cheeks grew…

He checked in the middle of the room, biting down on a feeling of irritation. Did she think he was crass enough to insist on his marital rights, after she had been so ill? But before he could begin to defend himself Heloise blurted out, 'Oh, I am so sorry, Charles, about what I said.'

'What exactly that you said are you apologising for?' He frowned, drawing a chair to her bedside and settling himself on it.

'For saying that I hate you! I thought you meant to force me to walk off that ship and try to behave like a lady, when all I wished to do was die. I never guessed you were going to pick me up and carry me. And I had spent the entire voyage cursing you, so it was hard to get myself out of thinking that everything was entirely your fault. Indeed, at that precise moment I think I did hate you. But of course now I have calmed down I fully accept it is not your fault that I have seasickness. And you weren't at all cruel to force me to go on that ship. It would only have been cruel if you had known how ill I would be—and how could you, when I never knew myself? For I have never been on a ship before!'

'Nor will you ever set foot on one again,' he said with determination.

She shuddered. 'Indeed not.'

He paused. 'You know, of course, that means you can never return to France.'

They eyed each other warily as the import of his remark sank in, each convinced the other must regret this truth, and each equally determined to conceal their hurts.

It was Charles who ended the impasse, by leaning back, crossing one leg over the other, and declaring, 'Since you do not hate me at this precise moment, perhaps this would be a good time to discuss our mode of life together?'

Recalling the way he had indicated he wished her to keep herself amused, and not interfere with his no doubt hectic social life, Heloise forced herself to nod, waiting to hear what further layers of humiliation he meant to heap on her.

'I don't wish to raise any speculation about my marriage by appearing to pack you off to the country as though I did not like you.' She would have to live with him in London, just to begin with, to prevent any speculation regarding their union. Not that he cared what people said about him. But he did not want her exposed to the sort of malicious gossip that was bound to hurt her. 'The season has not yet properly begun, but that will give you time to procure a suitable wardrobe and settle into your new role. I expect it will take you some time to find your feet, socially speaking, but until you have acquired your own circle of acquaintance I will ensure you always have a trustworthy escort to any event you may wish to attend.

'Naturally, I do not expect you to understand the British political system. All I expect from you is to be charming to those I introduce as my political allies, and reserved towards my opponents. Even though you may not like them, I shall expect you to be hospitable to the more important party members to whom I shall make you known, and their wives, when I have occasion to invite them to any of my homes. Do not worry, however, that I shall expect much of you as a hostess. I have excellent staff running all my properties, and a sterling secretary to whom you may apply, should you find yourself floundering in the political shoals.'

Heloise listened to that patronising little speech with growing indignation. If it would not give rise to the very speculation he wished to avoid, he would as soon pack her off to one of his country houses. Her poor little brain was no match for the intricacies of the English political system. She was not to interfere in the management of any of his households, which were all running exactly as he wished. And if she had any questions, he wished her to apply to his secretary rather than bother him!

'Heloise?' he prompted, when she had been sitting in simmering silence for several minutes. He sighed. She clearly felt overwhelmed by the idea of being a leading figure in society. 'You must tell me if there are any gaps in your education which may cause you difficulties.' He had no intention of throwing her in at the deep end and letting her sink or swim as best she could.

'G...gaps?' she gasped, flashing him a look so indignant even he could not misinterpret it.

'Don't fly into the boughs with me,' he retorted, annoyed that she should cling to her hostility when he was doing all in his power to smooth her entry into society. 'If you cannot dance then I need to know, so that I may engage a dancing master for you. If you cannot ride then there is no point in me acquiring a horse for you to show off its paces in the park. I would instead purchase a barouche, or landaulet, and employ extra grooms to take you about.'

Her cheeks flushing, she hung her head. 'I beg your pardon, my lord,' she said, as humbly as she could. She had to admit he was trying to make the best of a bad job. He was prepared to employ as many staff as it would take to ensure she would be able to carry off the role he expected her to play. Just so long as he didn't have to be personally involved.

'I have learned to dance,' she flashed at him. 'Though you probably never saw me stand up whenever we went to balls in Paris. For not many men have ever asked me to dance, and when I was with you it was in the role of chaperon, so it was not at all appropriate. As for the horse, it is true that I cannot ride.'

'Should you like to learn?'

'Do you wish me to?'

'I should never object to any activity which would give you pleasure, Heloise,' he said wearily. It was clear that he was not going to win his wife's trust overnight. And her mention of how he had neglected her, whilst showering attentions on her sister, reminded him she had a deep well of resentment from which to draw. 'I bid you goodnight.'

He placed a chaste kiss on her forehead and retreated before things deteriorated any further. She might declare she did not hate him, but she had withdrawn sufficiently to start calling him 'my lord' again.

All he could do was keep sufficient distance for her to forget to regard him as a tyrant, whilst maintaining a watchful eye on her. She would learn, eventually, that she could trust him.

Wouldn't she?

London was not at all like Paris. The streets and squares through which their carriage passed were so clean and orderly, giving an overall air of prosperity. She frowned. Although perhaps it was just that her husband inhabited one of the better areas. This, she surmised as the carriage drew to a halt outside an imposing mansion, whose doorway was flanked by two massive pillars supporting a portico, was probably the equivalent of the 'court' end of Paris. There were probably overcrowded and dirty alleys somewhere. It was just that as an English countess she would never set foot in them.

A footman dressed in blue and silver livery handed her from the coach, and she entered her new home on her husband's arm. Oblivious to the interested stares of the servants who had gathered to greet their new mistress, Heloise gazed in awe at the lofty dimensions of the hall. A marble staircase swept upwards, branching at a half-landing to serve the two wings of the first storey, then continued up by several more flights, as far as she could see. Light flooded in through a domed skylight at the very top. Walton House reminded her of one of the better hotels in Paris, though it was shocking to think one man lived here alone. In Paris, a house like this would be divided into several apartments, which would be leased to tourists to provide an income for the impoverished nobles who clung to the upper floors.

An upper servant approached, bowing. 'Begging your pardon, my lord, but Captain Fawley has requested the honour of making the acquaintance of your Countess.'

'Has he, indeed?' Handing over his gloves and hat, Charles wondered what new start this might be. 'How does the Captain fare today?'

'Restless, my lord,' the footman replied, wooden-faced.

'My lady,' Charles said to Heloise, placing his hand under her elbow. 'A word in private, if you please?'

Drawing her into a little ante-room, he shut the door to ensure total privacy. 'I have little time to explain, but I would request a further favour of you. I had planned on sparing you the worst of Captain Fawley's temper, but on this one occasion I would ask that you bear me company and back me up in whatever I say. Can you do that for me?'

'This Captain Fawley…he is the man you wished me not to meet, who lives here with you?'

'I have no time to explain it all, but the salient facts are these: Captain Fawley is my brother. He hates me. He hates the fact that since he was invalided out of the army he has been forced to depend on me. I fear he will use your presence in my life as an excuse to try to strike out on his own. He must not do so, Heloise.' He took her by the shoulders, his eyes burning with an intensity she had never seen before. 'He must stay in Walton House!'

'Of course I will do whatever it takes to prevent him from leaving, if that is your wish,' she replied, though it all seemed very strange to her. Whatever could have gone wrong between them? Was this to do with the rift Charles had referred to before, with certain of his family?

'Robert—that is Captain Fawley—occupies a suite of rooms at the rear of the house, on the ground floor,' he explained as he steered her out of the little ante-room and across the hall. 'His condition when I first brought him back from the Peninsula made it imperative that he not have to attempt stairs. Also, I had hoped that installing him in these particular rooms would encourage him to make free of the place. They have a private entrance, leading to the mews, which would have made it easy for him to come and go as he pleased.'

They reached a set of panelled doors, upon which Charles knocked. To her surprise, he did not simply enter, but waited until the door was opened by a stocky servant, dressed in a plain black coat and stuff breeches.

'Ah, Linney,' Charles said, 'I believe Captain Fawley has expressed an interest in meeting my bride?'

'Indeed he has, m'lord,' the stocky man replied, his own face as impassive as her husband's. Why, then, did she get the impression that both of them saw this as a momentous occasion?

It took Heloise's eyes a moment or two to acclimatise to the gloom that pervaded the room she walked into. Lit only by the flames of a roaring fire, it was clearly the domain of a man who did not care what his visitors might think. Her nose wrinkled at the smell of stale sweat, unwashed linen and general neglect that hung in the over-heated room. Unfortunately, it was the exact moment her eyes came to rest on a figure sprawled on a scuffed leather sofa, to one side of the soot-blackened fireplace.

For a second her heart seemed to stop beating. The man who regarded her with piercingly hostile black eyes was so very like Gaspard that she uttered a little cry and ran to him, her hands outstretched.

Leaning on his shoulders, she planted a kiss on each cheek, before sitting down next to him. When he flinched, she said, 'Oh, dear—should I not have done that? I have embarrassed you. It is just that you are so like my own dear brother.' In spite of herself, her eyes filled with tears. 'Who I will never see again. But now I find my husband has a brother, so I have a brother again, too.'

Somewhat overcome, she reached into her reticule for a handkerchief. While she was busy blowing her nose, she heard Charles cross to the fireplace.

'You haven't embarrassed me as much as I fear you have embarrassed yourself,' Captain Fawley snarled. 'Linney, perhaps you would be so good as to draw back the curtains?'

In silence, the manservant did as he was bade. Sunlight streamed in, illuminating the livid burns down one side of the Captain's face, head and neck, which the length of his unkempt hair did little to conceal. The left sleeve of his threadbare jacket was empty; the lower part of his left leg was also missing.

Perplexed, Heloise said, 'Why will drawing the curtains make me embarrassed?'

Captain Fawley laughed—a harsh noise that sounded as though it was torn from his throat. 'You have just kissed a cripple! Don't you feel sick? Most pretty women would recoil if they saw me, not want to kiss this!' He indicated his scarred face with an angry sweep of his right hand.

But, 'Oh!' said Heloise, her face lighting up. 'Do you really think I am pretty? How much more I like you already.'

The stunned look on Captain Fawley's face was as nothing compared to what Charles felt. Her face alight with pleasure, Heloise really did look remarkably pretty. He could not think why he had never noticed it before. Her eyes sparkled with intelligence, she had remarkably thick, lustrous hair, and a dainty little figure. She did not have the obvious attractions of her sister, but she was far from the plain, dull little creature he had written off while his eyes had been full of Felice. 'Captivating', Conningsby had said of her. Aye, she was. And she would be a credit to him once he had her properly dressed.

There was a certain dressmaker in Bond Street whose designs would suit her to a tee…

'You cannot mean that!' Robert began to curse.

A few minutes of such Turkish treatment was all he would permit Heloise to endure, then he would escort her to the safety of her rooms.

'Why not?' Unfazed, Heloise untied the ribbons of her bonnet and placed the shapeless article on her lap. Charles had a vision of wresting it from her hands, throwing it off a bridge into the Thames, and replacing it with a neat little crimson velvet creation, trimmed with swansdown.

'Well, because I am disfigured,' Captain Fawley said. 'I am only half a man.'

She cocked her head to examine him, in the way that always put the Earl in mind of a cheeky little sparrow. She missed nothing—from the toe of Robert's right boot to the puckered eyelid that drooped into the horrible scarring that truly did disfigure the left side of his face.

'You have only lost a bit of one leg and a bit of one arm,' she said. 'Not even a tenth of you has gone. You may think of yourself as nine-tenths of a man, I suppose, if you must, but not less than that. Besides—' she shrugged '—many others did not survive the war at all. Gaspard did not. I tell you now, I would still have been glad to have him back, and nothing would have prevented me from embracing him, no matter how many limbs he might have lost!'

'But you must want me to leave this house,' he blustered. 'And once an heir is on the way—' he rounded on Charles '—you can have no more excuses to keep me imprisoned here!'

Before he could draw breath to reply, Heloise said, rather stiffly, 'Is it because I am French?'

'Wh…what?'

'You reject my friendship because I am French. In effect, all this nonsense about being disfigured is the flim-flam. You don't want me for your sister.'

Faced with an indignant woman, Captain Fawley could do nothing but retreat from his stance, muttering apologies. 'It is not your fault you are French. You can't help that. Or being married to my half-brother, I dare say. I know how ruthless he can be when he wants his own way.' He glared up at Charles.

'Then you will help me?' Again, her face lit up with hope. 'Because Charles, he says it is not at all fashionable for a husband to hang on his wife's arm all the time. I have heard in Paris all about the season in London, with the masquerades, and the picnics, and the fireworks, which he will not at all want to take me to, even if I was not his wife, because such things are all very frivolous and not good *ton*. But I would like to see them all. And he said I may, if I could find a suitable escort. And who would be more proper to go about with me than my own brother? And then, you know, he says I must learn to ride…'

'Well, I can't teach you to ride! Haven't you noticed? I've only got one leg!'

Heloise regarded his left leg with a thoughtful air. 'You have only lost a little bit of the lower part of one leg. You still have your thigh, and that, I believe, is what is important for staying in the saddle. Do I have that correct? You men grip with your knees, is that not so? Whereas I—' she pulled a face '—must learn to ride side-saddle. I will have to hang on with my hands to the reins, and keep my balance while the creature is bouncing along…'

'Well, there you have it!' Captain Fawley pointed out. 'You have both hands. I have only one, and—'

'Oh, don't tell me you are afraid of falling off!' she mocked.

Charles suddenly felt conscious of holding his breath. For weeks before he had gone to Paris he had known Robert had regained most of his health and strength. There had been nothing preventing him from getting out and resuming a normal life but his own black mood. Had they all failed him by tiptoeing round his sensibilities?

'A brave soldier like you?' Heloise continued relentlessly. 'You are full of…of… Well, it is not polite to mention what you are full of!'

Captain Fawley turned for support to his brother. 'Tell her, Charles. Tell her that I just can't—'

Charles cut him off with a peremptory wave of his hand. 'You had as well give in graciously. Once she has the bit between her teeth, there is no stopping her. You cannot argue with her logic because it is of that singularly female variety which always completely confounds we mere males.' So saying, he swept her a mocking bow.

Robert sank back into the cushions, looking as though he had been hit by a whirlwind. Heloise was still watching him, her head tilted to one side, a hopeful expression on her face. And all of a sudden the dour cripple let out a bark of genuine laughter.

'I quite see why you married her, Walton.'

'Indeed, she left me no choice.'

'Very well, madam. I will come with you when you start your riding lessons,' he conceded. Then he frowned. 'Since I expect we will both fall off with monotonous regularity, I recommend we take our lessons early in the mornings, when nobody will be about to see us.'

She clapped her hands, her face lighting up with joy. Something twisted painfully inside Charles. Nothing he had ever done or said to her had managed to please her half so well.

'I dare say,' he said brusquely, 'you would like to see your rooms now, madam wife, and freshen up a little?'

Heloise pulled a face at Robert. 'What he means, no doubt, is that I look a mess, and that also he wishes to take me aside to give me a lecture about my appalling manners.'

'No, I am sure not,' Robert replied, regarding the stiff

set of Walton's shoulders with a perplexed frown. 'Your manners are delightfully refreshing.'

Heloise laughed at that, but once they had quit Captain Fawley's suite she turned anxious eyes on her husband.

He made no comment until he had taken her to the suite of rooms he'd had his staff prepare for his bride. On sight of them, Heloise gasped aloud. She had her own sitting room, with a pale blue Aubusson carpet upon which various comfortable sofas and chairs were arranged. Her bedroom, too, was carpeted almost to the wainscot. With a smile, Heloise imagined getting up in the morning and setting her bare feet on that, rather than the rough boards of the little room she had shared with her sister. No shutters on any of the windows, she noted, only heavy dark blue velvet curtains, held back with self-coloured cords.

'I hope you like it—though of course if there are any alterations you wish to make, you have only to say.'

Heloise spread her hands, shrugging her utter bewilderment at such opulence. 'How could I not like this?' she managed to say, when it became apparent that her husband was waiting for her to say something.

It seemed to have been the right thing to say, for some of the tension left his stance. 'I will ring and ask for refreshments to be served up here in your sitting room,' he said, crossing to the bell-pull beside the chimney breast. 'You may rest assured I shall not intrude upon your privacy. This is your domain. Just as the rooms downstairs are Robert's. The only time I shall enter, save at your express invitation, will be to bid you goodnight. Every night,' he finished sternly.

So that the servants would believe they were a normal husband and wife, she assumed. She sighed as a group of them came in and laid out the tea things. She supposed she should be grateful he wanted things to look right. At least she would get to see him once each day. Otherwise, the place being so vast, they might not bump into each other from one end of the week to the other.

Once the servants had retreated, Charles said, 'Come, Heloise, I can see you are bursting with questions. I have a little time to spare to indulge your curiosity before I must be about other business.'

There was no point in questioning their living arrangements. She had promised not to be a nuisance. But she would like to know what on earth had happened between the two Fawley brothers for them to come to this.

'Why does your brother accuse you of imprisoning him here? Is this something to do with the rift in your family you spoke of to me?'

'You do not need to have tea served if you do not like it,' he remarked, noticing the grimace of distaste with which she had set down her teacup after taking only one sip. 'The kitchen can provide anything you wish for.'

'Don't you wish to tell me? Is that why you talk about tea? If you do not want me to know about your family secrets then you only need to say, and I will not pry any further!'

'That is not the issue!' This was not a topic he found it easy to discuss. She would have to make do with a succinct account of the facts. 'Robert's mother was my father's second wife,' he bit out. 'In their zeal to protect me from her influence, when my father died the people he had nominated my guardians sent her back to her own family— with a modest annuity and penalties attached should she try to inveigle herself back into my life.'

'What was she, then, Robert's mother?' Heloise asked, fascinated. 'Something scandalous? An actress, perhaps, or a woman of easy morals?'

Charles smiled grimly. 'Worse than that, in the opinion of my stiff-rumped maternal relatives. She was a doctor's daughter.'

At Heloise's complete bafflement, he continued, 'She was, with her middle-class values, the kind of person who might have influenced me into thinking less of my consequence than they thought I should. They reminded me that my real mother was the Duke of Bray's granddaughter, and set about instilling me with pride in my true lineage. Rigorously.'

Heloise shook her head. What a miserable little boy he must have been. But worse was to come.

'I did not even know that I had a brother until, when I came of age, I began to go through all the family papers with my lawyers, instead of just ratifying them as my guardians assumed I would. I discovered that Robert had been born some five months after my father's death. Instead of having him raised with me, and acknowledged as second in line to my inheritance, they consigned him to the care of his mother's family. By the time he was sixteen, so vehemently did he hate my mother's relations that he began to refuse even the meagre allowance they had arranged for him. Instead he requested they purchase him a commission, so that he could make his own way in the world without having any need for further contact with relatives who had made no secret of the fact they wished he had not been born. Which they did—hoping, no doubt, that his career would be short and bloody. It was not long after that when I discovered his existence. And by then he was beyond my reach. He neither wanted nor needed anything from the brother he had grown up hating.'

'Oh, Charles,' she said, her eyes wide with horror. 'How awful. What did you do?'

He looked at her with eyes that had grown cold. 'I did as I was trained to do. I acted without emotion. I severed all connection with those who had systematically robbed me, my stepmother and my brother of each other.'

'And what,' she asked, 'happened to Robert's mother?'

'She scarcely survived his birth. The story he had from his family was that she died from a broken heart, at the treatment meted out to her whilst she was still in shock at being widowed.'

No wonder Charles appeared so hard and cold. The one person who might have taught him to embrace the softer emotions had been ruthlessly excised from his orbit. Then his relatives had taught him, the hard way, that there was nobody upon whom he could rely.

No wonder he had been able to shrug off the loss of a fiancée with such panache. Her betrayal was nothing compared to what he had already experienced.

And yet, in spite of all that, he had never stopped reaching out to the brother who repaid all his overtures with bristling hostility.

'Oh, Charles,' she cried, longing to take him in her arms and hold him. Tell him he was not alone any more. She was there.

She had begun to stretch out her hands towards him before recalling what a futile gesture it was. She could not be of any comfort to him, for he was only tolerating her presence in his life. Besides, he had already expressed his dislike of her propensity for being demonstrative.

'I am so sorry,' she said, swallowing back the tears she knew he would disparage, and folding her hands in her lap with a feeling of resignation. He had only confided in her so that she might understand the situation, and not create further difficulties with his brother.

He made that very clear by turning on his heel and stalking from the room.

What further proof, thought Charles, seeking the solitude of his own bedchamber, did he need that she now considered him more repulsive than Du Mauriac? Even though her heart had been moved by his tale, she hadn't been able to bring herself to so much as touch his arm through his coat sleeve. But she had run to Robert and managed to kiss him. On both cheeks.

Chapter Six

'I have brought my bride to you for dressing,' the Earl informed Madame Pichot, upon entering her establishment the following morning. 'She needs everything.'

Madame Pichot's eyes lit up. 'Walking dresses, day dresses, ballgowns, nightrail?' She swallowed. 'A court dress?'

'Naturally.' By the time such a grand toilette was complete, and Heloise had practised walking in the hoops, he would have found someone to present her in Queen Caroline's drawing room. It was not so great a hurdle as obtaining vouchers for Almacks. If she offended one of the six patronesses of that exclusive club, or if they decided her background failed to meet their exacting standards for membership, she would never be truly a part of the *haut ton*.

Noting Heloise's rather worn coat and battered bonnet, Madame Pichot ventured, 'I could have one or two items delivered later today, or possibly first thing tomorrow. Just to tide milady over, of course…'

The Earl nodded acquiescence. Heloise would find it

easier to think of herself as an English countess once she shucked off the serviceable clothing of a French bureaucrat's daughter.

'In future, should we require your services, you will present yourself at Walton House at my wife's convenience.'

'Of course, my lord,' replied the dressmaker, somewhat startled by the statement Heloise knew had been made primarily for her benefit. Whatever had been her habit formerly, a countess did not deign to visit a dressmaker's. She sent for such people to wait on her in the privacy of her own home.

'My wife will wear pastel colours. Rose and powderblue—and, yes, this primrose satin would suit my wife's colouring.' He fingered one of the swatches an assistant had brought for his inspection.

'Oh, but with *madame*'s dark hair and eyes, she could wear striking colours. This crimson would look ravishing.'

'I don't want her going about looking like a demi-rep,' he curtly informed the somewhat abashed modiste.

Heloise had just taken a breath to object and say that she was quite capable of selecting her own gowns, thank you very much, when her mother's warning rang loud in her memory. He would want her to look the part she had persuaded him she could play. That he had no confidence in her dress sense might be somewhat insulting, but then, he was the one picking up the bills. Feeling like a child's dress-up doll, she meekly tried on the few gowns that were already made up, and had never been collected by other clients, while Charles and the modiste between them decided which could be altered to fit, and which did nothing for her.

A trip to a milliner followed, and then to the bootmakers, where she had her feet measured for a last.

'You must be growing tired,' Charles eventually declared, when all his efforts to spoil his wife had met with supreme indifference.

Felice would have been in ecstasy to have had so much money spent on a wardrobe of such magnificence, not to mention his undivided attention in selecting it. But Heloise, he was coming to realise, cared as little for such fripperies as she did for him. He was not going to reach her by showering her with the kind of gifts that would win most women over.

'I have other business to attend to for the rest of the day,' he told her. 'But I shall be in for dinner this evening. Will you dine with me?'

Heloise blinked in surprise. He had spent hours with her today already. She had assumed he would have something better to do with his evening. But he had actually asked her to dine with him!

Struggling to conceal her elation, she had just taken a breath to form a suitably controlled reply when he added, 'Or would you rather remain in your room?'

Was that a veiled way of telling her that was what he wished her to do? Did he hope she would take the hint?

Well, she was blowed if she was going to take all her meals in her rooms as if…as if she were a naughty child!

'I will dine with you,' she said, with a militant lift to her chin.

As though she were about to face a firing squad, he thought, hurt by her response to a simple invitation.

'Until tonight, then.' He bowed, then stalked away.

The evening was not a success. Charles made polite enquiries about how she had spent the rest of her day, while they sat sipping sherry in an oppressively immaculate ante-room. He looked relieved when the footman came to inform them dinner was ready. She soon realised this was because they would no longer be alone. A troupe of footmen served a staggering variety of dishes, whisked away empty plates, poured wine, and effectively robbed the event of any hint of intimacy.

Her heart did begin to pound when Charles leaned forward, beckoning to her, indicating that he wished to whisper something to her. Only to plunge at his words.

'At this point it is the custom for ladies to withdraw. I shall join you in the drawing room when I have taken some port.'

Feeling humiliated that he'd had to remind her of this English custom, Heloise followed one of the younger footmen to a vast room that was so chilly her arms broke out in goose pimples the moment she stepped over the threshold. She sat huddled over the lacklustre fire for what seemed like an eternity before Charles joined her.

'Should you like to play cards?' he suggested. 'Some people find it helps to pass the time until the tea tray is brought in.'

He could not have made it clearer that this was the last way he wished to spend his evening.

'I enjoy cards as little as I care to pour that vile drink, which is fit only for an invalid, down my throat,' she replied rather petulantly.

'Most husbands,' he replied frostily, 'take themselves off to their clubs, where they find companionship and amusements they cannot find at home, leaving their wives free of their burdensome presence.'

As Heloise stormed up the stairs, she decided never to set foot in that horrible drawing room again. If Charles would rather go off to his club, then let him go! She did not care, she vowed, slamming her sitting room door behind her, almost knocking over one of the silly little tables dotted about the floor as she stormed across the room to fling herself onto the sofa.

She glared at it, and the collection of ornaments it held with resentment. She hated clutter. She would have to get a footman to move it against the wall, out of the way. After all, Charles had said she could do as she pleased up here.

A militant gleam came to her eye and she sat up straight. He had meant she could decorate as she pleased. But she could do much more than that. She dared not ask him for a proper drawing table, knowing how much he disapproved of her sketches, but if, under the pretext of reorganising her rooms, she had that one large desk moved to a spot between the two windows, to catch the maximum daylight…

Her spirits began to lift. Drawing was more than just a hobby to her. She could lose herself for hours in the fantasy world she created on paper. It had been a solace to her in Paris, where she had been such a disappointment to her parents. How much more would it comfort her here in London, as an unwanted bride?

Her fingers were already itching to draw Madame Pichot, with her peculiar accent that would only pass for French in England. She reminded her of a drawing she had seen in the Louvre, of a creature whose eyes stood out on stalks and which was said to change colour to match whatever type of background it walked across.

Though how she was to locate a really good shop where she could buy pencils, paper and brushes without Charles finding out, leave alone how she would pay for her materials, would pose quite a problem.

It was very late when Charles came up to bid her goodnight, as he had warned her he would do.

'Do you have everything you need?' he enquired politely.

'Yes, thank you,' she replied in an equally polite tone, her fingers plucking listlessly at the quilt.

'Then I will bid you goodnight,' he said, barely brushing his lips across her forehead.

Heloise glared at his back as he left, barely suppressing the urge to fling some pillows at it. She was not a child for him to come and kiss goodnight in that insufferably condescending manner! She was surprised he did not tuck her in and pat her on the head while he was about it!

But the sad truth was she was as inexperienced as a child. She had no idea how to encourage her husband to regard her as a woman rather than a girl. And there was no female to advise her. Her worst fear was that if she did try to breach his reserve she might only succeed in alienating him completely. She heaved a sigh as she sank down under the covers. At least *he* appeared content with the present situation.

Several evenings passed in an equally unsatisfactory manner before Heloise discovered a chink in Charles' armour.

When they met before dinner, and he enquired, as he always did, how she had spent her day, she told him that several outfits had arrived, and she had spent the afternoon trying them on.

'Was the riding habit among them?'

'Yes, and it is…' She bit her tongue. The pale blue gown with its silver frogging had instantly put her in mind of his servants' livery, and had made her crushingly aware that he only regarded her as just one more of his chattels. 'It is very pretty,' she finished in a subdued tone.

'If you are still determined to learn to ride, I could arrange for you to begin lessons with Robert tomorrow morning.' He frowned into his sherry glass for a few seconds, before saying softly, 'I bought him a lovely bay mare, very soft about the mouth, for Christmas. He has never even been to look her over. I shall be for ever in your debt—' he flicked her a glance '—if you could goad him into taking some form of exercise.'

'Of course!' she cried, immensely flattered that he had entrusted her with such an important mission. 'He must not stay in those dark rooms and moulder away.'

The rigid formality of the dining room was completely unable to dampen her spirits that night. For now she had a plan.

If she could be the means to help poor Robert get out of his rooms, Charles would be pleased with her. Riding lessons would only be the start. He could take her shopping for art supplies. And, though he might be sensitive about his scars, surely she could get him to take her to Vauxhall Gardens to watch the fireworks one evening? Buoyed up by the prospect, she received her husband's goodnight kiss with complaisance. Even though he was dressed in his evening clothes, and clearly on his way out.

One day, she vowed, snuggling down beneath the covers, he would take her with him on one of these forays into London's night life from which he had so far excluded her. If all went well with Robert in the morning, it might be quite soon!

The sound of the outer door slamming, not once, but twice, roused Charles from the pile of invitations he had been poring over in his study early the next morning. As the season got under way, more and more people were expressing an interest in meeting his bride. But he had no intention of exposing her to this collection of rakes, cynics, and bitches, he vowed, tossing a handful of gilt-edged invitations into the fire. It said something about his social circle that he thought it unlikely he would ever find a house into which he could take his vulnerable young bride without risk of having her confidence ripped to shreds.

'Stop right there!' he heard Robert bellow, just as he emerged from the study. Heloise, the back of her powder-blue riding habit liberally stained with mud, was fleeing up the stairs.

She did not even pause, but ran along the corridor to her rooms, from whence echoed the sound of yet another slamming door.

Robert, red-faced, had stopped at the foot of the staircase, clutching the newel post.

'Problems?' Charles drawled softly.

Robert spun round so swiftly the heel of his false leg slipped on the marble floor and he nearly lost his balance.

'Go on, then—order me to leave your house!' he panted.

Charles leaned against the doorjamb, folding his arms across his chest. 'Why do you suppose I should wish to do that?'

'Because I have insulted your bride,' Robert flung at him. 'I swore at her. Comprehensively and at length! You must have seen that she was crying when she fled up the stairs!'

Frowning, Charles pushed himself from the doorframe and advanced on his brother. 'If you have insulted her, it is for you to put right. This is your home. I shall not evict you from it.'

Glowering, Robert spat, 'And just how do you propose I make the apology? Crawl up all those stairs?'

Charles regarded the false leg his brother had, for the first time to his knowledge, strapped onto his mangled knee joint. Heloise was amazing. She had only been here a matter of days, and already she'd cajoled Robert out of his rooms, into his false leg, and onto the back of a horse.

'No,' he mused. 'Until she calms down, I dare say all that will happen is that she will inform you she hates you. Far better to wait until she has had time to reflect on her own part in your quarrel. I suggest you join us for dinner tonight, and make your apologies then.'

'Dinner?' Robert blustered. 'I had as well crawl to her suite now as to attempt ascending to any other rooms on the upper floors!'

'Then I will order dinner for the three of us in the little salon,' he replied, indicating a room across the hall. His heart beating with uncomfortable rapidity, he waited for Robert to protest that nothing would make him sit down and eat with the man who had been instrumental in causing his mother's death. Instead, he only glared mutinously before hobbling back to his own rooms and slamming the door behind him.

Upstairs, Heloise was blowing her nose vigorously. It was no good feeling sorry for herself. That her first riding lesson had been such a fiasco was not what upset her the most, though that had been bad enough. What really hurt was her failure to gain any ground with Robert at all. Charles would be so disappointed with her.

Startled by a tap on the door, she blew her nose again, annoyed to find her eyes were watering afresh.

'May I come in?'

Charles stood in the doorway, ruefully regarding his wife's crestfallen appearance. 'Was it the horse, or my brother?'

Waving admittance to the footman who hovered behind him, bearing a tray of what looked like His Lordship's finest brandy, Charles advanced into the room.

'I thought you might feel in need of a little restorative,' he explained, as the young man placed the silver salver on an elegant little table beside the sofa she had flung herself on when first she had come to her room. 'And, since I know of your aversion to tea, I thought I would supply something more to your liking.'

'You are m…most k…kind,' Heloise half sobbed, as Charles stooped to pick her riding hat up from the floor, where she had flung it not five minutes before. The feather that adorned the crown had snapped. He ran his fingers over it with a frown.

'Why is your hat on the floor? Is your dresser not in attendance?'

'I have not rung for her. I don't want her!' she snapped. Since he was already disappointed in her, she had nothing to lose by admitting she could not live up to his exacting standards. 'If I wish to throw my hat on the floor and…and stamp on it, then I have no wish to have her tutting at me as though I am a naughty child. It is my hat, after all, and I can do with it as I see fit!'

Instead of reprimanding her for her childish outburst, he merely smiled and remarked, 'I'll buy you another one,' tossing the crumpled headgear to the footman as he exited the rooms.

'I don't want another one,' Heloise said, perversely irritated by his magnanimity in the face of her tantrum. 'I am never getting on another horse again as long as I live.'

'I thought you scoffed at people who disliked falling from horses. I seem to remember you saying—'

'Yes, I remember very well what I said. If the horse had been trotting, or even walking, it might not have been so humiliating. But the horrid creature was standing perfectly still when I fell off. If I can fall off a stationary horse, which is being held at the head by a groom, I cannot think how much worse it will be should the brute try to move.'

'Are you badly hurt?' Charles frowned, suddenly wondering whether her tears and her evident discomfort might stem from more than wounded pride. 'Should I send for a doctor?'

So, after a perfunctory check, he was going to palm her off on another person? If they had the relationship a husband and wife ought to have, he would be running his hands over her bruises right now, assuring himself that nothing important was damaged. Instead of which he had handed her a drink, with a mocking smile twisting his lips.

'I don't need a doctor.' She sighed. I need a husband. A husband who would put his arms round me and tell me everything is all right, that he is not ashamed of his stupid little wife, or disappointed in her failure to help poor Robert.

Mutinously, she went to the bellrope and tugged on it viciously. 'I wish to change out of these clothes now,' she informed him. 'And take a bath. Unless there is anything else you wish to say to me?'

Charles bowed politely, remarking, 'Only that I hope, when your temper has cooled a little, you will endeavour to mend fences with Robert. I have invited him to dine with us this evening. It is the first time that he has agreed to do so. I would not wish it to be his last.'

Heloise glared at the door through which he departed. Not a word of thanks for her efforts, abortive though they had been. Only a stern warning to watch her behaviour at dinner this evening, so as not to offend his precious brother any further. He had not even bothered to find out what the boor had said to upset her!

Nothing she ever did would please him.

Very well, then, she would start pleasing herself. She

tore at the silver buttons of her riding habit with trembling fingers. She would dismiss the horrible dresser who looked down her nose at her. As a pair of housemaids came in, carrying towels and cans of hot water, she eyed them speculatively. Her husband seemed to employ dozens of staff. If she could not find one amongst them with whom she could strike up a tolerable relationship, then she would advertise for an experienced lady's maid and begin to conduct interviews. If nothing else, it would give her something to fill the endless monotony of her days.

And as for tonight… Oh, Lord! She sank into the steaming fragrant water of her bath and bowed her head over her raised knees. Charles would be watching her like a hawk. Robert would resent her for being the catalyst that had forced the two men to eat at the same table. She would be like a raw steak being fought over by two butcher's dogs.

By the time she entered the little salon Robert and Charles were already there, sitting on either side of the fireplace, sipping their drinks in a silence fraught with tension. Both, to her surprise, looked relieved to see her.

'I believe I owe you an apology,' Robert said, struggling to his feet.

She merely raised one eyebrow as she perched on the edge of the third chair which had been set before the hearth.

'All right, dash it! I *know* I owe you an apology. I should never have used such language to a female…'

'Not even a French female?' she replied archly, accepting the drink the footman handed to her. 'Who is not even of noble birth, is an enemy of your country, and most probably a spy to boot?'

Flushing darkly, Robert muttered, 'If I said any of those things to you this morning…'

'If?'

'All right. I admit I said a lot more besides the swearing I have reason to apologise for! But don't you think it is pretty disgusting behaviour to laugh at a cripple?'

'Oh, I was not laughing at you, Robert.' Heloise reached a hand towards him impulsively, her eyes filling with tears. 'No wonder you got so cross, if that was what you thought. It would indeed have been the most unforgivable behaviour if that was so!'

'But you were laughing…'

'It was the horse! When you went to climb onto him from the right side it looked so surprised. I have never seen such an expression on an animal's face before.' A smile twitched her lips at the memory. 'And it turned to stare at you, and it tried to turn round to place you on what it thought was the correct side, and the groom was dodging about under its head, and you were clutching onto the saddle to stop from falling off the mounting block…'

'I suppose it must have looked pretty funny from where you were sitting,' Robert grudgingly admitted. 'Only you have no idea how I felt—too damned clumsy to mount a slug like that, when I've always been accounted a natural in the saddle.'

'I'm sorry, Robert. But you have to admit I received just punishment for my thoughtlessness.'

He barked out a harsh laugh. 'Aye. You should have seen her, Walton. Laughed herself right out of the saddle. Lost her balance and landed on the cobbles at my feet…'

'With you swearing down at me while I was struggling to untangle all those yards of riding habit from my legs…'

'And the grooms not knowing where to look, or how to keep their faces straight…'

'It sounds better than the pantomime,' Charles put in

dryly. 'Ah, Giddings, it is good to see you back with us. I take it your presence indicates that our dinner is ready?'

Charles had tactfully arranged for the meal to be brought to a small round table set in the alcove formed by the bay windows, so that Robert had very little walking to do.

Linney took a position behind Robert's chair. When Charles' footman approached him with a tureen of soup, the man took it from him, ladling a portion into a bowl for his master himself. For the first time it occurred to Heloise just how difficult it must be to eat a meal with only one arm, and how demeaning it must be for a man in his prime to have to rely on someone else to cut up his food for him. How he must hate having others watching the proof of his disability.

Desperate to introduce some topic of conversation— anything to break the strained silence which reigned at the table—she asked Giddings, 'Did I not meet you in Paris?'

Although he was somewhat surprised to be addressed, the butler regally inclined his head in the affirmative.

'How was your trip back to England? I hope your crossing was smooth?'

'Indeed, once I was at sea I felt heartily relieved, my lady,' he unbent enough to admit.

'Did you dislike France so much?'

The butler looked to his lordship for a cue as to how he should answer. Instead, Charles answered for him.

'You have evidently not heard the news, my lady. Bonaparte has escaped from Elba. On the very eve of our marriage, he landed at Cannes with a thousand men and began his march on Paris.'

'Damn the fellow!' Robert put in. 'Has there been much fighting? King Louis must have sent troops to intercept him?'

Charles again gestured to Giddings, which the butler interpreted correctly as permission to tell his tale himself.

'The last I heard, every regiment sent for the purpose of arresting him joined him the minute they saw him in person.'

'It is no surprise, that,' Heloise said darkly. 'He has a way with the soldiers that makes them worship him.'

'By the time I reached Calais,' Giddings continued, 'fugitives from Paris were catching up with me, telling tales of the desperate measures they had taken to get themselves out of the city before he arrived. The price of any sort of conveyance had gone through the roof.'

'Thank heavens we married when we did,' Charles remarked. 'Else we might have been caught up in that undignified scramble.'

'Is all you can think of your precious dignity?' Robert retorted. 'And how can *you*—' he rounded on Heloise '—be so bacon-brained as to worship that Corsican tyrant?'

'I did not say *I* worship him!' Heloise snapped. First Charles had made light of the convenience of their marriage, and now Robert had jumped to a completely false conclusion about her. 'Do you think I want to see my country back in a state of war? Do you think any woman in France is ready to see her brothers and sweethearts sacrificed to Bonaparte's ambition? It is only men who think it is a fine thing to go about shooting each other!'

'Now, steady on, there,' Robert said, completely taken aback by the vehemence of her reply, and the tears that had sprung to Heloise's eyes. 'There's no need to fly into such a pucker...'

'Not at the dining table,' put in Charles.

'Oh, you!' She flung her napkin down as she leapt to her

feet. 'All you care about is manners and appearances. Men in Paris might be fighting and dying, but all you can do is frown because I speak to a servant as if he is a real person, and say what I really think to your so rude beast of a brother!'

'This is neither the time nor place—'

'When will it *ever* be the time or the place with you, Charles?' she cried. Then, seeing all hope torn from her— not only for her marriage, but also for her country—she burst into sobs and left the room.

For a few moments the brothers sat in an uneasy silence.

'Dammit, Walton,' Robert said at last, flinging his spoon down with a clatter. 'I didn't mean to upset her so.'

'I dare say she is anxious over the safety of her parents,' Charles replied abstractedly. Did she really think he was so shallow all he cared about was good manners? 'Giddings, give Her Ladyship an hour to calm down, then take a tray up to her room. As for you—' he turned to Robert with a cool look. '—I suggest you finish your meal while you consider ways to make amends for insulting my wife and making her cry for the second time in one day.'

Chapter Seven

'Charles, you will never guess what has happened!' Heloise greeted her husband, when he came in to bid her goodnight several nights later.

She was not clutching the sheets nervously to her chest for once, Charles observed. Sadly, the robe which matched the gossamer-fine nightgown she wore was fastened demurely across her breasts, rather than lying provocatively across the ottoman. Though she was getting used to him visiting her room, she had no intention of inviting him into her bed.

Still, it was a small step in the right direction. There were other indications that she was gaining confidence in her position as his wife, too. She had ordered some lower footmen to rearrange her furniture without asking his permission. She had dismissed the dresser and the maid he had engaged for her. Then, as though wondering just how far she dared push him, she had promoted the scrubby little girl who cleaned the grates and lit the fires to the position of her maid.

She had then gone to Cummings and asked how she might go about doing some personal shopping.

Was that what had put the sparkle in her eyes tonight? Discovering from his secretary what a generous allowance he had arranged for her to have?

He took his seat at her bedside with a vague feeling of disappointment.

'Robert is going to take me to Vauxhall Gardens to see the fireworks! Is that not wonderful?'

His disappointment evaporated. Her pleasure stemmed from mending a quarrel with his brother rather than a so far concealed streak of avarice.

'He said that he cannot take me anywhere by daylight, but if we kept to shadowy walks, so that nobody can raise objections to the state of his face, it might not be too bad. Charles, this is something I do not understand.' Her brow puckered with confusion. 'Nobody looks askance at a soldier on the boulevards of Paris, no matter how grotesque his injuries!'

'But you have had conscription in France for many years. Everybody feels more personally involved in the war. Anyone's brother or husband could easily suffer the same fate as those poor wretches.' He sighed. 'Heloise, you must understand that most people are basically selfish. They come to town to enjoy themselves. They want to gossip and flirt and dance. Seeing a man like Robert is a reminder that life can be ugly and brutal. And they don't want reminders that outside their charmed circle men are fighting and dying to ensure their freedoms.'

Heloise felt a twinge of guilt. She herself had become so preoccupied with her husband, and how she could win his approval, that she had not spared Bonaparte a thought for days.

'I trust you have not fixed tomorrow evening for your outing to Vauxhall?' Charles frowned. It had suddenly occurred to him that it would look very odd if her first outing in public was taken in the company of her brother-in-law. He rapidly reviewed the entertainments available to him for the next evening.

And wondered why he had never thought of it before.

'You will be accompanying me to the theatre.' It had worked well for them in Paris. Why should it not work here?

'I...I will?' Finally, *finally* he was going to permit her to appear in public as his bride!

And people would look at how small and plain she was, and wonder why on earth he had married her when he could have had any woman for the lifting of his finger.

Charles watched the joy drain from her face.

'Is the primrose satin ready?' he asked tersely, refusing to voice his hurt.

It was not her fault she regarded an outing with him as a duty to be borne, when a trip to Vauxhall Gardens with his half-brother filled her with eager anticipation.

When she nodded, he said, 'Wear it tomorrow.' Without further comment, he gave her the kiss which was always the prelude to leaving her room.

It was only after he had gone that she allowed herself to feel resentful that he had not bothered to thank her for getting Robert to venture out of doors. Nobody else had succeeded in so much as rousing him out of his rooms for months. But could Charles unbend towards her enough to applaud her achievement? Not he!

But she still, foolishly, studied his face for some sign of approval as she descended the stairs the following evening, dressed according to his dictates. She felt a little uncomfortable in the high-waisted gown which would have left her arms completely bare were it not for the matching gloves that came past her elbows. The neckline glittered with the most intricate beadwork Heloise had ever seen. The motif of thistle-heads and leaves was picked up in the self-coloured stitching on her gloves, and repeated around the three flounces on her skirts.

'Come into my study for a moment before we leave,' he said, crooking his finger imperiously. His guarded expression told her nothing. 'I have something I wish to give you.'

She followed him, her stomach feeling as though a nest of snakes had taken up residence there. She was thrilled he was taking her out, desperate to be a credit to him, terrified she would let him down, and agonisingly conscious of every single one of her physical deficiencies.

Walking to his desk, he opened a large, square leather case which had been lying on it, and pushed it towards her across the polished mahogany surface. Inside, nestling on a bed of black velvet, was a parure consisting of necklace, bracelet, earrings and an aigrette of pale yellow gems, in a rather heavy and elaborate setting of gold. From another box, which he produced from his pocket, he took a matching ring.

'I wished to have given you this sooner, but on returning to London and examining it I found it needed cleaning.'

'Oh?' Her eyes filled with tears as he slid the ring, which fitted perfectly, onto her finger. He had bought Felice a ring that matched her eyes. When he had given it to her, he had said no jewel could compare with them. He had merely had some old baubles he'd had to hand cleaned up for his plain and undeserving wife.

Still, at least she understood now why he had ordered her to wear the primrose satin. There were not many fabrics that could complement such unusually coloured gems as the ones he lifted from the box and fastened in her ears.

'Perfect,' he said, standing back to admire the effect of the earrings glittering against the curtain of his wife's dark hair.

Heloise stiffened her spine, stifling her momentary pang of self-pity. She had always known she was a second-best wife. Of course she would only get second-hand jewels! What had she expected? That her husband would begin to act out of character and forget that she was not the woman he had wanted to marry?

He was being very kind, considering the way she had acted since being installed in his home. He had never, for example, upbraided her for the scene she had created at dinner, when she knew such behaviour was what he deplored above all else. He had merely sent her food up to her room.

Because he was, she suddenly realised, a kind man underneath those chillingly controlled manners. It was why she had never really been able to stay afraid of him for longer than a minute at a time. Why she had been able to confide in him from the very first. She had even been secure enough to give way to the childish temper tantrums that her brother had predicted would drive any husband to give her a beating.

Charles would never beat her. He did not, she saw with a sinking heart, care enough about her to lose that glacial self-control.

'I couldn't have you going out without any jewellery, could I?' he said, fastening the necklace round her throat.

'No, I suppose not,' she replied. He might not care about her much, but he cared about his own reputation. His Countess could not appear in public without adequate adornment. The dress, the jewels—they were just the costume that made her look the part she was playing.

Charles was rather perplexed by Heloise's response. He

had just hung diamonds worth a king's ransom around her neck, and instead of going into raptures she seemed weighed down.

Could she be nervous at suddenly having so much wealth displayed upon her person? She had never owned much jewellery before.

Nor wanted it. She had not even been tempted to try on the emerald ring that had been her sister's.

'These are yours by right as my wife, you know, Heloise.' The set of yellow diamonds had been in his family for generations, handed down to each new bride upon her wedding—except for the ring, which was given upon the occasion of the betrothal. 'It never felt right that you had to wear that ring I bought in Paris.'

'I shall never wear it again,' she vowed. It must remind him of all he had lost! And while she had been complaining to herself of all that she did not have, she had entirely forgotten that her husband was still trying to recover from his broken heart. He was so good at disguising his emotions that it took moments like this to remind her how much he must still be hurting.

'What are we going to see at the theatre tonight?' she said, deciding that he would be more comfortable if they talked about trivial matters.

'The *beau monde*,' he quipped, taking her arm and leading her to the door. He was glad he had taken that moment to reassure her. Now that she had got over her initial reluctance to accept the family heirlooms, she might even be able to enjoy herself a little. 'As in Paris, we go to the theatre to see who is in the audience, not what is being performed upon the stage. I expect that during the intervals persons wishing for an introduction to my new Countess will besiege our box. They will probably think,' he remarked dryly, 'that they will be able to get to me through you. I hope you will not be taken in.' He frowned. 'It would be best if you did not associate with anyone without checking their credentials with me first.'

Heloise was virtually silent all evening. At first, Charles wondered if he had said something to offend her. She had lifted her chin as he'd handed her to her seat, and stared fixedly at the stage throughout the first act. Fortunately, this had left her oblivious to the stir her appearance, decked in the Walton diamonds, had created.

Gradually, he recognised that this was the Heloise he had first become acquainted with. The quiet, reserved girl that nobody noticed. Who observed but did not participate. This public Heloise was a far cry from the termagant who yelled at his brother, flounced out of rooms, slammed doors, and rattled on without pausing to draw breath.

He welcomed her return when they got into the carriage to go home.

'Charles,' she breathed, leaning forward and tapping his knee with her ivory-handled fan. 'Who was that dreadful man—the great big dark one who accosted us in the corridor during the interval?'

He smiled wryly. He had assumed it would be easier to control exactly whom he permitted to approach her if they went for a stroll, rather than sitting passively in their box and letting the importunate besiege them.

'Lord Lensborough,' he replied, no doubt in his mind as to who she meant.

The Marquis had stood directly in their path, blocking their progress. And when he had said, 'Allow me to felicitate you upon your marriage,' his hostility had been unmistakable.

'Is he one of the family you won't speak to because of what they did to Robert?'

'Far from it. If anything, he regards himself as Robert's champion. His own brother, who serves in Robert's former regiment, was so concerned about the Turkish treatment I would mete out, he wrote begging Lensborough to watch over him.'

'Oh. I am so sorry.' Heloise laid one gloved hand upon her husband's sleeve.

'For what?' It was ridiculous, he reflected with a frown, that his spirits should lift just because she had forgotten herself so far as to reach out and touch him.

'That people should so misunderstand you. What do they think you mean to do with Robert? Is he not your brother? Your heir?'

'Alas, from Lord Lensborough's reaction this evening, I fear they suspect that I mean to cut him out by siring an heir of my own. Through you.'

'Well, that just goes to show,' she said, snatching back her hand, remembering his reaction when she had made such an impulsive gesture once before, 'how silly they are.' Couldn't they see how devoted Charles was to his brother? Didn't they understand how outraged he had been by the way his guardians had tried to cut him out of the succession?

Charles sighed. The reminder that she would one day have to face this distasteful duty as a wife had brought about an instant withdrawal.

But at least when he went to her room later, to bid her goodnight, she seemed to be in good spirits.

'Thank you for this evening, Charles,' she said prettily, when he bent to bestow a chaste salutation on her forehead. 'I did enjoy it.'

'Really?' He frowned. 'I thought you seemed…abstracted.'

'Oh, well…' She fidgeted nervously with the ties of her robe, her cheeks flushing pink as she averted her eyes from his.

Ah! She was relieved it was over. But she did not wish to wound him by confessing as much.

She wanted him gone. Very well, he would oblige her! He would not force his unwelcome presence on her a moment longer. Turning on his heel, he stalked from the room.

Heaving a sigh of relief, Heloise flung back the covers and went to the desk which she had converted to a drawing table. She had nearly given the game away then. It was just that there had been so many odd people at the theatre. And the knowledge that there was, at last, a fresh sheaf of drawing paper and a selection of really good-quality pencils hidden in a box beneath her bed was like a tonic fizzing through her veins. Now that she was a countess, with an army of staff at her disposal, she did not have to search the shops for what she wanted. She simply sent her maid, Sukey, with a list, and *voilà*! After an hour or so the girl returned with exactly what she requested! And, since Sukey was so grateful for the meteoric rise in her status, she would rather cut her own throat, she had breathed dramatically, than ever betray Her Ladyship's confidence.

Heloise only felt a small twinge of conscience for continuing with a pastime Charles frowned upon. So long as he did not find out, it could not hurt him.

And so many ideas had flooded to her while she had been studying the crowds tonight. *Beau monde!* She scoffed as she pulled a stool to her desk and lit the two lamps she had placed there for moments such as this. There was nothing *beau* about the manners of some of those people! They ignored the efforts of the actors upon the stage for the most part, which was rude, since they had clearly gone to a great deal of effort for the entertainment of an audience that was interested only in its own members. Except for certain of the men, when the pretty young dancers came on. Then it was all tongues hanging out and nudging elbows, and comments which she was certain were coarse, though fortunately she had not been able to hear them. And as for that obnoxious marquis, who harboured such uncharitable thoughts towards both Charles and herself…well! She had seen the plump little blonde sitting beside him in his own private box, giving him sheep's eyes. A woman who was clearly not his wife. And he had the temerity to look askance at *her*!

Dawn was filtering through her curtains before Heloise began to yawn. Her excitement had driven her to fill page after page with initial sketches. Later, when she had the interminable hours of daylight to fill, she would add the detail and bring the scenes to life with judicious touches of watercolour paint. Yes… She yawned again, sloughing off her robe and letting it drop to the floor. There was much to be said about an evening spent at the English theatre.

And tonight the pleasure gardens of Vauxhall would provide even more material for her portfolio.

Robert was to dine with them both before taking her out. Charles had sent a note to inform her.

This time there were no arguments. There was scarcely any conversation at all. It was as though all three of them were determined to say nothing that might spark another confrontation.

Eventually, Charles remarked, 'I shall not be dining at home for the next few evenings, Lady Walton. I warned you before we married that I have an interest in politics. And at this particular time, with Bonaparte on the rampage again, you will appreciate that I must be busy in the affairs of my country.'

Of course she understood. In Paris, it was in the private salons of influential hostesses that statesmen decided which line they were going to take in public. Similar meetings must go on in London.

She nodded. Robert scowled.

She was not surprised when, the second they got into Walton's private carriage, which he had put at their disposal for the outing, Robert blurted, 'He's not going to back those fools who want to try and appease Bonaparte, is he?'

'I do not know,' she shrugged. They never talked about anything. 'All I know is what you heard him say. Charles will be too busy to bother with me for a while.'

Robert looked perplexed. 'I'm sure he did not mean that. You must admit, Bonaparte escaping like that, and winning over the army that was sent to arrest him, has caused the deuce of a panic all over Europe.'

She turned bleak eyes in his direction, though she could only make out his silhouette. Somehow, in the darkness of the jolting carriage, it was easy to let her hurt spill out. 'It is not a question of him suddenly being busy. He has never wanted to spend more time with me than he has to.'

'Cold-hearted wretch,' she heard Robert growl.

'No, you must not say such things,' Heloise protested. 'Really, he is most kind to me…'

'Kind! To leave you alone in your room, night after night, while he goes out on the town? Oh, don't think because I stay in my rooms I don't know what goes on in this house. The way he neglects you. Look.' He leaned forward, his earnest expression illuminated for a second as they passed under a street lamp. 'I may not be able to introduce you to the elevated set my brother belongs to, but I do have friends in town. You'd probably enjoy yourself a deal more with them, anyway, than at the stuffy *ton* gatherings Walton frequents. I'll…' He drew in a breath, as though steeling himself to go on. 'I'll introduce you to them. I will not,' he stipulated, 'escort you to picnics, or go boating, or anything of that nature. But once you get to know a few people you'll have no shortage of invitations to all the sorts of things females of your age enjoy.'

Sitting back, and running a hand over his perspiring brow, he grumbled, 'Why Walton hasn't seen to it himself beats me.'

Heloise was torn. On the one hand she wanted to defend Charles' actions. And yet there was no doubt she could use Robert's misapprehension to get him to renew contact with the friends he had shut himself away from for far too long.

It would take something as radical as his ingrained hatred for his brother for him to run the gauntlet of public reaction, she began to realise as the evening wore on. She lost count of the number of dandies who lifted their lace handkerchiefs to their noses as they sauntered past, eyes swiftly averted. She grew furious with the females who placed troubled hands to their breasts, as though the very sight of Robert was too distressing for their delicate sensibilities. She was beginning to wish she had not dragged Robert out and exposed him to such a cruel and humiliating reception.

Spying a bench, positioned in a secluded nook for the convenience of clandestine lovers, Robert limped to it and sat down heavily. His false leg might have been fashioned by the most skilled craftsman Walton could hire, but learning to walk in it was clearly no easy matter.

'Oh, Lord,' Robert moaned. 'Here comes another one of 'em.'

Heloise sat forward, to look round Robert and see who he meant, and spied Lord Lensborough strolling towards them, the plump blonde on his arm.

'I thought he was your friend.'

'No,' replied Robert shortly.

As he drew level with them, Lord Lensborough paused, eyeing them closely.

'My lady,' he said, bowing slightly. 'Captain Fawley. How…interesting to see you here, of all places.'

The blonde giggled, alerting Heloise to the fact that his sneering words could as well mean this particular secluded bench as Vauxhall Gardens. Beside her, she felt Robert stiffen.

'A word in private, if you please, Lensborough?' Robert growled.

The Marquis sloughed the blonde from his arm, taking a seat on the far side of Robert. The blonde seemed inured to such cavalier treatment, wandering off a few paces without expecting to be introduced, let alone take part in the general conversation. Indignant on her behalf at such rudeness, Heloise got to her feet, deciding she would go and introduce herself.

'Hello,' she said, offering her hand to the startled blonde.

Warily, she looked to Lord Lensborough for her cue. But since he had his head close to Robert, and they were engaged in such deep conversation that they were oblivious to what she might be doing, she protested, 'You didn't ought to be talking to the likes of me—a great lady like you.'

'Well, if I did not I would be sitting being ignored. Since you are being ignored as well, we might as well amuse each other, don't you think?'

The blonde smiled uncertainly.

'I saw you at the theatre yesterday evening, did I not?' Heloise asked, since the blonde still seemed unwilling to initiate any conversation.

'Yes, and I saw you too. With your husband. The Earl. Ever so nice you looked. That gown was from Madame Pichot's, wasn't it?' When Heloise nodded, she went on, 'Oh, I should love to have a gown from her. Your husband is ever so generous, ain't he? Mrs Kenton was always saying it, and when I saw those rubies he gave her…' She trailed off, suddenly looking guilty. 'I shouldn't be men-tioning the likes of Mrs Kenton, or what your husband gives her,' she continued, hanging her head. 'Jasper is always telling me I talk too much…'

'It is of no matter to me.' Gritting her teeth, Heloise smiled bravely at Lord Lensborough's ladybird. 'Men of his rank always have mistresses.'

When the nameless blonde smiled in obvious relief, Heloise knew that the simple creature had just inadver-tently revealed the name of Charles' mistress. She had always known he would have one. But it was a shock, all the same, to find out her name at a moment when she was least expecting it.

Feeling a little sick, she turned back to Robert.

'I wish to return home now,' she said, pointedly ignoring the Marquis, who had so far done the same to her.

'I shall be only too glad to take you. I'm devilish tired.'

To her surprise, as Robert struggled to get up, the Marquis also rose to his feet, and made her a respectably deep bow. Pinning her with an intent look, he said, 'I have

issued an invitation to you and my young friend for an
evening at Challinor House. Quite informal. A little supper,
some hands of cards…'

Though she felt certain the last thing the Marquis
wanted was to have her enter his home, she also knew he
had Robert's welfare at heart.

'I don't mind taking you to play cards at Lensborough's,' Robert admitted gruffly. 'But not the supper.'

She winced at the memory of Linney cutting up
Robert's food for him. 'It sounds delightful. I love above
all things to play cards,' she lied.

Her ineptitude at the card table was one of the faults for
which her father had frequently berated her. But people
were so fascinating when they forgot company manners to
concentrate on their game. Far more interesting than the
little pieces of board she held in her hand, or the points she
should have been counting in her head. However, Robert
needed to believe she wished to play, and wanted his escort.

Bowing to her with a tight smile, the Marquis gathered
up his companion and took his leave.

Neither of them was very talkative on the way home.
Robert's face had the waxy pallor of a man close to exhaustion. And Heloise was wrestling with the turbulence
of her thoughts.

She was not sorry, now, that she had let Robert think
badly of Charles. It would motivate him to take her out, so
that she could make her own friends. Which would leave
Charles free to live his own life.

With his Mrs Kenton.

Somehow she would learn to cope. At least if she concentrated on helping Robert to regain his self-esteem it
would stop her wallowing in her own unhappiness. It
would be her mission, she decided, squaring her shoulders.

It was not until they made to go their separate ways, in the hall of Walton House, that he turned to her and said, in a voice hoarse with emotion, 'My brother is a prize idiot not to see what a treasure you are. If he won't treat you as he should, then, dammit, I will!'

'Oh, Robert,' she said, rather tearfully. Nobody could force her husband to grow fond of her. 'It is enough that you agree to take me out now and again. I have been…' She paused as her breath hitched in her throat. 'So lonely since I came to London.'

Impulsively, she flung her arms round him, almost causing him to overbalance.

'I say—steady on!' Robert laughed.

'I cannot help it,' she declared with feeling. 'You are the only friend I have.'

Neither of them heard the door to the small salon close quietly as Charles withdrew behind it. He had been a little anxious all evening about how Heloise would cope with his irascible brother. Given the way things usually turned out whenever Heloise tried to 'help' his brother, he had been preparing to go and pour oil onto troubled waters. He had not, he thought, recoiling from the scene he had just witnessed, expected to see his brother make a declaration of that sort to his wife—nor for her to respond so enthusiastically!

Nor had he expected the searing pain that left him gasping for breath.

For a few moments he gripped the edge of the mantel, leaning his forehead against the cool marble and taking deep, steadying breaths, while his heartbeat gradually returned to something like normal.

Why in Hades was he so upset?

It was not as if he was in love with Heloise. It was a proprietorial thing. That was all. He had always felt the same disgust when one of his mistresses had shown affection for another man while under his protection.

Had he made it clear to Heloise, when laying down the terms of their union, that, while he was willing to let her lead her own life, he would not tolerate her taking a lover? At least not until after she had given him an heir.

It probably hurt all the more that it was his own brother who had so effortlessly breached the defences he had lain siege to weeks ago. He laughed bitterly. All he'd had to do was trim his hair, put on clean linen, and take her to watch some fireworks!

He strode to the salon door and flung it open. The scene he had witnessed was only the opening round in the dance that went on between a man and a woman. He would have to make Heloise understand that it must progress no further, he thought, as he pounded up the stairs to her room.

He gave only a peremptory knock before striding into her bedroom. She was not yet in bed, but standing by her dressing table in the act of disrobing.

At his entrance, the maid uttered a little shriek, her hands flying to her cheeks. Heloise's gown, already half undone, slithered to the floor, leaving her standing in just a flimsy chemise. She had already removed her shoes and stockings.

He had never seen so much of her. Slowly, his blood thickening, he examined every perfect inch of her—from her flushed cheeks, down her slender arms, past her shapely calves and ankles to the ten naked toes she was curling into the soft blue carpet. She was exquisite. And he wanted to stake his claim right now.

'Sukey,' she said in a reedy voice, 'hand me my wrap, then you may leave us.' Whatever Charles wanted must be important for him to be displaying such an uncharacteristic lack of manners.

His eyes flicked upwards. She was fastening the belt tightly, with fingers that trembled.

Moodily he paced to her desk, looking blindly at the sheets of paper scattered on it, seeing only the anxiety in her eyes when he had invaded the sanctuary of her bedroom.

'I am writing a letter to my sister,' she said, breathy with panic as she gathered the loose pages and stacked them neatly together before he got a chance to glimpse any of the sketches she had been working on lately.

Stuffing the pages into a drawer, she turned to him warily.

'You did not forbid me, so I have written several times. I suppose that now you will tell me I must stop?' she finished gloomily.

She still thought of him as a tyrant, he realised, reeling from her. Hadn't he made any progress with her at all? If she still believed he would forbid her contact with her family, no wonder she turned to his brother for comfort.

'Heloise,' he ground out, seizing her by her shoulders, 'didn't I tell you that all I want is for you to be happy as my wife?'

'N…no, you didn't,' she stunned him by stammering.

'Of course I did!' He paced away from her, running his fingers through his hair. He had made it absolutely clear, on more than one occasion. Hadn't he? 'Well, I am telling you now!' he exclaimed.

Why, when he had just told her he wanted her to be happy, was she shrinking from him like that?

There must be something he could do to drive that scared look from her face. Perhaps he could begin by reassuring her that he did not, as she assumed, frown on her corresponding with her sister.

'If you want to write to your sister, of course you may. Has Felice replied to your letters?' he said, in as calm a tone as he could muster. 'How is she?'

'She reached Switzerland safely, and—' she swallowed, loath to be the one to break the news '—she has married Jean-Claude.'

Charles struggled to find something else to say. How did a man go about gentling a nervous female? He didn't know.

He only knew that he had to get out of here before he tore the damned wrapper that she was clutching to her throat like a shield from her perfect, enticing young body, and proved conclusively that he was the monster of her imagination.

Muttering an oath, he beat a hasty retreat.

'Whatever has got into His Lordship?' Sukey said, as she emerged timidly from the dressing room, where she had taken refuge. 'I've never seen him in such a pucker.'

'I have no idea.'

All she did know was that for the first time since their marriage he had not kissed her goodnight. No. Tonight, with thoughts of Felice running through his mind, he could not bear to touch her at all.

He was probably already on his way to his Mrs Kenton, to seek the solace his unappealing wife was too naïve to know how to offer.

'No idea,' she repeated dully.

Chapter Eight

'I do not agree!' Heloise returned her soup spoon to the bowl, the consommé untouched.

Robert glowered at her across the table. 'I suppose you think all the other European nations should just let Bonaparte take up where he left off, then?'

'That was not what I said!'

It was at moments like this that she was at her most attractive, Charles reflected, sipping his wine. And he only ever saw her this animated these days when Robert was around.

On the few occasions she could spare time from her increasingly hectic social life to accompany him to a ball, or rout, she behaved with extreme modesty and decorum.

He got the 'public' Heloise.

Not this vibrant, intelligent woman who held such passionate views.

She picked up her spoon again, her mind so fully locked in the tussle with Robert she didn't notice that she spattered droplets of consommé across the snowy damask tablecloth.

'I just meant that there might not need to be another war. There has not been any fighting in France…'

'Only because anyone who might have opposed Bona-parte's return has turned tail and fled. Why do you think he's amassing an army, you silly goose? Do you think he means to march them up and down the Champs-Elysées to entertain the tourists?'

'There are no tourists left in Paris,' Charles pointed out pedantically. 'They have all run for their lives.'

Heloise and Robert turned to stare at him, his wife's face creased with frustration, his brother's lip curling in contempt.

Flicking his finger to Giddings, Charles indicated it was time to remove the cooling soup and bring on the next course.

To all intents and purposes things could not be progressing better. He had wanted Heloise to make her own way in society. He had wanted Robert to get well.

He had not imagined the two events, taken in tandem, would make him feel like an intruder in his own home.

'There was no need for the tourists to flee,' Heloise said to him carefully. 'Your Whig politicians are pressing to make the treaty with Bonaparte…'

'While the allies gathered in Vienna have just declared him an outlaw!' scoffed Robert.

Charles frequently heard them bickering like this when they returned home of an evening. He was growing increasingly resentful that it was Robert with whom she felt easy enough to speak her mind. But that was nothing to what he felt when he heard them laughing together.

What kind of fool resented hearing his wife enjoying herself? Or watched his own brother's return to health and vigour with a sense of dread?

His lips twisted in self-mockery as he dug into a dish of lamb fricassee.

Heloise took only a small portion of the stew, which was

on tonight's menu so that Robert would have at least one dish from each course that he could manage for himself. She glowered at him as Linney spooned onion sauce onto his plate. She wished Charles would not invite Robert to dine with them quite so often. He ruined all her attempts to impress her husband with her increasing grasp of British politics. She had spent hours poring over the newspapers and questioning Cummings, to no avail. Robert took her up on every point, arguing with her until she became hopelessly enmired and tripped herself up. Confirming her husband's opinion she was the greatest idiot he had ever met. She only had to see the mocking way he was smiling now to know what he thought of her intellectual capabilities.

Well, she would soon wipe that smirk off his face!

'So—this masquerade you take me to at the Opera House this evening. Will it be very disgraceful?'

She had the satisfaction of causing Robert to choke on his wine. He had lectured her at length upon the importance of *not* telling her husband where they were headed tonight. Charles would strongly disapprove of his wife disporting herself at a venue where ladies of quality simply did not venture, he had warned her.

'Of course it would be,' he said hastily, 'if anyone was to find out you had gone there. But I've taken all the precautions necessary to protect your reputation. We will both be wearing masks and cloaks, and travelling in a plain carriage.'

Though he addressed the last part of this to his half-brother, Charles' face remained impassive.

'I say, you don't mind me taking Heloise there, do you?' Robert put in uneasily.

'If it amuses her to go to such places—' he shrugged

'—who am I to deny her? I have told her she may enjoy herself exactly as she pleases.'

She felt as if he had slapped her. Robert was always saying how generous it was of her husband to leave the Walton coach and driver at her disposal, but she knew better. He didn't care how many servants he had to pay to keep her out of his hair. Oh, he went through the motions of squiring her to at least one event 'every se'en night or so', as he'd put it, 'for form's sake'. But she knew, from the very way he carried himself on those occasions, that he was not enjoying her company.

'Well, then,' she said, rising to her feet and tossing the napkin to the table, 'I shall go and fetch my cloak. Tonight, Robert, you will get the proof that all I have been saying is correct.'

Charles went cold inside. Had he just inadvertently given his wife the go-ahead to commence an affair with Robert by saying she could do as she pleased?

He heard Robert's chair scrape back, heard him mutter that he would wait for Heloise in the hall, but all he could see was her face—the defiant look in her eyes as she said, 'Tonight, Robert.'

Sweat broke out on his brow.

Tonight.

Around him the footmen were clearing away the dishes, removing the cloth, pouring the port.

He had instinctively known they couldn't be lovers. Not yet. Apart from the fact Robert was scarcely fit enough, Heloise was not the kind of woman to break her marriage vows so quickly.

She had never been able to deal in deceit. Her father had said it was because she was too stupid, but he liked to think it was because she was too honest.

But if he didn't do something to put a spoke in Robert's wheel it would happen. How could Robert not desire her when she turned those flashing eyes up at him, or laughed at one of his sarcasms? She was so full of life. It was all any man could do to keep his hands off her. And she was clearly growing increasingly fond of him. It was only natural. They were far closer in age, their tastes seemed to mesh…

He was damned if he was going to sit at home and let his brother seduce his wife out from under him!

Leaving his port untouched, he rose from the table and, like a man on a mission, made his way up to his rooms. He had purchased a domino and mask for a private masquerade himself, the previous autumn. If his valet knew where to lay his hands on the outfit, he would track his wife and brother down at the masquerade and observe them undetected. The grotesque devil's mask that would cover his upper face was of red satin, matching the lining of the black velvet domino. He would look nothing like his usual civilised, conventional self in that disguise. Hell, he scarcely recognised himself any more. What kind of jealous fool stalked his wife and spied on his half-brother?

After the dire warnings Robert had given her, Heloise was surprised to discover the Opera House was not the shabby, ill-lit lair of her imagination, but a rather elegantly appointed theatre. Four tiers of boxes, decorated in white and gold, surrounded a stage upon which people in a variety of disguises were dancing.

'It's still not too late to turn back,' Robert urged her. 'So far you have not stepped over that invisible line which separates you from scandal. But if you set so much as a toe across it, I warn you, you will unleash consequences so dire…'

She tossed her head. 'I am no coward, to cringe at the threat of these vague consequences! But if you are afraid...'

Robert drew himself up. 'If I am wary, it is not on my own account, I assure you.'

'Isn't it?' she taunted. 'Isn't it truly the prospect of the rejection of females that has you quaking like a blanc-mange tonight? For I cannot believe you are suddenly afraid of what Charles might do—not after some of the places you have been taking me to...'

'Only because you asked me to!' he protested, twitching her simple black domino over her evening gown. 'For God's sake, if we are going to stay, keep yourself covered up,' he urged, taking her arm and tugging her towards one of the boxes on the lowest tier. 'And don't do anything or say anything that might give anyone a clue as to who you are. If you think you can shock Walton into taking more notice of you, you need your head examining!'

She almost laughed aloud at Robert's misapprehension. She had long since given up any hope of making Charles regard her with anything more than bored indifference.

But Mrs Kenton was a different matter.

She was not going to permit That Woman to sneer at her and pity her and crow over her for being the one who had Charles in her bed every night!

It had been Nell, Lord Lensborough's plump blonde mistress, who had introduced the two women one evening, when Heloise had gone unaccompanied to a small party being held by one of Robert's friends. At the last minute he had confessed he was not feeling up to it, but, at the look of disappointment on her face, had told her there was nothing to stop her going alone.

From the outside, the house had looked completely respectable. It had only been once she had stepped inside she'd realised she ought not to have gone. The guests had nearly all been young, single military gentlemen, who had already been growing rather boisterous. She had intended to say hello to her host, a Mr Farrar, and slip away, when Nell had come bounding up to her. The dear silly creature had noticed her looking a little flustered upon coming into a room of virtual strangers without a male escort, and decided to look after her. Being slightly foxed, she had seen nothing untoward in introducing her to the statuesque brunette who'd stood at her side. For a split second neither lady had been sure how to react.

It had been Heloise who had recovered first. Later, when she had gone over the evening's events, she had been proud of the way she had behaved.

She had smiled gaily, holding out her hand to Mrs Kenton, who had been looking as if she wished to strangle poor Nell.

'Is it not fortunate for us both that Charles is not here? This is exactly the sort of scene which he would dislike above anything!'

'Indeed he would,' Mrs Kenton had replied faintly, taking Heloise's hand in a limp grasp.

Seeing Nell's brow finally pleating with concern, Heloise went on, with false bravado, 'I assure you, I do not in the least mind meeting the lover of my husband. It is only what I expected when I married an Englishman. It would be silly of me to pretend I do not know he has a mistress.'

And now that she had seen her she could understand exactly what drew Charles to this woman. Although she was a good deal older than Felice, she had the same dark hair, the same graceful carriage, even a sultry set to her lips that put her strongly in mind of her sister when she was not in the best of moods.

'At least he does not have two, like Lord Wellington,' she prattled on. 'Or parade them about in public while shunning his poor little wife. Why he brought her to Paris at all nobody could in the least guess, if he meant to humiliate her in that fashion!' Finally she paused to breathe, desperately hoping the bright façade she had adopted was successfully hiding her despondency.

For Mrs Kenton was wearing the ruby necklace. The stones were magnificent, gleaming like fire against the woman's milk-white skin, the large, central stone dipping provocatively into a cleavage that made Heloise fully conscious of her total inadequacy to compete in the bedroom stakes.

'Although I suspect, myself, that he wished to prove he had beaten Bonaparte upon all suits, and probably had no idea he had hurt her. Men!' she finished on a false laugh, fluttering her fan before her flushed cheeks.

'It is very…open-minded of you to say so,' Mrs Kenton said, with a puzzled frown.

'Oh, no—I am a realist, me. And it seems silly to pretend not to know how the world works.'

A knowing expression flickered across Mrs Kenton's face. She purred, 'Or to pretend that you don't mind?'

Heloise responded with a shrug. 'Why should I mind?'

The older woman's eyes narrowed on the parure Heloise was wearing, her expression growing positively feline.

'Why, indeed? He is such a generous man that any woman with an ounce of sense would always forgive his little…lapses.' She leaned forward conspiratorially. 'You are wise to pretend not to mind about me, my dear, just as I shall pretend not to mind about you. The one thing he cannot abide is a woman making a fuss. He hates to feel he might be losing control of a situation.' She chuckled—

a low, throaty sound. 'Well, you know how far he takes his *desire* for mastery.' She fanned herself, raising her eyebrows meaningfully. 'My, I grow heated just thinking about his skill between the sheets. It more than compensates for the coldness of his public manners, as I am sure you would be the first to agree.'

Heloise turned and stalked away. Round one had definitely gone to the courtesan. Though she wanted nothing more than to leave the party at once, she refused to let it look as though Mrs Kenton had driven her away.

The second bout was fought with rather more subtlety. Mrs Kenton followed Heloise to the lady's retiring room, where she had been trying to hide until a sufficient amount of time had passed to make it look as though she was not running away.

Pretending she did not know anyone else was in the room, Mrs Kenton remarked to Nell, who was with her, 'Isn't it a good thing that Walton's poor little wife is able to look after herself?'

Nell blinked owlishly, hiccupped, and subsided onto a sofa.

'Otherwise, who knows what would become of her? Everyone knows he is bored with her already.'

'Well, I like her,' Nell protested.

'As do I!' Mrs Kenton quickly put in. 'Which is why I feel so sorry for her. He never goes anywhere with her if he can avoid it. One can only wonder why he married her in the first place!'

That remark had struck her to the core. Charles had only married her to save face, and at her own suggestion. But it had been to no avail. The whole of London could already see that it was a mismatch!

Well, one thing they would not see. And that was a

bride who was not completely content with her lot. Heloise had determined there and then to prove to the whole world that nobody need feel in the least sorry for her. Particularly the patronising Mrs Kenton. From that moment she had taken pains to attend the sorts of places she was most likely to run into the woman, and demonstrate that not only did she know exactly what she was to her husband, but that it didn't affect her in the least. She would show them all she was a sophisticated Parisienne, well acquainted with, and impervious to, the base nature of men.

This bravado had carried her, over the next few days, to all sorts of places she had not enjoyed visiting in the least. But she would not back down. Not while that woman flaunted the rubies her husband had given her, while all she had to show for the marriage were some antiquated crystals he'd got out of a cupboard and dusted down so she would not look as though she had nothing! And if she could face down her husband's mistress at every turn, Robert could learn to deal with his own demons.

'Robert,' she said now, more gently, laying a gloved hand on his arm, 'your limp will not deter a woman who has a good heart.'

'Nor my face?' he scoffed.

'Ah, but tonight it is covered.' She reached up to adjust the set of his white velvet mask, which matched her own. 'Any woman you approach will see only your eyes, burning with admiration for her. She will see how determined you are to approach her, and she will think, My, how he must want me. You will not give her commonplace flatteries about the colour of her hair, or the magnificence of her figure—*non*! You will tell her that no other woman has such beauty of spirit. You will see beneath the trappings to the very heart of her. And her heart, it will be in your hands before the end of the very first dance.'

'I shall sound like a complete coxcomb if I dish out that kind of cant,' Robert grumbled. 'Then I'll probably catch my false leg in her skirts and trip her over.'

'Ah, no! The coxcomb is the one who pays tribute too prettily, not meaning half of what he says. You will let your lady see that you need her. Every woman wants to feel she is the only one who can answer the needs of her lover's heart.'

'Sounds like a load of hokum to me,' huffed Robert from the dark corner of the box where he was hunched. 'Shall I prove it? Shall I do as you have suggested, and make a complete fool of myself?'

'That,' replied Heloise with some asperity, 'was the whole reason for coming to a masked ball. So that you could try out the technique on some girl who does not in the least matter to you, rather than make the cake of yourself before your friends. There!' Heloise took his arm and indicated a female in a pink domino, who was casting them an occasional look from a box directly across the stage from where they sat. 'She is looking your way again. Go and ask her to dance!'

The masked damsel shot him a coy look, before turning away and fanning herself with vigour.

'Hell, what have I got to lose?' Robert finally said, pushing himself out of the chair.

It was not until he had left her alone in her box that Heloise realised just how vulnerable she was to the attentions of the masked revellers who leered at her over its edge. This was not the first time since embarking on her private little battle with Mrs Kenton that Heloise had felt completely out of her depth. But it was the first time she had sensed she could be in real danger. Even in private gaming hells there was a code of conduct which ensured her personal safety. But here the drunken bucks who made free with the females clearly felt they had the right to do so. For the type of females who came to such a place did not expect the same consideration as would a lady of quality. Indeed, she had not seen any woman here display reluctance towards any advances made upon her.

It was quite terrifying when a large male, clad in a black silk domino topped with a red devil's mask, stepped over the edge of the box without so much as a by-your-leave.

The domino parted as he took the chair beside her, revealing the stuff knee breeches of a tradesman.

'All alone, my pretty?' he slurred. 'How about a kiss?' He lurched forward, assailing her nostrils with gin fumes.

'*Non!*' she gasped, shrinking back into her chair.

'French, hey?' the stranger responded, cocking his head to one side. 'Not a good time to be a Frenchwoman in London, is it? Though you are the prettiest one I've ever seen. Let me see you better,' he said, reaching for the strings of her mask.

'You must not!' she cried, rapping him over the knuckles with her fan. It was imperative that her mask remain in place. Charles would be furious if he ever found out she had revealed her face at such a place as this!

'Why not?' The man chuckled, his hands dropping to her waist. 'It's what you've come here for, isn't it? To have a little fun?'

In a panic now, Heloise struck out at his devilish mask with her fan. He caught her hand easily, his reflexes surprisingly quick for a man whose slurred speech indicated he was heavily inebriated.

She could not think how to get rid of him. Admitting she was a respectable married woman would do no good.

He would not believe her. Respectable married women did not come to places like this. Not without their husbands.

If he knew she was the Countess of Walton, with a husband renowned for his vengeful nature, he would stop trying to paw at her like this! But she could not betray Charles by using his name! Nobody must ever know that she had disgraced him by coming to a place like this!

In desperation, she mentioned the only threat which she thought might hold sway with the drunken buck.

'I am not here alone! I am here with my…' Even if she mentioned her brother-in-law, it might give her assailant a clue as to her true identity. In spite of his domino and mask, it was impossible to disguise the full nature of Robert's injuries. Anybody who knew anything about the upper classes would have heard of the maimed soldier who lived with his half-brother and the French wife. 'My lover!' she declared, hoping this man had not seen Robert limp off towards the far side of the stage.

'Lover, is it?' the stranger hissed. 'Pretty careless of him to leave you here unprotected, then, wasn't it?' He placed his arm along the back of her chair, propping his leg up against the door of the box as he did so, effectively penning her in with him. 'I don't think he would care all that much if I stole a kiss or two…not if he's the fellow I saw going to the refreshment room with the little tart in the pink domino a moment or so ago.'

Heloise's breathing grew ragged. Robert could *not* have abandoned her! He would not do such a thing!

'You lie! He would die for me! And he was a soldier. If you dare to touch me he will kill you!'

The man's eyes glittered coldly through the slits in his mask. 'He would have to catch me first,' he sneered. 'Is that how you came to be his lover? He fought in France? Is that it? And brought you back with him? Spoils of war...' Almost casually, the hand which was not gripping her shoulder fumbled its way under the silken folds of her domino.

'*Non!*' she cried, trying to push his hand away. 'It was not like that!'

'What was it like, then?' His hand headed unerringly towards her breast. She couldn't believe how strong he was. It took both her hands and all her determination to prevent him from reaching his destination, and even then she was not convinced he hadn't stopped for some obscure reason of his own.

'It is none of your business!' she panted, seizing his wrist as his questing hand altered the angle of its exploration under the concealing folds of her domino, this time sliding to the low neckline of her gown, from whence he slipped it inside her bodice. 'Stop this! Stop it at once!' she shrieked, leaping up out of her chair with such haste that the neckline ripped. 'Oh!' she sobbed, pressing herself to the back of the box, her hands clutching at the torn edges of her gown. Thank heaven Sukey was utterly loyal to her. She would never be able to give a satisfactory explanation to Charles if he ever found out she had come home with the front of her gown torn. 'You will pay for this!'

'Since I'm paying, I may as well get my money's worth,' the man said, lunging at her.

He grasped her by the elbows, his body pressing hers into the thick crimson curtains that shrouded the shadowy depths of the box as his mouth crashed down on hers.

It was an angry, demanding kiss, and quite terrifying. Outraged, Heloise struggled against him with all her strength.

Until something quite unexpected happened. As the stranger's hands embarked on an assured exploration of her feminine contours, she began to compare him with Charles. He was of the same height and build, and though his voice was coarse, and his clothes that of a much poorer man, the eyes which glittered from behind the devilish mask were of a similarly cool blue.

If only Charles would kiss her like this. She groaned, and then, for a few crazy seconds, found herself pretending this man was her husband, and that he wanted her. She stopped struggling, sagging back into the suffocating folds of the drapery, her whole body trembling with a kind of sick, guilty excitement.

If only Charles would caress her like this! Would be so wild with desire for her that he would kiss her in a public place, even peeling the torn fabric of her dress away and pressing his lips to the exposed skin beneath as this man was doing now. She moaned. Oh, if this man did not stop soon, she would fling her arms round his neck and kiss him back!

And why should she not? Charles was doing something like this, maybe at this very moment, with the beautiful Mrs Kenton!

At the thought, a whimper escaped her throat.

The stranger's head jerked back. For a moment he simply stood, gazing down at her, his chest heaving with each hoarse breath he took. And then he astounded her by reaching out, almost tenderly, to brush away a tear that was trickling down her cheek.

She did not even know at what point during the assault she had started to cry.

'Aren't you going to slap me?' he mocked, withdrawing slightly.

Heloise grabbed the chair back as the world seemed to lurch crazily, flinging her completely off balance.

'*Non,*' she grated, shaking her head. 'I deserved it.' She

had just responded lustfully to a drunken stranger's lecherous groping! 'I am a slut,' she gasped in shock. Sinking to the chair, she buried her face in her hands and burst into tears.

Chapter Nine

Heloise flinched when a large male hand landed clumsily on her shoulder.

'Oh, Robert!' She sighed in relief on recognising it was his form looming out of the shadows, and not her assailant's. 'P…please take me home!'

She was still shaking with reaction, unable to form coherent replies to any of Captain Fawley's questions until they were safely shut inside the coach and on their way home.

On hearing the bald facts, Robert became so angry it was all she could do to prevent him turning the coach round and hunting the man down.

'It was my fault—all my fault,' she insisted. 'I never want to go to such a place again.'

'I did not want to go in the first place,' he retorted. 'From now on let me decide where we go, if you must go out with me and not your husband!'

As if she had any choice! The mere mention of her husband's neglect sent her into fresh floods of tears. When they reached Walton House she was in no state to argue when Robert steered her into his rooms, sat her firmly on the sofa, and pressed a drink into her hands.

'If you think you fared badly,' he drawled, easing himself onto a chair opposite her, 'you should hear what I suffered at the hands of the Pink Domino.'

She was sure that he was inventing more than half of the amusing story he went on to tell her, but by the time he had finished, and her drink was all gone, she had stopped shaking.

She even managed a wavering smile for him when, a little later still, she reached the half-landing and looked down to see him standing in the hallway, watching her with a troubled frown.

'I will be fine,' she assured him.

Though she did not believe the lie herself.

From then on, guilt and shame hung over her like a pall wherever she went, no matter how gaily she forced herself to smile.

If it were not for the importance of pushing Robert back into the circle of friends who were restoring him to health and vigour, she would have stayed in her rooms. Preferably in bed, with the covers drawn up over her head.

But she could not let him down too. She might be useless as a wife, but at least she was doing Robert some good.

She glanced across the crowded, stuffy room to the group of young men surrounding him tonight, earnestly discussing the latest news from France. Surreptitiously she crept away to find a quiet corner, where she could nurse her bruised spirits in relative peace.

Heloise did not notice the malevolent look Mrs Kenton arrowed her way, but the Honourable Percy Lampton did. Swiftly he made his way to Mrs Kenton's side.

'We have not spoken before—' he began.

'I am free to speak to anyone,' Mrs Kenton interrupted him, 'since I broke with Walton.'

Percy Lampton was a younger scion of the side of the family she had been strictly forbidden by Charles to have anything to do with, if she valued her position.

'Even his wife?' Lampton said snidely. 'I don't think he would like to hear how you've been tormenting her.' He clucked his tongue reprovingly. 'Letting her think you are still in his keeping. In fact, I wonder at your daring. It can only be a matter of time before Walton finds out what you have been about, and when he does…'

'Are you threatening me?' She wrenched her eyes from Heloise to glare at him.

'Far from it.' He sidled closer. 'I am just wondering how far you would be prepared to go in your quest for revenge. It is revenge you want, is it not? Though why you feel entitled to seek it…' He shook his head in mock reproof. 'You must have known he would marry eventually. And that it could never be to a woman like you.'

Tears of chagrin stung her eyes. 'It would not have been so bad if she had been beautiful, or wealthy, or even from a good family. But to think he cast me off for *that*!' She gesticulated wildly in Lady Walton's direction.

Snagging a glass of champagne from a passing waiter, Lampton drew Mrs Kenton into a small antechamber.

'And what am I left with?' she continued, having downed the drink in one gulp. 'I was completely faithful to him, let other opportunities slip through my fingers for him, and now I have to start all over again…'

'In direct competition with nubile young nymphs like Nell.' He nodded sympathetically.

'I am still an attractive woman!' she spat at him.

All he did was raise one eyebrow, and she subsided. They both knew her career was in terminal decline.

'If it is any consolation to you, I happen to know that

Walton married as he did purely to spite my family. Before
he took off for Paris there were moves afoot to bring him
back into the fold.' He smiled wryly. 'We had exactly what
you described—a beautiful young woman of good family,
who was also incidentally in our pockets—lined up to
marry him. Is it so surprising he went off and married the
first plain, poor foreigner he came across? She is Walton's
little rebellion, nothing more. It must be obvious to you
that Walton has no strong feelings for her personally. He
has done the bare minimum required to stem speculation
by arranging her presentation and squiring her to a few *ton*
events. But on those occasions the chilliness of his demeanour towards her has been marked.'

'Has it?' Mrs Kenton had never actually seen them
together, since she did not have an entrée to the upper
echelons of society.

'Most marked.' Lampton grinned. 'And can you wonder
at it? She is teetering on the verge of social ruin, coming
to places like this. All she would need is one little push…'

Her eyes flashing with malice, she purred, 'What do you
want me to do?'

'May I join you?'

Heloise looked up in annoyance. Just because she was
sitting on her own, why did men assume she would
welcome their attention? Did she have a sign pinned to her
gown, saying 'This woman is a slut. Feel free to insult
her?'

'I would prefer you did not,' she huffed, snapping her
fan open and waving it before her face.

'Ah, I see you recognise me,' the man said cheerfully,
taking the vacant seat beside her. 'But don't you think it a
little silly to carry the feud so far? I can understand why

Walton should not wish to have anything further to do with his mother's relatives, given their shoddy behaviour towards his brother,' the man persisted, 'but I had nothing to do with all that. I had not even been born!'

'You are of the family I am not supposed to acknowledge?' she guessed, examining his face properly for the first time. There was a strong resemblance, now she was looking for it. He was of the same height and build as Charles, though a good few years younger. His eyes were the same clear, pale blue, fringed with golden lashes. As they rested steadily on her, something about the coldness of his regard began to make her feel uneasy. And then, over his shoulder, she noticed Nell looking from one to the other of them, before scuttling off, wringing her hands in distress.

'Come, my lady,' he said, leaning closer. 'Why shouldn't we be friends? It is not as if your husband even has to know. I dare say he does not know the half of what you get up to, hmm?'

The knowing tone of his voice, the way he slid one arm along the back of her chair while extending one leg so that she felt trapped by his body, was jarringly familiar. Could this be the man who had kissed her at the masquerade?

'I am sure he does not know you attend bachelor parties alone, or that Captain Fawley has introduced you to gaming hells, does he?'

His smile was predatory, chilling her to the core. He must have been watching her every move, just waiting for the opportunity to strike.

'P…please, sir,' she begged him. 'Do not persecute me like this!'

'Oh, Lady Walton—there you are!' a female voice cut in.

Looking up, Heloise saw Mrs Kenton standing over them, with Nell hovering anxiously behind her.

'I have been looking for you everywhere. Have you forgot you promised to partner my friend at cards?'

'Oh, yes,' she replied, jumping hastily to her feet. She glimpsed a scowl marring the stranger's handsome features as she made her escape.

'Have you no sense?' Mrs Kenton hissed, as soon as they were far enough from her persecutor for him not to hear. 'Consorting with your husband's enemies? Don't you know how foolish it is to antagonise a man of his temperament?'

'I didn't know who he was when he sat down!' Heloise protested. 'And anyway, I tried to make him go away.'

'That was not what it looked like from where I was standing,' Mrs Kenton sneered. 'He had his arm round you! And you just sat there!'

What was she supposed to have done? Heloise had no experience of men approaching her with such determination and lack of respect.

Mrs Kenton would have known exactly how to put him off, a little voice whispered in her head. No! No, she would rather die than ask That Woman for advice. It was bad enough to suffer the humiliation of having to thank her for coming to her rescue. Which she could scarcely bring herself to do.

'I did not do it for you,' Mrs Kenton replied. 'But for Nell. She seemed to feel it was her fault Percy Lampton had cornered you. But if you will choose to loiter in secluded corners, what can you expect? Look, if you don't want predators like Lampton pawing at you, the thing to do is stay in full view, preferably in the company of several other people, engaging in some innocuous pastime like playing cards.'

She dragged Heloise into the card room, indicating the small knots of players grouped around the various tables. Plastering an alluring smile to her face, she approached two gentlemen who appeared to be waiting for her.

'Good evening Lord Matthison, Mr Peters,' she said, ushering Heloise towards the green baize table. 'I hope we have not kept you waiting too long?' Smoothing her skirts, Mrs Kenton took a seat opposite the older of the pair, a florid-faced, bewhiskered gentleman with a claret-stained cravat.

His companion, a dark, lean young man, regarded Heloise through world-weary eyes. 'May I hope you are at least a competent player?'

Heloise shrugged as she took her seat opposite him. Much as she hated to admit Mrs Kenton was correct, she would feel safer waiting for Robert in here, pretending to play cards, than falling prey to men like Lampton. 'I do not know. What game do we play?'

'Whist,' the whiskered gentleman grinned. 'And Lord Matthison boasted he could beat me, no matter who Mrs Kenton found to partner him!'

'Oh,' she sighed in relief. If her partner was such a good player, her lack of skill would not matter. 'I have never played whist before, my lord. Is it difficult to learn?'

Lord Matthison gave Mrs Kenton a hard look, before going through the rules with Heloise. They seemed fairly simple, and for the first few hands Heloise did not let her partner down too badly. She even managed to win a few tricks.

But then Lampton strolled into the room, a drink in his hand, and took up a position by the fireplace, from where he could observe her play at his leisure.

The looks he sent her were lascivious enough to make her squirm in her seat. She no longer doubted he was the man from the masquerade—the man to whom she had responded so shamefully! The longer he stood there, leering at her, the more worried she grew that he would use that interlude against Charles, somehow.

But what could she do to stop him?

'I think it is time to call it quits,' she eventually heard Lord Matthison drawl. 'It serves me right for not specifying that I could win were I partnered with any male. In future, miss,' he growled at her, 'you might try to remember that if you lead with a trump, your partner will assume you have a fist full of them. My congratulations, Peters—' he bowed to Mrs Kenton's partner '—on rolling me up so effectively.'

'Did I make you lose a lot of money?' Unsure of the value of what they had just lost at cards, Heloise began to chew at her lower lip.

'No more than I can afford,' he said shortly. 'And I hope the same goes for you. Though, judging by the pile of vowels Peters is holding, you may have to pledge your jewels until you can wheedle the cash from whichever poor sap paid for that expensive gown you have on.' Flicking her one last contemptuous look, Lord Matthison strode from the room, leaving her cringing on her chair.

He thought she was someone's whore! She hung her head. What else was a man to think, when it had been Mrs Kenton who had introduced them?

'Your bracelet,' she heard Mrs Kenton urging her in an undertone. 'Leave that as security until you can raise the ready.'

Still cringing at what she had led her whist partner to think, she peeled off the bracelet and dropped it onto the mound of IOU's she had written.

'How much is the total?' she asked.

'Five hundred guineas!' Mr Peters beamed.

'What the deuce—?'

At the sound of that voice, Heloise looked up to see Robert limping towards her, his face drained of colour.

'Heloise, you have never lost your bracelet at play?'

'It is just a pledge against what I owe,' she protested. 'I will get it back when I pay this gentleman.'

'You will oblige me by giving me your address,' Robert grated. 'I will deal with the matter on the lady's behalf.'

'With pleasure.' Peters grinned, scribbling on the back of a scrap of paper.

Robert did not speak to her again until they were safely tucked into Walton's closed carriage.

'I can't believe you dropped that bracelet on the table like that!'

'But I had run out of money. And I did not like to put any more vowels down. It is not as if the bracelet is all that valuable…'

'Not valuable! You little idiot! It is a family heirloom. A totally irreplaceable part of the Walton parure!'

'Y…yes, I suppose it would be difficult to match those funny yellow crystals…'

'They're not crystals, Heloise. They're diamonds. Extremely rare, extremely fine yellow diamonds.'

'I had no idea,' she admitted, beginning to feel a bit sick. 'But I have not really lost it. We can get it back when you pay Mr Peters what I owe.'

Robert subsided against the squabs, looking relieved. 'That's right. God!' He laughed. 'I wondered how on earth you had the nerve to wear those baubles at some of the places I took you to! I thought it was because you wanted to make Mrs Kenton jealous…' He shook his head ruefully. 'When all the time you had no idea…' He grinned. 'Never mind—it could be worse, I suppose. How much did you lose tonight, by the way?'

'Five hundred guineas.'

Robert went very still.

'What is the matter? Is that a great deal of money? I am not perfectly sure how many guineas there are to the pound, but I know it is not twenty. That is shillings…' She faltered. 'Or is that crowns?'

'I had thought I could bail you out,' he grated, 'if you had any difficulty raising the cash. But there's nothing for it now. You are going to have to go to Walton and make a clean breast of it. You have lost a small fortune at play, and left a priceless heirloom as security against the debt. Only a man of his means will ever be able to redeem it. My God,' he breathed, 'he'll kill you. No, he won't, though—he'll kill me! He'll know you've no more notion than a kitten how to go on in society. It's all my fault for not taking better care of you. I've taken you to the lowest places, let you consort with prostitutes—and not just any prostitutes, oh, no! He will think I did this on purpose. And just when… Oh, hell.' Suddenly he looked very weary.

'Then we must not tell him!' She could not let Robert take the blame because she had been such a fool. 'There must be some other way to find the money. I have an allowance which I draw from Cummings. He might let me have an advance against next quarter!'

Robert shook his head. 'The only way to get hold of that kind of money in a hurry would be to go to a money lender. And for God's sake don't do that! Once they get you in your clutches, you'll never get out. No, there's nothing for it. We'll have to throw ourselves on Walton's mercy.'

'No,' she moaned, burying her face in her hands. It was not just a question of the gaming debt and losing the bracelet. She knew, once Charles looked at her in that cool, superior manner of his, that it would all come tumbling out. How jealous she was of his relationship with Mrs Kenton. This was precisely what her mother had warned her she must never do—behave like a jealous, possessive wife! And she had promised, too, that she would never cause him any trouble. She had broken the terms of their agreement twice over. He would never forgive her.

The carriage drew to a halt and a footman let down the steps. Her heart was in her mouth as they entered the hall together. It seemed the inevitable end to a disastrous evening when, just as she had taken off her cloak and handed it to a servant, the door to Charles' study swung open and he appeared in the doorway.

'Tell him now,' Robert murmured into her ear. 'The sooner you get it over with, the better for all of us.'

'Tell me what?' said Charles, advancing on them. 'Whatever it is you have to tell me had better be told in my study.' He stood to one side, inviting them into his domain with a wave of his arm.

Robert limped forward immediately.

'Care to join us, Lady Walton?' said Charles.

She had never felt so scared in all her life. But it would not be fair to let Robert face her husband alone. It was not his fault she had been stupidly goaded into gambling away a fortune by Charles' mistress. It had been her own stubborn pride that had done that. Not that she should have known who Mrs Kenton was, anyway. And Robert was right. Charles would blame him for that, too. There would be another fight between the two men, and the rift between them, which had begun to heal, would be ripped even wider. She could not let it happen.

Garnering all her courage, she followed Robert into the study, and joined him beside the desk.

Charles took the chair behind it, and gazed upon them with cool enquiry.

Neither of them could tell how fast his heart was beating as he braced himself to hear what he assumed would be the confession of their affair. He had not needed to question Heloise for long when he had trapped her in that box at the masquerade. She had confessed that Robert was her lover. Though she'd clearly felt guilty, bursting into tears and castigating herself for her loose morals, hearing the confirmation of his suspicions from her own lips had stunned him. He had reeled away from her in agonising pain and found himself somehow back here—waiting, as had become his habit, until he knew she was safely home.

They had both gone to Robert's rooms, rather than parting at the foot of the stairs as they normally did. It had been some considerable time before she had emerged, with a little smile playing about her lips as she floated up the stairs. Robert had stood in the hallway, gazing up at her, with a calculating expression on his face.

'Well?' he rapped out, when they had stood shuffling their feet and exchanging guilty looks for several minutes.

'I have taken Heloise to several places you would not like—' Robert began.

'The truth is,' Heloise blurted out, determined not to let him sacrifice himself for her, 'that when we went to that horrid masquerade some man assaulted me!'

Robert turned to her with a look of exasperation on his face. 'Hang on, Heloise, that's not—'

'No, Robert! Let me tell this my own way!'

With a shrug, he fell silent.

'Robert only left me for a minute or two unprotected, I

promise you. It was not his fault. It was mine. I insisted that he ask a young lady to dance, since he had the idea that no woman will ever accept him with the injuries he has taken. And while he was engaged with her this man, whom I have never seen before, took me in his arms and… kissed me.'

'Did you enjoy the experience?' Charles enquired coldly.

Heloise gasped as though he had slapped her.

'What sort of question is that?' Robert put in, aghast. 'She was naturally terribly upset! The point is, I had no business taking her to such a place…'

'Is this all?' Charles enquired politely, looking down at a sheaf of papers on his desk. Frowning, he moved the top sheet, as though something of interest had caught his eye. Certain that they were about to confess what had gone on between them behind closed doors, under his very roof, he was filled with such cold fury he could not bear to look at either of them. The only hope left to him was that he might be able to salvage his pride by masking his true state of mind while he waited for the blow to fall.

'Yes, that is all!' Heloise flung at him, her face white with fury. 'Come, Robert. You can see that to him it is nothing!'

She flounced out, Robert hard on her heels.

'Heloise! Wait!' Robert cried.

She paused halfway up the stairs and glared down at him.

'I told you we would have to find another way!' she whispered, aware that the door to Charles' study was not properly closed.

'You haven't confessed the whole yet—'

'What would be the point? I would die rather than tell him what happened tonight. Besides, if he finds out I have thrown away something you say he values so highly, he will banish me to the country—or put me aside altogether…'

'No, he won't. A gentleman doesn't divorce his wife over—'

'Gentleman! I do not even know what you mean by that term any more. Except that it is a nature that is cold and proud and unapproachable! I will not beg him to rescue me ever again! I wish I had not done so in the first place! Du Mauriac is dead, after all, and I would have been able to stay with my parents, who, though they think I am an imbecile, at least let me draw what I wish!'

While Robert's brow pleated in perplexity at this statement he found incomprehensible, in his study Charles clutched his head in his hands.

He had known from the start that she should not have carried on with the marriage once Du Mauriac was out of the picture.

Stifling a groan, he went to the study door and closed it.

'I will find a way to raise the money myself!' Heloise declared defiantly, storming off up the stairs.

In his study, Charles paced the carpet, too agitated even to pause to pour himself a drink. It would not soothe him, anyway. Nothing could ever ease the agony of hearing Heloise declare she wished she had never married him.

He had done all in his power to reconcile her to her position. To demonstrate she need not fear him he had allowed her more freedom than even the most besotted of men would accord their bride. He had put no pressure on her to conform to his requirements, imposed no restrictions on her movements, no matter how close she had sailed to the wind. And for what?

As he passed the window, he caught sight of his reflection in the panes of glass. Could this wild-haired, wild-eyed man really be him? Within two months of being married his wife had reduced him to this?

He should never have kissed her. That had been his greatest error. Now that he knew what she felt like under his hands, his mouth, he could more readily imagine his brother's hands shaping her breasts, his brother's mouth plundering her soft, responsive lips.

A strangled cry escaped his throat as he whirled away from the reflection of a man whose blood was infected with a form of madness. For no sane man would experience such rage, such despair, such self-disgust! Where was the cool, untouchable man who had always believed that to give way to strong emotion was a sign of weakness?

He flung himself into his chair, dropping his head to his hands. He had to get a grip on himself.

Straightening up, he drew several long, deep breaths through flared nostrils.

He *must* look at this situation dispassionately. The facts were these: his wife, for whom he felt more than he had ever imagined he could feel for any woman, did not return his affection.

Second, in spite of his forbearance, she had decided to humiliate him by taking a lover before providing him with an heir.

Decided? He shook his head. Heloise was too impulsive a creature to decide upon such a course of action. She had just followed her heart. She had been brought up by parents who had eloped in the teeth of opposition, and had applauded her sister for jilting him for the sake of her 'true love'. She had not meant to betray him. In fact, letting him know she was going to that masquerade could have been a cry for help. She had known she was on the slippery slope to adultery, and her tender conscience had been troubling her.

But as for Robert… His fist clenched on the arm of the chair. Robert was getting the perfect revenge. Cuckolding his despised brother under his own roof, secure in the knowledge there would be no divorce to expose him for the scoundrel he was. And if Heloise fell pregnant Robert's child would inherit the property from which he had been excluded. For Walton would be obliged to acknowledge the bastard as his own if he wanted to shield Heloise from disgrace.

And he did. He lowered his head, his face contorted with anguish. He would not permit her to run off with Robert and live a hand-to-mouth existence as the whore of an invalid on a meagre army pension.

He got to his feet and strode to the door. He must tell her, and tell her now, that he would not permit that. Though she might not think so, she would do far better to give up her foolish dreams and accept her lot. She was staying with him!

He took the stairs two at a time, flung open the door to her suite, and crossed the darkened sitting room to her bedroom.

When she saw him, her eyes widened with apprehension. It infuriated him to see her draw the sheet up to her chin, as though he were the villain of the piece! Losing control of the ragged edges of his temper, he strode to the bed, ruthlessly yanking the covers from her fingers.

'You are my wife—' he began.

'Yes, I know, and I am so sorry! I never meant to—'

He laid his fingers to her lips, stopping her mouth. He did not want to hear her confess what he had already worked out for himself. She had only followed where her heart led.

'I know you couldn't help yourself.'

Beneath his fingers, her lips parted in surprise. 'You are not angry?' Had Robert told him everything after she had left? 'Oh, Charles,' she sighed, tears of remorse slipping down her cheeks. 'Can you forgive me?'

Cupping her face between his hands, he brushed those

tears away with his thumbs. Could he forgive her? Wasn't that asking rather too much? With a groan of anguish, he gathered her into his arms and buried his face in her hair.

And suddenly he knew, with blinding clarity, that if he could have her once—just this once—then his future would not be so unbearable. For he could make himself believe that any child she bore might be his.

And so he pushed the nightgown from her shoulders, grating, 'Just this once. Just tonight.'

'Yes,' she sighed, winding her arms about his neck and sinking back into the pillows.

It was her guilt that motivated her to offer him this comfort, he was sure. But he was desperate enough to take whatever he could get. Swearing to himself that he would never take advantage of her in this manner again, he followed her down and for the next few moments let his hot need of her sweep aside all his scruples. He forgot everything but Heloise: the sweetness of her lips, the softness of her skin, the heat of her breath pulsing against his throat.

And then, searing his soul like a whip cracking into naked flesh, the sound of her agonised cry as he took her virginity.

Chapter Ten

Charles could not credit that he had been so wrong about her.

'I beg your pardon,' he said lamely. Where was the rule of etiquette to cover an occasion like this? 'If I'd had any idea you were a virgin…'

She had been lying beneath him with her eyes screwed shut. Now they flew open, full of disbelieving hurt, as though he had struck her.

'Of *course* I was a virgin!' How could he think she would break her marriage vows? Didn't he know she would rather die than be disloyal to him in any way?

The shuttered expression on his face only added to her feeling of humiliation. She had imagined that he had finally come to her bed because he had begun to find her desirable.

Instead it had been an expression of his contempt. He thought she was the kind of woman who…

'Ooh!' she cried, pummelling at his shoulders. 'I hate you! I hate you!'

He reared back, appalled at the mess he had made of things.

Pausing only long enough to snatch up his clothes, he fled from her bedroom, chastened, sickened and shaken.

He might just have destroyed whatever slim chance there had been to make something of their marriage.

He sank to the floor, his back pressed to his bedroom door, his clothing bundled up against his chest.

'Heloise,' he groaned. 'My God, what have I done?'

Alone in the dark, Heloise rolled onto her side, drew her knees up, and let the tears flow.

He must have heard rumours about the places she had been, the company she had kept, and jumped to the worst possible conclusion.

And why wouldn't he? It was only what Lord Matthison had deduced within minutes of meeting her.

Dawn found her gritty-eyed from weeping. When Sukey came in with her breakfast, her throat was so hoarse she could barely croak a dispirited dismissal.

How could she eat anything, when she'd just had her last shred of hope ripped from her? And what was the point of getting dressed and going out, acting as if her life had meaning any more? He had come to her bed. For whatever reason, he had finally decided to make her his wife in fact as well as in name—and what had she done? Lashed out at him. Told him she hated him. Driven him away.

She lay under a black cloud of despair until noon, when Sukey came back, bearing yet another tray of food.

'I told you to leave me alone,' she sighed wearily.

'Begging your pardon, my lady, but His Lordship insisted you had something to eat when I told him you wasn't getting up today.'

His feigned solicitude ground her spirits still lower. Even though he regarded her as an infernal nuisance, he would always fulfil his responsibilities towards her in the most punctilious fashion. Appearances were everything to Charles.

He would not want the servants to know there was anything amiss between them. He most definitely would not want her confiding in Sukey that she wished she had never set eyes on him.

Forcing her lips into a parody of a smile, she murmured, 'How thoughtful,' and propped herself up on the pillows so that Sukey could place the tray across her lap.

For appearances' sake she picked at the food while Sukey drew back the curtains, tidied the room, and poured water into her washbasin. The sound made her aware of how sticky and uncomfortable she felt. She could at least cleanse herself, put off her ruined nightgown and dress in clean clothes.

In some ways, she thought some time later, sitting down at the dressing table so that Sukey could comb out her tangled hair, this would be the perfect time to go to him and confess what a scrape she was in. It was not as if he could possibly think any worse of her.

Could he? Her heart twisted into a knot at the prospect she could sink any lower in his estimation.

No, she would not tell him about the bracelet. Somehow she would get it back. She lifted her chin and met her own eyes in the mirror. He would not divorce her. Robert had been adamant about that. So she had a lifetime to reverse the poor opinion he had formed.

And, judging by the way things had gone between them so far, a lifetime would be how long it would take.

Still, Robert was so much better. She need not go anywhere with him again. Though most of his friends were completely respectable, if not of her husband's elevated status, women like Mrs Kenton hovered on the fringes of his world. She had no intention of locking horns with her again. She would just stay in her rooms if Charles did not require her presence at his side. If she grew really bored she would take the occasional walk in the park, with Sukey. And a footman for good measure. She would put Mrs Kenton right out of her mind, and concentrate on being such a model of rectitude that even Charles would be able to see he had misjudged her.

And in the meantime she would cudgel her brains until she came up with a way of raising enough money to pay off her gambling debts and recover the bracelet. Before Charles noticed it had gone missing.

She dismissed Sukey, needing to be alone to think. After pacing the floor fruitlessly for a while, she went to her desk and pulled out her supply of paper from under the layers of petticoats in the bottom drawer. 'Five hundred guineas', she scrawled across the top of a fresh sheet. How on earth could a woman honestly raise such a sum without going to money lenders?

As her mind guiltily replayed the way she had accumulated the debt, her hands instinctively began to portray that fateful game of whist. She drew herself first, as a plump little pigeon, being plucked by a bewhiskered gamekeeper with a smoking gun at his feet. In the background she added a caricature of Percy Lampton as a pale-eyed fox, licking his lips from his vantage point in a hedge whose leaves bore a marked resemblance to playing cards.

Suddenly she came out of that reverie which often came over her when she was sketching. People—artists like Thomas Rowlandson, for example—made a living by selling cartoons. She had seen them in bound copies in

Charles' library, and lying around the homes of Robert's bachelor friends. Depictions of sporting heroes, or lampoons of political figures were very popular. She recalled how amused the ladies from the embassy in Paris had been by the sketchbook that Charles had forced her to burn.

Her heart began to beat very fast. She dropped to her knees and scrabbled through the second to bottom drawer, where she stashed her finished works. Whenever she returned from an outing with Charles, she sketched the people who had particularly amused or annoyed her. Politicians, doyennes of society, even the occasional royal duke had all fallen victim to her own very idiosyncratic interpretation of their foibles. If only she could find someone to publish them, she was sure she could make money from her drawings!

She pulled them all out and rolled them up together, then went to the fireplace and tugged on the bell to summon her maid. She would need string, brown paper, and a cab. She was most definitely not going to turn up at a prospective employer's door in the Walton coach, with her husband's family crest emblazoned on the panels. Not only would that advertise her predicament, but his driver would be bound to report back to Charles where he had taken her. She hoped Sukey would know where to find a print shop, so that they could give an address to the cab driver.

Oh, Lord, she was *still* engaged in activities of which he would disapprove. She pressed her hands to her cheeks, taking a deep, calming breath. It would not be for much longer. Once she had paid off this debt she would never do anything Charles might frown at. Never again.

Charles twirled the pen round in his fingers, staring blindly at the rows of leatherbound books which graced the wall of the library opposite his desk. He had never felt so low in his life. Until now he had always been sure that whatever he did, no matter how harsh it might seem to disinterested observers, was the right thing to do.

He could not understand now, in the clear light of day, what had driven him to act in such a reprehensible, nay, criminal fashion last night.

If only he could go to her and beg her forgiveness. Wrap her in his arms and at least hold her while she wept. And he knew she was weeping. Sukey had whispered as much to Finch, the youngest of his footmen, when she had taken the untouched breakfast tray back to the servants' hall. He could not bear to think of her lying up there alone, with no one to comfort her. But he was the very last person she would wish to see this morning.

At midday he had insisted Sukey check on her again. To his great relief Heloise had nibbled on some toast and drunk most of a cup of chocolate. She had then risen, washed her puffy eyes in cold water, and donned her long-sleeved morning gown with the apricot lace flounces. Finch had yielded this information to Giddings, who had informed His Lordship when he brought a cold collation— which Charles had not ordered—to the library, from where he could not find the energy to stir.

Mechanically, he bit into the slice of cold mutton pie Giddings had slid onto his plate, only to leap up at the sound of small feet crossing the hall, followed by the noise of the front door slamming.

Wiping his mouth with his linen napkin, he strode into the hall, Giddings at his heels.

'Where has she gone?' Charles barked at Finch, who froze in an attitude of guilt by the console table.

'I am sorry, my lord, I do not know.'

'She did not order the coach,' Giddings mused. 'She must not intend to go far.'

Charles was barely able to restrain the impulse to race upstairs and check her cupboards, to see if she had packed her bags and left him. Good God, losing Felice was as nothing compared to what it would be like if Heloise should desert him.

Barely suppressing the panic that clutched coldly at his stomach, he fixed a baleful stare on the hapless Finch, and asked, 'What was she carrying?'

'Umm…' Finch thought for a moment. 'Well, nothing as I can recall. Though Sukey had what looked like a long sort of tube thing.' He frowned. 'Might have been a parasol, wrapped up in brown paper.'

A parasol? A woman did not run away from her husband armed only with a parasol, whether she had wrapped it in brown paper or not. He ran a shaky hand over his face as he returned to the relative sanctuary of his library. He could not go on like this. Whether she could believe in his remorse, whether she could ever forgive him, or even understand what had driven him to say what he had, was beside the point. He had to tell her he would accept whatever terms she cared to name so long as she promised not to leave him.

It was late when she returned. He decided to give her only sufficient time to put off her coat and take some refreshment before going up to her room with the speech it had taken him all afternoon to perfect.

Five more minutes, he thought, snapping his watch closed and returning it to his waistcoat pocket.

He looked up, on hearing a slight noise from the doorway, to see Giddings making an apologetic entrance.

'Begging your pardon, my lord, but there is a man who

insists you will want to see him. When I informed him you were not receiving, he told me to give you this.' Giddings laid a rolled-up piece of paper on the desk, concluding, 'He is awaiting your answer in the small salon. I would have left him in the hall, but he insisted that the matter was of the utmost delicacy, and that he did not wish Her Ladyship to see him.'

Charles' hand shot out to unroll the single sheet of drawing paper. He could see, after one glance, that it was his wife's work.

It was the night he had taken her to the theatre. The boxes that overlooked the stage were populated by various creatures, though the one which leapt out at him was a sleek black panther, with one paw upon the neck of the sheep who shared his box. It was Lensborough to the life, and the sheep undoubtedly the silly young lightskirt he currently had in keeping. The stage was populated by a flock of sheep, too, with ribbons in their curly fleeces, and all of them with wide, vulnerable eyes. The audience that filled the pit comprised a pack of wolves, their tongues hanging out as they eyed the helpless morsels penned on the stage.

Was this what Sukey had been carrying this afternoon when she had gone out with Héloise? Not a parasol, however disguised, but this picture, rolled up just as Giddings had presented it to him? And, if so, where had she taken it—and who was the man who had brought it back to him?

For the first time that day Charles recalled that Heloise had other troubles than being married to a man she'd grown to hate. Last night Robert had tried to make her tell him what they were. Instead of listening to her, he had totally lost his head and driven her away, confirming her opinion that he was 'cold and proud and unapproachable'.

'Send the fellow in,' he ordered Giddings. Seating himself behind the desk, he schooled his features so that they revealed nothing of his inner turmoil. That this man had one of his wife's sketches and had dared to use it as a calling card was enough to set his back up. If the scoundrel was in any way connected with whatever it was that was troubling his wife, he would soon learn he had made a bad mistake. Charles would destroy him. Slowly, painfully and completely.

'Mr Rudolph Ackermann,' Giddings announced, somewhat surprising Charles. This man was a reputable publisher, not the sort he would have expected to dabble in blackmail.

'Thank you for agreeing to see me,' Ackermann said, coming to stand before the Earl's desk. 'I apologise for the unorthodox method I employed—' he indicated the sketch that lay on the desk between them '—but I needed to get your attention.'

'You have it, sir,' Charles replied. 'State your business.' He did not invite the man to sit. Nor did he ask Giddings to bring in refreshments before dismissing him.

'Your wife came to my offices on the Strand this afternoon,' Ackermann began, the second the door closed behind Giddings. 'I would not have admitted her had she not brought her maid along. Indeed, at first, I assumed she wanted to make a purchase.'

He ran a finger round his collar, clearly growing uncomfortable under the Earl's hostile scrutiny.

'Instead, she produced a bundle of her own work, and asked me if I would pay her for them, and for as many more as would be needed to make up a volume for public sale. Since she was clearly a lady of quality, I thought it best to humour her by pretending to examine her drawings.

I was amazed at how wickedly comical they were. For a while I got quite carried away with the notion of actually bringing out a book along the lines of *The Schoolmaster's Tour.* We even discussed calling it *The French Bride's Season...*' His voice faltered under the Earl's wintry stare.

'Of course,' he blustered, 'I came to my senses almost at once.' He sighed, looking wistfully at Heloise's sketch of her night at the theatre. 'I realised that such a scheme would be abhorrent to a man like you.' He cleared his throat. 'Not that she told me her real name. Indeed, I was only completely sure of her identity after my clerk returned—that is, the lad I sent to follow her home—and he told me the address of the house she came into.'

The Earl's eyes bored into Ackermann's. 'You say my wife brought you a bundle of her work? I assume you are now going to tell me you hold the rest in safekeeping?'

Ackermann looked relieved. 'Precisely so. If I had not persuaded her that I would buy them all she would simply have taken them to another publisher. Someone who might not share my scruples.'

'Scruples?' the Earl repeated, his lips twisting into a cynical sneer.

'Yes.' Ackermann's face set in implacable lines as he finally understood what the Earl was implying. 'My lord, my business relies on the goodwill of men of your class. If I were to expose your wife to scandal I know full well you would break me. I have taken what steps I could, in good faith, to prevent Lady Walton's actions from coming to light. I gave her a modest payment, to ensure she would not think of going to someone who might enjoy seeing you humiliated...'

'A modest payment?'

'Five guineas.'

'You make a poor sort of blackmailer if all you require of me is five guineas.'

Ackermann looked as though he was hanging onto his temper by the merest thread. 'Whoever may be blackmailing your wife, it is not I. Though she is clearly trying to raise a large sum of money in a hurry.'

Charles stroked his chin thoughtfully. He took another look at the sketch, then at Ackermann's indignant posture, recalling his wife's distress in this very room the night before.

'How much money did she say she wanted?'

'Five hundred guineas.'

For several minutes Charles said nothing.

Heloise was in need of five hundred guineas, but she found him so unapproachable she would probably rather die than ask him for anything. Especially now.

And yet… He tapped on the arm of his chair thoughtfully. If he could somehow supply her with the funds she needed, in such a way that he did not appear as the tyrant of her imagination…

'Take a seat, Mr Ackermann,' he said. 'While I spell out exactly what I wish you to do for me.'

Chapter Eleven

Heloise did not know whether to massage her aching wrist or rub at the frown that felt like a hot knife welded between her eyebrows. She had sat up all night, putting finishing touches to any half-started sketches she could find, so that she could impress Mr Ackermann with her industry at this morning's interview.

Although if he was only going to give her five guineas per drawing, she had realised just as she was climbing into the cab, she would have to sell him another ninety-nine to clear the debt. It would take her months to raise five hundred guineas this way. Even if he agreed to buy everything she ever drew, which was hardly likely.

She slumped back into the grimy leather seat, chewing at her lower lip. She still had Felice's emerald ring. Charles had said it was quite valuable. Since she was never going to wear it, it might as well go the way her sister had originally intended.

And, since she was never going out again, she would not be needing all the expensive gowns Charles had bought her. In Paris she had thought nothing of going to peddlers of second-hand clothes. There was bound to be a similar market in London. Particularly for beautifully embroidered creations from the salon of Madame Pichot.

By the time the cab reached its destination Heloise was drawn tight as a bowstring. Since it was a bad business tactic to reveal her state of nerves, she pulled her shoulders down and raised her chin as she took a seat in Mr Ackermann's office. The drawings she had left with him the day before were already spread across his desk. He took her latest offerings, slowly perusing every single page.

Little shafts of hope streaked through her every time his lips twitched in amusement. He hovered for the longest time over her depiction of her presentation. At first glance it looked as though she had drawn a lily pond, surrounded by reeds amongst which elegant herons were poised, eyeing the fat carp drowsing in the shallows. The puffed-up toads squatting on their lily pads were easy enough to identify. It took him a little longer to work out which personage each fish or bird represented.

'Is this all you have?' he eventually asked her.

'Yes, but I promise you I can produce as many as you wish. I will work every hour of the day and night…'

'No, no.' He held up his hand to stop her. 'I shan't need any more.'

When her face fell, he swiftly explained, 'I am willing to give you five hundred guineas for what we have here.'

She gasped, pressing her hands to her cheeks as he slid an envelope across the desk towards her. 'You are giving me all the money now? Just like that?'

'Just like that,' he replied, with a wry twist to his mouth.

She grabbed the envelope before he changed his mind, and tried to stuff it into her reticule. It would not fit. Even folded, it was far too bulky. She clutched it to her bosom, bowing her head as a wave of faintness washed over her. It was terrifying to have so much money on her person. What if she lost it? She had to get home and hand it over to Robert at once. She leapt to her feet and made blindly for the door.

Once there, she turned back, gasping, 'I am sorry if I appear rude, but so large a sum of money…'

The strangest look flitted across his face. It was almost as though he pitied her. But his brisk, 'Good morning,' as he began to tidy her drawings from his desk-top was such a businesslike dismissal she decided that in her nervous state she must have imagined it.

As soon as the door had closed behind her, the Earl of Walton emerged from his place of concealment. Sparing only a second to nod his acknowledgement to Mr Ackerman for playing his part so well, Charles set out in hot pursuit of his wife.

He hated resorting to following her like this. But how else was he to find out why she needed five hundred guineas? He had abandoned the idea of simply demanding an explanation almost as soon as it had occurred to him. He would not give her any further grounds for accusing him of bullying her.

It was not long before it became apparent she was going straight home. He bit down on a feeling of frustration as he watched her climb the front steps. He might have to shadow her movements closely for some time before discovering what she intended to do with the money.

He slipped into the hall so soon after her that the footman did not even have time to close the door behind her.

And saw her disappearing into Robert's rooms.

She had flown straight to him!

It always came back, somehow, to Robert.

A series of images flitted in rapid succession through his brain. Heloise embracing Robert in this hall, telling him he was her only friend. Heloise wafting up the stairs with a smile playing about her lips after the masquerade.

Given her family's propensity for eloping at the drop of a hat, he could only draw one conclusion.

Thrusting his hat into the hovering footman's outstretched hands, he strode across the hall, pushing Linney aside as he plunged into his brother's rooms hard on his wife's heels.

And caught her holding out the envelope containing the money—his money—to Robert.

They both froze, looking at him just like two children caught with their hands in the biscuit barrel.

A vision of her in some French farmyard feeding chickens flashed into his mind. Robert emerged from a shadowy doorway, put his arm about her waist and kissed her cheek. She smiled up at him, the picture of contentment…

Charles could not bring himself to say a word. He felt as if he was teetering on the edge of an abyss, and one wrong move would send him hurtling eternally downwards.

Until this moment he had not really believed she hated him. She had said it once before, in the heat of the moment. When she had calmed down, she had admitted she had not really meant it.

But here was the evidence she could not bear to spend another moment as his wife.

It was his own fault. He had treated her abominably. He had left her shaking and crying at the masquerade. No wonder she had turned to Robert for comfort. He had practically driven her into his arms. And, worse, he had flung his mistrust in her face at the worst possible moment…

He drew in a ragged breath. This time, no matter what it cost him, he would hold his anger in check until he had learned the truth. All of it. Whatever it might be.

Only then would he deal with it—or rather find a way to survive losing both his brother and his wife in one fell swoop.

Like an automaton, he crossed the room to the fireplace and propped himself against the mantel, folding his arms across his chest.

Eyeing Robert, who was reaching for the crutches that were propped on the arm of the sofa on which he sprawled, he ground out, 'I think it is high time someone told me exactly what is going on.'

'Tell him, Lady Walton,' ordered Robert, letting the crutches fall.

'I cannot!' Heloise stood rooted to the spot, the money clutched in her hands, large tears welling in eyes that stared at him piteously from a pinched white face.

'Then I will,' Robert declared, pulling himself to a more upright posture. 'It's no use trying to hide it from him any longer. The game's up.'

'Robert!' she cried, rounding on him as though he had betrayed her.

'It is far better for Charles to act for you in this matter,' he went on mulishly. 'I said so from the start.'

Act for her? These were not the words of a man contemplating eloping with his brother's wife. Nor was his exasperated tone in the least lover-like. A great weight seemed to roll from Charles' shoulders.

'Perhaps you would find it easier to confide in me if I were to tell you that I know you were trying to sell your drawings, and that it was, in fact, I who supplied the publisher with the five hundred guineas in that package?'

Heloise let out a strangled cry, dropping to a chair and covering her face with her hands. She should have known no businessman would pay so much money for the dozen or so drawings she had given him. They were probably not worth a sou!

'I can see I have been even more stupid than usual,' she said, turning the packet over in her hands.

She would have to tell Charles everything. And then he would be so angry with Robert. He would say things that might alienate them from each other for ever. They were both of them so deucedly proud! Insults, once spoken, would not be easily retracted or forgiven by either. And it would all be her fault.

Perhaps if she could tell Charles alone, and he had time to calm down before confronting Robert…

'Robert,' she said, getting to her feet and dropping the mangled package onto the cushion beside him, 'you know what to do with this. Charles—' She turned to him, lifting her chin. 'If you will spare me a few moments, I will tell you the whole.' She took a few steps towards the door. 'In my sitting room.'

To her great relief, not a second after she quit Robert's rooms, she heard Charles' tread on the staircase behind her.

'Please—won't you sit down?' She waved him to a chair to one side of the fireplace once she had dismissed Sukey. Nervously, she perched on the one opposite. 'I p…promised you before we married that I would not be any trouble to you at all, but I have got into such a terrible mess! I do not know where to start.'

'Start with the pictures,' Charles said grimly. 'I should

very much like to hear why you felt obliged to run round town selling your work for a paltry sum…'

'It is not a paltry sum. Robert said it was a small fortune!'

'Well, I have a large fortune at my disposal. For heaven's sake, Heloise, am I such an ogre that you cannot even apply to me for funds when you need them?'

'It is not at all that I think you are an ogre. But that I have broken my word and did not want to admit it. Nor why I broke it! I have done all that is reprehensible. And then I lost all that money at cards…'

'Gaming debts.' Why had he never considered that she might have been fleeced at cards? He shook his head. 'I have even made you think I would not meet your gaming debts,' he said bleakly.

Wringing her hands, she plunged on. 'I am the imbecile. Maman warned me I must not mind about your mistresses, but when I saw her, with those rubies you chose for her, and her air of such sophistication, while I had only those horrid yellow stones… But then Robert said they were diamonds, and priceless, and I knew how angry you would be that I was such a ninny—but how could I know?' She got to her feet then, pacing a few feet away before turning to exclaim, 'You said you had got them cleaned, and handed them to me as though they meant nothing. I thought you could not bother to go out to a jeweller and buy anything just for me. I did not know,' she sniffed, dashing a solitary tear from her cheek, 'I swear I did not know how valuable that bracelet was, and if I had known what a vile place the Opera House was I would never have made Robert take me there. He warned me, but I would not listen, so it was entirely my own fault that horrid man kissed me—'

'Just stop right there!' Getting to his feet, Charles crossed the room and took hold of her firmly by her shoulders.

He had considered once before that there might be only one way to stop his wife when she was in full flow.

He employed it now. Ruthlessly, he crushed her lips beneath his own, knowing she would not welcome the kiss, but completely unable to resist. When he thought how close he had come to accusing her of infidelity again... He shuddered. Thank God he had managed to rein in his abominable jealousy!

'Ch...Charles,' was all she could manage, in a strangled whisper, when he finally pulled away. Why had he kissed her when he was clearly very angry with her?

As he looked down into her distraught face, he knew he still had a long way to go. Though she had not been planning to run off with Robert, he had still been the one she had run to in a panic, assuming she had nowhere else to turn.

Gently, he tugged her to sit beside him on one of her prettily brocaded sofas.

'Heloise,' he explained, 'anyone can get badly dipped at cards. You should have just told me.'

'I was too ashamed,' she admitted. 'I knew I should not have been playing at all, when I am so useless at counting, but when Mrs Kenton looked at me with such contempt I felt I had to prove I could be as good as her at something! And then, because it was the house of one of Robert's respectable friends, and not a gaming hell like some we had been to, I was not on my guard. And nobody told me a guinea was worth more than a pound!' she complained, as though the injustice of this had just struck her. 'Why must you English have crowns and shillings, and guineas, and everything be so complicated?'

'That is the second time you have mentioned Mrs Kenton,' Charles said sternly. 'Would you mind telling me how you came to make her acquaintance?'

Determined to protect Robert as far as she was able, Heloise said, 'Nell introduced us.' When Charles looked puzzled, she explained, 'Lord Lensborough's mistress. They are friends.'

'Yes, but how came you to be acquainted with a woman like Nell—if that is her name?'

'Why should it not be her name? She is entitled to a name, like any other person. Just because to earn her living she has to—'

Charles took the only certain method of silencing his wife once again.

'If you cannot keep to the point, madam wife, I will have to keep kissing you, you know.' He wanted more than anything to rain kisses all over her dear little face. But her reaction told him she would not be receptive to such a demonstration of affection.

She disentangled herself from his arms, her cheeks flushing mutinously. So he kissed her to punish her, did he? A perverse excitement thrilled through her veins. She only had to defy him, then, and he might kiss her again! Oh, if only she were not so determined to clear her name and prove she was not the amoral hussy that Englishmen all seemed to assume, just because she did not follow the stricter rules their society imposed on Englishwomen.

While she was still dithering between his kisses and his contempt on the one hand, or his respect with coldness on the other, he said, quite sternly, 'Heloise, you should not be socialising with women like Nell and…Mrs Kenton…'

'No, Maman warned me that I must pretend not to know about your mistress. But this was absurd when we walked into each other. How am I supposed to ignore a woman who is standing right in front of me?'

Felice would have done it with relish, he reflected. She

had a way of cutting people, a haughty tilt to her head sometimes when she took offence at something said to her, that had made it easy for him to envisage her as his Countess. She would have had no trouble ripping his discarded mistress to shreds. She could easily have become the sharpest-clawed of all the tabbies in town. He swallowed suddenly on the frightening prospect. But Heloise—his sweet, good-natured, straightforward little pea-goose—needed his support and his care in a way Felice would never have done. A feeling of hope warmed his veins. She had based at least some of her actions on a couple of misapprehensions about him. If he could clear those up, perhaps he could begin to redeem his character in her eyes.

'Heloise,' he said, steeling himself for the kind of conversation a man as fastidious as himself should never have to have with his wife, 'Mrs Kenton is not my mistress.'

'Don't lie to me, Charles! Everyone knows those rubies she flaunts were a gift from you.'

'She *was* my mistress. That much is true. But, for your information, those rubies were my parting gift. I gave them to her before I left for Paris. And now we will not mention her again. In that I have to agree with your *maman*. I should not have to discuss my mistress with my wife.'

Heloise did not question how she knew he was telling the truth.

But that cat had deliberately made her think the relationship was current!

Indignantly, Heloise leapt to her feet, pacing back and forth as she assessed how the woman had deliberately played on her insecurities, taunted her into playing beyond her means, and finally goaded her into parting with the bracelet she must have known was priceless.

'Oh!' she cried in vexation, flinging herself back onto the sofa. 'She has made a complete fool of me.' Suddenly sitting up straight, as another thought occurred to her, she exclaimed, 'And *he* was in it too! Percy Lampton!'

'Lampton?' Charles grated, his hackles rising. He might have known the Lamptons would do their utmost to hurt his chosen bride.

'Yes—he persecuted me until Mrs Kenton and her game of cards seemed like a perfectly reasonable means of escape. And he kissed me, too!' she concluded, remembering the assault at the Opera House.

'He *what*?'

A shiver of dread ran down his spine. Apparently Lampton would stop at nothing. Oh, he no longer feared Heloise would stray into an adulterous affair. He must have been mad to suspect her integrity for so much as a second! But a ruthless swine like Lampton would only have to get her into a compromising position, arranging things so that there were witnesses, and his wife's reputation would be in tatters.

It was no use hoping she would suddenly start trusting him enough to listen to any warning he had to give her. The only sure way to keep her safe would be to remove her from that man's reach altogether.

'We will have to leave London.'

He would take her down to Wycke, his principal seat. And while they were there he would make sure she spent at least some part of each day in his company. There were so few other distractions to amuse a city-bred girl like Heloise that she would soon welcome any company—even his. He would rein in his absurd jealousy, treat her with the kindness and consideration a young bride deserved, and maybe, just maybe, she might come to regard him as a patient, devoted husband rather than the unapproachable tyrant of her imagination. God, how he wanted to kiss her again! If only she didn't freeze whenever he took her into his arms, and then look at him with those bemused, wounded eyes when he let her go.

'I just need to clarify one point,' he said. 'Will the money you gave Robert today clear all your outstanding debts, or is there anything else I should know before we leave town?'

'Th...that is all,' she stammered, amazed that he was taking it all so calmly.

He nodded, relieved that she had at least had someone she could turn to for help—but, dammit! He swore to himself, rising to his feet. He should have taken better care of her!

She tensed as he turned his back on her. Did that outward calm only conceal a deep disgust of her failings?

'I am sorry, Charles—' she began.

He rounded on her, a strange gleam in his eye. '*You* are sorry?'

Her heart sank as she saw he was not going to accept her apology. He was not going to give her a chance to prove she had learned a valuable lesson and would never behave so foolishly again. He was just going to pack her off to the country, where she could not do his reputation any damage.

'I suppose,' she muttered mutinously, 'I should thank you for not threatening to cast me off without a penny.'

He flinched as though she had struck him. 'You are my wife, Heloise. A man does not cast his wife off for being a trifle expensive. I might scold, or preach economy, or...' Manfully, he strove to gentle his voice. 'The truth is, you are the least expensive female I have ever—' He broke off, cursing himself for this tactless turn of phrase.

But it was too late.

Stiffening proudly, Heloise replied, 'Yes, in that I should have listened to Mrs Kenton. She told me how generous you are.'

Damn Mrs Kenton, he thought, slamming himself out of the room. If she was here now, he would be sorely tempted to wring her neck!

Heloise watched a Dresden shepherdess on a console table beside the door rock dangerously before settling on its plinth. Could she never learn to control her tongue when she was with Charles? He had told her it was not suitable to speak about his mistress, and what had she done? Dragged her straight back into the conversation again.

No wonder he felt he had no option but to pack her off to one of his country estates. It was she, after all, who had put the notion into his head when she had suggested they should get married! She had actually *offered* to go and live in the country and keep chickens.

Uttering a cry of pure vexation, she seized the hapless shepherdess and flung her against the closed door, shattering her into hundreds of tiny shards. Nobody would ever be able to glue her back together again.

She knew her eyes were puffy from weeping. She knew her face was blotchy. She would much rather have stayed in her room than face her husband's disapproval so soon after that last devastating scene.

But Giddings had told her they would be dining *en famille* in the small salon tonight. And once Charles had deposited her in his country house and come back to town it might be months before she saw him again. As hard as it was to endure his presence, writhing inside as she was with humiliation, it would be far worse to sit alone in her room, knowing he was in the house and still, ostensibly, within her reach.

Charles and Robert were already there, standing on either side of the fireplace, so engrossed in conversation they did not appear to notice she had come in.

At least her time in London had not been a complete waste. When she had first come to England they had barely been able to stand being in the same room. Now, as they fell silent, turning to look at her with almost identical expressions of distaste on their faces, she could see that disapproval of her flighty, irresponsible ways had united these two proud men in a way that perhaps nothing else could have achieved.

'I am pleased we are all able to dine together tonight,' Charles said, as Finch proffered a tray containing a single glass of the sweet Madeira wine she had recently developed a taste for. 'This may be the last time we are all three together for some time. I am taking Lady Walton down to Wycke as soon as all the travel arrangements are in place,' he informed Robert.

'Sloughing me off?' his brother replied bitterly. 'Not that I can blame you, I suppose.' Eyeing Heloise with open hostility, he tossed back his drink, then held his glass out to Finch for a refill. 'Oh, don't look at me as though you're some puppy dog I've just kicked,' he growled, when her eyes filled with hurt tears. After downing the second drink, he sighed, rubbing his hand wearily across his face. 'Best sit down to dinner and forget I said anything.'

A wooden-faced Giddings pulled out her chair, assisting her to take her place when, in response to Robert's remark, Charles gave the signal to commence dining.

They ate their minted pea soup in silence. Heloise could think of nothing to say that wouldn't make everything ten times worse. She kept stealing glances at her handsome, enigmatic husband, a sense of awful finality lining her stomach with lead. While she had been dressing for dinner she had analysed every aspect of his behaviour towards her. She could better understand his attempt to consummate the marriage now she knew he had not, after all, been availing himself of Mrs Kenton's services. Assuming she was experienced, he had decided he might as well try her out 'just the once'. But, from the rapidity with which he left the room afterwards, it was clear she had fallen way short of his exacting standards.

And the fact that he did not seem to mind too much about the gambling debt must be because he was glad she had finally given him the excuse he needed to send her away. He had said they must spend some time in London just at first, to silence gossip. Well, now that time was at an end, and who could wonder at him taking her to the country and leaving her there?

He was only just recovering enough from his disappointment with regard to Felice to be thinking about having another woman in his bed. But once she was installed at Wycke he could come back to London and trawl through the women thronging Covent Garden, just as the other men of his class did.

She briefly wondered what he would look like with pea green soup dripping down his supercilious face. Perhaps fortunately for her, Giddings cleared away her bowl before she had summoned up the courage to indulge her vengeful daydream.

Linney leaned over Robert's plate to cut up the collop of veal that comprised the second course, provoking Robert into thumping his one clenched fist on the tabletop. His wine glass went flying, splattering scarlet liquid all over the pristine white tablecloth, onto his plate, and into the nearby dish of béchamel sauce.

'Dammit, dammit, *dammit*!' As he tried to push himself to his feet, Finch, who had sped to the scene with a cloth to mop up the spill, inadvertently blocked his clumsy manoeuvre. Linney caught him as he bounced off the strapping young man's frame, deftly deflecting him back into his seat. Then, without so much as a raised eyebrow, calmly carried on cutting up his master's veal.

'You'll feel much better, if you'll forgive me for saying so, sir, once you've got on the outside of some meat,' Linney observed. 'Been overdoing it today, he has, my lord.' He addressed Charles. 'Dashing all over town, knocking himself up, and getting into a pucker over the news.'

'Thank you, Linney. When I want you to speak for me, as well as cut up my food and put me to bed,' Captain Fawley stormed, 'I'll let you know!'

For the first time since she had come into the salon Heloise stopped thinking about her own problems and noticed that Robert looked really ill.

'Robert, what is the matter? Why have you been dashing all over town? Oh, please say it was not on account of my—'

'The news which has upset Robert, I believe,' Charles interrupted, hoping to avoid having his wife's gaming debts discussed before the servants, 'is—'

'Hell and damnation! Will you all stop trying to speak for me as though I'd lost my tongue along with an arm and a leg and my looks!'

'I beg your pardon,' Charles replied, calmly cutting up a portion of his own meat and spearing it neatly with his fork. 'By all means, repeat before my wife the news you related to me earlier.'

'Well, dammit, so I will!' he retorted. 'Grey lost the vote,' he told her. 'The government has finally decided to send British troops to support the forces the Prussians, Russians and Austrians have already assembled to put a stop to Bonaparte's ambitions. Britain is, in effect, at war with France again.'

He glared at her so ferociously that Heloise felt obliged to say, 'I know I am French, Robert, but I am not your enemy…'

He snorted in derision. 'But you're the only French citizen I'm likely to get anywhere near. Wellington and Bonaparte are finally going to meet, every able-bodied ex-soldier is volunteering, and what am I doing? Running errands for a French-born—'

'I think you have said enough,' Charles said.

Robert struggled with himself. 'Lady Walton,' he eventually said, 'it is not your fault you are French. I dare say the truth is that Linney is right. I have done too much today—knocked myself up. But if you had heard the way those fools were prating in the clubs! Laying odds on the chances of Wellington beating Bonaparte as though it was a cockfight! And all my friends, joining up and saying their farewells, and I'm stuck here—a useless wreck of a man. I just want to hit someone! I don't particularly care who. And I can't even do that,' he finished, glaring down at the empty sleeve which Linney had pinned neatly out of the way for dinner.

'Truth of the matter is I'm not fit company tonight, and I should never have come to this table,' said Robert, signalling to Linney to help him from his chair. 'I'll return to my rooms and stop casting a blight on your evening. Lady Walton.' He bowed to her. 'I carried out your little commission, as you requested. I gave the package to Charles.

I apologise for my filthy temper, and my boorish manners. And I trust you will enjoy your visit to Wycke.'

Heloise's mind began to race. 'Charles,' she said, turning to him the minute Robert had left, 'it cannot be good to go away just now and leave Robert all on his own. He might sink back to the way he was when I first came here.'

If she could postpone her exile, even for a few days, surely she could come up with some way to prove to Charles that he need not banish her? Even if it was only a stay of execution, she would at least have had a few more days with him.

'No,' he said, with such finality it dashed all her hopes to the ground. 'My mind is made up.' He had to remove Heloise from the dangers London posed for such an innocent. 'We will leave in the morning.'

She sat like a stone, picturing her lonely, loveless future, while the servants efficiently cleared away Robert's place-setting. In a space of minutes it was as if he had never been in the room. Even his chair was removed and placed against a wall, where it blended in amongst its fellows. Charles would no doubt have his servants eradicate all traces of his errant wife from this house just as efficiently.

'Do you require any help with your packing?'

She blinked. Charles was set on his course. She had no doubt that if she tried to resist he would order these efficient minions of his to pack her things for her. She had a brief vision of Giddings wrapping her in brown paper, securing her with string, and stuffing her into a trunk.

'No,' she said, folding her napkin neatly and placing it beside her still half-full plate. 'But what of Robert?' It had occurred to her that her exile might be easier to endure if she had a friend to share it. 'I cannot bear to think of him alone in those gloomy rooms. Could he not come with us?'

Charles set down his knife and fork. If Robert came with them it would ruin everything! He wanted Heloise to himself.

'Robert has a standing invitation to view Wycke any time he pleases. He is my heir, if you recall. But he does not care to go,' he warned her.

Heloise went cold inside. Charles had just reminded her he had no further use for her—not even to provide him with an heir. He wanted Robert to succeed him.

Frantically she grappled for something, anything, that might still win her a tiny place in her husband's good graces.

What if she could get Robert to travel to Wycke? Would that not please Charles? It had to be worth a try. For as things stood she was never likely to set eyes on him again. Once he had settled her into her new home he would feel free to pick a fresh, pretty new mistress, and within a month he would have forgotten all about her.

'I am finished here,' she said, pushing herself to her feet.

On legs that felt like cotton wool she left the salon and wove her way across the hall to pound on Robert's door. She had to persuade him to come to Wycke. It was her last chance to show Charles she had some worth as a wife.

Chapter Twelve

'Goodness!' Heloise exclaimed, leaning over Robert to peer through the window on his side of the carriage. 'How much land does Charles own?'

'More than half of Berkshire, I believe, besides swathes of land just outside London, and several minor estates dotted about the country.'

She sat back, a troubled frown on her face. 'I only meant how big is this estate of Wycke? It has been more than ten minutes, I think, since we drove through the lodge gates.'

'We have been driving through Walton's lands for the past hour and more,' Robert explained.

'All those farms and fields…the village we just passed through…'

'Did you not notice the name of the inn? The Walton Arms? The very vicar of the church is in your husband's pocket.'

He owned a village. And paid the priest. He was—she shuddered—the local *seigneur*. Just like her infamous grandfather.

She had always known Charles had a grand title. He had

told her he had a vast fortune. But she had never fully comprehended what it all meant until this moment.

Feeling very small, and very helpless, Heloise turned to look out of her own window, so that she could keep her feeling of shock from her travelling companion. And caught sight of Charles, mounted on his favourite hunter, breaking away from the cavalcade that was winding its ponderous way along the carriage drive and making for a belt of trees on top of a small rise. Did the house lie in that direction? In the middle of a forest?

She swallowed down a feeling of panic. He was going to abandon her here in the middle of all this countryside, with not a soul to talk to for miles.

The carriage wound round a right-hand bend, revealing yet another feature of Wycke's extensive grounds. On her side of the carriage the ground sloped down to a shimmering silver lake, containing an island complete with yet more trees, and a ruined castle.

It was a relief when the coach veered away from what looked suspiciously like the very sort of place a man would lock away an unwanted wife, and rolled along an avenue bordered by neatly clipped shrubbery.

The house itself was huge, naturally, and built of stone the colour of fresh butter.

'Oh, hell,' muttered Robert.

Following his gaze, Heloise registered that in order to reach the front door they were going to have to ascend a flight of about twenty steps.

By the time they stepped through the glass-paned double doors and into a bright, airy lobby, Robert's face was the colour of whey.

'Walton,' he gasped, addressing the figure emerging

from a green baize door to the rear of the hallway. 'Beg leave to inform you…'

But before he could finish, his eyes rolled back in his head. With a grunt, Linney took his dead weight, lowering him gently to the cool, marble tiled floor. Heloise dropped to her knees beside them, her hands frantically tearing away Robert's neck cloth.

'Finch! Wilbrahams!' Charles barked.

Heloise briefly lifted her head, registering her husband striding towards them with his jacket flying loose, his riding crop in his hand, closely followed by two footmen in the familiar blue and silver livery.

'Get Captain Fawley to his rooms!'

With Linney's help, the footmen manhandled Robert's dead weight towards a set of mahogany doors to the right of the grand staircase.

When Heloise scrambled to her feet and made to follow them, Charles caught her by the arm. 'Leave him to Linney,' he snapped. 'Your duty lies elsewhere.'

For the first time she noticed that the hall was crowded with servants, all of whom were watching her with avid curiosity.

From among them stepped a grey-haired lady, severely garbed in black bombazine.

'The staff wish to extend a warm welcome to your new bride, my lord,' she said dropping a respectful curtsey, though the expression on her face did not match her words.

Heloise was suddenly aware that as she had knelt to help Robert her bonnet had come askew, and that in rising she had caught her heel in her skirts, tearing loose a flounce. Her face felt sticky after the journey, and she was convinced there must be at least one smut on it.

'This is Mrs Lanyon, our housekeeper,' Charles said, his

fingers curling more tightly round her arm. He guided her along the line of servants as the housekeeper proceeded to name each and every one, along with their position.

Charles could not seriously expect her to remember the names of an entire regiment of household staff? Could he? Never mind the additional brigade of grooms and gardeners.

'And now I shall conduct you and your personal maid to your suite of rooms, my lady,' Mrs Lanyon intoned. 'There will just be time to refresh yourself and change for dinner,' she added, sweeping up the dark oak staircase. 'We have held it back against your arrival on this one occasion, although normally, of course, we do not keep town hours at Wycke.'

Heloise meekly followed, mortifyingly aware of the staff nudging each other and whispering behind their hands.

'I trust this is to your satisfaction, my lady?' Mrs Lanyon said, upon showing her into a set of rooms on the second floor.

'I am sure it is,' Heloise replied, loosening the ribbons of her bonnet. There had been something in the woman's tone that almost dared her to make any criticism. 'If you would show me where I may wash?'

Mrs Lanyon led the way across what Heloise had to admit was a very pretty, feminine sitting room, and opened a door. 'Your dressing room.'

'What a lovely washstand,' Heloise said inanely.

The top was of pink-veined marble. Standing upon its gleaming surface was a floral-patterned washing set, comprising ewer and basin, and a dish holding a cake of soap sculpted into the shape of a rose. Pristine linen sheets were draped in readiness over a free-standing towel rail.

'I shall feel so much better after a wash,' she said,

removing her bonnet and unbuttoning her spencer in the hope that Mrs Lanyon would take the hint and leave her in peace.

'Shall I send up some refreshments?'

'A glass of lemonade would be very welcome.'

'Lemonade,' Mrs Lanyon echoed faintly. Then, as though pulling herself together, 'If that is what you wish…'

'It is,' Heloise insisted, barely resisting the urge to stamp her foot. It had been a horrible day. Charles had been in one of his most unapproachable moods all day, the coach had been hot and stuffy, making the journey extremely uncomfortable, and she had discovered that her husband was not just Charles at all, but a man as important and influential as a French *seigneur*. This woman's thinly veiled disappointment in her new mistress was the last straw.

Only when she heard the door shut behind her did she permit herself to sink onto a striped day bed and toe off her sweat-stained pumps.

'Oh, Sukey,' she groaned, pressing her fingers to her throbbing temples. 'Did you ever see such a place? Or so many servants?'

'No, my lady,' she agreed, in a voice that was slightly muffled since she was peering into the wardrobe. 'Shall I pour the water for your wash now?' she asked, shutting it, and running her hand reverently over the beautifully carved door panels.

'You had better,' Heloise replied, prising herself from the sofa and padding to the dressing room in her stockinged feet. 'I dare not be late for dinner. You heard what that woman said. "We don't keep town hours at Walton."'

Sukey giggled as Heloise imitated the woman's voice almost perfectly.

'What shall I lay out for you to wear?'

'Whatever looks the least crumpled,' Heloise replied as Sukey went to work on the hooks of her gown. 'Oh, that feels so much better,' she sighed, as she peeled gown and stays from her perspiring body.

It felt better still to sponge herself all over with cool, delicately scented water. When she went back into the sitting room, wrapped only in a linen bath sheet, she found a tray containing lemonade and a plate of freshly baked biscuits on a little occasional table. Both were delicious, and very welcome.

'I've laid out that light yellow silk gown for dinner,' Sukey said, emerging from another door, which Heloise could see led to a bedchamber. She felt a queer tightening in her middle at the possibility there might be a door somewhere that connected her suite to her husband's rooms, just like in London. Should she ask Sukey? Or just go and look for herself later on? So it would not seem as though she had given the matter any thought?

'Since it has been such a hot day, I thought you would want something cool to wear.' Sukey explained her choice. 'But I've put the gold silk shawl out as well, in case it gets chilly later on.' She picked up Heloise's hairbrush. 'Shall I start on your hair while you finish your drink, to save time? And if I bring the plate of biscuits to the dressing table you can carry on eating, too.'

'A good idea,' said Heloise, settling on the low-backed chair.

'It's going to take me a month of Sundays to remember the names of all the people who work here,' Sukey muttered through a mouthful of hairpins.

'Me also,' agreed Heloise with a rueful smile.

'And have you ever seen so many trees? Not but what we don't have trees in London, but at least they are in nice straight lines along the side of the road, where they give shade in the summer,' she grumbled, swiftly working the brush through Heloise's tangles. 'I reckon they must be downright gloomy when it rains.'

'Do you dislike it so much here?' Just because she was doomed to misery, it was not fair to condemn her maid to the same fate. She felt a flicker of panic. 'If you want to return to London…'

'I dare say I will get used to it!' Sukey said hastily. 'I didn't mean to complain. I'd much rather be a lady's maid, even if it is stuck out here in the middle of all this nothing, than go back to blacking the fires in London!'

'I don't expect you will go back to blacking fires—not now you've become a lady's maid,' Heloise reproved gently. 'You have learned to do it so well! At least, I think you have.' She frowned. Then, seeing Sukey's downcast expression in the mirror, she explained, 'You see, I never had a maid—not before I married Lord Walton. In Paris I shared a room with my sister, and we used to help each other dress and do each other's hair.'

Absentmindedly, she nibbled on a biscuit. She had no experience with servants at all, if truth be told. In London, once she had discovered that Charles disliked her chatting to Giddings as though he were a real person, she had tried to ignore them. They had all helped her by taking care to be as unobtrusive as possible. They had certainly never all stood in one place at the same time, and stared at her as though she was some kind of fairground exhibit. Why had he not warned her they would all turn out to greet her like that? And why had he not told her what she should say? She had seen the expression of disapproval on his face when she had been struck dumb by the onslaught of all that curiosity. And she had felt the scorn emanating from Mrs Lanyon's stiff back as she had led her way up the stairs.

'I hope you won't leave me, Sukey,' she said, suddenly reaching for her maid's hand over her shoulder. She needed at least one ally amongst all these strangers.

'Of course I'll stay. It's not as if we'll be down here for ever, is it? Old Giddings was explaining to me that though His Lordship comes down here regular, he never stays for long. We'll soon be back in town, dressing you for parties and the theatre and the like!'

Charles never stays for long. She sighed, replacing her half-eaten biscuit on the plate. But she doubted very much whether she would ever see London again.

Just when he'd thought the day could not possibly get any worse, Charles discovered dinner had been laid out in the state dining room.

Nothing could have been more daunting to a woman like Heloise. His place was at the head of the table, while she sat at its foot, some twenty feet distant. There was no point in even attempting any sort of conversation.

He barely managed to stifle the irritation that had dogged him all day, reminding himself that the staff had clearly gone to a great deal of trouble to impress his new Countess. The meal was a culinary triumph. And he was sure Mrs Lanyon had not intended to intimidate Heloise the minute she stepped through the front door. It was just, he realised, that his guardians had inaugurated a devilishly formal atmosphere at Wycke. And he had never bothered to dismantle it. When he was in residence his focus was on the land, and his tenants. He did not care enough about household management to bother altering a routine into which he fell without thinking.

He should have given Heloise a hint, though, about how to deal with that welcoming party. He had meant to, but when he had gone out to the coach and seen Robert sitting in it he had been so angry that the only way to avoid an unpleasant scene had been to have his hunter saddled up and claim he preferred to ride in such warm weather. So instead of spending the journey warning Heloise that their housekeeper liked to do things 'properly', he had flounced off in a right royal huff. He should have been pleased that she had somehow cajoled Robert into finally accepting an invitation to come and view the place where he should have grown up.

All he could think of was that his plans to get Heloise to himself had been ruined. He would have to divide his time between wooing his reluctant bride and initiating his recalcitrant brother into the ways of Wycke. And in giving way to anger he had done them both a disservice. Not only had Heloise's inadvertent recoil offended Mrs Lanyon, but he had not taken sufficient care of a man who was still far from well. It would probably take Robert days to recover from the journey down here.

He rose to his feet when Heloise left the table, morosely noting how swiftly she fled his presence.

He had the devil of a job on his hands with both Heloise and Robert. And, he reflected, gulping down port that should really have been sipped and savoured, he was damned if he knew how to proceed with either of them.

Heloise took the stopper from the perfume bottle she had found on her dressing table and sniffed tentatively. It was floral, but with an underlying hint of musk that was quite sensual. She dabbed a little onto each wrist, and behind her ears. Then, feeling very daring, between her breasts.

She had already dismissed Sukey, claiming with complete honesty that she would not need her any more. For seducing her husband was a thing a woman had to do for herself.

During dinner she'd had ample opportunity to study her distant spouse and form a plan. He seemed very much at home here, in this house that ran with the precision of a clockwork toy. He was not the sort of man to break any habit he had formed without good reason. So she could probably expect him to come and bid her goodnight.

Gazing along the length of polished mahogany that had symbolised the vast gulf that separated them, she had noted that he was able to enjoy the meal for which she had little appetite. He was a healthy man in his prime, with healthy appetites—at least one of which had not been met since they had married, so far as she could tell. And they were miles from anywhere. And he was not the sort of man to dally with the housemaids.

Which was why she had got Sukey to fetch her most revealing nightdress under the pretext that it was a very sultry night. And doused herself with the only perfume she could lay her hands on.

Finally, with great daring, she arranged herself in what she hoped was a seductive pose on top of the covers.

And waited nervously for Charles to come to her.

It was hard to resist the instinctive desire to preserve her modesty by pulling the covers over herself when she heard the knock that presaged his arrival. Her sense of vulnerability increased when he strode into the room fully dressed.

His reaction was not what she had hoped for either. He glanced only briefly to where she knew her nipples were just visible through the filmy fabric of her nightgown, then, his jaw tightening, fixed his eyes firmly on her face.

'I must apologise,' he said, sitting on the chair beside her bed and crossing his legs as though he had not noticed she was barely decent, 'for the reception you received from the staff. Mrs Lanyon meant well. I was remiss in not preparing you for the formality with which things are done here,' he added, thinking of the dreadful atmosphere at dinner. 'Mrs Lanyon has ruled the roost for a long time.'

Far too long. It was well past time some changes were made. Mrs Lanyon presided over the routine his guardians had inaugurated. But he could remember that Wycke had had a far more relaxed, happy atmosphere when his father had been alive.

'I hope you will make whatever changes you feel are necessary to make this a comfortable home.'

Heloise bit her lower lip. Before they had married he had told her that his staff were efficient, and that he did not want her altering anything. That had been before he had discovered she was such a liability he would not be able to tolerate living in the same household. That he was now granting her permission to make whatever changes she wished here at Wycke, so that she could be relatively comfortable in her exile, was a generous concession on his part.

'You must be tired,' he said. 'It's been the devil of a day.'

He kissed her swiftly, and left so abruptly he might just as well have slapped her.

It was only after he had gone that she worked out what she should have done. When he had bent to kiss her she should have put her arms about his neck and kissed him back. Not on the lips, she had not the courage to be so brazen. For if he had recoiled from such a kiss she would have died of the humiliation. But she could have given him an affectionate peck on the cheek. She frowned. Though he had warned her he did not like displays of affection.

Oh, damn the man! She knelt up and flung a pillow at the door through which he had retreated. Then buried her face in her hands. The barriers which separated them were impenetrable. Especially since he bolstered them every way he could. She should just give up before she totally humiliated herself.

Charles' mood the next morning was even blacker than it had been the night before. Heloise had looked so tempting, lying on her bed in that confection of lace and moonbeams, that it had been all he could do to keep his hands off her. The wary look on her face had reminded him just in time what a disaster that would have been. The speech he had spent so long carefully preparing had evaporated like morning mist at the sudden hot flare of lust he'd had to disguise by sitting down quickly, crossing his legs, and clasping his hands in his lap.

He'd spent a sleepless night, remembering how she had looked reclining on that bank of pillows and wishing he could be beside her. Racking his brains to think of some way he could achieve that goal.

While he had been shaving, he'd had a brainwave. For a couple of days he would have Heloise to himself, while Robert was recovering. He could make a start by showing her over the house. And while he was doing that he would persuade her that it might be a good idea to learn to drive the estate gig. The narrow seat of the two-wheeled vehicle could only accommodate a driver and one passenger. They would have to go out on their own. He would have to take hold of her hands to teach her how to use the reins. She would get used to him touching and holding her, under the guise of accepting instruction, and slowly she would cease to feel threatened by him. When they reached that point he would slide his arm about her waist, or her shoulder. He would inform her that her bonnet was most becoming, and drop a kiss on her cheek...

A less contained man than he would have whistled on the staircase as he went down to breakfast.

And would then have thumped Giddings for informing him that his bailiff was already waiting for him in the estate office.

Why had he forgotten that he always spent his first day at Wycke going over the estate accounts? And damn the place anyway, for its relentless routine which ground any hope of spontaneity into the dust!

Heloise checked on the threshold of the breakfast room when she saw the thunderous expression on his face. A stickler for good manners, he got to his feet and bade her a gruff good morning, but it was evident he had not expected her presence at the breakfast table.

The room was far nicer than the one where they had dined the night before. It was smaller, for one thing, and the floor-to-ceiling windows gave a view over a gravelled parterre in the centre of which an ornamental fountain played. The table was round, and lacked formal place-settings. If Charles had not retreated behind his newspaper, indicating his preference for solitude, she could have sat next to him.

'I had thought you might like a tour of the house this morning,' he said, as she helped herself to some chocolate from a silver pot which stood on a sideboard. 'Unfortunately I have pressing estate business to see to, else I would have taken you around myself.'

'It is of no matter.' Heloise shrugged. She would have years to explore this horrid house, and would probably come to detest every inch of it. 'I will go and make a visit with Robert, see how he does. And after I shall take a walk through the gardens.'

'I have another suggestion,' he put in hastily. He had to wean her from the habit of turning to Robert. 'Have Mrs Lanyon take you over the house this morning. She knows far more about its history than I, in any case. She has made quite a study of it. And, you know, it would be a good opportunity to get on terms with the woman.' They had not got off to a good start. 'You are going to have to deal with her on a regular basis…'

Yes, Mrs Lanyon was to be her jailer! Breaking open a bread roll with rather more force than was necessary, Heloise considered her husband's advice. It was bad enough that she was going to have to live in this wilderness, let alone with a woman who despised her. One who wielded such immense power over the staff as well.

'You are right,' she sighed.

'Then I shall arrange it. Also,' he added in a deceptively casual tone, 'one day soon, since the estate is so large and you do not ride, I shall teach you to drive a gig. Then you will be able to get around more independently.' He studied her downbent head with a growing feeling of disquiet. It was almost as if she sensed his suggestion was merely a ruse to get her alone, and was thinking of excuses to put him off. 'It would be a great pity to be restricted to the house when there are so many delightful vistas just a short drive away,' he went on, in some desperation. 'Once you become proficient I should not object to you driving yourself into the village on occasion—provided, of course, you took your maid.'

Heloise could hardly swallow her bread and honey for the lump which formed in her throat.

He might not be able to feel any affection for her, but

he was clearly not going to leave her here until he was fairly sure she had the means to be comfortable. He was intent on smoothing her way with the formidable Mrs Lanyon, and had come up with a plan to ensure she had a degree of freedom when he was no longer there.

Though he did own a village, and held the lives of so many people in the palm of his hand, he was by no means a tyrant. His strict sense of duty ensured he looked out for the welfare of all his dependants, be they tenants or injured and estranged brothers, or ill-chosen wives. How could she help loving him?

She sighed. It would take a remarkable woman to earn his regard. She did not know why she had even thought it was worth trying.

There was no point in her wearing transparent night-gowns and dousing herself with perfume to try to titillate his manly impulses. Or trying to worm her way into his busy life by interrupting him at the breakfast table when he clearly would much rather be reading his paper. She would revert to the routine they had set in London and keep out of his way, as she had initially promised.

She lifted her chin, laying what remained of the honeyed crust on her plate.

'You do not need to teach me to drive. I shall get Robert to do it. It will do him good to get out in the fresh air. Besides, I am sure he wants to explore the estate, but nothing would let him admit as much. If he has the excuse of having to look after me, it will mean he can get out as often as he wants.'

He was still groping for some objection to her very logical suggestion when she rose from her chair and glided from the room without a backward glance. Somehow she had managed to slip through his fingers yet again.

* * *

'And now we come to the portrait gallery,' Mrs Lanyon intoned.

She certainly knew a great deal about Wycke, and the family who had lived there since it had been built, in the latter days of Queen Elizabeth. She liked nothing better, she had confided on collecting Heloise from her rooms, than showing interested parties around.

Wycke was mentioned in guidebooks, and visitors to the county always put it at the very top of their itinerary, she had further declared, with pride.

'This is the first Earl,' she said of a life-sized portrait of a man with a ruff round his neck and a fierce expression on his face that put Heloise in mind of Robert.

Each successive Earl and Countess Mrs Lanyon introduced her to gazed down at her with varying degrees of disdain.

'The late Countess of Walton,' Mrs Lanyon said, jerking Heloise out of her introspection.

'Which one?' she dared to ask, her interest reviving for the first time since 1724.

'I mean to say, is it the Earl's mother, or his stepmother?'

Mrs Lanyon drew herself up to her full height before saying frostily, 'His mother, naturally. She was the grand-daughter of the Duke of Bray.'

She looked as though she might have been, Heloise mused. The weight of generations of breeding sat heavily on the slender shoulders of the young woman who looked out of her gilded frame with a somewhat pained expression. The glossy curls which peeped from under the brim of her hat were of a similar colour to Charles' hair, and her eyes were blue, but her mouth had a petulant droop to the lips that she would never associate with him.

'My grandfather,' Heloise blurted in a spirit of rebellion, 'was among the very first to go to the guillotine.' Her father might be only a government functionary, but her mother's blood was as blue as any of these ancestors of Charles'.

'Dreadful!' gasped Mrs Lanyon, her hand flying to her throat.

'Yes, he was. He doubled the taxes during a period of famine, causing great hardship to the peasants. Something that Charles,' she declared with conviction, 'would never do.'

Having finished her tour of the house, Mrs Lanyon handed her over to Bayliss, the head gardener. Thoroughly oppressed by so much history, and aware she had spoken too controversially for Mrs Lanyon's comfort, Heloise was glad to get out of doors.

To her dismay, the Walton family, and in particular the ladies, pursued her through the grounds. A knot garden was the work of the first Countess; a rose garden was the inspiration of the third. She could see why the place attracted visitors, for it contained a great deal that was beautiful. But it was more like a museum than a home.

Spying a familiar figure lounging on a south-facing stone terrace, Heloise escaped from her guide.

'Robert!' she cried, running up the steps and bounding to his side. 'You are better today, yes?'

'Just sitting out enjoying the fresh air,' he groused. 'Don't go pestering me to go anywhere today, because I have no intention of stirring from this terrace. Which is mine, by the way.'

'How do you mean, yours?' She sat on a wooden bench next to him, her eyes alight with curiosity.

'I mean just that. The windows behind me lead directly into my rooms. Nobody is supposed to disturb me out

here. Do you know you have to walk across I don't know
how many lawns to get to those steps you ran up?'

'Only too well!' she snorted. 'For I have walked across
them. Oh,' she said, suddenly registering what he had said,
'you wish me to leave you alone.' From his eyes she met
the hostility of generations of Waltons. 'I understand.'

Leaping to her feet, she ran back down the steps and,
without knowing where she would end up, headed away
from the house. Anywhere, she fumed, blinking back tears,
as long as she was out of everyone's way! She blundered
through a dense shrubbery to emerge on the lip of an em-
bankment. To her amazement she discovered she had come
out just above the curving carriage drive, and that beyond
it a flower-sprinkled meadow undulated down to the lake.

Perhaps the grounds were not so large as she had first
assumed. She would never have guessed, when she had
driven along this particular stretch of the drive the day
before, that she was so near the house.

She eyed the ruined tower on the island in which she
had imagined Charles might lock her away. He might just
as well. The servants had despised her on sight, and now
even Robert, whom she thought of as a brother, had said
he wanted her to stop pestering him.

Very well! She would not pester Robert to teach her to
drive after all. She would get one of the grooms to do it.
And prove to Charles that she did not need him—no, not
for anything.

And then he could go back to London and forget all
about her.

And she…no, she would never forget Charles. She
would spend every minute of her long, lonely exile wondering what he was doing.

And who he was doing it with.

Chapter Thirteen

Charles paused in the doorway of the state dining room, which tonight was looking its most magnificent. The staff had polished the massive epergnes to mirror-brightness, filling them with banks of freshly cut flowers that filled the air with their perfume. A footman was going round lighting the candles already. Once he had finished, the china and crystal would glitter like jewels set against the yards of spotless damask linen tablecloth.

'It all looks splendid—as ever,' he said to his house-keeper. Within a week of his arrival Mrs Lanyon had reminded him that he always sent out cards of invitation to his neighbours. It was just one more tradition he wished he had never allowed to become set in stone. 'Though in future you should expect Lady Walton to oversee events of this nature.'

Fortunately for her, Mrs Lanyon refrained from making the comment which would have brought her instant dismissal. Though the way she pursed her lips told him exactly what she was thinking. Heloise had played no part in the organisation of this dinner whatsoever. Whenever Mrs

Lanyon had consulted her, she had replied she must do exactly as she wished.

Though it hurt to think she disliked him so much she could not even pretend to show an interest in his social life, he could not be angry with her. Being on display for his neighbours would be an ordeal for a woman of her shy, retiring disposition. If he could only have thought of a way to cancel the dinner without insulting his neighbours he would have done so. But in the end he had decided it would be better to just get the thing over with as soon as possible. Far better for them to find out that his wife was a little gauche than for them to imagine she was unfriendly.

He had never been so irritated by the number of obligations his position brought him before. But since they had come down to Wycke every chance he might have had to get closer to Heloise had been thwarted by estate business in one form or another.

Still, he had dealt with all the most pressing business now. And once this annual county dinner was over he could devote himself almost exclusively to wooing her.

As he went along the corridor to the red salon, he wondered what lay behind her decision to get Grimwade, the head groom, to teach her to drive rather than Robert. Strolling to the window that overlooked the carriage drive, he rubbed his hand across the back of his neck. To his knowledge, Robert had not stirred from his rooms since his arrival, although Linney assured him his master was recovering nicely from the journey. He barely repressed the urge to fling the window open. Though the room felt stuffy, the air outside was even hotter, and heavy with the threat of an approaching storm. He hoped it would not break too soon. The last thing he wanted was for his guests to be stranded, so that he would be obliged to offer them hospitality.

* * *

'Do I wear the Walton diamonds?' Heloise was anxiously asking Sukey. 'Or will it look as though I am showing off?'

One did not dress so elaborately in the country. Even she knew that. Which was why she had chosen the simplest evening gown she had. But, since she had no other jewellery, it was either wear the Walton parure or nothing. She did not think Charles would wish her to look dowdy.

Though how could she look anything else? She had neither Felice's emerald eyes, nor the voluptuous figure of Mrs Kenton. With a small cry of distress, she whirled away from the mirror.

'Don't be nervous, my lady,' Sukey said brightly. 'You are the highest-ranking lady in the district, and nothing anyone might think will alter that.'

She was right. The women she'd seen wearing the Walton diamonds in portrait after portrait might disapprove of her, but she was as much the Countess as any of them. Because Charles had married *her*. Not the graceful Felice, nor the experienced Mrs Kenton, but plain, naïve little Heloise Bergeron.

Anyway, these hard cold stones were all she had to prove this marriage was real. Especially since the arrival of her monthly courses, a few days earlier, had robbed her of even the faint hope that she might have conceived a child during that one brief coupling.

Straightening her shoulders, she walked across to the table on which the ancient jewel case squatted. 'I will wear the diamonds,' she said. 'All of them.'

She did not care if anyone thought she was overdressed. She clipped the earrings to her earlobes with a grimace. Though she wanted to make a good impression on the people who would form her new social circle, she had an even greater need to bolster her flagging self-esteem.

Before long she was ready to join Charles in the red salon, where Mrs Lanyon had told her he always greeted his dinner guests.

He looked magnificent in his evening clothes. He was always so immaculately dressed, so correct in all his behaviour. She itched to reach up and tousle his neatly brushed hair, to mar that perfection which threw all her own faults into stark relief. When his guests started to arrive, and saw them standing side by side, they were bound to wonder at the Earl having made such a mismatch.

The breath hitched in Charles' throat as she trailed slowly across the room to join him beside the empty hearth. She was so lovely. The simply cut gown she had chosen became her slight figure far more than some of the fussy creations he had seen adorning the so-called leaders of fashion in London. And with the diamonds glittering about her throat and wrist she looked every inch the Countess.

He was on the verge of telling her so, when she began to twist her hands together at her waist. He had got used to seeing her drooping disconsolately about the place, but this new symptom hurt him abominably. She could not bear to come within three feet of him!

He turned from her abruptly. It took him a moment or two to get himself in hand. And then he found he was standing by the sideboard. He did the only thing that came to him which might just help her. He poured a small glass of Madeira and carried it back to her.

Heloise tossed it back, wondering in what way she had failed to measure up this time, for him to walk away from her with such a grim expression. Had it been a mistake to wear the full parure? Had it reminded him of how very nearly she had lost part of it? Or did he just think she was overdressed? And if he thought so what would his guests think? Perhaps she should run back upstairs and change? Oh, but there was no time. The front door was being opened, she could hear Giddings greeting someone, and already there was the sound of more wheels crunching over the gravel drive.

Her heart pounding against her ribs, she held out her empty glass to Finch.

'Get me another,' she pleaded, avoiding her husband's gaze. It was bad enough knowing she disappointed him without encountering the full wintry blast of his eyes.

The room rapidly filled with about thirty people who had known Charles and each other all their lives. There was only one person amongst them who did not totally overwhelm her. Her name was Miss Masterson, and her father was a retired colonel. Heloise empathised with the way she sought out a corner away from the more ebullient guests, and made sure the circulating footmen did not overlook her. When Charles had gone back to London she would call on the girl, who looked as if she was of a similar age, and see if she could make a friend of her. If, that was, she could bear to enter the house of the Colonel and his bulldog-faced wife.

'Hoped to be able to meet your long-lost brother,' Colonel Masterson was booming at Charles, as though he was yards away across a parade ground. 'Military man, ain't he? Was hoping to have a jaw with him about developments in the Low Countries. Wellington's been given charge of the allied armies, d'you know? Got it from Viscount Brabourne on his way through to his hunting box in Wiltshire. Damned shame we're at war with your wife's country again. Though I'm sure,' he said turning towards her, 'you want to see Bonaparte brought to book, eh? Must support the Bourbons. Walton wouldn't have married you unless you was a Royalist, now, would he?'

'You are mistaken,' she replied, cut to the quick by his barely concealed speculation as to what on earth could have induced an Earl to marry her. 'I am very far from being a Royalist.'

She did not realise that she should have taken the time to explain she despised fat Louis and his inept government almost as much as she detested Bonaparte's ruthless efficiency until she heard the Colonel confide to his wife, in what he must have thought was a whisper, as they were processing to the dining room, 'Outrageous! He's brought a Bonapartist amongst us!' His wife managed to hush him, but she could not stop him casting suspicious looks her way throughout the meal.

Lord Danvers, who was sitting to her right at the foot of the table, opened the conversation over the soup by enquiring if she hunted.

She made the fatal error of confessing that she could not ride at all.

'Not ride?' He looked at her as though she had confessed to a crime.

Swiftly she tried to vindicate herself. 'It is considered unpatriotic, in my country, to keep a horse. Like our sons and brothers, they belong to the army of France.' The malevolent glare this comment drew from Colonel Masterson suggested he now believed she must have come to England for the sole purpose of winkling state secrets from her husband. Now he would never allow her to befriend his daughter.

After that, the conversation at the foot of the table became painfully stilted. And yet Heloise dreaded the moment when she would have to rise, signalling it was time for the ladies to withdraw. While they were confined to their seats and occupied with their food only the nearest handful of guests could attack her. She had the feeling that once she got to the music room it would turn into a free-for-all.

Lady Danvers fired the opening salvo.

'Do you play the pianoforte, Lady Walton?' she cooed. 'Or perhaps the harp? Or have you arranged something particularly French—' she tittered '—to entertain the gentlemen when they join us?'

'No,' she replied bluntly. She did not ride, she did not play any musical instrument, and she did not have a lively personality. She sighed. And if only it were true that she had ensnared her husband by the sort of French naughtiness this abominable woman implied.

With a triumphant gleam in her eye, Lady Danvers went to the sofa where Lady Masterson was sitting, settled beside her, and murmured something in her ear that caused the older lady to regard Heloise with even deeper hostility.

'Perhaps our dear Countess has other talents,' suggested the vicar's wife. 'We are all good at something. Even if it is only the art of putting the poor at ease when visiting. Or the clever arrangement of flowers. Or embroidery. Or…' Looking more and more desperate as Heloise shook her head at every suggestion the kind lady put forward, she eventually subsided.

'You mean to tell me you have no accomplishments whatever?' Lady Danvers drawled.

'I do not tell you that at all,' Heloise snapped, her patience finally running out. 'I am an artist!'

'An artist?' Lady Danvers quirked one eyebrow in distinct mockery. 'You mean you dabble about with paint?'

'No, I draw,' she replied, her heart suddenly plunging to her dainty satin slippers. Charles would hate it if these people ever found out she had tried to make money from the sale of her work. Work of which he strongly disapproved.

'But I do not have a portfolio to show you. It was lost…' Well, at least most of it was 'lost', burnt, actually '…when I left France.'

'Oh, how disappointing,' drawled Lady Danvers sarcastically. 'I am sure we have missed a rare treat.' She exchanged a knowing smile with Lady Masterson.

Heloise gasped. The woman was accusing her of being a liar to her face!

Lydia Bentinck, one of a trio of elderly spinsters, sniffed loudly before saying, 'There is more to being a lady of quality than being able to draw, or play the piano, or ride a horse. I have always held that good manners are an absolute prerequisite.' She looked pointedly at Lady Danvers. 'So sadly lacking in many these days.'

Lady Danvers' eyes snapped with fury. While she struggled to find a suitably cutting come back, Diana Bentinck turned to Heloise and enquired, 'What sort of drawings do you do?'

'People. I do sketches of people.'

'Oh, how charming. Would you do a sketch of me and my sisters? I should love to have a likeness. Or would it take too long?'

She was on the point of refusing, out of deference to Charles' views, when she caught sight of Lady Danvers' lip curling in derision.

'I would be glad to sketch you,' she declared defiantly. 'Please to take seats close together, while I find some materials.'

By this time one of the other ladies, a Mrs Goulding,

had taken a seat at the piano, and while Heloise unearthed some sheets of writing paper from a desk drawer she began to pick out the bare bones of a Haydn sonata. From her reticule, Heloise produced the sliver of charcoal which she was never without. While the Bentinck sisters fluttered about the three chairs they had decided to pose on, arguing as to which order they should sit, either by age or by size, and whether one should stand behind the other two to make an interesting group, Heloise's nimble fingers flew across the page. By the time they were settled she was able to walk over to them, holding out her finished work.

'Why,' exclaimed Lydia, 'this is quite remarkable!'

Three grey heads bent to examine the sparse lines on the creamy vellum. They could see Lydia standing over her two seated siblings. Diana was holding out her hand, palm upwards, while Grace had her head tilted to one side, a pensive frown knitting her brows. Though each pose denoted a certain amount of conflict, each woman was also expressing a strong affection for the other two, so that the overall impression was one of harmony.

'I cannot believe you did that so quickly!' Diana Bentinck cried.

'It was not so quick.' They had been bickering gently for several minutes, and she had always found it a simple matter to reproduce an accurate physical likeness.

'I am sorry that it is only on writing paper…' she began.

But, 'Oh, no!' the three sisters cried simultaneously. 'This paper has the Walton crest on it. What a lovely reminder it will be to us of a delightful evening spent at Wycke!'

The vicar's wife had now sidled up to her. 'Oh, I should love to have a sketch drawn by you, Lady Walton,' she gushed.

'As you wish,' Heloise replied, picking up her charcoal.

Fortunately, she had not had time to study these people too closely, and so link them inextricably in her mind with some member of the animal kingdom. So she managed, with some application, to repress her imagination and stick to a strictly literal likeness of her next subject. The resultant sketch was exclaimed over, passed round, and generated such excitement that several other ladies asked if she would do their portraits too.

She became so deeply absorbed that she noticed neither the passage of time nor the arrival in the music room of the gentlemen. All she did see, when she handed Miss Masterson her finished sketch, was the smile which lit up her face.

'Do I really look like that?' the girl exclaimed, running a finger wonderingly over the smudged lines of her portrait. Her face clouded. 'I think you must have been flattering me.'

'Not in the least,' Charles said, startling Heloise. She'd had no idea he was standing behind her chair. 'My wife never flatters her sitters. She has the knack, though, of putting something of the subject's personality in beyond the physical likeness. Perhaps that is what you recognise in your own portrait, Miss Masterson?'

Heloise did not know what to make of this remark. Perhaps his oblique reference to the way she habitually portrayed people as the animals they reminded her of was a warning to behave herself?

'You must do my son,' Lady Masterson said. 'Now that you have managed to make my stepdaughter look so fetching.'

Heloise hesitated. She would have been thrilled at winning over one of her major opponents so easily, were she not so scared of offending Charles. Warily, she looked to him for guidance. But his expression gave her no clues.

She pulled a fresh sheet of paper from the drawer of the writing desk as young Thomas Masterson took the seat his older sister had just vacated.

Why did she never think about the consequences before acting? she berated herself. It had been just the same in that stupid card game. Only tonight it had been Lady Danvers who had goaded her into losing her temper and acting in a way that was guaranteed to displease Charles. Gripping the charcoal tightly, she paused to examine the young man's features for a moment or two before setting to work.

Charles watched in fascination as her fingers flew across the paper. He had never seen her drawing before. She had pitched her work this evening in a way that was guaranteed to please their guests. His heart swelled with pride. She could so easily have taken revenge for the various snubs she had borne earlier, by accentuating the uglier aspects of her neighbours. Instead, she brought out the best in them. She had even managed to make the dreary Miss Masterson look interesting, transforming her habitually vacant stare into the dreamy reverie of a *savant*.

She was so talented. He ached to tell her so. He pondered how best to word the compliment, savouring the knowledge that it was the very one he could pay her that would please her.

And while they were on the subject he must ask her pardon for forcing her to burn that sketchbook. If she could forgive him that one transgression… His heart-rate picked up dramatically. Had he finally found the key that might unlock his wife's heart?

He could hardly wait for the last of his tedious guests to leave so that he could make his declaration.

'I am sorry you did not have an easy time of it this evening,' he began, his expression sobering as he recalled

Colonel Masterson's rudeness, and imagined the barbed comments he was sure the spiteful Lady Danvers must have let fly. 'But I believe most of our guests went away having been tolerably well entertained.'

His words struck at her like a blow from a fist. Though she had very nearly disgraced him, he seemed to be saying, his neighbours had been gracious enough to overlook all her inadequacies.

'Then may I go to my room, now?'

'Very well,' he conceded, battening down his eagerness to put his new plan of action in train. He followed her into the hall and watched her ascend the stairs. He would give her a few minutes before following her, and then…

'A word, if you please, Walton!'

Robert's harsh voice abruptly shattered his fantasies. He turned to see his half-brother emerge from the shadows beneath the bend in the great staircase.

'Ashamed of me, are you?' Robert began, with no preamble.

'I beg your pardon?' Why did he have to pick such an inappropriate moment to pick a quarrel? 'You'd better come into my study.'

Striding past his brother, he flung open the door and went in. He was not going to participate in any kind of a scene in the hall, where angry words would echo up to the rafters.

'What is it?' he said with impatience, going from habit to the side table on which rested a decanter of fine cognac and several glasses.

'I want to know why you excluded me tonight,' Robert began, stumping angrily along in his wake. 'Why the devil drag me down here if all you do is shut me away like some…?'

Abruptly his words petered out as he caught sight of the portrait that hung above Charles' desk.

'That's my mother!' he exclaimed in indignation. 'Why have you got a picture of my mother in your study? Why isn't she up in the gallery with all the reputable Waltons?'

'When have *you* been up in the picture gallery?'

Robert looked a little discomforted, but did not admit that he had bribed Finch to show him round at times when he knew neither Giddings nor Mrs Lanyon nor Charles would discover he had done so.

'Well, I am glad you have been exploring your home, though had I known you wished to do so I would gladly have been your guide…'

'Oh, would you?' he sneered. 'When you hide me away from your neighbours as though you are ashamed of owning such a brother!'

'I have done no such thing! I had nothing to do with the arrangements. Heloise…' He frowned. She had left the whole thing to Mrs Lanyon. Did the housekeeper have a problem with Robert's presence in the house? Might she even have some lingering loyalties to the Lamptons?

'Oh, hell,' said Robert, casting himself into a chair and easing the position of his wooden leg with his good hand. 'My cursed temper! I've upset her. I wondered at the time…though normally when I rip up at her she gives it me back threefold.'

'Here.' Charles pressed a glass of cognac into his hand and settled behind the desk.

'I wish you wouldn't be so damned reasonable all the time,' Robert grumbled. 'If only you would shout back at me just once in a while, instead of being so…icily polite, I shouldn't feel so…so…'

Charles shrugged one shoulder. 'My guardians did a

sterling job of raising me after the pattern of my own mother's irreproachable forebears. Although…' he swivelled in his chair to gaze at the portrait that hung there '…when I gaze upon your mother's face I can remember a time when things were very different here at Wycke. It was only from the day they ousted her it became this cold, inhospitable mausoleum. They told me she had abandoned me.' He took a large gulp of the cognac. 'I was eight years old. She was the only mother I had ever known. She had always seemed warm and loving, to both me and my father. Suddenly it was as if I had never known her at all. How could a woman turn her back on a child who had just lost his father?'

'She didn't!' Robert defended her. 'They sent her back to her family and then threw all their weight into crushing her spirit!'

'For which crime I shall never be able to forgive them.'

His eyes grew so cold that Robert took a swig of his cognac to counteract the chill that pervaded the whole room.

'You should have grown up here, with me. We should have climbed trees, fished in the lake, and played at Knights and Saracens in the ruined tower. If your mother had been here she would have made sure I went to school rather than being walled up here with a succession of tutors.'

'I never appreciated you may have felt like this.' Robert frowned into his glass. 'I always assumed that the quarrel you started with the Lamptons when you came of age was to do with money…'

'Money! Oh, no. They were always scrupulously honest when it came to my finances. It was something far more valuable they robbed me of.' His eyes returned to the portrait of the dark-haired woman smiling down at her boys. 'Something irreplaceable. My childhood.'

After an awkward pause, Robert managed to mumble, 'Grown up in the habit of hating you, but I have to concede of late you have been very generous to me…'

Charles made a dismissive gesture with his hand. 'I have done nothing but restore what should always have been yours. How our father managed to make such a botch of his will…'

It was the opening he had longed for since the day he'd discovered he had a brother. As the level in the brandy bottle steadily dropped, the two men managed to discuss, for the most part relatively cordially, the woman they had both called mother, and the events that had led up to her tragic demise.

By the time Charles went upstairs and softly entered his wife's room she was fast asleep.

'Oh, my darling,' he murmured, bending to kiss her sleep flushed cheek. 'Thanks to you, my brother has been restored to me.'

Gently, he brushed one stray lock of hair from her forehead, before retreating to his own room. If she did not come down for breakfast in the morning he would send a note, requesting she join him in his study as soon as she was awake. He had learned a valuable lesson from his long, and painful interview with Robert. His brother had attributed nefarious motives to all his actions. It was not until he had spelled out exactly why he had taken what steps he had that Robert had finally managed to let go of years of resentment.

He needed to have just such a conversation with his wife.

Heloise stared at the curt little note she held in her hand with a sinking heart. Charles requested her presence in his study as soon as she woke. Pushing her breakfast tray to one side, she swung her legs out of bed. He must be so angry with her for flouting his wishes the night before. She did not wish to make him any angrier by keeping him waiting. She went straight to her washroom, pulling off her nightgown and tossing it aside in her haste to begin her toilette.

'Please to lay out my clothes while I wash,' Heloise said, when Sukey gaped at the sight of her mistress pouring water into the basin for herself. 'My green cambric walking dress.'

She was halfway down the stairs before she wondered what on earth she was doing. She could well imagine what he wanted to say to her. He was ready to go back to London. And, since she had let him down so badly, he had no intention of taking her with him. She had lived in dread of this moment ever since they had got here.

She stood, clutching the banister for support, as tears began to roll down her cheeks.

Stifling a sob, she hitched up her skirts and, instead of meekly going to the study, she ran down the passage that led to the back of the house and fled into the gardens.

And she kept on running. From her pain, from her loneliness, from her sense of utter failure. Across the lawns, through the shrubbery, down the bank and across the meadow. Only when she reached the lake did she veer from her course, following the shoreline until her strength gave out and she crumpled to the ground, giving way to the misery she had bottled up for so long.

She had no idea how long she lay there, curled up like a wounded animal, her utter misery cloaking her in a dense shroud of darkness.

It was only when the first great fat drops of rain began to strike her back that she sat up, suddenly aware that the darkness was not only inside her. The storm which had been hanging over Wycke for days had finally broken. She gasped as rain struck the ground around her like a hail of bullets, spattering her dress with sandy ricochets.

Her first instinct was to seek shelter. But she could not bear to go back to the house. She could see herself standing before Charles' desk, her hem dripping water onto his polished floor, her hair hanging in rats' tails round her face, while he informed her, his lip curling with disdain, that he never wished to set eyes on her again.

She pushed herself to her feet and made her way back to a wooden footbridge she remembered running past. It led across a narrow strip of water to the island on which stood the ruined tower. She would wait there until the storm had passed.

Maybe by then Charles would already have left Wycke, so that at least she would be spared the ordeal of suffering his dismissal in person.

Stumbling over a large piece of masonry half hidden by nettles alerted her to the fact she was nearing her goal. She lifted her head, brushing back the streamers of wet hair clinging to her face. The tower stood defiantly amidst the mounds of crumbling stones, all that remained of what might once have been an impressive set of fortifications. It still possessed a door, though it was almost completely obscured with a tangled growth of ivy. Grabbing the iron ring that served as a latch, Heloise turned it and pushed with all her strength.

The door yielded by perhaps two feet, grating over the stone-flagged floor within. She squeezed inside, grateful to have found shelter so quickly. It was dry inside, though almost pitch-black. Only the faintest glimmer of light filtered in from a source far above her head. It originated from the head of a wooden staircase, set into the outer wall of the tower.

She wrinkled her nose at the smell of decay that hung in the air. What was she doing in this dark, dirty ruin, when she could be sitting before a nice warm fire in her pretty sitting room, sipping hot chocolate? She could at least be comfortable, even if she would not feel any less miserable.

She wrapped her arms round her waist as a shiver racked her body. The rain had soaked right through her dress and flimsy indoor shoes in a matter of seconds. Charles would think she was an idiot for running in here instead of returning to the house.

Well, she *was* an idiot! She had been told as much for as long as she could remember. She sniffed. But the most foolish thing she had ever done was fall in love with a man that even a child could see should never have married so far beneath him!

And the worst of it was she had no right to admit she was miserable because he did not love her. Love was never supposed to have been part of the bargain they had made.

She wiped her hand across her face, not sure if it was rain or tears that were running down her cheeks, as a gust of wind blew in through the partially open door. She retreated from the storm, deeper into the gloom, and felt a sharp stab of pain in her shin as she stumbled over a broken chair which was lying on its side next to a battered wooden trunk.

Perhaps she would be better off up on the next floor, where it was a bit lighter. And there might not be so much rubbish lying about, she thought, making for the stairs. There was a metal railing fixed into the wall, onto which she clung as she tentatively began to climb. After only a few steps the air began to feel fresher, and as her head came onto a level with the upper floor, she saw that the room was indeed a great improvement on the rubbish tip the ground floor had become. Though the floor was a bit dusty, there were several pieces of quite sturdy-looking furniture, arranged to face a floor-to-ceiling window which, though grimy, was fully glazed.

She was just congratulating herself for making the decision to explore, when without warning the step upon which she had just placed her foot gave way with a sharp crack. Her foot went straight through, and if she had not been clinging to the handrail she would have fallen. Shaking with shock, she pulled her leg carefully up through the splintered tread.

Then realised, with horror, that it was not just her body that was shaking. The whole staircase was quivering under her weight.

And then, with a sound that reminded her of the ship's timbers creaking as the craft had plunged its way across the Channel, the whole structure parted company from the wall.

Chapter Fourteen

Charles pulled his watch from his pocket and frowned as it confirmed what he already knew. It had been three hours since Sukey had put his note into Heloise's hands, and still she had not come to him.

'You sent for me, my lord?'

Charles looked up to see Giddings standing in the doorway.

'Yes.' He snapped his watch shut and tucked it back into his waistcoat pocket. 'Have luncheon served in the breakfast parlour, and send someone to find out if Her Ladyship will be joining me.'

Perhaps she was unwell. Although, if that were the case, surely she would just have replied to his note with one of her own, apprising him of the fact.

No, he could not shake the conviction that this prolonged silence was a message in itself. He sighed. It had been too much to hope that he could put things right with his brother and his wife on the same day.

He went to the window, leaning his forearm on the sash as he gazed out at the rain which had begun to fall not long after Robert had left in the family coach, bound for London. He accepted that Robert needed time on his own, to come to terms with the new understanding they had reached in the early hours of the morning. And when Robert had haltingly given his reasons for wishing to return 'home', his heart had leapt, knowing that this was at last how he thought of his rooms at Walton House.

He turned at the sound of a knock on the door.

'Begging your pardon, my lord,' said Giddings. 'But Sukey does not seem to know Her Ladyship's whereabouts. Apparently she dressed in a great hurry and left her rooms quite early this morning, as soon as she received the note Your Lordship sent her.'

Charles felt as though a cold hand had reached into his chest and clamped round his heart. It could not be a coincidence that Heloise had disappeared the same morning his brother had returned to London.

'Will that be all, my lord?'

'What? Oh, yes—yes,' he snapped, dismissing his butler with a curt wave of his hand.

He had been standing in this very room, he recalled, the last time he had received news that had rocked his world to its foundations. Though he had only been a child, and standing on the other side of this desk, when his maternal uncle had told him he was never going to see his stepmother again. He stared blindly at the desk-top as he felt that same sense of isolation closing round him all over again.

His stepmother had kept a little singing bird in a cage in the sitting room that now belonged to Heloise. He had been able to hear it singing clear up to his schoolroom. But not that morning. When she had left she had taken it with her, and a dreadful silence had descended on Wycke.

And now, though Heloise had never really belonged to

him, her absence would reverberate through every corner of his existence.

How could she have betrayed him like this? How could Robert?

He drew in a deep breath, forcing himself to sit down and consider his situation rationally.

Though jealousy would have him believe his wife was the kind of woman who would run off with another man, his saner self knew her better than that. Though she had made her marriage vows in haste, and soon come to regret them, he could not believe she would break them so easily. Her conscience was far too tender. Look how she had berated herself for supposed lack of morals that night he had kissed her at the masquerade, when she had still been a virgin!

No, if she had left with Robert, it was not to embark on an affair.

She could not do it.

The only thing that would ever induce her to break her marriage vows was if she fell in love with someone else. And there was no evidence to indicate she had done so.

And as for Robert… No, he could no longer believe that he would deliberately conspire against him either. What he could imagine was Heloise going to him and begging him to take her back to London, where she would be safe from her cruel husband. A man would have to have a heart of stone to refuse her.

He would give her a few days' respite from his loathsome presence before following her to London. Though follow her he would. For he would not be able to rest until he could look her in the face and tell her…

He sucked in a sharp breath as the truth hit him. He had fallen in love with his wife. Fallen. He groaned. What an apt term! A fall was something you had no control over. It happened when you least expected it. It shook you up, and took your breath away, and it hurt. God, how it hurt. Especially when the woman you loved could not bear to be in the same room—nay, the same county!

What was he to do now?

Why, he mocked himself, take luncheon as if there was nothing the matter, of course. It was what he did best—act as though nothing touched him.

He went to the breakfast parlour, sat down, and methodically worked his way through the food that was set before him.

When at last he rose from the table, he went to the windows. For a while he just watched the rain trickling down the panes, observing how it was drowning his entire estate in tones of grey. But at length something impinged on his abstracted mood. There was a thin plume of smoke rising from the trees on the island. Who on earth would be foolish enough to try lighting a fire, on his private property, in such weather as this?

His heart quickened. He knew only one person foolish enough to be outside at all on a day like today. He could not begin to imagine what Heloise was doing out on the island, nor did he question how he was so certain she was the one responsible for raising that defiant plume of smoke. He only knew he had to get to her.

Flinging open the French windows, he strode along the parterre, vaulted over the stone parapet, and broke into a run. He sprinted across the lawns and through the shrubbery, skidding down the slope and landing in an inelegant heap on the carriage drive.

He scrambled to his feet and pounded his way across the bridge, not stopping until he reached the foot of the tower, from which, he had soon realised, the smoke was rising.

'Heloise!' he roared as he forced his way through the half-open door. 'What the devil do you think you are doing in here?'

'Charles?'

He looked up to see her head and shoulders appear over the lip of the upstairs landing. It took him only a moment to work out what must have happened. All that remained of the staircase was a heap of rotten timbers scattered across the floor.

Heloise's face looked unnaturally white, and her hair was plastered to her face. Just how long had she been stranded up there, alone and afraid? When he considered how he had tucked into a hearty luncheon, bitterly imagining her guilty of all manner of crimes...

'I'll soon have you down from there!' he vowed, looking wildly about for something he could use to climb up to her. He had to get her to safety, take her in his arms, and wipe that agonised expression of dread from her face.

There was a chest which he knew contained croquet hoops and mallets, a table kept specifically for picnics on the island, and several chairs and other boxes used for storing all manner of sporting equipment. Hastily he piled them up against the wall where the stairs had been, and began to climb.

'Oh, take care!' Heloise cried, when the pyramid of furniture gave a distinct lurch.

'It is quite safe, I assure you. Give me your hand and I will help you climb down.'

She shook her head, backing away. 'Charles, I don't think I can...'

He was just about to offer the reassurance he thought she needed when his improvised staircase separated out into its component parts. The chest went one way, the chair another, and he gave one last desperate push upwards, to land sprawled at his wife's feet on the upper landing.

Before he could do more than push himself to his knees, Heloise had flung her arms around his neck.

'Oh, thank heaven you made it safely! I was so afraid you were going to fall,' she said, pulling back just far enough to be able to gaze up into his face. Her eyes were full of concern.

Charles looked down into her tear-streaked face with a sense of wonder. She cared about him. Oh, maybe not as much as he cared for her, but nevertheless...

Taking ruthless advantage of her momentary weakness, he wrapped his arms about her and hugged her to his chest.

'I am fine,' he said, and in fact he could not remember when he had ever felt better. 'But what about you? Are you hurt?'

'Only a graze on my leg where my foot went through the stairs.'

'Let me see.' As he pulled her onto his lap, he suddenly registered that she was wrapped in what looked like a large, dusty sheet.

'What on earth is this?' he asked, pushing a swathe of material away from her leg. He winced as he saw the gash on her shin, and the blood which smeared her skin right down to her toes. Her bare toes.

'It is a curtain. I hope you do not mind, but I was so wet and cold, and I did not know how long it might be until somebody came to rescue me, and then I found the tinder box, and there was already some kindling in the grate, and I am sorry, but I also smashed one of the chairs, but only the littlest one, to get a fire going...'

Looking over her shoulder, he saw various items of feminine attire draped over a semicircle of chairs arranged in front of the fireplace. A muddy gown, a dripping petti-coat, torn stockings…

His hand stilled.

'Are you completely naked under that curtain?' he asked throatily.

She nodded, her cheeks flushing. 'That is why I could not have climbed down to you. I was going to explain that if I let go it would just fall away, for I have no pins to secure it, nor a belt…'

She had simply wrapped the curtain round her shoulders like a cloak, and was maintaining her modesty only with the greatest difficulty.

'Your feet are cold,' he said, having forced his hand to explore in a downward direction, when all it wanted to do was slide upwards, underneath the curtain. Her ankles were so slender, he noted, gritting his teeth against the sudden surge of blood to his groin. He could almost encircle them with his fingers.

The rest of her was not cold at all—not any longer, she thought. As his hand gently stroked her injured leg, it sent fire coursing through her veins, making her feel as though she was melting from the inside out.

'And I fear I am making you wet again,' he said, suddenly pushing her off his lap.

Guilty heat flooded her face as she wondered how on earth he could know what his touch was doing to her. But when he stood up and stripped off his jacket she realised he had not been saying what she thought he had at all.

For as he draped it over the back of the chair which already held her stockings, he remarked, 'My waistcoat is a little damp, too, but apart from my neckcloth—' which he deftly unwound and hung beside her petticoat '—my shirt is quite dry.'

Her mouth went dry when he untied the laces and pulled it over his head.

'Here,' he said, holding it out to her. 'Put this on. You will be more comfortable and…er…secure than wrapped in that curtain. Which looks none too clean, by the way.'

She got up and moved towards him. The flickering fire-light seemed to caress the planes of his face, the powerful sweep of his shoulders. His hair was a little mussed from having pulled off his shirt, his shoes were caked in mud, and his breeches were grass-stained. For the first time since she had met him he did not look in the least forbidding.

As her eyes strayed to the enticing expanse of male flesh bared to her avid gaze, her lips parted. Instead of taking the shirt he was holding out, she found herself reaching out to touch the very centre of his chest. The hair which grew there was coarse and slightly springy. His body was so intriguingly different from hers. Where she had soft mounds of flesh, he had slabs of hard muscle. Her hand slid over, and down, until Charles abruptly stopped her exploration by clamping her hand under his own.

'What are you doing?' he rasped.

Shocked at her own temerity, she tried to pull her hand away. But he would not let it go. Keeping it firmly pressed to his waist, he declared, as though in wonder, 'You want me!'

She could not deny it. But nor dared she admit it, only to suffer the humiliation of being rejected all over again. She turned her face away, biting down on her lower lip as she wondered how on earth she was going to come up with an explanation for what she had just done.

'You don't need to be shy with me. I'm your husband,' said Charles, taking her chin firmly between his thumb and forefinger and turning her face upwards. 'If you really do want me, I will be only too happy to oblige.' He smiled, and lowered his head to kiss her.

His mouth was so gentle. For the first time he was kissing her as she had always imagined a lover would kiss his woman.

And it was all she could ever have dreamed of. As he let go of her hand to pull her closer she slid it up his side, finally feeling she had permission to explore the rugged contours of his body. He was so big, so powerful. Yet so gentle as he lifted her and laid her down on a rug by the hearth.

She basked in the wonder of his touch, not even registering the moment he unwound the curtain from her body until he reared up to gaze down at her nudity.

It was too much for her. Shyly, she pulled a corner of material over her hips, stammering, 'I cannot…we cannot… it is broad daylight! Somebody might discover us!'

'Nobody will even think of beginning to search for us until we do not appear for dinner,' he pointed out. He could not bear it if she were to draw back now. 'We have hours. Hours and hours…' he murmured, bending to kiss her into submission again. But she was no longer so pliant under his ministrations.

Eventually he knew he would have to make some concession to her shyness. In desperation, he got up, went to the window, and tore down the one remaining curtain.

'Here,' he said, draping it over them both as he lay down beside her. Though he would have enjoyed being able to look at her while they made love, the most important thing was that he got her past this first hurdle.

She wrapped her arms tight about his neck, pressing her lips to his throat as though in gratitude, and he sighed with contentment.

She had been so scared when he had got up and walked away, a frown on his face as though he had grown impatient with her. It was such a relief when he came back she could have wept. She would make no more foolish protests. Whatever he wanted to do, whatever he asked of her, she would comply.

Even though to begin with she felt a little shocked that there were so many places on her body he wanted to kiss, or lick, or nip with his teeth, or pluck at with his clever, sensitive fingers.

But before long he'd roused such a tide of sensation in her that it swept all modesty aside. She writhed and moaned, kicking the curtain away as her whole body throbbed with heated pleasure. Then his fingers plucked once more, sending her shooting high into a realm of such exquisite sensation she cried aloud at the glory of it.

'Ah, yes,' he murmured into her ear. 'You liked that.' He was elated by her response. He had hoped she might grant him some concessions eventually, after a long period of wooing. He had been prepared to play on her sense of honour, reminding her she had a duty to give him heirs, if nothing else worked. Yet she had just yielded completely. And it was typical of her to give so much when he deserved so little. Especially considering how he had insulted her on the night he had taken her virginity. He should have been gentle and considerate of her inexperience. Instead of which…

'I was less than chivalrous last time,' he ground out. 'I will not be so careless of your needs in future, I promise you.'

She was so beautiful, lying in sated forgetfulness in the aftermath of what he knew must have been her first orgasm.

'But I have needs of my own,' he said, moving over her and into her, revelling in the soft warmth of her welcome.

Her eyes fluttered open as he began to move gently, her hands lifting to his waist as, unbelievably, she began to respond to him all over again.

He forced himself to go slowly, introducing her to the next level of lovemaking with an entirely different repertoire of moves.

'Charles!' she cried, and he felt her throbbing with release.

Hearing his name rise to her lips as she came to completion was all that was needed to send him tumbling over the edge. And, when he was spent, a feeling of such intense peace washed over him he dared not say one word for fear of shattering their first experience of harmony.

It took Heloise quite a while to come back down to earth. Charles had given her such intense pleasure. She could never have imagined her body was capable of anything so wonderful.

She turned her head to look at him. He had fallen asleep. Not surprisingly, she smiled. For he had done all the work.

'He likes to have the mastery between the sheets,' she remembered Mrs Kenton gloating, fanning her face, and just like that her joy was snuffed out. He was always like this in bed with a woman. It was nothing special to him.

And, she recalled, a feeling of sick dread cramping her stomach, he had only done this to 'oblige' her. She had approached him, blatantly stroking his chest, with her mouth hanging open at the sight of his semi-nudity. He knew they would not be rescued for hours, so it had seemed like as good a way to pass the time as any other. And he had needs, as he had pointed out as he had taken what was on offer.

She turned onto her side, pulling the curtain up over her shoulder, wondering why she should feel so cross. After all, not many nights ago she had worked out for herself that he would need a woman soon, and then made that spectacularly unsuccessful attempt to seduce him. She should be crowing in triumph, not blinking back tears. For she had got what she wanted, had she not?

It made her feel even more cross when he awoke with a smile on his face. When he saw that she was sitting hunched in front of the fire, the curtain clutched to her chin defensively, he cheerfully broke up another chair, tossing the pieces onto the fire until it was ablaze. It annoyed her that he was so much more successful at coaxing warmth from a fire she had only managed to get smoking damply. And it made her resentful when he began to tell her all about how this room had been used by former countesses to take tea, since it overlooked a particularly pleasing view of the lake, as though she were a guest he had to entertain.

It was a relief when, as dusk fell, she heard footsteps approaching the tower. Charles went to the landing, informing the servants who had come looking for them what had happened, and telling them to fetch a ladder. Hastily, while his back was turned, she fumbled her way into her damp clothing under cover of the dusty curtain.

Charles wished there was something he could do to ease his wife's discomfort. He could see she felt guilty for having enjoyed herself so much with a man she did not love. She had only married him to escape the horrific subjugation she would have suffered at Du Mauriac's cruel hands. It was futile to point out that plenty of people enjoyed the sexual act without any emotional involvement whatsoever. What they had just shared fell far short of her ideal.

She had succumbed to a fleeting moment of desire. Probably brought on by relief at surviving a frightening ordeal. He had disrobed before her, she had already been naked, and nature had taken its course.

He wanted to tell her that this mutual attraction was only the beginning. That love could grow from here. But she did not look as though she would be receptive to anything he had to say—not yet. She was clearly quite annoyed with him for taking advantage of her moment of weakness.

But he was not in the least repentant. They were lovers now, and there was no going back. She could not pretend his touch repelled her any more. They could have a good marriage. For even if she did not love him, he loved her— more than he had thought it was possible to love any woman, he reflected, as he helped her down the ladder. He would show her, he vowed, sweeping her up into his arms when she made to leave the tower on her own two feet, how good marriage to him could be. No bride would ever be as spoiled as she would be.

Ignoring her shocked gasp, and the amused looks of the two footmen who were holding the ladder, he kissed her, lingeringly, full on the mouth. And quelled her feeble protests that she was capable of walking back to the house.

'You are far too weak to make the attempt. You have not eaten anything all day. And you spent the entire afternoon making love.'

She subsided into his arms with that mutinous little pout he was beginning to love so much, saying not a word until he laid her down on the sofa in her own sitting room.

And then, when she drew breath to make the first of what he was sure would be a litany of complaints, he forestalled her.

'Sukey! See that Her Ladyship has a hot bath, and tend to the grazes on her shins. Then put her to bed and bring her some hot soup, bread and butter, and some of that apple pie she enjoyed so much at dinner the other night, if there is any left. And don't forget a pot of hot chocolate. I,' he said, dropping a kiss on his wife's parted lips, 'will return when I have had my own bath and a shave, and put on clean clothes. And, Giddings?' He turned to address the butler, who had followed them up the stairs on seeing the bedraggled state of his master and mistress. 'No visitors for the next two—no make that three days.'

'Very good, my lord.'

'And don't glare at me like that,' he advised Heloise. 'I have dealt with all the most pressing estate business, I have given my duty invitation to the neighbours to meet my Countess, and now I am entitled to enjoy my bride.'

Heloise let out one cry of vexation as Giddings turned, red-faced, from the room. First he had made it obvious to those two grinning footmen what they had spent the afternoon doing, and now he had scandalised Giddings with a statement of what he intended to spend the next few days doing. Where had all his rigidly correct behaviour gone, just when she could have done with it to spare her blushes?

Though in many ways she enjoyed his attention over the following week, just as much as he seemed to be enjoying hers, she never quite got rid of the feeling that it could not last. In desperation she grabbed what happiness she could, whilst privately waiting for the axe to fall.

It fell one morning while they were at breakfast, and Charles was reading one of the newspapers he had couriered up from London daily.

'My God,' he breathed, his eyes scanning the printed columns. 'There has been a battle.' Though he lowered the paper, it was as though he was looking straight through her. '*The* battle—the decisive battle. The losses have been disastrous.'

'Wh…who won?'

'Nobody.' His face was grim. 'The cost in human life was too great to call it a victory for Wellington. The losses from Robert's regiment alone...' He appeared to pull himself together. 'I will have to return to London. He should not be alone to deal with this.'

She went cold inside. He was going back to London. Just as he had always planned.

She could not let him walk out of her life like this. Not without a fight! Before they had become lovers she had fled out into the gardens rather than humiliate herself by confessing he was the centre of her universe. But now the thought of trying to survive without him was even more unbearable than the prospect of begging for a tiny place in his life.

'Please,' she began hesitantly. 'Please let me come with you.'

She saw disbelief in his eyes, and her heart began to thunder. She was breaking the terms of their agreement.

'Yes, I know I promised I would never cause you any trouble. But really, truly, I will not get in your way. I might even be able to help you,' she argued in desperation. 'I managed to help Robert before when nobody else could! Surely I could be of more help in London than stuck down here in the middle of nowhere? Please, Charles, let me try. Let me come with you. Don't leave me here alone!'

Chapter Fifteen

'Leave you here?' Charles frowned. 'Why would I do that?'

'B…but that was why you brought me down here! Because I had become too much trouble in London…'

'Because you had been *having* too much trouble in London,' he corrected her. 'I hoped that by the time we returned we might have come to a better understanding. So that you would feel you could come to me when you were in a scrape.'

'You never planned to leave me here?' Her eyes filled with tears. 'Truly?'

'I have never lied to you, Heloise,' he replied sternly. 'I never will.'

'But you were so angry…'

'Yes, I was angry the day we travelled down here. But that was not your fault.'

'Oh, but it was. I promised I would never give you any trouble, and I was in such a tangle…'

'I hold myself responsible for that. I should have taken better care of you. I knew there would be people that would try to hurt you in order to score off me, and I did nothing to protect you. Can you forgive me?'

'F…forgive you? There is nothing to forgive!'

He felt shamed that she should take such a generous attitude. Most women who'd found themselves tied to such an unsatisfactory husband would have done nothing but complain. Some would even have taken a lover—for consolation if not revenge.

Yet she seemed to be poised for him to mete out punishments for the most trifling faults… He blinked, remembering the day she had first come to him with her proposal. She had assumed from the very first that he would find her so irritating he would end up beating her.

She had no idea of her own worth.

And as yet he had done nothing to demonstrate just how much he valued her.

But all that was about to change…

'Well, now we have that misapprehension cleared up, we should make all haste to leave. Both of us,' he said firmly.

She scurried from the breakfast room as though his remark contained some kind of threat. She was so ready to believe the worst of him, he sighed. Just as Robert had been.

She had declared she found him cold and proud and unapproachable.

It was true that he had an abhorrence of expressing his feelings, especially when they were as turbulent as the ones Heloise aroused in him. Fortunately, he had already taken steps to show his regard for her.

But it was not just his reserve or her own lack of self-esteem he had to counter. As he climbed into the carriage beside her, and caught the expression of trepidation on her face, it hit him afresh that her plea to return to London was not in any way due to a wish not to be parted from *him*.

She had only spoken of her desire to help Robert. And when he reflected how miserable she had been during her stay at Wycke, it was perhaps only natural she should want to return to the city. He frowned as the carriage rumbled through the lodge gates and out into the lane. Her dislike of the place was yet another hurdle he would have to overcome. For he had a duty to his tenants and neighbours to visit the place more than once each year. And he was not going to leave Heloise alone and unprotected in London while he dealt with estate business. Besides, his heirs would be born there. And he wanted them to grow up there. He could picture a brood of perhaps three or four, tumbling over their mother's lap under the shade of the yew tree on the south lawn. Heloise would be such a good mother— loving and loyal.

He reached for her hand abstractedly, raising it to his lips and kissing her fingers as he focussed on how he was to bring about a state in their marriage where she would look up and smile as he approached, rather than shrink from him in expectation of a scold, as she did now.

The regime at Wycke would have to change before they visited again. Of that he was certain. He did not know if he should go so far as dismissing Mrs Lanyon, but sadly he feared that might be necessary. She seemed to harbour some kind of grudge against Robert, and, though he had always appreciated her efficiency in the past, he now saw that she was singularly lacking in compassion. A kinder woman would have helped Heloise grow accustomed to her position, instead of increasing her feelings of inadequacy.

He had not been aware how long they had been sitting

in silence until he heard Heloise sigh. It struck him forcibly that if it had been Robert sitting beside her she would no doubt have been chattering away merrily. He turned to look at her, noting the dejected slump of her shoulders. Except for a few brief moments when she forgot herself, in his arms in bed, that air of sadness hung round her like a persistent mist.

He drew in a sharp breath, turning away from her to look out of his own window as he felt a stab of fear that he might never be able to totally lift it. Even if she grew content with what he could offer her, it would never be the grand passion she had so admired her sister for harbouring for that penniless young engraver. Her parents had eloped, too, setting love above their personal safety. Whatever understanding they eventually reached, would it always seem like a poor substitute for the real thing?

Well, he might never move her heart to any great degree, but he could prove his solid worthiness.

He cleared his throat. 'When we return to London, things will not be between us as they were before.'

She turned to look at him, a little frown pleating her brow.

'There is no need to look so alarmed. It is your well-being that I am thinking of.'

He would need to deal with Lampton and Mrs Kenton in person before he could permit Heloise the same degree of freedom she had enjoyed before.

It was not just the personal vendetta the Lamptons held against him that might prove dangerous to her, either. After the losses incurred at Waterloo, there might well be some antagonism towards her simply because of her nationality. Until he had tested the waters for himself, and made sure she would be absolutely safe, he was not going to permit anyone anywhere near her.

Nor, to begin with, would he be free to escort her anywhere. The political map of Europe was going to change radically, if he was any judge of matters, and, while he had no intention of forcing Heloise to cross the Channel so that he could participate fully in negotiations, he could be busy laying the groundwork for those who would go in his stead.

'It might be a good idea if, just at first, you did not move about too much in society.'

Was there anything more annoying, she thought, than being told to act in a way she had already decided upon for herself? Why, it had been weeks since she had determined to be such a model wife that she would scarcely even venture out of doors! She knew she ought to be grateful that he was permitting her even a tiny place in his life, yet the longer he lectured her about what she was and was not permitted to do, and trotted out excuse after excuse for why he would be behaving much as he had done before, resentment began to smoulder inside her.

Charles noted that the nearer they drew towards London, rather than being reassured by his promises to take far better care of her than he had done before, she looked increasingly strained.

'Is something worrying you?' he eventually asked her.

Smiling determinedly to conceal her increasing feelings of resentment, she replied, 'Of course there is! I worry about Robert. It is for him that we return to London after all,' she reminded herself.

Charles was glad to get out of the carriage when at last it pulled up outside Walton House. He knew she was not in love with Robert, yet to hear of her concern for another man filled him with such unreasonable jealousy that it was all he could do to keep it leashed.

Heloise drooped into the house in his wake. He seemed

so relieved the journey was finally over. Oh, he had tried manfully to be what he seemed to think she would want— holding her hand, forcing himself to make conversation to keep her amused. As though she was a child and he a rather stern guardian, pointing out that he was going to be busy with important matters of state, and she must behave herself until he had a few minutes to spare!

He surged into the house, making straight for Robert's rooms. Just before he reached his door, he turned, as though recalling her tiresome presence, and said, with an exasperated expression on his face, 'I think you should go up to your rooms, Lady Walton, while I see how my brother fares. I cannot say when I may join you.'

She lifted her chin as her heart sank even lower. 'Of course.' Whatever had made her hope he might appreciate having his silly little wife at his side? Or that she might be able to help him through this crisis? He just wanted her to keep out of his way.

'I will see to my unpacking. As long as Robert is being cared for, that is all that matters.'

He turned from her so swiftly she was sure he had already relegated her from his thoughts. As he pushed open Robert's door, she caught a glimpse of booted feet sprawled at ungainly angles, and empty bottles lying on the floor.

She caught her breath. She really was silly to feel slighted because Charles did not dance attendance on her when his beloved brother was going through such a terrible time.

Feeling slightly ashamed of herself, she went up to her rooms.

'There is a parcel for you, my lady,' said Sukey, as soon as she saw Heloise trail in.

Frowning, Heloise went to the bed, on which the flat,

square package lay. She did not think she had any orders outstanding with the modiste. Wondering what it could be, she tore open the brown paper wrapping to find it was a leatherbound book.

She opened it at random, and gave a gasp of surprise. She was looking at one of her own sketches. Crossing to the desk by the window, she laid the book out flat and flipped through the pages.

'These are all mine!' she said to Sukey, who was peering over her shoulder. All the drawings she had left with Mr Ackermann were bound, here within these beautifully tooled leather covers. Just as though they were the work of a real artist.

She turned back to the very first page, and read the words: '*A collection of original watercolours, penned by the hand of Lady Heloise, beloved wife of Charles, 9th Earl of Walton...*'

Beloved wife? She ran a trembling finger over the printed words. This flowery language was not at all the kind of thing Charles would ever say, never mind cause to have written. He must have left the exact choice of words to the printer.

'Charles,' she whispered, wishing with all her heart that the words were true.

It was scarcely half an hour later that he came in and found her sitting on the bed, the book clasped in her arms and tears streaming down her face.

'Don't you like it?' He felt as though an iron fist had squeezed his heart. He had been so sure she would love seeing her work professionally bound.

'Like it?' she raised tear-drenched eyes to his. 'I love it. Did you...?' She stopped, shaking her head. If he had not meant the words, she did not want to hear the denial from his own lips. Far better to cling to the illusion that he felt some affection for her than to have her dreams shattered.

Hesitantly, Charles took a step towards the bed. 'I wanted to do something to demonstrate how sorry I am for forcing you to destroy that other sketchbook. It was quite wrong of me.'

'Oh!' Her head flew up, her eyes looking curiously wounded.

He clasped his hands behind his back. He would have thought his apology would comfort her. Perhaps it had only reminded her what an unfeeling brute he could be.

'I was acting completely out of character that night,' he admitted. 'My state of mind at that time was not… That is, Heloise…' He swallowed, searching for the words that would convince her, once and for all, that he was not the tyrannical bully he had shown himself to be during those few mad days in Paris. 'You have a remarkable skill. I admire it greatly. I have no wish to stifle your talent. I know I made a great deal of fuss, saying I did not want people to see your work, but that is not how I feel about it now. Now I have come to know you better, I know you would not do anything to embarrass me, or the name of Walton.'

'Not deliberately!' she cried, kneeling up and moving towards him, her hands outstretched. 'I did not mean to make a spectacle with your neighbours at Wycke…'

'You did not!' he vowed, taking the final step that brought him within touching distance. Taking her hands in his, he said, 'I was proud of the way you managed to make some of the most cantankerous, narrow-minded provincials look like rational, attractive people. With only a stub of pencil and some rather ancient writing paper!'

'Truly?'

He sat on the bed next to her, drawing her hands close to his chest. 'Heloise, when will you learn that I never say anything I do not mean? In fact, the next time we go to the country I hope you will spend some time making sketches of my favourite vistas. It is long past time that I put up some original artwork in this place.' His gaze flicked round the uninspiring collection of oils that graced her walls, and he grimaced. 'Your work would at least have the bonus of being amusing.'

'I draw people, though, not scenes,' she protested.

He cut her off with a smile. 'You do scenes. And you capture the atmosphere of a place. Have you forgot this?' He leaned down and flicked through the pages of the book until he came to the depiction of their first night at the theatre. 'Looking at it brings back the atmosphere of that night so vividly I can almost smell it.'

'But it is the people that create the atmosphere...'

He shook his head. 'Heloise, you have more talent than you give yourself credit for. I know you focus on the people, and regard the background only as the setting for your caricatures, but even in the few strokes you begrudged the curtains round Lensborough's box you captured the very texture of the velvet. If you wanted, you could capture not just the scenery of my home but its very essence. When you know it better. I feel sure that even now, should you decide to draw the ruined tower...'

Their eyes met and held as they remembered that afternoon they had become lovers. The book slid to the floor, forgotten, and they moved into each other's arms.

'I shall ring and have supper sent up,' Charles said, much later. 'There is no point in dressing for dinner now. And we would be eating it alone, wherever we took it. Robert is in no fit state to appear before you, my love.'

Rolling onto his side, he propped himself on his elbow.

'We had no need to fear that Robert would suffer alone. While the bells rang out all over London to celebrate the nation's victory, those who could not stand the pain of their bereavement gravitated to his rooms and made a valiant attempt to drink my cellars dry. You may be surprised to hear Lord Lensborough himself is one of those currently nursing a hangover down there.'

Heloise was beyond making any response. He had praised her work, taken her to bed in broad daylight, and called her his love. Yet downstairs Robert and his companions were mourning the shameful waste of so many young male lives. It was wrong to experience any measure of happiness when so many were grieving.

'I will visit with him tomorrow,' she declared. Tonight was just for her and Charles.

'Tomorrow will be soon enough,' he agreed, making her heart soar. 'Robert's rooms are no fit place for a lady at the moment. But now he knows we have returned, it may be the push he needs to begin sobering up. And his friends will feel they may safely leave him now that we have come home.'

Her brief moment of joy dissolved. Charles was not thinking of how delightful it would be to have a romantic supper in bed with her. His priority was still Robert's well-being.

'You are not upset, are you, that I will be otherwise engaged tomorrow?'

As if she were a spoiled child who had to be constantly amused!

She lifted her chin. 'I do not need you to dance attendance on me,' she declared proudly. 'Even when I first came to London, did I not manage to amuse myself?' Flushing darkly, she added, 'Perhaps that is not such a good thing to remind you of. But I will do better now. I will not go to gaming hells, or masquerades, or gamble with military gentlemen again, I promise you!'

'Even if you should do all of those things,' Charles declared, 'I should not banish you to the country. If you get into any sort of trouble you must tell me straight away, and no matter what you have done I will help you.'

'I have just told you,' she snapped, 'that I won't get into trouble!'

'Well, we'll see, shall we?'

Crestfallen that he still assumed she would get into some sort of trouble the minute his back was turned, she rolled over and pretended to go to sleep.

Over the next few days Heloise was carried along by a determination to prove to Charles that in spite of his misgivings she *could* behave herself when the need arose.

She usually slept in until quite late. For, although she scarcely saw Charles during the hours of daylight, whatever time he came home, he never failed to come to her bed.

Once she had washed and dressed, she liked to take an airing in the park, although she made sure both Sukey and a footman always properly escorted her. When she returned there was always some little gift from Charles for her to unwrap—proof that he was appreciative of her efforts to reform. She spent the hours before dinner either reading the poetry, or pressing individual blossoms from a posy—or, once, attempting to put together the cleverly designed portable easel he had purchased. And she spent the hours after dinner waiting impatiently for him to come home.

She might even have felt a measure of contentment if only she'd had Robert to keep her company during the long, dull evenings. But whenever she went and knocked on his door there was always already a group of grim-faced young men sprawled about the rooms, and a distinct aroma of alcohol in the air. The fact that all conversation ceased the moment she walked in made her feel increasingly awkward about intruding. He had friends about him. That was the main thing. And who better than those young men, with military backgrounds, who could understand far better than she could what he was going through?

She was selfish to wish he would at least let her in for half an hour, so that she had someone to talk to. She sighed now, picking up the latest novel that Charles had sent her. Did she not have so much more now than the last time she had been in London? She might not go out, but then she had not really enjoyed many of her outings anyway. Particularly not once she had locked horns with Mrs Kenton.

She shivered, applying herself to words that she had a vague recollection of reading before. It was not an easy story to get into, but she wanted very much to be able to tell Charles that she was enjoying it. Even though she was having difficulty working out what the story was supposed to be about, she sighed. Still, though the story itself was not very interesting, she did love the fact that Charles had bought it for her. He was so generous.

'…so generous that it quite makes up for the coldness of his public manners…' she heard Mrs Kenton whispering.

That Woman! The moment her mind strayed in her direction, her words flooded her mind with her poison all over again.

She shut the book with a snap, and went into her

bedroom. She would sketch until Charles came home. That always made her feel better.

But though she sat at her drawing desk, and took the charcoal in her fingers, her mind remained devoid of inspiration. She could not think of a single thing she wanted to draw. She had not been anywhere or seen anyone since returning to London to fire her imagination at all.

There seemed to be nothing but a great emptiness all around her. When Charles came in, far earlier than she had expected, she was so relieved to see him that she flew into his arms. She knew he would not rebuff her these days. On the contrary, he seemed only too keen to strip her naked and kiss and caress every inch of her, until she was mindless with pleasure and he was completely exhausted.

She looked down at him, as he lay sleeping beside her later, a troubled frown creasing her brow. If only she had never met Mrs Kenton. For then she would be completely happy, thinking that the way he behaved was an indication that he felt something for her. But she *had* met Mrs Kenton, and she knew that he took similar pride in his performance in bed, no matter which woman shared it.

And, on reflection, she could not read very much into the fact he sent her gifts every day, either. Mrs Kenton had told her how generous he was to his mistresses.

He had never given her a single thing before he had taken her to his bed. With a pang of shock, she realised that, far from being a mark of his approval, those gifts were more like payment for services rendered.

He was treating her just like he would treat his mistress!

No, on second thoughts he was not even treating her so well as that. At least a mistress got an outing every now and again. She had met Nell in the theatre, and at Vauxhall Gardens, and although everyone said Lord Lensborough was a hard man, even he had given Nell her own carriage and pair to drive about in the park.

She sat up, hugging her knees to her chest as she grew more and more upset. He had said before they married that as his wife she would move in the first circles. But she didn't. She never went anywhere. It was as if he was ashamed of her!

She could barely look at him when he rose the next morning to be about his business. Business which, she thought huffily, he could as well conduct at home, if he had a wife he trusted. If he really was engaged in politics. She sniffed. For all she knew he could be out carousing with his friends, or even trawling Covent Garden for a new mistress.

'Heloise?' he said gently, noting the stiff set of her shoulders under the blankets. 'I can see you are not happy with me this morning.' Or indeed any morning. 'This state of affairs cannot continue.' Fortunately he would be able to conclude his involvement in party affairs today. And then he would be able to devote himself entirely to getting his wife to admit that being a partner in a marriage of convenience was not the end of the world. 'When I return tonight, you and I need to have a serious talk.'

She shut her eyes tight on the wave of pain that assailed her. She had known it! She had known it from the first! She had only ever been a poor substitute for Felice, and now he could not even continue to use her as he would use a mistress. He was tired of her.

Had he already found her replacement? Was that where he went every night, when he said he was engaged in state affairs? *Affaires*, more like! And she, rather than demanding he treat her with respect, had welcomed him into her bed whatever time of the night he rolled in, with open arms, like the lovesick fool she was! She should have known when she'd had to go to such lengths to seduce him that he would not stay faithful for long. If he had ever found her in the least bit desirable he would have made the first move!

'In the meantime, I should like you to have this.' He went to his jacket, which was hanging on the back of a chair, delved into the pocket, and extracted a black rectangular box. 'I had meant to give it to you last night, but…' He smiled wryly at the memory of her flying to his arms, and more or less dragging him into bed.

'Don't remind me!' she flung at him waspishly.

He frowned as he approached the bed, where she was sitting with her knees hunched up, a mutinous glare on her face. He faltered, wishing with all his heart that she did not feel so ashamed of experiencing desire without love.

'Here,' he said, proffering the jeweller's box.

Until now, the gifts he had bought her had been trifling things, meant to amuse her and remind her he was thinking of her, though he could not be with her. But he had never forgotten her face when she had spoken about the Walton diamonds. She had thought he did not care because they were old. She seemed to have thought that if he cared about her he would have bought her something new. And so he had sought to redress that error in the purchase of these pearls. Pearls for purity. For she was the purest woman he had ever known. Besides which, he could not wait to see how the ear drops would look against the glorious silk of her dark hair.

As he opened the box to reveal the long strand of perfectly matched pearls, her eyes widened in horror.

'How dare you?' she cried, drawing back as though he was holding out a snake. 'I won't be treated like this! No—not one minute more! Oh, yes, I know I promised I would not stop you from amusing yourself, however you wished, but I have to tell you that I cannot keep to that stupid bargain we made one minute longer!'

He went cold with dread as he heard her telling him their marriage was over. And all because he had given her pearls? He looked down at the box, lying open in his hand, wondering where he had gone wrong this time.

He was about to find out. Flinging the covers aside, Heloise rose from the bed, completely forgetful of her nudity, and advanced on him, her eyes spitting fire.

'I am your wife! Your *wife*!' She swiped at the box, knocking it from his nerveless fingers. 'And if you think you can pay me off with pearls, when even that Mrs Kenton got rubies, you are the greatest imbecile! And I know you never made *her* stay within doors, not to mingle with your so perfect friends. Even poor little Nell gets trips to the theatre every now and again. And you think, you *really* think, that I will walk out of your life quietly after you give me the kind of jewels that a mother would give to her daughter when she makes her first curtsey in society? Well, I tell you, *no*! I am not going back to Wycke, and I am not going to sit at home any more while you go out and amuse yourself without your embarrassing wife hanging on your arm. And if you think I am going to do nothing while you set up another mistress, then you are very much mistaken. If you dare…if I find out where you are keeping her…I shall…I shall…'

For much of the tirade Charles had been too bemused to take in more than the fact that she was furiously angry and gloriously naked. But at last some of her meaning began to percolate through.

'What,' he said, his heart pounding, 'will you do, Heloise, if you find out where I have set up my mistress?'

'Oh!' She drew back, as though him saying it made it real. Her eyes filled with tears. She began to shake. 'I shall do something terrible,' she whispered, her face grim. 'Of that you can be sure.'

'Thank God,' he sighed, drawing her into his arms. She loved him. She must do to be experiencing such fierce jealousy. It was a feeling he recognised only too well.

'No!' she whimpered, struggling to break free. 'You shall not subdue me with your kisses again. I won't let you. I hate you!' she cried, raising her fists to beat at his chest.

'No, you don't,' he countered. 'You hate feeling weak and helpless under the force of your feelings. But your feelings for me are not hatred. Ah, no—don't cry, my little love,' he crooned, scooping her up and carrying her back to bed. 'I have not set up a mistress. I promise you,' he said, kissing her forehead.

'You…you have not?' she hiccupped, frowning up at him through tear spiked lashes.

'Of course not. Why ever would you think I would do such a thing?'

'Well, I know you are only putting up with me…you only married me, after all, to save face so that no one would know Felice broke your heart. I…I know you will never love me like you loved her.'

'That much is true,' he said dryly. 'For I was never in love with her at all.'

'What? That is not true. When she ran off with Jean-Claude your heart was broken!'

'Actually, no, it was not. Not in the least. The truth,' he said ruefully, 'as you pointed out with such perspicacity at the time, was that she had severely dented my pride. You see,' he said, taking her hand, 'Felice was such fun to be with. I had never met anyone like her before. When I was with her she made me feel as though there was something about me as a person that she valued, since she made no secret of the fact she despised the aristocracy as a class. She was not forever hinting that she wanted me to buy her things, either.' He shook his head, a frown clouding his brow. 'And I was in a peculiarly vulnerable state of mind at the time.'

Though Heloise still seemed oblivious to her state of undress, he felt obliged to reach down and pull the coverlet up, tucking it round her shoulders as he considered the best way to explain.

'I had suffered a series of shocks. Discovering I had a brother. Learning that the men I had trusted throughout my youth had perpetrated a crime against him and my stepmother…and then finding that I was totally unable to escape their pernicious influence!' He laughed bitterly. 'I could cease seeing them, but I could not undo my training. No matter how much I wished it, I could not find the least desire to behave with anything less than complete decorum. And then I took Robert into my home and endured his scorn, while seeing how very much he was valued by his friends… In the end I fled to Paris looking for…well, I don't know what I was looking for, to tell you the truth. I only know that for a while I felt that Felice was the answer. She made me feel as though I could slough off all that I had been and make a fresh start. It was my dreams of becoming a better man she stole, not my heart, Heloise.'

He stopped fussing with the coverlet and looked her straight in the eye as he confessed, 'My heart belongs to you, Heloise. It is a poor, stunted thing, I know. But, such as it is, it beats for you alone.'

'But when…? But how…?' She sat up, an intent expression on her face. 'When you brought me to London you left me utterly alone. After giving me a long list of things I was not supposed to do and people I was not to talk to, as though I was a complete nuisance!'

He took her face between his hands. 'Do you know how much it hurt that you never understood?' He took a deep breath. 'You always put me in mind of a little bird. And when I saw that picture you drew of yourself, chained in an intolerable marriage, I knew I did not want it to be like that between us. I know I said a lot of damn fool things at the start, but once you were mine I did not want you to feel you were caged, or chained. I wanted you to be able to fly free and come to me because you wanted to come to me, not because I compelled you.'

'I…I thought you did not care what I did. And I felt as though my heart was breaking. Because I loved you so much…'

'You said you didn't!' he protested, rearing back. 'When you suggested we get married…'

'I don't think I did—not at that precise moment. Or perhaps I had not allowed myself to, because I thought your heart belonged to my sister. But by the afternoon, once I knew you were to be my own husband, I could not bear the thought that you might want any other woman. And then, when I feared Du Mauriac would kill you, then I was sure. I was so scared! I had to get you away from France to safety, no matter what it cost me!' She reached up and stroked his cheek, her expression full of remembered concern. 'I told myself I would not care if you never loved me back so long as you were safe. Oh, but when we got to London, and you were so cold, I made such a fool of myself trying to win your approval,' she finished ruefully.

'You were trying to win my approval with all that

time you spent with Robert?' he groaned. 'While I was trying to show you how tolerant I could be, letting you do as you liked!'

'Oh, don't be tolerant any more, then,' said Heloise. 'It made me so unhappy!'

'Very well, since you ask,' he growled. 'From now on I shall be the most intolerant—' he kissed her hard on the lips '—jealous—' he pulled her down until she lay flat on her back '—possessive husband that ever drew breath! In fact I will never let you out of my sight again. When I think of the torment I suffered when I thought you planned to leave me...'

She looked perplexed. 'When was that? I never thought of leaving you!'

No... The day he feared she had run back to London with Robert she had in fact been stuck in the tower. And the day he had assumed she was trying to raise money to elope with him she had been trying to sell her pictures to pay off her gambling debts. Even in France, when he had thought she would want to flee an intolerable marriage, she had already been in love with him!

She had never thought of leaving him. Nor had his step-mother, come to that. And at that revelation something inside him seemed to unfurl and blossom. He felt tears prick his eyes. Somewhat appalled, he blinked them away, before burying his face in the silken cocoon of her hair.

'I love you,' he said, for there was nothing else that summed up so neatly the enormity of what he felt at that moment.

Her answer, 'I love you too,' was exactly what he needed to hear.

Some time later, she whispered, 'And you promise you really won't send me away and take a mistress?'

'I would not dare,' he groaned, rolling onto his back and

pulling her into his side. 'Besides, you would not let me—would you?'

'How could I stop you if you really wanted to?'

He chuckled. 'Are you serious? Don't you know how powerful you are?'

'Powerful? Me?' she squeaked.

'Yes, you. You have been able to mould me like putty in your hands from the first moment you set your sights on me. When I had vowed to have nothing whatever to do with your family you persuaded me to marry into it. I had decided nothing would induce me to leave Paris until my lease expired, and scarcely a day later you had me racing for the coast like a lunatic. And worst of all, when I had always believed love was a debilitating emotion from which I would never suffer, you wrung it from my stony heart. Nobody else could have done it.'

'Are you sorry?' she asked in a small voice.

'Sorry?' He snorted. 'I have never been more glad of anything in my life. You are my life, Heloise,' he said softly. 'The light of my life. If you had never bullied me into marrying you I would have been the coldest, loneliest man in London. Instead of which...' He paused, his eyes suspiciously bright with moisture. 'Ah, don't talk any more,' he groaned. 'Just kiss me.'

'With all my heart,' she sighed. 'With all my heart.'

* * * * *

Captain Fawley's Innocent Bride

Chapter One

'Oh, no,' Susannah grumbled to her friend, Miss Deborah Gillies, snapping open her fan and raising it to conceal the lower part of her face. 'Here comes Captain Fawley, hobbling over to ask me to dance again. And I cannot. I simply cannot.'

Deborah compressed her lips to hide her own revulsion—oh, not at Captain Fawley. The poor man could not help the way he looked. He had lost the lower part of one leg, and his left hand in the same explosion which had so badly disfigured his face. His left eyelid would for ever droop into the scarring that covered his whole cheek, twisting his mouth into a permanently cynical expression. No, she could feel nothing but compassion for him.

It was Susannah's behaviour that upset her.

Captain Fawley bowed over her friend's hand, his dark eyes raised to hers with dogged determination.

'Good evening, Miss Hullworthy, Miss Gillies.' Though he included Deborah in his greeting, he shot her only the briefest glance. 'I was hoping I might prevail upon you to dance with me this evening.'

'Oh, dear,' said Susannah, with just the right amount of regret in her voice to sound convincing. 'I am afraid my dance card is already full. And here comes my partner for the quadrille.' She looked over Captain Fawley's shoulder, a smile stretching her lips into a pretty pink bow as Baron Dunning came to claim her hand.

Deborah supposed it was not Susannah's fault that the rules of conduct required a lady to repress her true feelings under a cloak of civility. But surely it would be kinder to Captain Fawley if she could just tell him how he made her feel. Then he wouldn't keep on approaching her, and being rebuffed so prettily that he had no idea that the very thought of him touching her made Susannah feel nauseous.

She flicked him a soulful glance as he watched Susannah walk to the dance floor on the arm of her portly young partner. Captain Fawley must have been strikingly handsome once, she sighed wistfully. Dark haired, as well as dark eyed, with features that were still discernibly pleasing, even under that horribly reddened and puckered skin.

Whereas there was nothing handsome about Baron Dunning. He had a weak chin, made more noticeable by a mouth full of prominent teeth, and his skin was a greasy broth of suppurating pustules.

'Many people suffer from spots,' Susannah had remonstrated when Deborah had pointed out that Baron Dunning's complexion was no better than Captain Fawley's. 'He cannot help that!'

Besides which, he had a title. All the poor Captain had to offer was his devotion. And Susannah might protest that she would hate to look ridiculous hobbling about the dance floor with a man who had a false leg, but she never worried what it looked like to dance with the doddery Earl of Caxton. The *on-dit* was that the cadaverous widower was on the lookout for wife number three, and Susannah was plainly ready to stifle her squeamishness for the sake of a coronet.

The impecunious Captain Fawley could expect no such consideration.

'How could I let him touch me, with that false hand?' Susannah had whined only the previous night, when they had been preparing for bed at the end of an arduous day of husband hunting. It had occurred to Deborah, as her friend applied pineapple water to her skin, that it was most apt to refer to the early weeks of spring as 'the Season'. Débutantes stalked their prey as ruthlessly as sportsmen on a grouse shoot, flushing unsuspecting bachelors from their covers with a swirl of silken skirts, then bagging them with a volley fired from a pair of sparkling eyes. Or lured them into traps baited with honeyed smiles and coaxing words.

'It is very hard to tell it is a false hand, it has been so well made,' Deborah had pointed out. 'It looks just like any other gentleman's hand, covered with an evening glove.'

'I would know it was a dead thing, resting on my arm.' Susannah had shuddered. 'Eeugh!'

As the orchestra began to play, Captain Fawley came back to himself. Turning to Deborah, he inclined his head and held out his arm. His right arm. She had noticed on previous occasions that if he offered a lady his arm, it was never what remained of the left one.

'Shall we take a turn about the room?'

Deborah smiled, and laid her hand upon his sleeve. As she glanced up, it occurred to her that placing her on his right side also had the effect of presenting the unblemished side of his face to her scrutiny. A pang of sympathy smote her. He was sensitive enough to his appearance, without girls like Susannah rubbing his nose in it. He had even grown his hair longer than was fashionable, sweeping part of his fringe over the left side of his forehead, in an effort to conceal the worst of the scarring.

They set out along the edge of the room, in the area behind the pillars that marked the boundaries of the dance floor. Captain Fawley's gait was a little uneven, she had to admit in fairness to Susannah. But by no means did he hobble! And though she had never danced with him, she was certain he would look no worse than many of the men here tonight, lumbering about with straining waistcoats and florid faces.

'I can see you would much rather be on the dance floor,' said Captain Fawley, noticing the direction of her gaze, 'than bearing me company. I shall escort you to your mother, and—'

'Oh, please do not!'

He eyed her curiously.

'I would m…much rather be promenading, than left to wilt on the sidelines.'

Her dance card, unlike that of her friend, bore very few names. If Captain Fawley abandoned her, it would be humiliatingly obvious that she had no partner.

She felt as though the only time she ever got to dance lately was when one of Susannah's admirers took pity on her, as Captain Fawley was doing now.

And unlike some of those gentlemen, Captain Fawley was invariably attentive and polite, almost managing to make her believe he was enjoying talking to her.

And what was more, she was sure he would never take part in the kind of conversation she had overheard not half an hour since. Not that she could blame Baron Dunning for comparing her unfavourably with Susannah. Although both of them had dark hair, Deborah's curls would have gone limp by the end of the evening. Her eyes, though as brown, were more often lowered bashfully than sparkling with wit. Her complexion, thanks to an inflammation of the lungs she had suffered over the winter months, might, she accepted, by candle-light look somewhat sallow. And when she stood next to the shorter, shapelier Susannah, she supposed she could see why Mr Jay had scathingly likened her to a beanpole.

Not that knowing they had said nothing untrue made their comments any less hurtful, which was why she felt so grateful that Captain Fawley was deigning to spend these few moments with her.

When she thought of the adventures he must have had, in his soldiering days, she was amazed he could talk to her so kindly about the trivial concerns of a plain, provincial miss like her.

He gave her his wry, lopsided smile, which somehow always managed to make her own lips want to rise in imitation.

'Then let us go and sample the refreshments,' he suggested, turning her towards a door at the far side of the room from where the orchestra was playing.

'Thank you, I should like that.'

She hoped very much that he would linger while she drank a glass of lemonade. Conversation would be limited, for after her initial burst of pleasure in securing his attention, she would doubtlessly become tongue-tied. He had experienced so much, when she had scarcely set foot outside her father's parish before this trip to London. Not that he had personally related how he had fought his way across the Peninsula before suffering the horrific injuries at Salamanca that had left him hovering between life and death for months. No, that information had been gleaned from her mother's friends, who made it their business to know everything about everyone.

They had shaken their heads, expressing pity as they related what they knew of his history, but she could only admire the determination with which he had clawed his way back to his present state. He did everything an able-bodied man did, though it must take him twice the effort. Why, he had even learned to ride a horse. She had glimpsed him on a couple of occasions, cantering through the park in the early morning, before many other people were about. He seemed to her to be so much more manly than the fashionable fops who lounged their languid way through London's drawing rooms. He had overcome whatever life had thrown at him, which you could see, just by looking at him, had been a great deal.

She felt that first betraying blush sweep up her

cheeks, which always assailed her at about this point in their meetings. For what could she say that might be of interest to a man like him, a man who had really lived? Though she knew that, whatever she said, he would never give her one of those condescending looks, which so many eligible bachelors seemed to have got down to a fine art. He was so kind, so magnanimous, so…

'Tell me,' he said, as they sauntered towards the table on which a large punch bowl sat, 'just what a man has to do to secure a dance with your friend?'

Deborah's flight of fancy exploded in mid-air, plummeting to earth like a spent rocket. He had not sought out her company because he wished for it. She was only a means by which he might be able to approach Susannah. Of course a man like him would not willingly spend time with a drab, nondescript, foolish, ignorant, penniless, plain…and let us not forget shy, awkward, dull…

She pulled herself together with effort, and pasted a polite social smile upon her face, as Captain Fawley continued, 'I purposely arrived early tonight, and still her dance card seems to be full.'

'It was full before ever we arrived,' Deborah temporised. It was not her place to tell him that, no matter what he did, Susannah would rebuff him. Not only did she find him physically repulsive, but she had her sights set on a title. Forming an attachment with an impecunious commoner was not part of Susannah's plan at all.

'Before you arrived?' Captain Fawley signalled a waiter to pour Deborah a glass of lemonade.

'Yes,' she confirmed, her heart plummeting as the waiter handed her a drink in a tall glass. It would take for ever to drink it down, and, for some reason, she no longer wanted to spend a moment longer with Captain Fawley than she had to. There was an acid heaviness in her stomach, her throat ached, and, to her annoyance, her eyes had begun to prickle with what she was afraid were burgeoning tears. She did not want him to see her cry. Lord, she did not want anyone to see her cry! What kind of ninny burst into tears at a ball because every man there wanted to dance with her friend and not her!

She took a gulp of the drink, appalled when the glass rattled against her teeth. Her hands were shaking.

'Are you quite well, Miss Gillies?' Captain Fawley looked concerned.

Her heart performed a peculiar lurch as she thought how like him it was to be so observant. 'I…' Lying was a sin. She would not do it. And yet, she desperately wanted to escape. If she was to twist the truth, just a little…there could be no harm in that, could there? 'I think I would like to return to my mother, and sit beside her after all, if you do not mind?'

'Of course.' Captain Fawley took her glass and placed it on a convenient window ledge. He tucked her hand into the crook of his arm, pulling her hard against his body so that he could support her wilting form as he ushered her towards the door. She had never been held so close to any man before, except her father. It made her heart race to feel the heat of his body seeping through his uniform jacket. She could feel the flex of his muscled frame with every step he took, and a slight change of pressure every time he breathed in or out. And if she could feel him, then he must be aware she was trembling. Oh, pray God he would put it down to physical weakness, and would never guess that he had devastated her with his careless remark.

Her mother was sitting on a bench with several other chaperons, ladies whose task it was to ensure their charges maintained that delicate balancing act between doing their utmost to entrap an eligible bachelor into matrimony whilst simultaneously behaving with sufficient decorum to avert scandal.

'Mrs Gillies,' said Captain Fawley, executing a polite bow, 'I fear your daughter is feeling unwell.'

'Oh, dear!' Her mother's eyes shot past her, to where Susannah was twirling merrily around the floor with Baron Dunning. 'We have only just arrived, and Susannah is having such success…she will not wish to leave. Do you really need to go home?' She shifted to one side, so that Deborah could sit next to her. Taking her hand in hers, she gave it a squeeze. 'Deborah was so ill over Christmas, I almost decided to put off coming to London at all. But Susannah was so keen…' she explained to Captain Fawley.

'I shall be fine, Mother. If I may but sit quietly for a while….'

'Perhaps a turn about the garden, to get some fresh air?' Lady Honoria Vesey-Fitch, an old friend of her mother's suggested with an arch smile. 'I am sure the Captain would oblige.'

Oh, no. It was bad enough that he did not wish to dance with her, never mind dragging the poor man round the garden on what would be a fool's errand. For no amount of fresh air was going to make her feel any better. On the contrary, knowing that Captain Fawley would wish himself anywhere rather than with her would only serve to make her feel ten times worse.

'Oh, no!' To Deborah's immense relief, her mother instantly vetoed the suggestion. 'The cold night air would be most injurious to her health, after the heat of this stuffy room. I do not want her to catch a chill on top of everything else!'

Everything else? Had her mother guessed that her only daughter had been smitten by a severe case of hero-worship? Though how could she, when Deborah had only just worked it out for herself? It could be the only reason why her heart twisted at the look in Captain Fawley's eyes every time Susannah turned him down, the little leap it performed when he turned, albeit with resignation, to her.

'Is there nobody who could escort Miss Gillies home?' Captain Fawley said, then, looking pensive, he ventured, 'Or perhaps you could take your daughter home, if you would entrust Miss Hullworthy to my care. I assure you, I…'

That did it. He would gladly think of an excuse to shovel her out of the way, so that he could have Susannah all to himself. Pulling herself upright in her chair, she said, 'There will be no need for anyone to leave, or any alteration made to our arrangements. I will be fine, if I may but sit quietly, for a while.'

'Oh, but thank you for your concern, Captain,' her mother put in quickly. 'Please do call on us tomorrow if you are still anxious over my daughter's health.'

An arrested expression came over his face. 'I shall certainly do so,' he said, a gleam coming to his eye.

Deborah glared down at her hands as she clasped them in her lap. He did not care a fig for her health! He had just worked out that, if he called, he would be able to ascertain which social events Susannah might be attending the next evening. For all his manly attributes, he was clearly inexperienced at wooing society women. He often arrived at a ball quite late, looking flustered, as though he had searched several venues before hitting upon the right one. But now he had cottoned on to the mysterious means by which his rivals had stolen a march over him. They called during the day, and by means of cajolery, flattery or downright bribery, wrought promises from their darling before even setting foot in the ballroom.

Tomorrow, he would join the ranks of admirers who called to deliver posies and drink tea whilst vying for Susannah's favours.

She rather thought she might have a relapse tomorrow. She did not think she wished to witness his humiliation.

There was a smattering of applause as the music ended, and the dancers began to leave the floor. Baron Dunning returned Susannah, very correctly, to Mrs Gillies. Flicking her fan open, she waved it briskly before her face, pointedly ignoring Captain Fawley.

'It is so hot in here,' she complained.

'Indeed,' he put in, in an effort, Deborah was sure, to draw her sparkling gaze in his direction. 'Miss Gillies has been quite overcome with the heat.'

'Really?' Instantly Susannah dropped what Deborah thought of as her ballroom manner, and looked at her with concern. 'Oh, don't say you are going to be ill again, Debs.'

'I am not going to be ill,' she grated, flustered at becoming the centre of attention. 'I will be fine, if everyone was to just leave me alone.' To her mortification, the tears that had long been threatening welled up; despite blinking furiously, one spilled down her cheek. Hastily, she wiped it away with her gloved hand.

'Oh, Debs,' said Susannah, her own eyes welling in sympathy. 'You really are unwell. We must go home at once.'

'No, no, I do not want to spoil your evening.'

'And you have so many distinguished names on your dance card,' put in Mrs Gillies. 'You don't want to disappoint so many eligible gentlemen....'

'Oh, pooh to that!' said Susannah, bending forward and taking Deborah's hand. 'I can dance with them all tomorrow. Or the next night. But I would never forgive myself if Deborah sacrificed her health for my pleasure.'

Deborah was swamped by a wave of guilt. No wonder the men all preferred Susannah to her. Not only was she far prettier, but she was a much nicer person too.

Captain Fawley certainly thought so. His eyes were glowing with admiration as he organised a footman to bring their carriage round. He was falling deeper and deeper under Susannah's spell with every encounter. Just as she, Deborah realised, stifling a sob, was growing more hopelessly infatuated with him. She had experienced an almost overwhelming urge to *cling* to him when he finally handed her over to her mother. To fling her arms around him and beg him to forget Susannah. In a ballroom!

She allowed Susannah and her mother to hustle her to the ladies' retiring room while *they* waited for their carriage and *she* grappled with the revelation that she had carelessly lost her heart to a man who scarcely noticed she existed.

'I am so sorry,' she said when they got into the carriage. 'I have ruined your evening, Suzy, and it is not as though I feel that unwell.'

Susannah grasped her hand. 'I shall not mind having an early night myself, truly, I promise you. Just lately, things seem to have become a bit of a whirl. It was easier, in some ways, when we first came to London, and hardly knew anybody.'

That was before Susannah had become such a hit. Her success had astounded Mrs Gillies, who had warned her not to expect too much from society. For though Susannah was so pretty, and so charming, and had so much wealth, that wealth came from trade.

'I can introduce you to a certain level of society,' she had explained. It was the reason that Deborah's mother was acting as chaperon, after all. Her own lineage was impeccable. Her only problem was lack of money. Since Susannah's family had plenty, they had come to a mutually beneficial arrangement. Mrs Gillies would introduce Susannah alongside her own daughter, and Susannah's parents would foot the bill for both girls. 'But there is no guarantee you will be accepted.'

Indeed, for the first few weeks of the Season, they had stayed in more often than they had gone out. Now, they had so many invitations, they had either to reject some, or attend several functions each evening.

And naturally, since Susannah's parents were meeting their costs, Mrs Gillies felt obligated to ensure that she had the opportunity to mingle with the sort of men she considered marriage-worthy.

They were not at all what Deborah wanted. She had hoped that she might meet a young man who did not mind that she was not very wealthy. He would be looking for a helpmeet. A girl who would not demand he keep her in splendid indolence, but be prepared to run his household on a tight budget, and raise his children with a cheerful demeanour. There must be many younger sons of good families who wanted a dependable, resourceful wife. When they had first come to London, she had held out hopes of meeting such a man. But not now they were beginning to mingle in somewhat higher social circles, to satisfy Susannah's ambitions.

Deborah sighed heavily more than once as the carriage took them the few streets to their rented house. In the small market town where she had grown up, she would have scorned to ride such a short distance, when she was perfectly capable of walking. But in London, she was subject to all manner of ridiculous restrictions. A footman grasped her arm as she stumbled in the act of clambering out of the coach. Hired for the Season, naturally, just like the town house they had rented in Half Moon Street. She missed being able to hold a conversation without wondering if the servants, who were strangers she could not trust, were listening. She missed being able to go for a walk without one of them trailing behind, for the sake of propriety. And really, how silly was it to stipulate that a footman was necessary to knock on the door of whatever house they were paying a call at? As though a young lady's knuckles were far too delicate for the task?

She barely restrained herself from shaking him off, but when, upon climbing the steps to their front door, she experienced a moment of dizziness, she was glad she had not. A little later, she blinked, to find herself sitting in the armchair in her pretty bedroom, a maid kneeling at her feet removing her slippers, and Susannah hovering over her, fanning her face. Her mother was behind her chair, hastily loosening her stays.

'Did I faint?' she asked, feeling thoroughly confused.

'Not quite,' her mother replied, 'but your face was as white as paper. You must get straight into bed. Jones,' she addressed the maid, 'go to the kitchens and fetch Deborah a drink.' When the woman looked a little put out, she continued ruthlessly, 'Miss Hullworthy and I are quite capable of getting my daughter undressed and into bed. What she needs from you is a drink of hot chocolate, and some bread and butter. You have lost weight this last couple of weeks,' she said, clucking her tongue at the sight of Deborah's bony shoulder blades as she removed the stays and gown. 'You have been racketing about, growing more and more tired, and only picking at your food....'

'I am so sorry,' Susannah put in at this point. 'I should have noticed. Please say you forgive me for being so selfish. I have been so full of myself. My success has quite gone to my head....'

'I think,' said Mrs Gillies, raising her daughter to her feet, and supporting her towards the bed, 'that it will do both you girls good to spend a few days at home quietly. We may put it about that it is on account of Deborah's indisposition, but really, Susannah, I have been growing quite concerned about you too.'

'Me?' Susannah plumped down on to a bedside chair as Mrs Gillies rolled up Deborah's nightdress and pushed it over her head, just as she had done when Deborah had been a little girl, back home in the vicarage. It was almost worth being a little unwell, Deborah decided, to be rid of that maid, and have her mother and Susannah to put her to bed as though she was herself, and not this prim débutante she had to pretend to be in order to trick some poor man into matrimony.

'Yes, you. You know, Susannah, that I would never countenance any of those fellows making up to my Deborah.'

At this statement, both girls blinked at Mrs Gillies in surprise.

'You may think you are doing well to attract the attention of several men with titles, but I have made it my business to find out about them, and the sad truth is that they are fortune hunters.'

'Well…' Susannah pouted '…I have a fortune. And I want to marry someone with a title.'

'Yes, but I think you could show a little more discernment. Over the next day or so, I think it would be wise to consider the gentlemen who have been paying you attention, very carefully. Baron Dunning, for example, is only obeying his mama in paying you court. She wants him to marry, so that she will not have to make the drastic economies that his late father's reckless gambling have necessitated. He will not be any kind of a husband to you once he has got you to the altar. Why, he is hardly more than a schoolboy!'

'Don't you think he likes me?' said Susannah in a very small voice.

'Oh, I think he likes you well enough. If he has to marry a fortune, of course he would rather it came so prettily gift-wrapped. But don't you think,' she said in a more gentle tone, 'you deserve better than that?'

Susannah bowed her head, her fingers running along the struts of her fan.

'And as for the Earl of Caxton…'

But Deborah was never to find out what her mother thought of the Earl of Caxton. The maid had returned, bearing a tray laden with a pot of chocolate, a plate of bread and butter, and a small glass of what smelled like some form of spirituous liquor.

'Ah, just the thing for a faint!' Mrs Gillies remarked cheerfully, startling Deborah even further. Her father, the late Reverend Gillies, had lectured his flock frequently, and at length, upon the evils of drink. And there was never anything stronger than ale served at his table. 'That was very thoughtful of you, Jones, thank you. And now, Susannah, I think it is high time you went to bed, as well.'

She bent to kiss her daughter's forehead, pausing to smooth back a straggling lock of hair before turning her full attention to her other charge. Susannah paused in the doorway to pull a face at her friend, knowing she was about to endure one of her mother's patient, but excruciatingly moving lectures.

Under Jones's watchful eye, Deborah consumed the plate of bread and butter, then, holding her nose, she downed what she had been told was brandy in one go, like the vile medicine she considered it to be, then snuggled down against the pillows to enjoy her chocolate.

A pleasing warmth stole through her limbs as she sipped the hot drink, and she could feel herself relaxing. She must have been quite wrung out, what with one thing and another, she reflected, yawning sleepily. Perhaps, after a day or two spent recouping her strength, she would be able to put the unsettling feelings she had towards Captain Fawley into proper perspective.

And the next time she saw him, she would be able to smile upon him with perfect equanimity. Her heart would not skip a beat, her breathing would remain orderly and she would not blush and grow tongue-tied. And if he took her arm, she would not succumb to the temptation to lean into him and revel in the feel of all that masculine strength and vitality concealed beneath the fabric of his dress uniform.

She was far too sensible to give in to the first infatuation she had begun to harbour for a man. Only a ninny would let her head be completely turned by a scarlet coat and a roguish smile, she told herself sternly. She must nip such feelings in the bud. She was the sensible, practical Miss Deborah Gillies, who could be relied upon to behave completely correctly, no matter what blows fate dealt her. Had she not stood firm when her mother had collapsed after the sudden death of the Reverend Gillies? Though she, too, had been grief-stricken and shocked to discover her loving father had left them with scarce two farthings to rub together, she had dealt with the legal men, assessed their budget, found a modest house and hired the few servants they could now afford. She had shaken hands with the new incumbent, who had wanted them to move out of the vicarage within a month of her father's death, and even managed to hand over the keys of the only home she had ever known to his pretty young wife with dry eyes.

In comparison with that, this inconvenient yearning she felt for a man who was unattainable was nothing.

Yawning again, she pulled the covers up to her ears, reminding herself that she did not have the energy to waste on weaving dreams around the dashing Captain Fawley anyway. What she ought to be worrying about was what she and her mother would do once Susannah had bagged her eligible, and they no longer had any reason to let the Hullworthys foot their bills.

If tonight had taught her anything, it was that she might as well stop hoping to meet someone who would want to marry her and miraculously make everything right. And she had long since known that she could not simply return to Lower Wakering at the end of the Season, and continue to be a drain on her mother's scant resources.

It was about time, she decided as her eyes drifted shut, to come up with some plan to settle her future for herself.

By herself.

Chapter Two

Deborah yawned, opened her eyes and stretched languorously. And sat up abruptly. She could see sunlight burning through the curtains, so the day must be far advanced. Why had Jones not come to wake her?

Then the events of the previous night filtered back to her consciousness. After the dizzy spell, the near faint, and, of course, the scene she had almost caused in the ballroom, her mother had probably decreed she should be left to sleep for as long as she needed. She swung her legs out of the bed and went to the washstand. The face that gazed back at her from the ornate gilt mirror was drawn, her eyes looking incredibly large against the pallor of her skin. Yes, she decided wryly, she had been trying to do too much, too soon after her illness. The fact that she had been unable to control her emotions in public was an indicator of how pulled she must be.

Once she had recovered her strength, she decided, splashing her face with cold water, she would be much better able to control those ridiculous feelings she had been experiencing around Captain Fawley. And the uncharitable ones she had been harbouring towards Susannah.

She rang the bell for the maid, deciding that she would have her breakfast in bed for once, just like a lady of fashion. While the Hullworthys were paying the bills, she might as well make the best of it. This would very likely be the last time she would have the opportunity to experience such luxury.

After a hearty breakfast of ham and eggs, washed down with liberal amounts of coffee, she fell asleep again, not waking until the day was far spent.

This time, when she rang for her maid, she decided she must get up and get dressed.

'I'll put out the long-sleeved morning gown, the one with the green sash, shall I, miss?' said Jones. 'There are several gentlemen callers downstairs, and you will be wanting to look your best.'

'Will I?' she said bitterly, causing Jones to frown at her. It would hardly matter what she looked like, she reflected, raising her arms for Jones to drop the delicate muslin over her head. They would all be there for Susannah.

'Perhaps I am not well enough to leave my room, after all,' she muttered darkly, settling on her dressing table stool so that Jones could arrange her hair. She had thought she had recovered her equanimity, yet the minute she was out of bed, she was beginning to feel jealous of Susannah again.

'Oh, no, miss, I think it would do you good to go and drink a cup of tea and eat a little something.'

There was that, she agreed, as her stomach rumbled

loudly. After brushing her hair briskly, Jones took a length of green ribbon in her hand.

'No sense in heating the curling tongs, if you are only going to be out of bed for an hour or so,' Jones said, deftly securing her hair off her face with the ribbon. Deborah wondered if she had infected the woman with her own pessimism, or whether Jones had come to the conclusion that, since her charge would never match up to the pretty Miss Susannah, there was no point in making much effort.

Funnily enough, Deborah approved of the new style Jones had created out of sheer laziness. She had not tried to torture her hair into the fussy mass of curls that had only ever made her face look even more pinched. It simply cascaded down her back. She looked far more like herself than she had felt since she had come to town.

'Let's not bother with the tongs again, Jones,' she said, making for the door. If the London bucks did not find her attractive enough to propose, she was no longer prepared to exhaust herself trying to get them to notice her.

As she descended the stairs to the first floor, she felt more cheerful than she had for some time. The result of all that extra sleep, or her decision to stop hankering after the unobtainable? She did not know. She only knew that she wanted a cup of tea. And some sandwiches. And maybe a few of the delicious little macaroons the cook always put out for afternoon callers.

She was not going to bother attempting to engage any of Susannah's suitors in conversation. She was tired of trying to discover some speck of intelligence in the fops and fribbles who were crowding her drawing room lately. No wonder she had begun to think so highly of Captain Fawley. He stood out from the herd whose minds were full of the cut of their coat, or the latest way of tying a cravat. Nor was his conversation peppered with tales of his exploits on the hunting field.

Oh, Lord, she thought, setting her hand to the doorknob with a self-deprecating smile, *here I go again*!

Susannah saw her the moment she entered the drawing room, and leapt to her feet, squealing 'Deborah!' in a most unladylike display of pleasure. 'I had begun to think you were going to sleep the clock round. Are you feeling better? Do come and sit by me.' She gestured towards the sofa seat next to her, causing the swain sitting there to scowl. 'Mr Jay will not mind making room for you.' She turned her sweetly smiling face to his, and the scowl miraculously disappeared. 'You can fetch Miss Gillies a plate of sandwiches from the sideboard, while I pour her a cup of tea.'

Deborah bit her lip to prevent herself from giggling. The last thing Mr Jay wanted to do was fetch and carry for a pasty-faced girl he would not have passed the time of day with, given the choice. But to win favour with Susannah, his pained look seemed to convey, he would walk across hot coals.

As she followed his progress across the room, her eyes snagged on the figure of Captain Fawley, lounging against the mantelpiece. He had been looking distinctly surly, but, on seeing her, the expression on his face softened somewhat.

In spite of her resolution not to allow herself to be

affected by him again, her unruly heart began to thump as he picked his way through the throng to reach her side.

'I am glad to have had the opportunity to see you before I take my leave, Miss Gillies,' he said. 'Miss Hullworthy gave me to understand that it was unlikely.'

Out of the corner of her eye, Deborah saw Susannah blush and look a little uncomfortable. She wondered if her friend had tried, at long last, to make her dislike of this particular one of her suitors somewhat clearer.

'Are you feeling better?'

'Yes, much, thank you,' she replied.

'I did peep in once or twice,' said Susannah, handing her a cup of tea, 'in case you were just resting and in want of company…'

'Never tell me you stayed in all morning! I thought you meant to go to Hatchard's, for some new books!'

'Oh, well, I could not go out and leave you until I was sure you were not really ill. If your mother had needed to send for the doctor—' Susannah broke off, chewing at her lower lip.

Deborah could not help noticing how the Captain's eyes fixed intently on that little gesture, his own lips parting slightly.

'Your concern for Miss Gillies's well-being is most commendable,' he said. 'Not many young ladies would forgo their pleasure, to sit at home and tend an invalid.'

'Nonsense!' Susannah replied robustly. 'I do not think of Deborah as an invalid. She is my dearest friend,' she said, taking Deborah's hand and squeezing it. 'She has been kindness itself to me, when I needed her, and if she was not here with me in London now, I should consider myself most unfortunate.'

Deborah returned the squeeze, remembering some of the grim times the Hullworthys had endured when they had first moved into Lower Wakering. The local gentry had closed ranks against the common upstarts, excluding them from their select gatherings. It was presumptuous, they all agreed, of the Hullworthys to buy the bankrupt Lord Wakering's estate, shocking of them to demolish the ramshackle mansion that had been his ancestral home and downright vulgar to replace it with a purpose-built colossus equipped with every luxury and new-fangled convenience. For some time, the only locals who had not been hostile had been the vicar and his family. And it was entirely due to their influence that the Hullworthys had gradually found a measure of acceptance.

Once more, Captain Fawley's eyes glowed with admiration. He appeared to think that Susannah was just being gracious, thought Deborah with a spurt of annoyance, when she had only spoken the literal truth. If her mother had not agreed to sponsor Susannah, she would not have the entrée to the circles in which she was now moving. Especially not if either of her parents had come with her. They would have ruined Susannah's chances, as Mrs Gillies had wasted no time in pointing out to them. Dearly though she loved them, there was no getting round the fact that Mr and Mrs Hullworthy were not at all genteel.

'I hope…' He checked himself, then went on, 'That is, I shall be asking the dowager Lady Lensborough to call on you soon, to extend an invitation to Lord Lensborough's engagement ball. I hope you will be able to attend. And that you will save me at least one dance.'

Susannah gasped, her grip on Deborah's hand growing uncomfortably tight.

'L…Lensborough? The Marquis of Lensborough?'

For a moment, Deborah thought she saw a flicker of amusement in Captain Fawley's eyes. Did he know that an invitation to such an event was the one sure way to capture Susannah's interest? She looked at him keenly. Perhaps it was not only débutantes who cast out lures to catch their prey. He had certainly baited his hook with the one worm that could make Susannah bite. She was almost obsessed with gaining an entrée to the *haut ton*.

'The same,' he said, his fleeting trace of amusement replaced with an air of gravity.

'Oh, well, that would be wonderful!' Susannah sighed rapturously. 'If you can indeed promise me an invitation, you may be sure I shall save at least one dance for you!'

'That was just what I thought you would say,' he replied, bowing over the hand she had extended, for the first time to Deborah's knowledge, willingly.

'Now I will take my leave,' he said, nodding curtly to Deborah. 'I am glad to hear you are recovering from your indisposition. And I hope you will accept the small token of my good wishes in the spirit in which it was given.'

'Token?' Deborah felt totally mystified.

'Oh, Captain Fawley brought you a posy. It is over there.' Deborah looked where Susannah had pointed, to see the usual mound of floral tributes piled upon the little table by the door. Her heart leaped to think that, at long last, one of them was for her!

'Miss Hullworthy informed me that you would not be able to accept it from me personally, so I left it with the other tributes to the beauties of Half Moon Street,' he said drily.

'Which one is it?' she asked, her pulse fluttering wildly.

'The orangey-coloured one,' he replied vaguely. 'I know not the names of the flowers. I just thought they were something like the colour of the ribbons you were wearing in your hair last night.'

All the breath left her lungs in a great whoosh. He had brought her a posy. And he had noticed what colour ribbons she had been wearing in her hair! She wanted to rush across the room, gather the flowers to her bosom and breathe in their fragrance. How silly of her. He had not brought it because he harboured any tender feelings for her. It had been expedient to arm himself with it, that was all, and feign concern over her health to gain entry to the home of the woman who really interested him. Rather stiffly, she said, 'I am sure Susannah would have brought it up to me, had I not got out of bed today.'

'Yes, of course I would!'

'Of course you would,' he agreed wryly. 'But now there is no need. Miss Gillies is much recovered, and I am sure in a day or so, will be well able to withstand the rigours of the ballroom at Challinor House.'

'Where is Challinor House?' Susannah asked, the minute he had left. 'And what has it to do with an invitation to Lord Lensborough's engagement? And what is his connection with the family?'

'Hush, Suzy,' Deborah murmured. 'Wait till your callers have gone. Then we may ask my mama.'

* * *

Her mother was very well informed about the noble families of England. It never ceased to amaze her how a woman who had spent the majority of her life in a rural backwater had managed to keep her finger on the pulse of London gossip.

'Challinor is the family name, dear,' Mrs Gillies explained, when Susannah eventually got the opportunity to question her about the Marquis of Lensborough. 'And you say Captain Fawley is to use his influence with the dowager Lady Lensborough to get you an invitation to her son's ball? Hmm…' She sank on to her favourite chair, her finger tapping her chin as a frown came to her brow. 'Of course!' Her face lit up. 'Her younger son served in the same regiment as Captain Fawley. Dead now, of course, like so many of them after that dreadful affair of Waterloo…' She sighed, shaking her head. 'But I believe shared grief has created something of a bond between your Captain Fawley and the Marquis. I know for a fact that he trained a horse especially to cope with his…umm… disadvantages. He is bound to be on the guest list already….'

'But I heard that the engagement ball is one of the most exclusive events of the Season so far!' Susannah protested. 'Why should they include a penniless nobody like Captain Fawley?'

'Now, Susannah, my dear, I have told you before about judging a man too hastily. There is nothing wrong with his background. He is half-brother to the Earl of Walton, after all.'

Deborah's heart sank as Susannah's eyes lit up. She suddenly felt incredibly weary.

'If you do not mind,' she said, 'I would like to go and lie down again before dinner.'

'Of course, my dear,' said her mother. 'And do not be thinking you will be left alone this evening. If you do not feel up to coming down and keeping company with us, one of us will come and read to you. Won't we, Susannah?'

To her credit, Susannah betrayed not the slightest sign of petulance, though Deborah knew she had been looking forward to the theatre trip planned for that evening. Instead, she leapt to her feet, saying brightly, 'Shall I come up with you now? We could have a good gossip while you have a lie down. For you surely don't need to sleep any more today, do you?'

Deborah mentally braced herself. She knew that the gossip would consist of hearing Susannah dissect every single one of her suitors—their dress, their manners, their connections and fortune—and she was not sure she was sufficiently in control of the frayed edges of her temper to hold it together.

'Fancy Captain Fawley being the brother of an earl!' Susannah sighed the moment they had shut the chamber door behind them.

'Yes, only fancy,' Deborah muttered glumly, sitting on a low stool to ease off her pumps.

'Why did you not tell me?'

'Would you mind helping me with the hooks?' Deborah prevaricated, turning her back to her friend. While Susannah was thrilled to find one of her suitors so well connected, so far as Deborah was concerned, it only seemed to put him further from her reach than ever.

While Susannah dealt with the fastenings of her dress, she confessed, 'I had no idea his father was an earl.'

'Which changes everything, of course. Do you think he is a viscount, as well as being a captain?'

'Don't you dare toy with him, Susannah!' Deborah whirled round, her eyes blazing with fury. 'He has suffered enough!'

'I wouldn't…' Susannah gasped.

'You may not mean to hurt him, but I have seen the way his eyes follow you round the dance floor, while you are making up to your latest conquest!'

'Well, I…'

'Oh, you do not need to tell me—you cannot bear to look at him!'

'With that face?' Susannah shuddered. 'Can you blame me?'

Deborah struggled to control her temper. 'I admit he has been knocked about a bit. But only consider how he received his wounds. Fighting for his country. He is worth ten of that fribble Baron Dunning, whom you hang upon because he has a title. He worked his way up through the ranks, earning promotion through merit….'

Drawing herself up to her full height, Susannah said quietly, 'Your mother has already made me revise my opinion of Baron Dunning. I see what this is, Deborah— you have designs upon Captain Fawley yourself.'

Deborah's mouth opened, then closed, as she sought to refute Susannah's argument, but realised she could not in all conscience do so.

'I do not have designs upon him,' she eventually

managed to say. 'But that does not mean I am prepared to stand by and watch you break his heart. I think you are a better person than that, Suzy.'

Susannah's eyes narrowed. '*If* you do not have your sights set on him, and *if* you are only thinking of what is best for him, then I would have thought you would be glad that I have finally relented towards him. He is intelligent enough to know what my ambitions are. He knows I intend to make a brilliant match. Agreeing to go to one ball as his guest, letting him have one dance with me, is all he aspires to, I assure you. I won't encourage him to dangle after me.'

'I...I hope you will not.'

'Of course I won't! What do you take me for?' She laid one hand upon Deborah's arm. 'Goose. I think you must really need to lie down if you are as snappish as this.'

'Yes,' Deborah mumbled, hanging her head guiltily. 'Yes, I think I must.'

Though she felt wrung out after that episode, sleep remained far from her as she lay rigidly on top of the counterpane, her fists clenched at her sides. She did not know what was the matter with her. Why had she got so angry with Susannah? Oh, if only this Season was over, and she could leave London and all its painful associations behind.

As soon as Susannah's future was settled, she would begin to scour the papers and apply for every post suitable for a lady of gentle birth.

She was never going to get married.

She did not want to get married!

Not if it meant playing the sort of games Susannah was indulging in.

* * *

A week later, as she entered the portals of Challinor House, Deborah was glad she had allowed Susannah to talk her into buying a new gown.

'Papa will pay for it!' she had airily promised. 'And don't think of it as charity. He has hired your mother to bring me to the notice of the best families, and I am sure he will think the cost of one gown well worth it to have us both looking our best when we walk into the house of a marquis!'

That had been all it had taken to sway Deborah. They both had to look the part, not just Susannah. If Deborah merely refurbished one of the few ballgowns she had, or remade one of Susannah's cast-offs, as she had first intended, every woman there would know she was purse-pinched. And then they would look at Susannah, decked out in her finery, and see the true state of affairs. A girl who had to hire someone to launch her into society would not be looked upon with the same indulgence as one who was being sponsored, out of friendship, by a family with as good a pedigree as the Gillies.

Still, seeing the diamonds that glittered at the throats and ears of so many of the other guests as they slowly made their way up the stairs, made her feel as though it was she, and not Susannah, who was the impostor here. Though her ballgown was quite the finest thing she had ever owned, a superbly cut satin slip, with an overdress of gauze embroidered with hundreds of the tiniest beads whirling in intricate patterns, little puffed sleeves and a demi-train of spangled lace, her only jewellery was a single strand of pearls that had been her mother's.

'I don't need such gewgaws at my age, dear.' She had smiled as she clasped it about her daughter's neck just before they came out. 'In fact, I prefer to conceal as much of my neck as I can!' She had recently taken to wearing an assortment of floaty scarves draped about her throat. The one she had on tonight was a delicate wisp of powder blue, which, Deborah had to admit, somehow managed to put the finishing touch to an outfit that was as elegant as anything that the other older ladies were wearing.

At length, they came to the head of the receiving line, and she finally came face to face with her host and hostess. The Marquis of Lensborough bowed his head in greeting to her mother, expressed the appropriate sentiments to her, but then merely looked at Susannah as though…she gasped—as though she had no right to be there. As his features settled into a decided sneer, Deborah took a strong aversion to him. Why on earth did Susannah want to ingratiate herself with people of his class, who would only ever look down their aristocratic noses at her? And his fiancée, a tall, rake-thin redhead, was no better. She had the most haughty, closed expression of any woman Deborah had ever met. It was a relief to get past them and make for the ballroom.

'Ah, there is Gussy!' said her mother, spotting the dowager Lady Lensborough holding court from a sofa in an alcove just off the ballroom proper. Deborah felt her lips rise in a wry smile. It had come as a shock when, not two days after Captain Fawley had made his promise to get them an invitation, the dowager Marchioness of Lensborough had swept into their drawing room, and proceeded to treat her mother as though she was a close friend. She soon learned that this was not so very far from the truth. They had known each other as girls, and though their paths in life had taken very different directions, they had kept up a sporadic correspondence.

She had made both girls stand, and turn and walk before her, before she deigned to hand over the coveted invitations.

'I will not have any chit in my ballroom who will not do it credit,' she had said outrageously. 'You are both pretty enough, in your own ways.' She had raised her lorgnette and frowned at each in turn. 'It is a great pity that your daughter has not her friend's looks and fortune, Sally. But then again, *she* has not the advantage of breeding. But there…' she sighed '…that is always the way of things. And there is no real reason why either of them should not marry well. My own son has gone for character, over beauty, in the choice of his bride, as I am sure you will discover when you meet her.' She clicked her tongue in exasperation. 'Men are such odd creatures. No telling what will take their fancy.'

Susannah and Deborah followed closely in her mother's wake, like chicks seeking the warmth of a mother hen. The dowager's evident pleasure in seeing the girls served as a welcome antidote to their frosty reception, and reassured the other guests that these two girls were persons worthy of notice. Soon, Susannah's hand was being solicited for the dancing that was about to ensue. She very correctly saved the first dance for Captain Fawley, but when he came to claim her hand,

Deborah was somewhat startled to find he had brought a tall, fair-haired man with him.

'Permit me to introduce my half-brother, Miss Gillies,' he said to her. 'Lord Charles Algernon Fawley, ninth Earl of Walton.'

He looked nothing like Captain Fawley. Not only was he fair-haired and blue-eyed, but there was nothing about their facial features to suggest they could be related at all.

Deborah curtsied. He bowed, then shocked her by saying, 'Would you do me the honour of allowing me to partner you for the first dance?'

It was with mixed feelings that she allowed Lord Walton to lead her on to the dance floor. It had been so kind of Captain Fawley to ensure she was not left on the sidelines, while Susannah formed part of the set that opened such a glittering ball. She had never danced with an earl, never mind such a handsome one. She should have been giddy with rapture. But as they trod the measure of the stately quadrille, she could not help being agonisingly aware that, though she formed part of the set that contained Captain Fawley, she was not his partner. Nor could she help but be aware of the satisfaction that gleamed from his eyes every time he linked hands with Susannah.

On the whole, she was glad when the exercise was over, and Lord Walton led her back to the bench where her mother was sitting, chatting happily with a bevy of dowagers.

As Susannah's next partner came to claim his dance, Captain Fawley bowed stiffly to Deborah. His face looked a little strained as he said, somewhat defensively, 'I am not going to ask you to dance, Miss Gillies. But may I have the pleasure of your company during the next set, if your card is free?'

In spite of all the stern lectures she had given herself, her heart began to beat a tattoo against her ribs in response to his request. In truth, she would much rather spend time talking to him, than treading prescribed steps in time with the music. Especially since she could tell that performing the quadrille had cost him quite dearly. Lines of tension bracketed his mouth, and his eyes were dulled with pain.

'Yes, thank you. I should like that.' She smiled, laying her hand upon his arm as he held it out. 'In fact,' she suggested, sensitive to his evident discomfort, 'I should quite enjoy sitting and watching the dancers.'

He quirked one eye at her. 'You sound just like Heloise—that is, my sister-in-law, Lady Walton. As an artist, she likes to observe the *ton* at play. Do you sketch?'

'Oh, no, not really. No more than any young lady is supposed to.'

He suddenly frowned. 'Of course, you are not in the best of health, are you? Here, let us sit on this sofa, so that you may rest.'

'I do not need to rest. Not tonight. I am not generally invalidish,' she retorted. Then could have kicked herself for being so insensitive. He had probably homed in on her precisely because he thought she was frail, so that he could have the opportunity to sit without making it look as though it was what he needed to do.

He settled her on a cushioned window seat, far

enough from the swirling crowds so that they could engage in conversation, yet still within sight of the chaperon's bench.

'Are you enjoying your Season?' he enquired politely, ignoring her last tactless remark.

'In some ways.' She sighed. She did not want to waste her few precious moments with him in polite nothings. Yet he did not look as though he was really interested in her answer. 'I am certainly glad to see my mother enjoying herself so much.' She looked across the room to where Mrs Gillies was dividing her time between chatting with her acquaintances and watching Susannah's progress with obvious satisfaction. 'From the moment we heard that a Season in London was going to be possible after all, it was as though she came back to life.'

'Your father died not long ago, I seem to recall?'

'Yes, and it hit her very badly. For several months she seemed to lose interest in everything. I had to…' She paused. She did not want to sound as though she was complaining. 'Well, we were not left in very comfort-able circumstances. But look at her now.' She smiled fondly at her mother across the room. Her cheeks were pink and her eyes were bright. 'It has done her so much good to launch Susannah. And finding so many of her old friends in London has successfully distracted her from her problems.'

'But what of you?' he persisted. 'I can see your friend is enjoying her triumph. And that your mother is in her element. But how does the delicate Miss Gillies fare in the hurly burly of London society?'

'I have told you before, I am not in the least delicate!

It was only because…' She tailed off, blushing as she realised she was on the point of divulging just how desperate their straits had been before the Hullworthys had come to their rescue.

The little cottage, which had seemed perfectly charming when they had moved in during the summer, had revealed all its inadequacies during the first autumnal storm. The roof leaked, the windows rattled in their casements, and the chimneys smoked. Her mother had shrunk into herself as though finally realising that she was going to eke out the rest of her days in penury. Feeling as though she had contributed to her mother's state of mind, by not having managed to find somewhere better, Deborah's health had broken down.

That, at least, had roused Mrs Gillies from her apathy. Fearing that she might lose her daughter, as well as her husband, within the space of a few months, she had put pride to one side and finally accepted the Hullworthys' offer of rooms up at the Hall so she could nurse Deborah back to health in warmth and comfort.

Even though it meant they had become charity cases.

Deborah was only having this Season at all because she felt she owed the Hullworthys her very life. She had not wanted to come, especially not at their expense, but Susannah wanted her mother to launch her into society, and Deborah was necessary to make the whole thing look right.

'If you must know, this whole thing seems…unreal. Wasting entire days shopping so that we may fritter away the evenings dancing, or doing something equally frivolous…it is a bit like living a dream, from which I am waiting to awake, so that I can get back to my real life again.'

'Do you dislike it so much?' he frowned.

'Oh, no. It is quite a pleasant sort of dream…' she sighed '…for the most part.' She frowned down at the dainty satin slippers that peeped from beneath the hem of her gown, wondering what on earth had possessed her to speak so frankly. Yet having begun, she felt a compelling urge to unburden herself to the one person she thought might understand her sentiments.

'It is just that I cannot ever permit myself to enter into it all in quite the same way as Miss Hullworthy does. She is here to catch a husband, whereas I…' Her breath hitched in her throat.

'You do not wish to marry?' Captain Fawley looked puzzled.

'Of course, marriage would be my preferred option. But being of a practical nature, I have to consider what I will do when my time in London is over, should I not have received any offers.'

'And what decision have you come to?' he asked, with a smile.

'That I shall have to find some kind of paid position, of course. Either as a governess, or teacher. I would prefer to secure a post as a housekeeper, for I know that is a job I could do really well. However, I do not think anyone would employ a girl as young as me for such a responsible post.'

'Would anyone employ a girl of your background for a teaching post, either?' She shot him a look of chagrin. But there was nothing in his face to suggest he was mocking her. On the contrary, he only looked as though he was curious.

'I think they might, yes,' she retorted, lifting her chin. 'All I shall need to do is teach other young ladies the very same things I have had to learn. I can do household accounts, and bake, and sew. And, what is more, Papa taught me Greek and Latin,' she finished proudly.

'Do many schools for little girls have Greek and Latin on the curriculum?' He laughed.

'They might have,' she replied, fixing him with a challenging look. 'There might be some schools that work on the ethos that girls have a right to learn all the things that boys do, and not restrict them to sewing, and deportment, and drawing.'

'Are you equipped to teach them to fence and box, by any chance?'

Part of her wanted to take offence at his words, but the smile in his eyes as he teased her was so appealing, she found herself laughing instead.

'Oh, very well, not perhaps everything, but you know what I mean.'

'Yes, I rather think I do.' He smiled, getting to his feet. 'Pray forgive me, Miss Gillies, but I must take my leave of you. Now that I have had my dance with Miss Hullworthy, and spent this delightful interlude with you, it is time I was elsewhere.'

Delightful interlude. He had said this had been a delightful interlude.

She stared up at him, her heart sinking as she noted the blankness of his face as he bowed his farewell. It was just the sort of nonsense men spouted all the time. Something to say. He hadn't really meant it.

'Goodnight, then, Captain Fawley,' she managed to say, though she could not muster the smile she should have raised to go with the polite utterance. Nor could she tear her eyes away from him, as he limped away. As he bade farewell to his host, Lord Lensborough's face darkened. And after he had gone, the Marquis turned and glared at Susannah, as she made her way down the current set, his fists clenching as though he was restraining the urge to seize her and throw her bodily through the nearest window.

At first, his demeanour shocked her. But then she reminded herself that she did not like the way Susannah treated Captain Fawley, either. Lord Lensborough might not be a very pleasant man, but he was clearly capable of loyalty towards those he considered friends.

And it *was* hard to sit and watch Susannah enjoying herself, when Captain Fawley, who had been responsible for bringing her here, had just slunk out, alone, into the night.

Oh, why could not Susannah appreciate what it was costing Captain Fawley to court her? He found it physically painful to dance, and yet he had persistently begged for the privilege of doing so with her, so ardent was his admiration. He could not even bear to remain in this ballroom, when he knew his own case was hopeless. He had laid himself open to rejection, time and time again, and yet it all meant nothing to her! Why couldn't she see that the esteem of a man like him was worth far more than landing a title? What did it matter if his body was no longer completely whole? It was the heart of a man that mattered.

And Captain Fawley's heart was Susannah's for the taking.

Susannah's.

She must not forget that. Not for an instant.

Snapping her fan open, Deborah rose to her feet, and made her way rather unsteadily to the bench on which her mother was sitting.

Chapter Three

It was a glorious afternoon. Though there was hardly a cloud in the sky, a deliciously cool breeze skittered playfully through the chestnut trees, making the air beneath their boughs sweet enough to drink. Sadly, Deborah's pleasure in being out of doors was dimmed somewhat by the company she was in.

Although Susannah no longer viewed Baron Dunning with much enthusiasm, she had not turned down his invitation to promenade through Hyde Park during the fashionable hour. Particularly since he had been thoughtful enough to bring along his friend, Mr Jay, to escort Deborah. The girls had both hoped that having male escorts would make the walk rather more like the brisk outings they were used to taking in Lower Wakering. But the men were no more willing to stride out than the hired London servants were. They strolled along at a snail's pace, pausing frequently to acknowledge acquaintances or point out persons of interest who were bowling along the carriage drive in smart barouches or landaulets.

Deborah's heart sank as yet another friend of Mr Jay's called out a greeting, then, upon catching sight of Susannah, pulled his rather showy chestnut mare alongside them.

'What brings you to the park at this hour, Lampton?' Mr Jay asked him as he swung down from the saddle. 'Wouldn't have thought it was quite your thing.'

'Oh, you know,' Mr Lampton said vaguely, his attention riveted upon Susannah. 'Won't you introduce me to your charming companions?'

Deborah's first impression was that he must be one of the most handsome men she had ever seen. He was tall and well built. A lock of fair hair strayed from under his curly-brimmed beaver hat, but she would have guessed at the colouring anyway, from the fairness of lashes and brows that framed forget-me-not blue eyes.

'Oh, this is Miss Gillies,' Mr Jay said briefly. 'Miss Gillies, the Honourable Percy Lampton.'

'Charmed to make your acquaintance,' said Mr Lampton, turning on a smile so patently false, it immediately put Deborah's back up. Men as handsome as this were not charmed to make her acquaintance. They usually ran their eyes over her swiftly, assessing her scrawny figure, the cheapness of her dress, and then the expression in their eyes became dismissive, or sometimes even downright scornful.

'Mr Lampton,' she repeated, making the proper curtsy, though she found it hard to muster up a reciprocal smile.

'And who, pray, is the dasher upon young Baron Dunning's arm?' he enquired, turning to make an exaggerated bow to Susannah.

While the introductions were made, the horse became quite skittish.

'You were correct about this brute,' Mr Lampton said to Mr Jay, tugging ineffectually on the horse's reins while its hindquarters surged across the path. 'Too high spirited by half.'

'Yes. I say, don't you think you ought to…?' Looking somewhat alarmed, Mr Jay let go of Deborah's arm and darted under the horse's tossing head. Shooting a look over his shoulder, he said to Baron Dunning, 'Perhaps you should move the ladies a little further away.'

While he set about calming the horse, with a competence Deborah had to admire, Baron Dunning linked arms with her and moved her out of range of those potentially dangerous hooves.

And somehow, once the incident was over, Mr Jay had the horse, Baron Dunning had Deborah on his arm, leaving Mr Lampton in sole possession of Susannah.

That was how it remained, all the way home. And Baron Dunning, far from exerting himself to be pleasant to Deborah, could not disguise his annoyance at being so neatly cut out by the newcomer. Deborah felt amused, rather than offended, only wondering how on earth Susannah would decide between all her suitors in the end. Although, if she could not make up her mind, there was nothing to stop her from returning to London again the next year. She was wealthy enough to be choosy. Her parents would not mind in the least if she went home without a husband in tow. So long as she enjoyed herself, and did not throw herself away on a nobody.

She sighed, remembering their conversation the morning after the Marquis of Lensborough's ball.

'I am not to throw myself away on a nobody,' she had said defiantly, when Deborah had challenged her for asking her mother to make further enquiries about Captain Fawley. 'Even if he is not what I thought him at first, I must not encourage him if he does not have any prospects.'

Sadly for Captain Fawley, it had not taken her mother long to discover that his prospects were non-existent.

'The eighth Earl of Walton married twice,' she had explained. 'The first marriage was arranged by his family, while he was scarce out of his teens, to ensure the succession, for he was the only son. They matched him with one of the Lampton girls, who, eventually, presented him with a healthy boy. He chose his own wife the second time he married, for reasons of sentiment, rather than duty. There was some sort of scandal about the time he died, which I have not been able to get to the bottom of, but the upshot was that the boys were parted and reared separately. The current Earl,' she said, leaning forward in her chair to dispense her nugget of gossip in a thrilled tone, 'scoured the battlefields of Spain to find Captain Fawley when he got news of how severely injured he was. He brought him home, and spent a fortune having him nursed back to health, thus effecting their reconciliation.'

'So,' said Susannah, getting to the nub of the matter, 'does that mean he is eligible, or not? If he is truly the younger son of an Earl, he must have a title, as well as his rank of captain from the army, must he not? And…'

She bit at her lower lip as she hesitated over broaching the indelicate topic of money.

But Mrs Gillies knew what interested her charge, without having to have it spelt out for her.

'No, he was never officially recognised as the eighth Earl's son. Nor did the old man leave him anything in his will. It all went to the current Earl. All Captain Fawley has is his army pension.'

'That's shocking!' cried Deborah, her fists clenching in indignation. 'Why was he cut out of the inheritance? It is not as if the present Earl cannot afford to spare a little. He must be one of the wealthiest men in England!'

Susannah laughed. 'Don't be such a goose, Debs. Isn't it obvious? Haven't you wondered why the two so-called brothers bear not the slightest resemblance to one another? No wonder the Lamptons threw the second wife out.' Picking up her cup of tea, and taking a dainty sip, she added, 'Well, that rules him out, for certain. Papa would never countenance me marrying a man who was born on the wrong side of the blanket.'

'Now, Susannah, dear, I hope you won't go around suggesting that I even hinted that Captain Fawley might not be legitimate. The Earl of Walton gets most upset with anyone who repeats that old scandal. He guards his brother's reputation zealously. And if you offend a man of his standing…'

Susannah had shrugged, calmly putting Captain Fawley out of her mind now that she had no further use for him.

It was a relief to get home from their walk in Hyde Park and slough off the disappointed suitors who would, if etiquette had not forbidden such tactics, have cheerfully shoved Mr Lampton off the pavement in order to pry Susannah from his side. Deborah was not surprised when, upon entering her mother's room, her friend's first words were of her latest conquest.

'What do you know about the Honourable Percy Lampton?' she said, perching on a chair beside the bed, where Mrs Gillies had been taking her afternoon nap. 'Is he one of the Lamptons who are related to the Earl of Walton? He looks as if he might be!'

Mrs Gillies struggled into a sitting position, while Deborah plumped up her pillows.

'From the way you have bounced into the room, I assume he has taken your fancy?' said Mrs Gillies, with a yawn. 'Of course, he will probably be a handsome devil, if he is anything like his father.' Her eyes took on a dreamy look as she delved back into reminiscences of her youth. 'And, yes, he is cousin to the present Earl. Very good *ton*, the Lamptons.' Suddenly, her eyes snapped back into focus. 'Eminently respectable family. Pride themselves on it, in fact. I do not know exactly how young Percy is situated financially, but if you like, I shall find out.'

Susannah leant forward, giving Mrs Gillies an impetuous hug. 'Thank you!'

Deborah and her mother watched her practically dance out of the room, with similarly thoughtful expressions.

'I think Susannah may have met her match,' said Mrs Gillies, at length.

Remembering the ruthlessly charming way he had outmanoeuvred his two rivals in the park, Deborah was forced to agree with her.

* * *

'What the devil is Lampton playing at, that is what I want to know.' Captain Fawley scowled at his brother, across the dining table, some ten days later. 'The way he is monopolising Miss Hullworthy is becoming the talk of the clubs. And don't tell me he is thinking of marrying her, for I won't believe it. Apart from the fact he enjoys his bachelor status far too much to hazard it for any woman, no Lampton would stoop to marrying a cit's daughter.'

The Earl of Walton frowned thoughtfully into his glass of port. 'He lacks only four months to his thirtieth birthday,' he said at length, enigmatically.

'What has that to say to anything?'

The Earl sighed, then looked his younger brother full in the face. 'What is Miss Hullworthy to you, Robert? Do you care for her?'

'I certainly don't want to see her ruined. Good God, you know what a menace Lampton is around women. Only remember the trouble he caused Heloise when she first came to London!'

Percy Lampton had joined forces with the Earl's discarded mistress in an attempt to soil his young bride's reputation. The marriage had very nearly foundered before the Earl had got wise to what was going on.

'I don't forget it,' said the Earl crisply. 'Although, in this particular case, I think I can see what motivates him.'

'Well, I cannot! Much as I dislike the man,' he said with a pensive frown, 'he strikes me as too fastidious to get embroiled in the kind of scandal that would erupt if he really did seduce her....'

'He won't need to go so far. All he means to do, I think, is to keep her away from you until he attains the age of thirty.'

'What has his age to do with anything?'

The Earl sighed. 'Upon his thirtieth birthday, Percy Lampton will come into a substantial inheritance.'

'But what has that to do with me? Or Miss Hullworthy, come to that?'

'You brought her to his notice, Robert, by pursuing her so hotly. Inviting her to Lensborough's engagement ball caused the devil of a stir.'

'That was my intent,' Captain Fawley replied brusquely. 'But why should Lampton think my affairs are any of his business?'

'Because of my Aunt Euphemia's will, I should think,' he said wryly. 'Which rather ambiguously named either you, or Percy Lampton as her heir.'

Captain Fawley went very still. 'I have been named in the will of some woman that I have never heard of? Why has nobody informed me of the fact until today?'

The Earl shifted uncomfortably in his seat. 'Aunt Euphemia died not long after I brought you home from Spain. My mother's family always regarded her as something of an eccentric, but when her will was finally read out, they declared she must have been unhinged. I do not think so. And nor did her lawyers or her doctors. Naming you as her beneficiary was not an irrational act, but rather her attempt to redress the injustice she felt her brothers had done to you over the matter of your upbringing.'

'*Felt* they had done?'

The Earl acknowledged his brother's objection. 'Did

do. We both know your mother should have been moved to the dower house and granted an annuity, and that you should have been brought up at Wycke, along with me.' He clenched his fist on the tabletop. 'They would have contested Aunt Euphemia's will, too, if I had not convinced them I had the resources to fight them tooth and nail until there would have been nothing left for anyone to inherit. Eventually, we reached a compromise with the trustees of her estate, which ensured that at least her fortune would remain intact until such time as one of you met with certain conditions.' He swirled his port round in his glass, staring into it meditatively. 'I rather think they ceded to my terms, instead of embarking on what would have been a protracted legal case because, at that time, nobody really expected you to survive.' He smiled mirthlessly.

'All right,' Captain Fawley grated, 'I accept that at the time this will was read, you acted on my behalf, since everyone thought I was about to stick my spoon in the wall. But I have been living under your roof for nigh on two years. Why is this the first I have heard about the will?'

'Would you believe me if I told you I did not think it would do you any good?'

'Not do me any good? I have a substantial sum of money owed me—at least I must assume it is, or the Lamptons would not have considered contesting the will to get it—and you say it would not do me any good?' Captain Fawley got to his feet, blood surging hotly through his veins. This was not the first time he had felt such hatred for his brother. No, he checked himself, only his half-brother. Though they shared the same father, his mother had never quite made the grade with the Earl's starchy relations. They had evicted her from his father's home before he was cold in his grave, threatening her with all sorts of dire consequences should she try to claim anything from her late husband's estate. Bereft, pregnant and without powerful friends to advise her, she had quietly returned to her middle-class family and dwindled away.

'What are you about, Walton? You pretend to act in my interests, but how can I forget that your mother was a Lampton too?'

Walton barely reacted to his brother's thinly veiled accusation.

'You forget, perhaps, that I mentioned there were conditions attached to you inheriting anything,' he said with icy calm. 'Until a few weeks ago, nobody, least of all myself, could have guessed you might want to meet them.'

'If I had known what they are, I would have been able to make the decision for myself!'

'Then do so now,' the Earl stated coldly. 'If you truly wish to escape the ignominy of living on my charity, all you have to do is make a respectable marriage. For one thing my aunt made resoundingly clear. She had no wish to have a bachelor living in her house. But do not tarry, Robert. If you are not married by the time Percy attains the age of thirty, then the trustees have decreed everything will go to him. He is, after all, a blood relative, which you are not.'

Robert felt as though the wind had been knocked out of him. No woman in her right mind would marry him. He knew it. Charles knew it. *That* was why he had not told him about the legacy. Knowing that a fortune lurked for ever just beyond his reach would only have added a further layer of torture to his existence.

He slumped back into his chair. Once again, he had lashed out at his brother, who had only ever had his welfare at heart. And sadly, though they both knew he hated having to subsist on his brother's charity, they also knew there was no viable alternative. Charles had offered on numerous occasions to make over to him the estates and trusts that should have been his, as the younger son of the Earl of Walton. Had he inherited them from his father, he would have been glad to live the life of a gentleman farmer, pottering about his acres. But the old man had not named him in his will…how could he, when he had not even been aware his wife was pregnant when he had died so suddenly? To accept them now, from his brother, out of some kind of misguided charity… He grimaced with distaste. No, he had been brought low enough, without stooping to accepting handouts, like some beggar on the streets.

If only he could be independent! His mind revolved over what Walton had just told him about this will. All he had to do, apparently, was to persuade a respectable female to marry him. Yes, that was all, he reflected bitterly. Persuade some poor woman to wake up to the nightmare of his face upon her pillow every morning.

Yet, Lampton must have thought he might have been able to persuade Miss Hullworthy to marry him. Or why would he have gone to such lengths to detach her from him?

'Damn him!' He lurched to his feet. 'Damn all the

Lamptons. And damn you too.' He rounded on his half-brother. 'Oh, yes, you claim you acted for the best, but because you decided to keep me in the dark, Percy Lampton is dangling that girl on a string. If only I had known, I would—' He stopped, bitter rage roiling in his gut. 'You have a lot to answer for, Walton,' he grated, turning on his heel and striding from the dining room.

He crossed the hall and slammed into the suite of rooms Lord Walton had set aside for him in his London residence. Linney, his manservant, who had been with him since his days in the army, was sitting at a table covered with newspaper, a tankard at his elbow and a pair of boots across his knees.

When Captain Fawley slumped into the chair opposite him, Linney reached under the table for a stone bottle, wiped round the rim of a rather smeared glass tumbler with the sleeve of his shirt and poured his master a full measure.

Captain Fawley drank the bumper off in one go, and pushed it across the table for a refill. He could not let Lampton get away with this! Apart from the fact he hated all the Lamptons on principle, the way he was falsely raising Susannah's expectations was downright dishonourable. Was there nothing that family would not stoop to, to increase their already substantial personal wealth?

It was not even as though Percy Lampton needed the money as much as he did. Lampton lived a comfortable, independent bachelor lifestyle, whereas he was completely dependent on his brother. His half-brother, he corrected himself.

He leaned his forehead on his hand, struggling against

the sense of resentment that thoughts of his half-brother still roused, even after all the man had done for him.

Too much! That was half the trouble. Walton always claimed he was acting in his best interests, but he was effectively robbing him of any choice. Smothering him!

If only there was some way out. Or, at least, some way he could prevent the blackguard getting his hands on his Aunt Euphemia's fortune.

He damned the Lamptons volubly, and comprehensively, before addressing his second glass of brandy.

He had hated the name of Lampton for as long as he could remember. They had destroyed his mother, blighted his childhood with their insinuations of his illegitimacy and made no secret of the fact they had hoped he would die in some foreign country while he was on active service. The French had done their damnedest, but he was not an easy man to kill. He had survived an explosion, two amputations, a fever and gruelling months of rehabilitation.

Even in his darkest hour, when he had felt he had nothing left to live for, he had refused to let them beat him.

And he was not going to let them beat him now.

If Percy Lampton thought he was going to sit back while he waltzed off with his inheritance, then he was very much mistaken.

He would find a way to best all the Lamptons.

His face twisted into a mask of hatred.

And he didn't much care how low he might have to stoop to do so.

Deborah started at the sound of someone knocking at the front door. Susannah had gone out for a drive in the park with Mr Lampton, and she had been looking forward to spending a peaceful afternoon reading. She had already become engrossed in her book, and was a little annoyed that she would be obliged to put it aside, and entertain some dull man who would be crushingly disappointed to find his quarry flown. Her mother, who was sitting on a chair by the window to get the best light for her embroidery, let out a sigh.

'Oh, dear,' she said, having evidently caught sight of the visitor as he waited on the front steps. 'He will be so disappointed to have missed Susannah.' Turning to Deborah, she said, 'Ring for some tea. We must make the poor boy especially welcome, must we not?'

It was only when Captain Fawley walked through the door that Deborah understood what had prompted her mother's sympathy. She had not approved of many of Susannah's suitors, before Mr Lampton had come on the scene, but she had a soft spot for the Captain. It was the way he looked at Susannah, she had confided to Deborah one evening not long after they had first made Mr Lampton's acquaintance. So wounded, so bitter, so tragically certain he had no chance against a man who was everything he was not. For not only was Mr Lampton staggeringly handsome, he had expectations. It was common knowledge that he stood to inherit a substantial fortune upon reaching the age of thirty. So he could not be pursuing Susannah for her money. He would make a better match for Susannah, Mrs Gillies had decided, than an ageing earl, or a spotty young baron. Nor would her parents look askance at him, even though he had no title, since Susannah herself seemed to have her heart set on him. And he was being so particular in his attentions, it was surely only a matter of time before he proposed.

Deborah laid her book to one side, as her mother said, 'Oh, Captain Fawley, how good it is of you to call on us this afternoon. We are all alone, as you see, and so dull! Please, do sit down. We have ordered some tea. I am sure you will stay and drink a cup with us, even though Miss Hullworthy is not here…' She faltered, looking a little self-conscious as she alluded to the Captain's disappointment.

'Thank you, Mrs Gillies,' he replied, though he remained standing stiffly by the door, rather than advancing towards the seat she had indicated he should take. 'I was aware that Miss Hullworthy was out. In point of fact, I waited until I was certain she would be. It is your daughter I have come to see. Miss Gillies,' he said, his cheeks flushing as he turned towards her, 'I know this is a little unorthodox, but might I have a few words with you in private?'

Deborah did not know how to answer him, nor to even begin to guess what on earth he might wish to say to her that would require privacy. Besides, it was completely improper! She was sure her mother would not allow any such thing.

'Why don't you two take a turn about the garden?' her mother stunned her by saying. 'But stay in sight of the windows. I am sure if Captain Fawley feels he needs to speak to you privately, he has a very good reason,' she said, in answer to Deborah's puzzled look. 'I will take a seat in the back parlour, from where I will have a good view of the lawn. Will that be acceptable, Captain?'

'Most acceptable. Thank you for your generosity, madam,' he said, opening the door and indicating that Deborah should accompany him.

One of the reasons for hiring this particular house was that it had a good-sized garden, by London standards. There was a narrow strip of lawn, bordered by low, shrubby sage plants, interspersed with clumps of sweet-william. Against one of the walls that separated their garden from the neighbouring property, some chairs had been set out around a wrought-iron table in a position to catch the early-morning sun. The area could still be used for sitting out later, too, since a pergola had been placed to provide some shade at the height of the day. And the roses and honeysuckle clambering over the structure in a marvellously scented tangle made it a pleasant place to sit well into the evening.

Captain Fawley headed unerringly towards the flowered arbour, making sure Deborah was sitting down before glancing back towards the house. When Mrs Gillies waved to him from the window, he bowed in her direction, before turning to address Deborah.

'Before I broach the matter I have come here to discuss, may I have your assurance that you will hold everything that passes between us in the strictest confidence?'

He returned her mystified gaze with a scowl so ferocious, Deborah began to feel a little nervous.

'If it means so much to you,' she answered, touched by his intention to confide in her, 'of course I will. Though I should not like to keep anything from my mother….'

'There will be no need to keep her in the dark for long,' he assured her. 'But I must insist that you do not reveal anything, not even to her, until I give you leave.'

'That sounds a little high-handed.'

'If I cannot trust you, then say so now, and that will be an end to it!'

Deborah scarcely paused to think. It would be quite impossible to let him leave without discovering why he had thought it imperative to breach etiquette by seeking an interview with her alone and then swearing her to secrecy. She would die of curiosity.

'You can trust me,' she vowed.

For a minute or two, he frowned down at her, searching her face as though he needed to be absolutely sure before committing himself any further. Finally, he squared his shoulders, as though coming to a decision about her, and muttered, 'If I did not think I could trust you, I would never even have considered coming to you. One thing I have noticed about you—you seem to possess more integrity than most girls of your age. I know that you have endured much during this past year, and borne it all with fortitude.'

Deborah filled up with pleasure at his praise, though gruffly delivered.

'You have also confided in me that when your Season comes to an end, you will have little to look forward to. I hope you will not take it amiss if I speak bluntly?'

He was about to trust her with some burden that he carried. How could she object if, in his extremity, he phrased it bluntly?

'You may speak freely to me,' she assured him.

'Well, then,' he said, taking the seat beside her and staring earnestly into her face, 'not to wrap the matter up in clean linen, the facts are these. You have neither the wealth, nor the looks, nor the wiles required to snare a wealthy husband.'

Deborah gasped, wounded to the core by his harsh assessment of her complete want of feminine allure. But he did not even pause in his catalogue of her failings.

'You might, perhaps, have secured the interest of a more ordinary man if you were not so frail. But I have no need to tell you that a man who must earn his own living, as, say, a soldier, or a diplomat, will want a wife in robust health, with the stamina to raise his family, and order his household in possibly less-than-comfortable circumstances.'

She was about to point out, in no uncertain terms, that she was not some frail creature that could not withstand a little hardship. And argue that, while such a man as he had spoken of was exactly the sort of husband she had come to London to find, Susannah's ambitions had catapulted her into spheres where such men did not venture. She was quite sure, that if she ever met such men, *they* might see she had some redeeming features. But he gave her no opportunity to say a word.

'You have admitted to me that you do not expect to receive any proposals of marriage,' he ploughed on with brutal candour, 'and that at the end of the Season, because of your straitened circumstances, you will have to seek paid employment. If you do not become a governess, you must serve as a teacher, for ever confined to some stuffy classroom. You will be quite miserable, for you would much rather marry, and be mistress of your own establishment than be for ever at the mercy of some other family's spoiled brats.'

Deborah's heart was pounding hard. She could not remember any man ever insulting her so comprehensively. Even though all he had said was true, it was cruel of him to fling it in her face. How dare he taunt her with her wish to marry, having told her she stood no chance of snaring a man!

'I do not think I wish to continue with this conversation,' she said, rising to her feet and turning her back on him.

'Miss Gillies, do not turn me down before you hear the whole.'

Turn him down? She froze. What was he trying to say?

'The…the whole?' Reluctantly, she looked at him over her shoulder.

'Yes. Miss Gillies, I have recently discovered that if I can but persuade some respectable female into marriage, I will inherit a substantial property.' He got to his feet, reached for her upper arm and spun her to face him. 'I thought you, of all women, might overcome your revulsion for such a man as I am in return for lifelong security.'

'You are asking me to marry you?' Deborah's heart was pounding with quite another emotion than she had been experiencing a moment earlier. She might have known his intention had not been to deliberately hurt her. He just obviously thought of himself as such a bad bargain for any woman, he had to highlight what he thought her alternative to accepting his proposal would be. 'The devil or the deep blue sea,' she whispered, her eyes filling with tears. Oh, how could he think no woman could love him!

'Don't dismiss the idea out of hand,' he implored her. 'Please, hear me out.'

Deborah's heart soared, even as she lowered her head to fumble in her reticule for a handkerchief. She did not know why she was crying, really. It was so silly when it felt as if a huge dark mass, which had been crushing her hopes and dreams, had finally rolled away, leaving her giddy and dazed. The man she loved had asked her to marry him!

She dropped back down on to her chair. The only reason, she now admitted to herself, that she had decided to forswear marriage and seek work was that she could not see herself marrying anyone except Captain Fawley. If she had received a proposal from any other man, she would have been gratified, but she did not think she could really have accepted it. But of course she would marry him. In a heartbeat! As soon as she had got this ridiculous urge to weep tears of relief under control, she would tell him so....

'Miss Gillies, I know I have little to offer you myself. But consider the property that comes with the marriage.' He sat down next to her, leaning forward as he put his case. 'I believe it would make an ideal family home. There will be room for your mother. I am sure you wish to be able to provide for her in her old age. I know her pension to be so meagre you thought it would be better to work than be a burden on her. And would you not rather raise children of your own than be paid to teach other people's? I would even permit you to hire a fencing master for our daughters, if that is what you wish,' he added, the touch of humour reminding her of the conversation they had shared at the Marquis of Lensborough's ball.

Though his reference to children was made in a jocular fashion, she knew he was spelling out to her that he was offering her a real marriage, not just a convenient arrangement. She had a brief vision of a boy and a girl capering about a broad, sunlit lawn, waving wooden swords at each other, while Captain Fawley, lounging beneath the shade of a gnarled oak tree, shouted instructions to them. Another little boy, with a grubby face, grinned down from the branches of the tree, while her mother, seated on a rustic bench nearby, smiled contentedly at her grandchildren. She watched them all from the windows of a rambling stone house, a tiny baby nuzzling at her breast. And then the Captain Fawley on that sun-drenched lawn turned to look at her. And he smiled at her. And his expression was not that of the bitter, careworn cripple who was putting this proposition to her, his eyes full of hopeless entreaty. He had become a contented family man.

She scanned the harsh features, scarce six inches from her own face. The warmth of his breath fanned her cheek. She could smell the faint aroma of bergamot, a scent she had associated with him since the night when he had supported her, half-fainting, from the heat of that crowded ballroom. Her hands remembered the texture of his sleeve, and, through it, the strength of the arm that it clothed.

How she longed to be the one to wipe away those lines of suffering that a lifetime of disappointments had etched so deeply on his face! To make those eyes, that burned with suspicion, glow with contentment or light with laughter.

Oh, she knew he was only asking her to marry him out of disappointment in losing Susannah to a rival. But she could empathise with the streak of practicality in his nature that had him reasoning that if he could not have the woman he had set his heart on, there was no reason that he should forgo the property, as well. Had she not planned her own future along similar lines? Having given up hope of marrying the man she loved, she had decided she would at least stand on her own two feet and not be beholden to anyone.

Though it was depressing that he thought so poorly of her. He saw her as a girl with so little going for her that she would be grateful for the chance to live in comfort, even if it meant allying herself to a man he assumed no woman could look upon with anything but revulsion.

'If any other man had asked me in such terms,' she declared, determined to justify her intention to accept him, in spite of his insults, 'I would have turned him down flat. Don't you know that the way you just addressed me was hurtful, almost beyond bearing?'

'If that is what you think,' he said, rearing back and making as though he was about to stand up, 'then I will trouble you with my unwelcome attentions no more.'

She regretted her impulse to put him straight, as soon as she saw the pain in his eyes. She had never intended to hurt him. Oh, blow her stupid pride. It was not worth defending if doing so wounded him.

'Your attentions are not unwelcome,' she hastily re-assured him. 'And of course I will marry you. It was just the way you put it…'

He got to his feet, looking down at her with an expression so fierce she felt almost afraid of him.

'You must not expect honeyed words, or any insincere flattery from me, Miss Gillies. I may not have put my proposal with any great eloquence, but at least you know exactly what it is I am offering. I am offering you financial security, a chance at a good, comfortable future. You are about to marry a man who has been a soldier all his adult life. A man who has fought hard and lived rough. I am not going to spout some silly romantic nonsense to try to deceive you into expecting what I cannot give.'

She blinked in astonishment. Hurt tears sprung to her eyes. Had any woman ever received such an insulting proposal or had her acceptance met with such a stinging rebuke? If she had a grain of sense, she would tell him what he could do with his proposal, and walk away.

But then she would never see him again.

She would become a teacher, just as she had planned, but with the knowledge that, had she had more courage, she could have been Captain Fawley's wife.

She could have endured that lonely life of drudgery, had he never proposed to her. But now, such a future would be unbearable.

A cold hand seemed to reach into her bowels, and twist them into a knot as another horrible thought occurred to her. Seeing the ruthless way he had tried to bludgeon her into a marriage he was convinced she could not want, was he not bound to bully some other hapless female into taking him on, so that he could get at his inheritance? She could not deceive herself into thinking she was anything more to him than the first on a list of prospective wives, drawn from the pool of available females in desperate straits.

'I do not expect anything from you,' she said despondently. How could she have forgotten, even for a second, that he was in love with Susannah? She might have fanciful visions of creating a happy family with the man she loved, but as far as he was concerned, she could be any female.

A means to an end.

Chapter Four

A sense of elation swept over him, so strong that it made him almost dizzy. Vengeance, for all of it, was almost within his grasp! He could not believe it had been so easy. He had all those fools to thank—the fools who had made this lovely girl believe no man could want her.

He sank down on to the chair next to her, and would have seized her hand in gratitude, had he not been aware that she saw acceptance of his proposal as the lesser of two evils. Poverty and drudgery on the one hand, or marriage to a man no other woman could stomach on the other. What was it she had murmured, tears in her eyes? The devil or the deep blue sea!

So what if she felt she had made a bargain with the devil? She would soon learn that though he might not be the kind of husband most girls dreamed of, she would most definitely enjoy the comfortable lifestyle marrying him would bring her. From what he had been able to glean from his brief visit to the lawyers, to verify exactly what he needed to do to inherit, the old woman had left a tidy sum of money, as well as the property that would become their home.

'Thank you, Miss Gillies. I cannot begin to tell you what this means to me.' He almost winced at his own choice of words. He had been deliberately economical with the facts. For he never wanted her to discover that he had taken advantage of her vulnerability in order to exact revenge on a Lampton. Such knowledge was bound to chafe at her tender conscience.

He had suspected, before he came to put his proposal to her, that she would refuse him outright if she knew that marrying him would be tantamount to ruining another person's future. She seemed capable of putting everyone's happiness before her own. Look at how pleased she had been to observe Susannah's success. She had displayed no trace of envy, though Susannah had totally eclipsed her more understated beauty, denying her a chance to attract her own suitors. And she had been pleased that the London Season, which was clearly sapping her strength, was helping her mother to get over her grief.

No, he had no intention of burdening her with the knowledge that he was determined to deprive Lampton of a fortune the man had always regarded as his.

But he had to secure it swiftly. Lampton was bound to take steps to prevent him marrying if he got wind of it.

'We must marry at once.'

'Must we?' she replied, in bewilderment.

'Yes, for if I do not fulfil the terms of the will, within a specified time, I may lose out on the inheritance altogether.'

'Oh,' was all she said, but he could hear acceptance in her tone. Relieved to have surmounted yet another hurdle, he braced himself for her objections when he stipulated, 'And I must insist that we send no announcement to the papers until after the ceremony. Nor tell anyone who is not directly involved either when, or where, it is to take place.'

She looked at him with a troubled frown. 'You want me to marry you in secret?' She shook her head. 'No…that would be…quite repugnant to me.' To marry in secret, as though there was something to be ashamed of…it did not bear thinking about.

'It seems so underhanded,' she persisted.

'I know I am asking a great deal of you. But, please, look at it from my point of view.'

Sometimes, a battle had to be fought with subtlety, using whatever stratagems necessary to outwit the enemy. He was not exactly lying to Deborah. Only throwing a little dust in her eyes. It was no worse than lying in ambush for an enemy who had superior numbers, rather than meeting him on open ground, where defeat would have been inevitable.

'I do not want there to be any more witnesses to our wedding than are absolutely necessary.' That much was the literal truth. But then, relying on her sympathetic nature, he added, 'Do you think I enjoy having people stare at me? Wondering what on earth I had to do to induce a beauty like you into taking on a wreck like me?'

'Beauty?' she gasped indignantly. 'You just said that you were not going to spout silly romantic nonsense! So don't resort to insincere flattery just to get your own way. I would much rather you kept to the plain speaking you say you pride yourself on.'

'Miss Gillies, I am being perfectly sincere. You posses an inner beauty that any man with an ounce of sense—'

'Oh, inner beauty,' she snorted in derision. That was how a man always tried to cajole a plain girl into doing his bidding. Well, he would soon find out that she was not as biddable as all that. She must tell him she simply could not act in a way she felt was morally reprehensible.

She took a deep breath.

'I refuse to keep this news from my mother, or marry without her to attend me….'

'Well, naturally,' he said, taking the wind out of her sails. 'Miss Gillies, I am not asking you to enter into a secret marriage. Only a very private one. There will be nothing havey-cavey about it. I shall be asking my brother to stand up with me. And once the ceremony is over and we are on our way to our new home, I will be only too pleased to advertise the fact.'

That did not sound too unreasonable, she supposed.

'However, I would rather you did not tell your mother that we are to marry, until you are in the coach and on the way to the ceremony.'

Deborah blinked.

'It is the only way to be sure she does not let slip what is about to take place. She is clearly very fond of Miss Hullworthy. Would she be able, do you suppose, to keep the news of your marriage from her? Would she be able to keep it from anyone? Most mothers are so pleased to know their daughters are to wed, they cannot keep a still tongue in their head.'

Deborah chewed on her lower lip as she pondered this aspect of the case. Her mother would indeed be thrilled to hear she was getting married, doubly so that it was to Captain Fawley. And if she knew that he planned to take her into the marital home, and care for her in her old age, nothing would keep her from flinging herself on his neck and weeping all over him, before she proudly announced to all her cronies what a splendid son-in-law she had managed to net.

And as for keeping the news from Susannah… She sighed. Captain Fawley would not want her to be present at the ceremony that represented a final farewell to the woman he loved. In fact, if she was honest with herself, having Susannah there would ruin the event for her, as well. It was bad enough knowing she was a poor second-best, without having her husband's first choice there in person to remind her what a second-rate marriage he was embarking upon.

She hated subterfuge, or anything that smacked of dishonesty in any form, yet refraining from telling her friend her news would certainly save both Captain Fawley, and herself, some pain.

'How long would you expect me to keep our engage-ment from my mother?'

She could not miss the flare of triumph that lit his eyes as he recognised her capitulation to his terms.

'Now that I have your promise, I can obtain the special licence required to marry without the need for banns. We will have to meet with the lawyers who are acting as executors of the will of which I am a benefi-ciary too. It is no use marrying without their prior knowledge and agreement. Providing all goes well, the ceremony itself can take place the day after tomorrow. We shall leave town immediately after the ceremony. Walton can send the notice to the *Morning Post* once we are safely out of the way.'

'Just a minute—what will happen if the lawyers do not give their agreement?'

'I am sure they will. You have no need to worry. I did not mean to imply they might not approve you. I just need to make sure I fulfil all the terms to the letter, so that nobody may contest my claim.'

'Contest your claim? Is that likely?'

What would happen to her, if she did not fulfil the requirements of this will? Or if someone contested his claim? He had only proposed because he wanted to inherit this property. He would have no use for her at all if the lawyers decided she was not fit for some reason. She went cold inside. What would he do in such an event? Take her home and wash his hands of her? Could he be so ungallant?

Was that why he had sworn her to secrecy? So that she would not be able to complain that he had proposed and then jilted her? For she had too much pride to admit to another living soul that she had done something so improper as entering into a secret engagement. Suddenly, she felt very alone, and very afraid.

But then, to her surprise, Captain Fawley reached out and placed his hand over hers as she twisted them together in her lap.

'I know it will not be easy for you to creep out of the house, without your mother's knowledge.'

She had not even considered the practical aspects of attending an appointment at the lawyers' office without her mother's knowledge until that moment. Now she had another worry to add to those already tormenting her!

'But only think how happy she will be when she finds out it was all in a good cause,' he cajoled her. 'And you will not have to keep her from our plans for more than a day, if all goes well.'

If all went well. But would it? It would be the longest day of her life. Lying to her mother, dreading that something might occur to prevent the wedding taking place....

'Trust me,' he said, giving her hands a little squeeze. 'I will arrange everything.'

Trust him? Oh, how she wished she could!

'It is only one day, Miss Gillies. I am sure you have the courage to endure just one day. You have gone through far worse since your father died, and emerged unscathed.'

She blinked up at him. He had said he would never resort to honeyed words, and yet here he was uttering another compliment. Did he mean it? He must do, for he had declared he could only speak the plain truth. He must think she had fortitude.

Yes, this was an aspect of that dratted inner beauty he had claimed to admire.

'Just one day.' She sighed. It would not seem all that much to him, for he did not know that she loved him. He assumed her torment would end, after that one day, whatever the outcome.

She looked up into his face, wondering whether this was the moment to tell him the truth. Surely he would not abandon her, even if she did not pass the examination of his lawyers, if she told him she loved him. He could not be so cruel….

But if she pressured him into keeping to his vow to marry her, how would they live? They would not have a feather to fly with. Every time a bill landed on their doorstep, he would resent her for preventing him from marrying a woman who would have enabled him to inherit that property.

Better for her to become a lonely, desiccated teacher, and know that at least she had not robbed him of his happiness, than to endure his hatred.

She would have to keep her feelings for him to herself then, until after they were married.

'It will only be for a day,' she said again, returning the pressure of his hand. Even if it meant a lifetime of misery for her, she would not let him down. Was that not what love meant? Putting the beloved's happiness before one's own?

'You will not regret it,' he declared fervently.

But she was regretting it even before she got back to the house. Her mother was bound to want to know what had passed between them in the garden. What was she to tell her?

In the event, she told her mother as much of the truth as she felt she could, without betraying Captain Fawley's confidence.

'He spoke to me on a…on a financial matter, Mother,' she said, fiddling with one of the tiebacks of the drawing-room curtains. 'And he asked me to keep the matter in confidence.'

'A financial matter…' Mrs Gillies frowned. 'Not a personal matter?'

'Mother, I promised not to speak about it until…until he gave me leave.'

Seeing how red her daughter's face was turning, Mrs Gillies let the matter drop.

Deborah was glad, for once, when Susannah returned and filled the room with an endless stream of chatter, which required very little input from anyone else. Her mother had not questioned her further, but kept darting her troubled looks, and taking a breath, as though she was about to speak. Then she would shake her head, and purse her lips, as Deborah felt her cheeks grow red at the prospect of returning another evasive answer. Susannah was a welcome buffer from the tension that steadily mounted all afternoon.

Both mother and daughter concentrated on conversing with her, rather than each other, during their outing to the theatre that night. But as the evening dragged interminably on, Deborah began to resent the situation Captain Fawley had placed her in. It was all very well for him to say she would not have to deceive her mother for more than one day, but while his day would be filled with activity, dashing about getting the licence and arranging appointments with lawyers and vicars, she would have nothing to do but count the minutes, while her mother kept looking at her with those mildly disapproving eyes until she would feel she was guilty of some heinous crime.

It was a relief to get into bed, where she did not have

to encounter her mother's reproachful looks any more. But by then she was too wound up to sleep. She thumped her pillows, and threw off the covers, furious at his cruelty in placing her in this untenable position. But it was not much later that she sat up, shivering in the chill night air, and dragged the covers back over her shoulders. The conviction that it would all come to nothing filled her with a cold sense of dread. Then she sank back into her pillows, her eyes searching the shadowy alcoves of her room. How on earth was it possible to love him, yet resent his behaviour with such ferocity, all at the same time?

By the time morning came, she felt almost wretched enough to declare she intended to stay in bed. She did not think she could cope with either her mother's suspicious looks or Susannah's self-centred oblivion to her distress.

But her mother took her hand when she tried to evade the social obligations of the day, saying in a firm voice, 'It will be much better if you got up, and kept busy, my dear. Distract your mind from...whatever it is that ails it. How long, by the way, did you promise to keep Captain Fawley's confidence?'

'Just for today, Mother,' Deborah replied, a little uneasy that her mother had so perceptively linked her distress to the conversation she'd had with Captain Fawley. 'By tomorrow, I should be able to...'

'Give him an answer.' Mrs Gillies nodded. 'He has a deal of pride, that young man.' She leaned down and kissed her daughter on the forehead. 'But my advice to you is to carry on as best you can, as though you did not have...a decision to make. If he has asked you to keep the matter confidential, you must act as though you were not considering…umm…whatever it was you discussed so intently in the garden yesterday.'

Deborah could not believe her mother had so nearly guessed at the truth. From her knowing smile and meaningful nods, she made it obvious she thought Captain Fawley had proposed to her, and was giving her time to consider her answer. She sat up straight, in alarm.

'Mother, you won't speak of this to anyone else, will you?'

'Of course not! Especially if you decide not to… umm…that is, I am sure you would not wish it to be known that you… And naturally, he will not want anyone knowing that you would not… No, no! Far better to keep the whole thing under wraps, until you have decided you will… I mean, when we may speak freely, without risk of hurting anyone's pride.'

Deborah felt much better, knowing that her mother had an inkling of what was in the air. It would be much easier to tell her the whole once they were on the way to her wedding than if she had to spring it on her out of the blue.

It would be easier to make some excuse to go out to the lawyer's too. She would assume she would be meeting Captain Fawley secretly, in order to give him an answer.

She rose early in the morning, after another restless night, wondering how he would manage to communicate with her. He could hardly come to fetch her himself. They could not just go out, without a chaperon of any sort. But she could not imagine how she was expected to find the lawyer's office unless he sent her a message. Her stomach roiled at the thought he would send her a letter, which she would have to somehow keep from the curiosity of both her mother and Susannah. They normally read all the post over the breakfast plates, discussing the various invitations they received, or comparing news from home. She shook her head, a nagging pain building across her forehead, which, she realised, had been ridged with worry almost since the moment he had made his proposal.

But in the event, Captain Fawley had, as he had promised, arranged things so she did not have to tell any lies at all. They had scarcely risen from the breakfast table, when the butler strode into the room, looking full of self-importance.

'The Countess of Walton is here, Miss Gillies,' he said, handing her a card. 'I have shown her into the front parlour.'

All three ladies gasped at the unexpected honour of having such a grand person visit them, especially at such an unsocial hour.

'Go on, go on,' her mother urged her, making shooing motions with her hands. 'Do not keep her ladyship waiting. We will join you as soon as we have…' She trailed off, straightening her cap as Susannah scurried to the mirror, where she patted her curls and tugged at the neckline of her gown.

'Oh, no, is that a smear of butter on my dress?' Deborah heard her saying, as she followed the butler from the room. 'I had better go and change!'

'Ah! Miss Deborah!' the Countess greeted her incorrectly, in a decidedly French accent, as soon as she entered the room.

Deborah had been introduced to the Countess at Lord Lensborough's ball, and had spent a few minutes trying in vain to think of some topic of conversation that might interest the diminutive and rather vague-looking woman. She had learned later, from her mother, that the Countess was generally considered something of a failure, socially speaking, although the universally poor opinion of the Earl's choice of bride had mellowed somewhat when she had eventually fallen pregnant.

'Alone too!' she beamed, leaping to her feet, and taking Deborah's hands to pull her down on to the sofa next to her. 'This is good! For I come from Robert, to bear you to him who is waiting at the office of his lawyers. He has told me how I must keep this a secret, and how I am to say to your mother that we are to go shopping, that I admired the gown I saw you wearing at Lensborough's ball, or some such piece of nonsense. As though anyone would believe I would wish to spend the day shopping when I am this size!' She indicated her clearly visible pregnancy with a rueful moue. 'But there, that is Robert for you!'

The countess was dressed in layers of pink muslin, which draped over, and emphasised, the roundness of her tummy. Together with her chirruping voice and her fluttery hand movements, she put Deborah in mind of a chaffinch hopping about her drawing room. This impression was reinforced when her mother entered the room, and Lady Walton briskly folded those hands in her lap, regarding the newcomer with her head tilted to one side.

'Mrs Gillies?' she enquired without preamble. 'You do not mind that I borrow your daughter for the morning to go shopping? It is a fancy of mine.' She checked, an expression of inspiration coming to her face. 'Yes! For we women who are *enceinte*, we get these fancies, you know. Nothing will do, but to have the delightful Miss Gillies to come shopping with me this morning. We met at Lord Lensborough's ball. I have very few friends in London,' she finished, with an abstracted air. 'Except for Robert, of course, who is quite like a brother to me. I mean to say, Captain Fawley,' she explained, at the mystified look Mrs Gillies gave her.

Deborah decided she would have to get the woman out of the house before she blurted out something that would give the game away. How could Captain Fawley have entrusted such a delicate mission to such a scatterbrained creature as this? She dashed upstairs, gathered her coat and bonnet, almost tripping on the hall carpet in her haste to get back to the drawing room.

Both women heaved a sigh of relief when the door of the Walton carriage shut behind them, and they set out on their mission.

'Oh, this is so exciting!' Lady Walton trilled, settling herself into a corner and regarding Deborah out of a pair of black, beady eyes. 'To think that I should be able to help Robert to outwit that vile Lampton, at last!' She checked herself, going a little pink in the cheeks when Deborah looked at her in astonishment.

'Lampton? What has Lampton got to do with this?'

'Oh, dear, now I have ruined everything. Robert will

be so cross with me. I promised I would not spill any beans and now I have done it before we even get to see the men who control his fortune. Miss Gillies…' she leaned forward, her face creased with distress '…please tell me that you will not turn him down, now that you know he has done what you must think reprehensible.'

Deborah felt a strange sensation in her chest, as though someone was squeezing her there, making it hard to breathe. 'Reprehensible?' she echoed. 'I do not know what you mean. What has Captain Fawley done?'

'He has done nothing! It is that vile worm of a pig, Percy Lampton, who has tried to steal everything from him. Please, if you care anything for him at all, do not side with his enemies today. From much he has recovered in the past, but not this, I think. It has been so hard for him to summon the courage to ask a woman even to dance with him, thinking himself so ugly, but to beg for your hand… You cannot think what courage he had to summon to approach you.'

She took Deborah's hands between her own. 'You see beyond the scars, to his heart, do you not? You have not just agreed to marry him because you wish to have a big house in the country and not to have to become a governess? I would not have agreed to take part in this deception if I did not believe you were worthy of him. But I saw how you looked at him at Lensborough's ball. You love him, don't you? Please tell me I have not this all wrong?'

'Y-yes, I love him,' Deborah breathed, tugging her hands out of the Countess's grip. 'But I don't understand….'

'You don't need to understand! Only love him. Trust him! Men...they do the foolish things sometimes, because they think to protect us. Wrong things, perhaps. But Robert will be so good a husband to you. I know it! He is so grateful that you give him this chance....'

'I don't want his gratitude!' Deborah snapped. The funny feeling in her chest was developing into a burning pain. She had felt from the outset that there was some-thing not right about all the secrecy Captain Fawley had insisted on. Now the Countess had confirmed that it was not just his sensitivity to the way he looked that had made him insist the wedding should be held in secret.

But the worst thing of all was knowing that he had taken this ninny completely into his confidence, even to telling her all about her plans to become a governess, when he had kept her in the dark. It had been bad enough when she had thought she came in a poor second to Susannah. Now she had to accept she did not even come in second. This woman, his sister-in-law, stood closer to him than she did.

She blanked out the Countess's persistent chirruping as the coach bore them into the City, as she tried to make some sense out of what she had let slip the moment they had got into the coach. She remembered the look of contempt Captain Fawley had directed at Percy Lampton the first time he had seen him with Susannah. And the malicious smile Lampton had returned. At the time, she had thought it was odd, but now she saw it was the look of two long-standing adversaries. She recalled the way Lampton had ridden up to them in Hyde Park, requesting an introduction, as though the meeting was purely accidental. She remembered her instant distrust of his charm. And felt certain that he was not merely another in Susannah's long line of conquests. Could his pursuit of her been deliberately calculated for the sole purpose of preventing Captain Fawley from marrying her, and thus gaining his inheritance?

She alighted from the carriage in a daze. Captain Fawley was waiting for her on the steps of a functional building in a narrow, though cleanly swept, side street. He looked tense.

As well he might. He was using her as a weapon in his ongoing struggle with the Lamptons in general, and Percy Lampton in particular.

And it hurt.

'Thank you for coming,' he said, limping forward to offer her his arm. 'I was beginning to think my ruse would not work. Heloise is such a pea goose. A dear little pea goose, but sadly featherbrained.'

'I heard that, you ungrateful beast!' Lady Walton put her head out of the carriage window to inform him, her eyes full of laughter. 'Now you will have to wonder if I will return, in Walton's carriage, to take your Miss Gillies home, or if I will take offence and wash my hands of you once and for all!'

'You wouldn't do anything so hard-hearted,' he returned, with a fond smile. 'Besides, you will be burning with curiosity to discover how this interview turned out.'

'Pig!' she answered, slamming the window and thumping with her parasol on the roof to indicate the driver should set off.

Could she really believe the Countess would connive at doing something that was really reprehensible? Though her words had set alarm bells ringing, the insouciant way she had driven off, after laughing and joking with Robert, made it sound as though she were participating in some kind of prank, at the very worst.

She shook her head, too hurt and bewildered to do more than follow meekly where Robert led her, which was into a narrow hallway and up a wooden staircase to the cramped office of the lawyers, Kenridge and Hopedale.

As they entered the room, two men looked up from behind a desk almost obliterated by the mounds of papers and files stacked upon it. One, a kindly-faced, stout gentleman, got to his feet, indicating that she should take the ladder-backed chair set out for the convenience of his clients. As Captain Fawley took his place directly behind her, the other lawyer scowled at them over the top of a pair of half-moon spectacles.

'Now, then, Miss...Gillies, is it not?' the cherubic lawyer muttered, shuffling a sheaf of papers in front of him. 'We just need to ask you a few questions.'

She felt Captain Fawley place his hand upon her shoulder, as though offering her reassurance. She felt an almost overwhelming urge to shake it off. Why had he not been open with her about his real motive for wishing to get married? Could he imagine for one second that she would side with the family who had wronged him even before he was born? She could not believe a man as starchy as the Earl of Walton would acknowledge a man as his brother, if there was even a hint he might be illegitimate. The Lamptons must have deliberately robbed Captain Fawley's mother, and him, of what should have been theirs. Now Percy Lampton seemed to be trying to do the same thing, all over again!

'We only need to know that she is of age, and entering into marriage with Captain Fawley freely,' the acid-faced lawyer interrupted. 'Are you?' he shot at her.

But before she could answer in the affirmative, the kindly lawyer shook his head. 'No, no, we must establish not only the legality, but also the suitability of this union. The marriage must be watertight. We do not want the Lamptons thinking they might have any possible grounds for contesting our decision to wind up the trust. If she does not come from an impeccable background, they might—'

'Codswallop!' the thin lawyer snapped. 'It is quite clear that Euphemia Lampton intended all her estate to go to this young man. Her nephew never even got a mention in the original will. Not even to a keepsake. You and I both know that she only added the codicil under duress.'

Something like a cold dart shot through Deborah at the use of the word *nephew*. Nephew to a Lampton? Could this other legatee mentioned in a codicil be…Percy Lampton? Was this the inheritance he had been fully expecting to come into? If so, what Captain Fawley was doing was worse than she had imagined. Not only was he using her to get his hands on this legacy, but it was a property that morally belonged to somebody else. Or at least…she chewed at her lower lip… Lampton had always assumed it belonged to him. So he would feel as though he was being robbed. Now she felt like an accessory to a crime.

The plump lawyer's cheeks went a little pink. 'Now, now, we do not need to mention specifics in front of this young lady….'

'Why not? You are practically demanding she provide references!'

The plump lawyer lost his cherubic look, his brows drawing down in an angry V as he swivelled to face his partner. 'Only in order to satisfy a legal point. Normally it *is* preferable for a property to go to a blood relation than somebody who has no connection with the testator.'

'The connection is there. You heard what Miss Lampton told us when we drew up the original will—'

'Excuse me,' Deborah said, rising to her feet, her pulse tumultuous with agitation. 'But I am quite able to vouch for my suitability to marry any man I choose,' she said, addressing the plump lawyer. 'My mother is granddaughter to the Earl of Plymstock, through the female line. You may check her lineage in *Collin's Peerage*. My father was a Gillies of Hertfordshire. Again, check away as meticulously as you please. Third son of Reginald and Lucinda Gillies, of Upshott. Not perhaps a noble family, but old.'

She drew in an indignant breath. Not only had Captain Fawley been dishonest in the manner of his proposal, but he had exposed her to this piece of impertinence!

'You may also investigate as long as you please, and you will discover I have *never* done anything that would give *anyone* any justification for claiming I was not completely respectable. My father was a man of the cloth. As his child, he taught me how important it was not to let him down by so much as an unseemly gesture.

Go and inquire in the town of Lower Wakering, where I grew up. You will not find anybody who could cast an aspersion on my moral rectitude. And as for the other matter, yes, I am of age! At my last prayers, in fact,' she said, her face twisting with bitterness as she recalled that it was precisely this fact Captain Fawley had used to lure her into what he thought was her last chance of ever marrying. 'And do I marry Captain Fawley of my own free will?'

She whirled round to glare at him. She felt humiliated, used, deceived. He held her regard without the slightest sign of guilt or remorse. There was only what might have been interpreted as a slightly mocking challenge in his eyes.

Trust him, the Countess had urged her. Do not side with his enemies.

She swallowed. Furious as she was with him, right at this moment, could she really back out of this horrible tangle, having come this far? Would he not see it as a betrayal, far worse than anything that had been done to him to date? He would regard her as an enemy. He would hate her.

Shaking with impotent fury, she turned back to the lawyers, who were awaiting her answer with quills poised.

'Yes,' she croaked, her voice clogged with emotion. She cleared her throat. 'If I do not marry him, I shall not marry anyone,' she declared firmly.

Then, her eyes full of humiliated tears, she whirled from the room and stumbled down the stairs into the dusty street. Leaning against the wall, her forehead grinding into the brickwork, she fought to regain her composure.

What was she doing, allying herself to a man who could deceive her, use her without regard for her feelings? Condemning herself to a lifetime of hurt, that was what!

'Miss Gillies!' She blinked as the Walton coach drew up at the kerb, and the countess leaned out, her face puckered with concern.

'Miss Gillies!' She heard another voice, a masculine voice, calling her from within the lawyer's offices. Captain Fawley must be making his way down the stairs, of necessity slowly and carefully.

A footman jumped down from the box and opened the carriage door for her. She strode across the pavement and got in.

'Where is Robert?' the Countess asked, peering behind her.

'I don't think we ought to be seen together, do you?' Deborah said, on a flash of inspiration. 'Wouldn't want to give the game away!' she finished bitterly.

The Countess's face lit up. Clapping her hands, she gave the order for the coach to set off.

Just as Robert emerged from the doorway, his face as dark as a thundercloud.

Chapter Five

'Oh, isn't the Countess coming in?' Susannah wailed in disappointment as the Walton carriage pulled away the moment Deborah had entered her front door. 'I was so hoping to meet her. What is she like? Where did you go? You have been an age, and I am dying with curiosity!'

'She is rather like a small, determined whirlwind,' Deborah answered, thinking it typical of Susannah to display that unfamiliar emotion on a day she was least willing to satisfy it. 'She whisked me off in her coach without waiting for a proper introduction to you both. I am so sorry,' she said, joining her mother and Susannah in the front parlour, where they were partaking of a light nuncheon. 'But I did not like to keep her ladyship waiting….'

'That is quite all right, my dear,' Mrs Gillies replied, pouring her a cup of tea. 'Since she is French, we cannot expect the same standards in her manners as if she had been brought up properly, can we?'

'I have been consumed with jealousy all morning!'

said Susannah, heaping ham on to the plate in Deborah's place setting.

'Jealous? You?' she gasped, taking her seat at table.

'Yes! It is one thing having men dangling after one. But what really gets one into society is to make a friend of some influential or aristocratic female.' She placed a slice of bread and butter to Deborah's plate, adding, 'I don't blame you for dropping everything and dashing off after her. If she takes you up, you will be made.'

'Oh, I don't know,' Mrs Gillies interposed. 'She is not exactly a leader of fashion. And she will not be much use to Deborah after another month or so anyway, since she is increasing.'

Deborah paused in the act of lifting a slice of ham to her lips, a troubled frown knotting her brow.

'One does not just make friends that can be of use, surely!' she protested. She had never liked this side of Susannah's nature, and was appalled to hear her mother speaking of connections in similar terms.

'But it is always a point to take into consideration,' said Susannah, popping a slice of tomato into her mouth. 'You are too unworldly for your own good, sometimes.'

'Unless…she may be looking for a companion to go with her, when she has to return to her country estate for the lying in,' Mrs Gillies pondered. 'Her husband is bound to insist his heir is born at Wycke, and I have heard that she detests the place. She grew up in Paris, you see, in such exciting times, and finds the countryside tedious.'

'Oh!' cried Susannah. 'Perhaps, if she does take a fancy to you, she will take you with her, to keep her amused.'

'Like a pet monkey,' Deborah remarked sourly.

Susannah began to giggle.

'I can just see you in a little knitted c-cap, with a Spanish j-jacket, like the one we saw dancing in the park that day....'

Her mother's mouth, too, twitched with amusement and from then on, by applying a little ingenuity, Deborah was able to ensure that the conversation never returned to exactly how she had spent her morning. By the time they rose from the table, her mother was ready to take her afternoon nap, and Susannah declared she simply had to write to her parents, since she had not done so for two days.

Deborah escaped to her room with a feeling of profound relief.

It did not last long.

Once she was on her own, there was nothing to prevent her from dwelling on what a dreadful situation she had got herself into. She had known it would be quite wrong to turn Captain Fawley down in the lawyer's office, while she was so angry with him. She needed to consider the situation rather more dispassionately, and make the decision which would affect her whole future, with a clear head. Concentrating her mind on fielding Susannah's curiosity had certainly helped her to calm down somewhat, but now she was alone, and free to think as she would, all her doubts and anxieties came flooding back with a vengeance.

Could she really marry a man who showed so little regard for her, who was embroiling her in some scheme about which she had the deepest suspicions?

She sank on her bedside chair, her head in her hands.

No, the real question was, could she live with herself if she spurned him? It hardly mattered what had motivated him to ask for her hand, even though she now had some evidence to suggest he was using her as an unwitting accomplice in snatching a legacy from some person. Some person that she refused to assume was Percy Lampton. That would be too dreadful a coincidence.

Oh, how she wished she had not promised to keep the whole matter from her mother! She would have known all about the family connections, and been able to give a name to the poor wretch who was expecting to inherit the property she and Captain Fawley were about to…steal from him. It amounted to that!

Though…the cross-looking lawyer had said that the lady who had died had wanted everything to go to Captain Fawley to begin with. So she was not stealing anything from anybody. She was only helping to fulfil the dying wishes of a poor elderly lady with no children of her own….

She sat up, pushing a stray wisp of hair from her forehead. She had only a few hours to make her mind up about what she should do. During the carriage ride home, Lady Walton had informed her that the marriage was going to take place that very evening, at six of the clock, in the library of Walton House.

While everyone who aspired to be fashionable was promenading round Hyde Park, she would be sneaking into a private room, to take part in a clandestine marriage, which would rob some other poor fellow of a substantial inheritance.

It was morally repugnant!

She got to her feet and paced to the window.

Yet how could she back out? If she refused to go along with Captain Fawley's plan, *he* would be the poor fellow who had his inheritance snatched from his grasp. She paced back to the chair.

Perhaps the issue was not so bad as she was imagining. Lady Walton had said she should trust Robert.

Robert. Hot jealousy had her pacing back to the window, her fists clenched at her side. Lady Walton called him Robert. She had not even known it was his given name, until she had prattled on about all the confidences he had shared with her! It would serve him right if she did jilt him!

No, no, it wouldn't, she gasped, searing pain almost doubling her over as she thought of the effect such an act would have upon him. Jilting him would wound him irreparably. How hard it had been, Lady Walton had said, for him to beg a woman for a dance, let alone for her hand in marriage! He would not understand why she had refused him. He would think it was because he was too deformed, even for a woman as desperate as her, to marry!

She could not do it to him.

She did not want to hurt anyone.

She paced back to the chair, sat down and wrapped her arms round her waist. Since somebody was clearly going to lose out because of the actions she took today, she would rather it was this faceless, nameless nephew, than Captain Fawley.

And even if the other legatee of the will turned out to be Percy Lampton, as she suspected…well, she had never liked him. In fact, she wouldn't put it past him to have sought Susannah out on purpose to prevent things from progressing to the point where Captain Fawley might have proposed to her. He had already lived with the unnecessary stigma of illegitimacy all his life because of the Lamptons' lies! And now, they were trying to prevent him from inheriting his own fortune.

She was not going to side with them. She was on Captain Fawley's side, no matter what!

Getting to her feet, she stomped to the wardrobe and yanked open its doors. Now, what kind of dress did she have that would be suitable for taking part in a clandestine wedding?

No sooner had Susannah set out for her ride round Hyde Park in Percy Lampton's high-perch phaeton, than Deborah urged her mother to get her bonnet and pelisse on.

'The Countess is returning for us both,' she explained. 'She is going to take us to Walton House....'

'And she did not want to include Susannah in the invitation?' Mrs Gillies frowned. 'Is her husband so high in the instep that he will not admit someone from her background into his home? I do not think I wish to encourage you in this friendship, if that is the case.'

'No, no, Mother, that is not it at all. Only please hurry to get ready, and I shall explain it all on the way.' She cast a significant look in the direction of the butler who came with the house, and Mrs Gillies subsided at once.

They waited for the Countess to arrive in tense silence. When the Walton town coach finally drew up outside their door, Deborah was surprised by a sharp pain that shot across the back of her hand as she leapt to her feet. Looking down, she saw she had been twisting the strings of her reticule so tightly they were cutting through her gloves into her flesh.

Lady Walton beamed at them as they scrambled into the coach before her footman even had time to climb their front steps and knock on the door.

'Oh, I am so glad you have decided after all to come! Robert has been in the state most terrible since this morning after that he came home from the lawyers. He said you were so cross, you would not go through with it. But I knew you would come! For you love him enough to forgive him anything, is that not so?'

She turned to Mrs Gillies, who was regarding her with frank amazement.

'Ah, you have not told your mother yet? But, no, since that silly girl who could not see how wonderful Robert is has only just left the house, I suppose you have not had a chance.'

'Er…Mother…' Deborah began.

Mrs Gillies made a dismissive sound as she dived into her reticule for a handkerchief. 'You have decided to marry Captain Fawley, after all. I am happy for you,' she said, blowing her nose, 'if you are happy?'

'Thank you, Mother,' Deborah fudged, unwilling to admit that right at that moment, she was not at all sure she was going to be happy marrying a man who had so clearly demonstrated how little he valued anything about her, except as a name on a piece of paper.

'I take it we are going to meet with the family and

discuss settlements?' Mrs Gillies got out, stuffing her crumpled handkerchief back into her reticule. 'Though, really, this sort of thing should be done through a man of business. I am sure Mr Hullworthy would be only too happy to act for you, if you applied to him.'

Deborah laid her hand firmly on her mother's sleeve. 'There will be no need for that. We went to see some lawyers this morning. We are getting married today. Now. In the library at Walton House.'

'But…without a man of business to see to the settlements? Really, Deborah, dear…'

'Mother, I have no dowry, so what good would a lawyer do me?'

'But you cannot have considered what a fragile thing life is. What if he dies and leaves you widowed? He has hardly a penny to his name. Your portion might be so slender that—'

'Mother, you have no need to worry. I told you that we discussed the financial side of things on Tuesday afternoon, did I not? Once I marry Captain Fawley, he will qualify for a substantial property. We will be able to live very comfortably. Indeed, he has even agreed that, should you wish it, you may come and live with us….'

'Oh, the dear boy!' Mrs Gillies cried, digging her handkerchief out of her reticule once again. 'So long as it is not entailed, this property?' she said sharply, crushing the damp piece of lace between her arthritic fingers.

Deborah saw that she had taken a great deal on trust. Far too much. She had no idea what kind of allowance Captain Fawley was likely to settle on her, nor how she would fare should she indeed be widowed. Not bringing in some man of business to negotiate all these points had been extremely foolish of her. But she was not about to burden her mother with her doubts.

'I am sure there is no need to worry about anything, Mother. We can trust Captain Fawley to do the right thing.' She only wished she could have felt the conviction she tried to put into her words. She was almost positive he was not doing the right thing, in marrying her secretly this afternoon.

Lady Walton, who had been watching them both, her beady eyes flicking from one to the other as she followed the conversation, clapped her hands, beaming at Deborah.

'Of course you may trust Robert! He may not have the polished manners of so many of the men who think themselves so attractive, but he has what they have not. The integrity. Yes, and the courage to fight for what is rightfully his!'

To fight for what was rightfully his. Yes, Deborah mused, settling back into the luxuriously soft leather squabs, that was what he was doing this afternoon. Lady Walton clearly knew all the details in regard to this inheritance, and regarded it as a just fight.

Perhaps it was understandable that he had not taken her fully into his confidence. He did not know her all that well. Besides, what was it Lady Walton had blurted out, earlier, on the way to visit the lawyers? That men sometimes did not explain why they were acting in a way that might be interpreted as a bit questionable, in an attempt to protect their women. She certainly had moral qualms about what she was doing. Had he been trying to protect her from going into a questionable situation, to spare her conscience?

A warm glow began to melt the knot of ice that her insides had become over the past few days. His woman. She was Captain Fawley's woman. Of course he was attempting to shield her from anxiety. Of course he would provide generously for her. For today, by marrying him, she was going to stand shoulder to shoulder with him in his fight, though he had deliberately kept her ignorant of the details.

By the time they reached Walton House, Deborah was glowing with the kind of happiness any bride might display on her wedding day. Her mother was still dabbing at her eyes as they mounted the front steps, just as the mother of a bride should do. When they went into the hall, one footman produced a fresh handkerchief for her mother, while a second presented her with a posy of roses and honeysuckle. Her heart almost stopped. They had been sitting in an arbour perfumed with roses and honeysuckle when he had proposed to her. He had remembered! Just as he had remembered the colour of the ribbons in her hair the other time he had bought her flowers.

This time, she did bury her face in the blooms, inhaling their scent with a mounting sense of elation. She drifted through the magnificent hallway in a haze of romantic hopes. It seemed like an omen that the bonnet and gloves she had picked out were the exact shade of pink as the centre of the honeysuckle blooms. How could she fail to love Captain Fawley? Even though he did not return her regard, he was perceptive and considerate. She was sure he would do his utmost to be a good husband to her.

Two massive double doors swung open, and she wafted into a library. But she scarcely registered anything about the room, save for the fact that it housed a lot of books. For Captain Fawley was standing in one of the window embrasures, watching her approaching him, and all she wanted to do was fill her eyes with the sight of him, as she had filled her lungs with the fragrance of her wedding bouquet.

He looked drained. But some of the tension that rode his shoulders slackened when he saw her enter the library. With a pang, she realised the way she had flounced out of the lawyers' offices must have contributed to his worries. Hadn't Lady Walton told her he had not been at all sure she would turn up today?

For a second or two they just stood there, looking at each other. Deborah felt so guilty for thinking only of herself, and adding to the lines of care upon his face that only days before she had dreamed of erasing. She could not interpret the expression on his face as he examined her in his turn. If she did not know better, she would think that the initial relief that her arrival had prompted was turning into a look so cynical it was almost akin to disappointment.

The Earl of Walton cleared his throat, breaking the tense silence that had bound them immobile.

The ceremony got under way.

Deborah marvelled that the words in the prayer book described so aptly, yet so poetically, exactly what marriage meant to her. She already loved Captain Fawley, and from that emotion sprang the will to honour and obey him. And, oh, how she longed to offer him comfort and become a companion in whom he would confide. They had already spoken of their plans to raise children. He had vowed she could have an input into their education beyond what most husbands would allow. She knew he did not love her yet. But she would be such a good wife to him—he was bound to grow fond of her eventually, wasn't he?

Though as he began to make his vows, she found herself clutching at the posy increasingly tightly. Captain Fawley sounded so angry, so bitter.

Her foolish romantic dreams evaporated like the morning dew in the first blast of the sun's rays. How could she have forgotten that he was in love with another woman? If it had been Susannah standing here, he would have gazed into her eyes with adoration as he spoke of worshipping her with his body. Instead, he shoved the ring on to Deborah's finger, his jaw working as he paused before declaring he endowed her with all his worldly goods, emphasising to her, at least, that this was all that could have induced him to marry such a poor specimen of womanhood as he considered her to be.

And suddenly she wanted to weep.

They were man and wife. But when Captain Fawley was given the opportunity to kiss the bride, there was an awkward little pause.

Then Lady Walton rushed up to her, gave her an impulsive hug, and said, 'Now you are like a sister to me!

Of all the women Robert could have brought into the family, I am so glad it was you!'

'Yes, welcome to the family, Mrs Fawley,' said the Earl, shaking her solemnly by the hand.

Her mother, just as Deborah had predicted, flung her arms about her new son-in-law's neck, almost overbalancing him in her enthusiasm, crying 'Oh, you dear boy! You dear, dear boy!'

It seemed that the only two people who did not wish to embrace one another were the bride and groom.

A butler, who must have been standing in the background somewhere during the ceremony, began to pour champagne, while Lady Walton tugged Deborah over to a table on which lay a selection of delicacies.

'We cannot linger,' Captain Fawley announced to the room in general. 'We have a long journey, and I wish to use what hours of daylight we have left to get as far from London as I can today.'

The Earl nodded, looking serious as he replied, 'I took the liberty of having a message sent down to the mews as soon as your bride arrived. The carriage should be ready for you by now.' Then in a voice so low only his brother could hear, he added, 'You don't need me to tell you how I shall relish dealing with the aftermath of this day's work.'

'Then, if you have no objection,' Captain Fawley said to Deborah, plucking her untouched glass of champagne from her fingers, 'we will leave at once.'

Deborah could think of plenty of objections. The first rose to her lips before she could prevent herself.

'I did not realise we were to leave town tonight. I have not packed a bag—'

'Oh, but I have!' Lady Walton put in cheerfully. 'Everything you will need for tonight, and a day or two, is already in the coach. Your mother and I can pack the rest of your things and have them sent on to you.'

Once again, he had taken Lady Walton into his plans, leaving her firmly out in the cold. 'I don't even know where we are going!' she protested, as Captain Fawley took her by the arm and propelled her towards the door.

'Our new home,' he grated. 'That is all you need to know.'

'Oh, how romantic!' she heard her mother cry, as he hustled her across the hall and down the front steps.

But she did not feel it was in the least romantic to be dragged away from her wedding breakfast, to who knew where, without even being permitted a proper leave-taking from her mother. 'How do you know what I need to know?' she complained, as he tugged her across the pavement to where a smart post-chaise and four awaited them.

'Do not be difficult,' he replied curtly, as a burly individual with a face like a potato leapt out of the carriage, let down the steps and held the door open for them to get in.

To her surprise, as soon as they were settled inside, the potato-faced man got in with them.

'This is Linney, my man,' said Captain Fawley when she looked the question at him.

She supposed she ought to feel grateful he had bothered to introduce her at all. Not that he bothered to tell Linney who she was.

No, she thought resentfully. For he already knew all

about her. So—here was yet another person her husband took into confidences he denied his own wife!

Alone in a carriage with two silent, grim-faced men, she had never felt so isolated in all her life. It was bad enough to whisk her away from the wedding breakfast without letting her take even one sip of the celebratory champagne, but now here he was, positively glowering at her as though she was an unexpected, and very expensive, bill he had to pay.

She was angry, and humiliated and, yes, a little afraid too.

Fortunately, the tremor of fear went from her mind entirely when it occurred to her that he had no right to stare at her with such marked hostility when she had just done him such a tremendous favour. If she had not agreed to marry him, he would still be a pauper. Instead of which, he was setting out to claim a property that would keep him in comfort for the rest of his life!

Narrowing her eyes, she shot him one look that she hoped told him exactly what she thought of his treatment of her, before lifting her chin and staring out of the window, determined to ignore him, and his manservant, for the rest of the journey.

Captain Fawley did not know which he wanted to do more—throttle her or kiss her. Naturally he could do neither with Linney present. Though the cheering thought struck him that, should he decide to murder his wife, he could rely on his man to help him dispose of the body, no questions asked.

He had no idea how far he could trust his wife.

He looked at her determinedly averted profile, wondering how long she could maintain this pose of affronted dignity. Not long, he would guess. Women were just not capable of keeping a still tongue in their head. They were the natural enemies of silence. Whenever they encountered it, they felt they had to fill it with chatter. It did not matter if they had nothing of import to say.

Linney folded his arms, closed his eyes and shoved his bulky body sideways so that he was wedged into the corner. There! A practical solution to dealing with the tedium of a journey. Use it to get some rest. Women always complained that they were tired after undertaking a long journey. They wouldn't if they just stopped talking and made a profitable use of the time!

But there she was, sitting ramrod straight, forced to clutch at the strap to keep her balance when they went over a pothole instead of letting the cushions absorb the impact.

But then, she was a foolish creature. She would not be sitting in this coach with him at all if she had an ounce of sense. She would have traded on her looks, on her family connections…good God, when she had parroted off her antecedents to his lawyers he was amazed she had entertained his proposal for a second!

Mutton-headed, that's what she was, to have accepted the first proposal she had received, out of some kind of panic that she might never get another.

But that was women for you. So determined to escape the stigma of spinsterhood they would sell themselves to a hunchbacked dwarf—isn't that what he had told Lensborough, when he had complained women only saw his title, and wealth, but never the man he really was?

He slouched a little deeper into his seat. Those very words had come back to haunt him already today. Namely when she had sashayed into the library, looking like the cat that had got at the cream, and it had hit him like a blow to the midriff that she was as avaricious as they came.

Why had he not seen the warnings earlier? She had not shown a flicker of interest in his proposal of marriage until he had described the extent of the property she could become mistress of. After that, she had been willing to roll over and give birth to his children.

A shaft of heat darted from his stomach to his loins.

He had to shift in his seat to accommodate his body's inconvenient reaction.

This was not the first time he had experienced such stirrings of lust in regard to Miss Deborah Gillies. That memorable occasion had been the afternoon when he had gone to her house, to offer Miss Hullworthy the one sure piece of bait that would have her clamouring to dance with him, and Deborah had tripped into the room, dreamy-eyed from sleep, with her hair flowing about her shoulders and down her back. She had looked so natural, so…yes, innocent. So out of place amongst the plotters and schemers who filled the room.

His reaction then had surprised him, to say the least. It had been a very long time since he had felt even the faintest stirrings of desire towards a woman. So long, that he had begun to wonder if his injuries had completely unmanned him.

That was why, when he had decided to lay claim to his inheritance, he had known Miss Gillies must be the woman he took to wife.

He had always liked the unaffected way she had spoken to him, as though she did not care what he looked like.

But then, he reflected sourly, she was always pleasant to everyone.

Whereas what he had discovered he really wanted, he grimaced, was the reality of that image she had created when she had breathed her vows. That was when he had begun to get really angry with her—when she had promised to love and obey him in a voice quivering with emotion. Who had she thought she was fooling, with that sickening show of pretence? He knew she did not care a rap for him. She couldn't. Not to have stormed out of the lawyers' offices, at such a crucial moment, without so much as a backward glance. She had sent no word as to her intentions. He had spent the entire day almost paralysed by dread she had gone for good. He'd had to tell everyone to carry on with preparations for the ceremony as though it was all settled, when for all he knew he was about to face the ultimate humiliation of being jilted.

And worse than that, had been the slowly dawning realisation that, if she did not show up, it would destroy him. He would never have the stomach to browbeat another female into an engagement. He would remain eternally dependent on his brother's charity.

A beggar, that is what he would become.

So when she had strolled in, mingled with relief that she had shown up at all, was a good deal of resentment that he had somehow allowed this slip of a girl to gain such a hold over his life.

While all she seemed to have on her mind was playing the part of blushing bride to the hilt.

Which brought him back to the question—why did she feel she had to pretend anything? Why did she have to wound him by giving him a glimpse of what it might have been like to find a woman who…?

Breathing hard, he turned to glare at her stubbornly averted profile.

Oh, yes, she had dropped the act the minute there was nobody to see it!

But what made him angriest of all was the fact that though he knew she cared nothing for him, somehow, by some strange process of alchemy, she had the power to stoke him to this seething pitch of arousal merely by sitting there with her shoulder turned to him and her nose in the air.

Did she expect him to attempt to cajole her out of this mood?

If he started down that road, he would soon be reduced to the state of supplicant, begging for her favours.

Well, she was about to learn he would never beg her for anything!

'There is no sense in maintaining this ridiculous stand off,' he growled.

'I have no idea what you mean,' she replied stiffly, darting a glance in Linney's direction.

'Do you object to having Linney with us?' He scowled. 'You had better not. Linney is my right-hand man, I go nowhere without him—' he began, then checked himself, looking down at his empty jacket sleeve. 'Perhaps it would be more accurate to say, he is my left arm. I cannot do without him. I need him to help me into and out of the coach. And when we stop for the night, he will cut up my food, undress me, wash me and put me to bed. He is an integral part of my day-to-day routine. And will become an integral part of yours. Get used to it!'

'I beg your pardon,' Deborah said, abashed. She had not considered her husband's disability. He seemed so much more of a man than any other she had ever encountered, that she had completely forgotten how awkward certain aspects of his life must be.

'In fact, while we are discussing my daily routine, I had best inform you that under no circumstances will I permit you to have your own bedchamber.'

He'd had to accept that she had only married him for his money. Now she must accept the conditions under which she would earn it. The time for play-acting was over. There were a few grim realities it was about time Deborah faced.

'We will sleep together, in the same bed, right from the start. Once Linney unstraps my false leg, and I lay my crutch aside on the nightstand, I will have difficulty leaving it, unaided. You must surely see how impractical it would be, should I feel the urge, and you were sleeping in some distant chamber? Would you not feel humiliated if I were to ring a bell and summon you, then send you packing when I had done with you, as though you were a whore? Or perhaps you imagine Linney will help me into your bed, wait until the deed is done, then assist me back to my own?'

From the dull flush that was creeping across Linney's cheeks, Deborah could tell he had heard every word.

'May we not speak of this in private?' she begged, shocked that he could discuss such an indelicate matter in front of his servant. Why was he in such a foul mood? She could understand he was hurt that he'd had to settle for marrying a woman it was becoming more and more obvious he felt little for, but he was embarrassing his serving man into the bargain. Linney did not deserve that, even if Captain Fawley thought she did.

'You are embarrassing your man.'

Captain Fawley turned to look at Linney, who was keeping his eyes resolutely shut, maintaining the pretence of being asleep.

He shrugged.

'So long as you understand that we *will* have this con-versation. And that there will be no point in you ever trying to defy me.' He was not going to suffer any more days like today, spent aching and uncertain, dependent on her whim for his peace of mind. He leaned forward, murmuring in her ear, 'If you refuse to accede to my wishes, I will have no compunction about sending Linney to fetch you from your virginal chamber, when I have need of a woman, and carrying you to me, if needs be, kicking and screaming. And don't think he will not obey such a command. For he will.'

Deborah flinched from the harshness of his words. She had no idea why he would think she would object to sharing a bed. That was what married people did. Her mother and father had always done so.

No, what shocked her was the idea that he would

compel his servant to manhandle her if she did not submit to his every dictate. That did not sound at all like the image of what she thought a husband should be to his wife.

Perplexed, and repulsed by the vision of marriage his words were beginning to conjure up, she shrank as deeply into the cushions as she could, averting her eyes so that he should not see the hurt tears that were gathering there.

Chapter Six

Deborah felt quite perplexed when the landlady of the coaching inn where they were to break their journey led her into a chamber quite separate from her husband's.

'I think there has been some mistake,' she said, recalling his insistence she must share a room with him.

'No mistake,' she heard his harsh voice ring out from a shadowy alcove, which turned out to be a connecting door to another room. 'Walton sent a man ahead to book us a suite. That will be all, thank you,' he informed the landlady, who bobbed him a deferential curtsy and left.

She must have looked as perplexed as she felt, for he explained, 'Unless you expect Linney to help you get undressed and into bed, as well?'

She gasped, appalled at the very idea.

'No, I thought not,' said her husband. 'A girl who works in this establishment will come to see to your needs. I will ring for you when I am ready for you, then you will come to me.'

Having delivered his edict, he turned and stomped from the room.

Deborah had always thought of herself as an even-tempered person, but right at that moment, she experienced an almost overwhelming urge to smash something. Or stamp her feet and scream.

Being far too much a lady to yield to either temptation, she settled for flinging herself into a chair and scowling at the door her irascible husband had just gone through.

If the Earl had not booked a suite for them and arranged for a maid to help her come and undress, would he really have been beastly enough to humiliate her by making his man undo her hooks and eyes?

She was his wife, she sniffed, untying the ribbons of her bonnet and lowering it to her lap. Just this afternoon, he had promised to cherish her.

She heaved a shuddering sigh, fighting back a wave of self-pitying tears. So far there had been precious little cherishing going on. On the contrary, it felt as if he had gone out of his way to demean her. She was tired and hungry and totally disoriented. She had no idea what town she was in, nor which direction from London they were heading. Even the news that the Earl had taken a hand in these wedding-night arrangements made her feel of less value to her husband. Everyone seemed to have had more input into the arrangements for her wedding than she had. Her wishes, her preferences, seemed to count for nothing!

A tap on the door heralded the arrival of a buxom young chambermaid, who said, 'Would you be wanting a wash before I bring your supper up to your private parlour, madam? I can fetch a can of hot water in a trice.'

'Oh, I…I am not sure…' A private parlour? Supper? And if the maid did bring hot water, was there any soap? Had Lady Walton packed a towel in the little bag of essentials that sat on the ottoman at the foot of her bed?

Something of her confusion must have shown on her face, for the maid said, 'Your wedding night, isn't it? If you don't mind me saying so, you will feel much more the thing once you've had a bit of a wash. And you'll take a glass or two of wine with your supper, if you take my advice. Help you calm down, it will. Make it much easier for you.'

'What!' Her spine stiffened. She might be feeling bewildered and isolated, but surely she was not such a poor specimen that even a serving girl felt she needed to give her advice.

'Was only saying, that's all,' the girl pouted.

'Yes, well, thank you. I would like a wash, I think.'

She did not know if she did or not, but at least sending the girl for the promised hot water got her out of the room. And while she was gone, she could hunt through the overnight case and find out exactly what it contained.

Though she was most definitely not going to face her wedding night in a state of inebriation. Lord knew Captain Fawley was hard enough to deal with when she had all her wits about her!

At least once she had washed and got the maid to help comb out the travel tangles from her hair, she felt a little less nervous about facing her husband across the supper table.

Her husband did not rise when she entered their

private parlour, but merely motioned to Linney to help her into a chair facing him. She was just racking her brains to think of some suitably haughty remark, which would indicate her refusal to feel intimidated by the set-up, when her stomach rumbled loudly.

Linney shot her a startled look, then, his mouth working as though he was trying not to laugh, remarked, 'Hungry, miss? I mean, madam?'

'Yes. Ravenous, actually.' She shot her husband what she hoped was a darkling look. 'I have not had a chance to eat anything since noon.' She felt satisfied that the dart had gone home when he looked a little chagrined.

A tavern servant brought in a tureen of soup and set it on the corner of the table. Linney dismissed the man, serving her first, and then his master.

It was a delicious, wholesome broth containing a lot of pearl barley and a small amount of mutton. She slathered butter on to a deliciously fresh bread roll, and once she had finished, leaned back in her chair with a contented sigh. She had been trembling when she had come to the table, but her hands were quite steady now. She did not even feel anywhere near so cross with her husband now she had taken the edge off her appetite.

Linney rang for the next course, which turned out to be a whole roast chicken, and a game pie, along with several side dishes of vegetables.

It was not until Linney began to cut up the food he had placed on Captain Fawley's plate into tiny pieces, that Deborah had any inkling of just how awkward her husband found it to feed himself. She lowered her eyes to her own plate as he scooped up a mixed portion of meat and vegetables with a spoon.

Now she knew why he never stayed to supper at any of the gatherings where she had met him in London. He must feel so clumsy, so…so exposed to the pitying stares or snide comments of others.

She raised her eyes to his, briefly, and met a challenging, almost hostile look. It was as though he was daring her to make any comment. Startled, she realised that, in having her to sit down and eat with him, he was permitting her to witness a vulnerability that he normally never revealed to anyone. True, he was uncomfortable with her being here, but it was a start. She dropped her eyes at once, flustered by a strange feeling of intense intimacy.

'That was delicious.' She sighed once she had demolished the contents of her plate. Raising her eyes to his, she attempted a smile. 'No wonder Lord Walton hired rooms for us here, if he has sampled the cooking.'

'I see that it was certainly to your taste. I only wonder, having witnessed that demonstration of just how much you manage to put away at one sitting, that you manage to stay so thin,' he replied, cuttingly.

Deborah eyed him with sadness. It was as if he was determined to rebuff her attempts to lighten the atmosphere or establish any sort of rapport with him. He confirmed that suspicion by then saying, 'If you are finished, you may return to your room until I send for you.'

He did not even wish to while away the last few moments of the day in conversing with her. Where had the man who used to be so kind to her, at the balls where she had been a wallflower, gone?

Puzzled and hurt, she pushed back her chair, and left him in solitary possession of the dining parlour.

Why bother to send for her at all? Or insist he wished her to share his bed? It was not as if he wanted to cuddle her, or talk over the problems of the day, which was what her parents had always told her was the main purpose of having their own big bed. He did not seem to want her as a companion at all.

And when he saw her in the nightdress Lady Walton had packed for her, he would probably laugh out loud. She was far taller than the Countess, and much thinner. She had known that the confection of silk and lace was entirely insufficient to keep her warm in a draughty inn, from the first moment she had set eyes on it. But once she had put it on, and seen how little of her it managed to cover, she felt positively annoyed. Why had Captain Fawley not warned her he intended to leave town at once? She could have packed her own, warm nightgown, and the thick flannel wrapper that would have covered her from neck to toe. Even the Countess's wrapper exposed more than it covered, she grimaced. Once she had dismissed the maid, she went to the bed, seized the coverlet, and wrapped it round herself like a cloak. Then she padded barefoot to one of the armchairs that flanked the empty fireplace—for, naturally, the Countess had not thought to pack her a pair of slippers—and curled up in it. Before she knew it, she had pulled her plait over her shoulder, and begun chewing on the end of it.

Disgusted with herself for reverting to a childish habit she had firmly believed she had grown out of, angry with her husband for pushing her until her nerves had reached such a pitch, she spat it out, got to her feet and padded over to the window.

Night had fallen while they had been eating supper, but the yard below her window was still a hive of activity. With a determination born of desperation, Deborah concentrated on the little figures bustling about, refusing to allow her mind to drift back to her own sense of ill usage. She did not wish to arrive in her husband's chamber in an angry frame of mind. Their first night together would set the tone for the whole of the rest of their married life.

She forced herself to remember that she had married him because she thought she loved him. It was not easy to dredge up any fond thoughts of him, after the abominable way he had treated her today, but she could refuse to allow her mood to teeter over into downright hostility. She frowned down into the bustling yard, wondering what demons had driven him to act as he had done.

At the supper table, she had glimpsed how uneasy he felt to have her sharing something as simple as a meal. Unwittingly, she slipped the end of her plait into her mouth again, chewing at it absently as she struggled to make sense of his attitude towards her. She already knew that he was convinced he was ugly, and clumsy and that no woman could possibly like him, never mind love him. How could she make him see that she did?

She sighed. She had thought she could tell him she loved him, once they were married, but right now, she was so upset with him, she knew such a declaration would ring hollow. And she was afraid that if she tried to show her affection in a physical way, he would rebuff her. Her mind went back to the day when she had caught a party of village boys scrumping apples from her orchard. In their haste to escape, one of them had fallen out of a tree and broken his arm. When she had gone to his aid, he had pushed her away, the belligerent expression on his face almost exactly like the one she had seen in her husband's eyes today when she had been watching Linney cut up his food.

'An injured male is a dangerous creature,' she remembered her mother explaining to her when she had asked why the boy had been so rude, when all she had been trying to do was help him. 'Rather than accept sympathy, they are inclined to lash out. Just like a wild animal, which would bite your hand should you try to help it escape from a trap.'

Suddenly everything he had done and said today made sense. Far from being grateful to her for helping him to achieve financial independence, he resented the necessity of having her involved at all. He equated admitting to any kind of need as a slur on his masculinity. That was why he had behaved with such uncharacteristic unkindness, she decided, letting her plait fall from her mouth. Though how she could convince him to cease hostilities, she could not imagine. The little village boy's hostility had been obdurate. In the end, she had been obliged to leave him in a crumpled heap at the foot of the tree and go and fetch a doctor.

She rather thought her husband's hurts were of the sort no doctor could treat. While she was still pondering how she could express her regard, without wounding his male sensibilities any further, there was a knock on the door, followed by the gentle cough, announcing Linney had come to fetch her.

He said not a word, merely opening the connecting doorway, and ushering her through. If anything, he seemed even more embarrassed than she felt as she marched past him, the coverlet clutched to her chin.

'What the deuce have you got on?' were her husband's first words when she entered his chamber.

'A blanket,' she replied, as Linney softly closed the door on his retreat. She noticed that a fire was smouldering gently in the grate, and though she had vowed not to give in to her sense of ill usage, she could not help saying, 'My room is really cold. And you should have seen the ridiculous get-up Lady Walton packed for me to wear!'

'I should like to see it,' he agreed. 'Knowing Heloise, it was probably intended to show off rather more than it covered.'

'How did you know that?'

He shrugged one shoulder, with a knowing smile.

'How any woman could consider wearing such an impractical outfit to bed mystifies me completely. Never mind lending it to a friend. What was she thinking?'

'Impractical,' he said, an arrested expression on his face. 'How do you mean, impractical, exactly?'

She advanced on the bed, in which he reclined against a bank of pillows. His right hand lay on top of the coverlet. His left arm, the one which she knew ended just below his elbow, was concealed beneath the blankets. A single candle burned in a holder on a nightstand, to the right of the bed, illuminating his uninjured side, and casting his left into deeper shadow. Her heart went out to him. Just having her invade his room was a monumental concession for him. In fact, she frowned, she did not really know why he was forcing himself to go through this torment.

'Well, it is certainly not designed to keep a body warm. There is hardly anything to it. And what there is, you can see right through! What is the point of donning a covering that does not cover anything?'

'I expect she thought I would keep you warm tonight.'

'Oh!' She looked dubiously at his chest, which was completely bare. Her father had always worn a nightshirt to bed. And usually a cap too. And had drawn thick velvet hangings round the battered old four-poster, to keep out the draughts. 'You don't exactly look as though you will be very warm tonight, either,' she said with concern. 'Were you in too much of a hurry to remember to pack a nightshirt?'

It was slowly dawning on Captain Fawley that his wife was a complete innocent.

'Did your mother never explain what went on in the marriage bed?'

'Not exactly, no.'

He bit down on a savage oath. He had been so intent on rushing the ceremony through in complete secrecy that he had forgotten she might need to learn a thing or two from her mother before sharing a bed with a man. Only now did her mystified looks when he had spoken of dragging her to his bed make sense.

To his surprise, while he was wrestling with the concept of having to explain to a naïve virgin what a man generally did with his wife, whilst repressing the overwhelming desire to just get on with it, she smiled, and shrugged off the blanket.

'I suppose we will just have to keep each other warm, then, won't we? At least there is a fire in here.'

His mouth went dry at the sight of her in her borrowed nightwear. The bodice consisted of a few slivers of peach-coloured silk holding together panels of lace, which were strategically positioned to entice a man's gaze.

He gazed. And saw the skirt was split to her thigh, revealing tantalising glimpses of her pale slender legs with every tentative step she took towards him.

She hesitated in the act of climbing up into the bed, her face turning bright pink as he growled when the silk slithered from her bent leg in sinful invitation.

'What is the matter?' she whispered. 'Do I look dreadful in this gown?'

He saw the uncertainty in her face, the need for re-assurance.

And something dark and bitter welled up within him. *She* was seeking reassurance from him, for the way *she* looked! Didn't she know she was perfect? Perfect face, perfect body, perfect skin. No man looking at her, in that seductive outfit, could fail to react as he was reacting at the sight of that bared thigh. He was rock hard. Sweating.

'Take it off,' he growled.

She flinched back, an expression of shock on her face.

'I said, take it off,' he repeated, as a fine tremor began to ripple through the blighted arm he had hoped to conceal from her sight by placing a pillow over the mangled stump where his hand ought to be.

'You don't like it,' she said, shaking her head ruefully. Then, lifting her chin, added, 'Nor do I.'

She kept her gaze fixed on his bare chest, as she reached for the ties that bound the wrapper over her breasts. He probably felt naked, and vulnerable, without the artificial limbs his servant had removed to make him comfortable for the night. In his mind, it probably seemed fair that she, too, should be stripped of some of her dignity.

She wondered if he was completely naked under the covers. A strange shiver went right through her at the thought of lying next to all that hair-roughened flesh. Her knees had gone weak, her heartbeat had fluttered when she had leaned up against him the night she had almost fainted. Being in such close proximity had affected her profoundly, even through her clothing and his. What would it be like with no barriers at all?

Her legs began to tremble as her heartbeat accelerated. Her fingers shook so much that she was convinced she would tear the delicate garment in her clumsy haste to divest herself of it.

Finally, as she stood completely naked before her husband, she drew the courage to look into his face. His expression was stark, unyielding—not at all welcoming as he flicked back the covers, indicating that it was time to get into the bed and join him.

'Wait!' he said, just as she began to climb up on to the bed for the second time.

She paused, one knee already bent on the mattress, her hands splayed out to balance her. Had she misinterpreted his wishes? He certainly did not look at all pleased to see her attempting to scramble in beside him. Slowly, she retreated and stood up, catching her lower lip between her teeth at the dreadful prospect that he was going to send her back to her room after all. He had tried, but when it came to the crunch, he just could not bear to have her near him. Just as he did not like anyone to see him eating, he probably hated anyone except his trusted manservant getting a good look at the full extent of his injuries.

She wanted to reach out and put her arms round him. But, remembering the reaction she had got from that village boy, she sensed it would only make him resent her all the more.

She shifted her weight from one foot to the other, wondering what on earth she ought to do.

'Undo your plait,' he growled, settling back into the pillows.

'My plait?' she echoed, at a loss to understand what could possibly lay behind that request.

'You promised to obey me this afternoon, woman,' he growled. 'Undo your plait. I want to see your hair down.'

Giving a mental shrug, she reached over her shoulder and undid the ribbon that held the ends of her hair in place. His eyes roamed her body as she worked the strands loose, the expression on his face growing fiercer by the second. By the time she had freed her hair, she was trembling from head to foot. He did not appear to like what he saw at all. She knew she must compare unfavourably with Susannah, the woman he wished was here with him tonight. She felt a strong urge to cover the breasts that were so much smaller than her friend's.

She felt gangly, and awkward and ashamed of the ribs and hipbones that were so clearly visible through her skin, instead of being covered by the feminine lushness of a woman in the peak of health. She was not sure how much more of this testing she could take before she ran back to her room and gave way to the tears of humiliation that were only an eyeblink away.

If she did not love him…if he did not need to reduce her to the level of exposure he was suffering, by having her invade his personal space…

'You are shivering,' he finally observed. A wave of goose pimples had swept across her body, tightening her nipples into the hard peaks that also betokened arousal. He knew she was not aroused. She was just plain scared. Her eyes were huge in her pale face, fixed on him as though he were a wolf, and she Little Red Riding Hood.

He felt wolfish. He wanted to devour her. Claw at her and bite her, and hear her cry out as he sank into her soft warm flesh.

Yet he also wanted to wipe away that look of uncertainty, and replace it with yearning, and wonder and rapture.

She knew nothing of what went on between a man and a woman. How could she? She was standing there, completely naked, completely bemused by his request to take down her hair. She shifted her weight from the foot she had been favouring, stroking the sole over the arch of the other, chewing at her lower lip, like a little girl, completely unaware of what the sight of her naked body was doing to him.

Any man with a shred of decency would let her grow

accustomed to intimacy by gradual stages, he sighed. Not plunge her straight into the sort of torrid encounter he had planned to subject her to tonight.

'Get into bed now,' he said, ashamed of himself for toying with her like this, 'and I will warm you.'

'Th…thank you,' she breathed, scrambling in beside him with alacrity, and pulling the covers up to her chin as she lay down. 'I am all over goose bumps.'

'I saw.' He put his arm about her waist, pulling her closer. 'Is that better?'

'Mmm…' She nodded, the top of her head bumping the underside of his chin. She kept her arms demurely by her sides, knowing he would not wish her to hug him, dearly though she wished to. But the entire length of her leg rested against his. He was warm, and hard and his skin was covered all over, it seemed, with coarse hair that made her want to rub herself against him—twine herself about him like a cat. Each breath he took, expanding his chest, brought him temporarily, tantalisingly closer to her upper body and made her yearn to roll on to her side, and press herself up against him, till there was not a single inch of air between their naked bodies. She wanted her breasts pressed against his chest, her legs entangled with his. She wanted the right to put her arms about him, and kiss the scars on his face, and, yes, the ones she had briefly glimpsed bubbling down the left side of his chest. She wanted to plunge her fingers into his overlong hair, while she kissed him with all the love she felt welling in her heart.

But she was so afraid he would repulse her.

He gritted his teeth, lying rigidly upon his back,

while he felt his naked young bride shivering with cold, and probably a large dose of trepidation, against his side. He did not know where to start. Not so long ago he had feared he would never want to lay with a woman again. Yet now he was experiencing a hunger so fierce he scarce knew how to hold it back. The things he wanted to do to this innocent young woman were so brutal they even shocked him. He gritted his teeth, knowing she needed a gentle introduction to a pastime she scarce knew existed. Not a clumsy, blundering cripple, who, even at his peak, had never known an innocent. His encounters, as a soldier, had been of the mercenary kind. Pleasurable enough for him, but not exactly good training for the polite coupling that he guessed ought to go on in a marriage bed.

She deserved far better than to marry a wreck like him. She had made it possible for him to have everything he had ever wanted. A home of his own, financial independence and revenge on the perfidious Lampton family.

And all she was getting in return was a bad-tempered cripple, who had scant idea how to initiate a virgin. Perhaps he ought to tell her to put her nightgown back on. If she was not naked…but then he imagined her getting out of bed, and bending over to retrieve that seductive confection of textures from the floor, raising her arms to slide it over her head…he would just want to rip it straight off her again.

He stifled a groan.

'Is aught amiss?' she asked, peering up at the rigid lines of his throat.

'No, nothing that need trouble you.' He sighed,

shifting so that no part of him quite touched any part of her any more. There was no way he could talk to her about what her marital duties would entail, not tonight. It was bad enough just thinking about it. If he tried to verbalise exactly what was going through his mind, he would end up wanting to give her a demonstration. And end up traumatising her, no doubt. For he was pretty sure he was not going to be able to take it slowly enough not to hurt her.

'Go to sleep.'

There was a short pause. Then she said, in a very small voice, 'May I kiss you goodnight?'

She must have felt him tense, because she added hastily, 'My mother and father always used to kiss each other goodnight. And we are married now, so, should I not kiss you?'

'Only if you really want to.' He was sure no woman could really want to kiss him. 'You do not need to,' he said, suddenly angry with Deborah's need to do her duty, as she saw it. 'It is not required.'

'But I do want to,' she stunned him by saying. Raising herself on to one elbow, she looked down into his face, right into his eyes, adding uncertainly, 'If you don't mind. It is what married people do, is it not?'

'Part of it,' he grated, his heart breaking into a gallop as her hair brushed across his chest, and he thought of what else married people did. And people who were not married, either, when the urge took them.

He had arranged it so that she was lying on his left side, his injured side. But she did not think he would like her to kiss the scarred side of his face. So she leaned across him, and placed a gentle kiss on his right cheek. As she did so, her breasts grazed across the hair-roughened surface of his chest. He sucked in a sharp breath.

'What did I do wrong?'

His eyes were squeezed shut. 'Nothing,' he grated. 'Lie down. Lie down at once.'

Chastened, she did so.

And shifted away, until she was right on the very edge of the mattress. But he could feel the warmth emanating from her skin. Could hear her breathing. Shaky, uneven breaths, as though…

'You are not crying, are you?'

'Of course not!' came her muffled response.

He rolled on to his side, raised himself up on his injured arm and looked down into her face with concern.

'Yes, you are…' he groaned '…and it is all my fault. I have been a complete b-beast today, have I not?'

'N…no…'

'Yes, I have. I know it.' When he thought back over the way he had treated her, he was amazed she had not given way to tears much sooner. What kind of man forced a timid young virgin to strip naked on her wedding night? Repulsed her so curtly after she had drawn the courage to place a shy kiss on his ravaged face?

'Forgive me, Deborah?' He ran his thumb along the poor, bruised lower lip that she had been chewing more and more as the stresses of the day had piled up.

'Of course I forgive you.' She sighed, looking up at him solemnly with tear-drenched eyes.

God, but he wanted to kiss her. If he could manage to be gentle, could she manage to stomach it? He thought she, of all women, might really be brave enough. Look at what she had already endured at his hands. All day long she had borne the brunt of the emotions that churned inside him. And had stoically maintained a dignified mien.

He lowered his head and gently sucked her lower lip into his mouth, soothing it with his tongue.

He felt a tremor run through her, and broke the kiss, with a feeling of intense regret. He should have known she would recoil.

'Are you afraid of me?' he asked ruefully, looking down into her face. Her hair had fanned out across the pillows, making her look…he gulped…incredibly alluring. He gritted his teeth as a fresh flood of desire surged through him. 'You do not need to be. Though I don't suppose after today's performance you will believe me….'

'No!' she replied, as he made to shift away from her. 'I am not afraid of you. Not at all. Only—' She broke off, and began chewing at her lower lip again.

'What are you afraid of?'

'That I might not please you,' she admitted, her eyes darting away from his.

'There has been no pleasing me today, has there?' he admitted, brushing his thumb over the lip she seemed so intent on abusing. As he recalled how soft her mouth had felt under his own, his breath hitched in his chest.

'I am sorry,' she said solemnly. 'I wish I knew…'

'You have nothing to be sorry for!' he insisted. She could not help the way she was. He did not even know now why seeing her in her true light should have hurt him so deeply. Women were none of them what they appeared. Even Lensborough's wife, a woman who had a reputation for being shy and demure, had turned out to have a sordid secret buried in her past. Before that marriage could proceed, they'd had to deal with a villain who had been blackmailing her for years.

'Truly?' she asked, with a hopeful expression. 'Even the kiss…' she persisted. 'Was that all right?' Her face fell. 'You did not seem to like it all that much.'

'The kiss was perfect.' He thought of the way her breasts had brushed across his chest, the way her hair had hung round both their faces like a curtain of living silk, cocooning them in a moment of dark intimacy. And how he had wanted to pull her fully on top of him, hold her in place and thrust up inside her. He swore under his breath.

'I wish to God I could trust myself to kiss you again.'

She frowned up at him. 'I don't understand. If you want to kiss me, then why don't you?'

'Because, my sweet little innocent, it will not stop at kisses. You would be shocked if I were to tell you…to show you…' The breath hitched in his chest again as his mind flooded with a series of images so erotic, he was amazed the sheets did not go up in flames.

'No, I won't,' she assured him in a breathy little voice. 'You said kisses were only part of what married people do. And…I don't want to stop at kisses. I want all of it.'

'You don't know what you are asking,' he growled.

She looked crestfallen. 'And you don't want to show me,' she said, turning over on to her side.

'What!' He pulled her over so that she lay on her back. 'What I want right now, is…what I want…' He groaned, finally abandoning his attempts to hold back. He plundered Deborah's mouth, plunging his fingers into her hair to anchor her against the force of his kiss. Need ripped through him, sweeping aside any thoughts of restraint. He looped one leg over hers, pinning her body beneath his, wanting to feel the softness of her skin against the full length of his own hardened need.

She arched up against him. For one terrible moment he thought she was trying to push him off. But instead, she looped her arms round his neck and kissed him back for all she was worth.

It was like striking a spark into dry kindling.

Just as he had known it would, any hope of initiating her gently went up in smoke. Amazingly, she seemed as greedy for sensation as he felt. She matched him, kiss for kiss, touch for touch, until the moment when he went to push her legs apart. Though she opened for him willingly, and he found her lusciously ready for his possession, it still hurt her. He felt no regret when she gave a yelp of pain, only a soaring triumph at the audible proof she was his now, utterly his in a way no other woman had ever been. And when she began to move against him again, winding her legs about his waist, her little hands clawing at his back, he felt a rush of power, that he had somehow, miraculously, against all the odds, brought her to this pitch of wild abandon.

He felt as though their rising pleasure was fusing them together. It was swifter, more intense, than anything he could ever have envisioned. For a blinding second or two, when he felt her convulse around him, crying out her rapture, he felt as though he had left the hell of his existence behind, and found a slice of heaven. When he came back to earth, he was shocked to find his face was wet with tears. He had to bury his face in her neck to stifle the shuddering sobs that shook his whole body.

How could a mere woman reduce him to this? He pulled away, rolling on to his back and flinging his arm over his face. He could not let her see what she did to him. If she said one word that mocked him, gave him so much as one look that showed she knew the power she could wield over him, he would make her rue the day she was born!

When he had regained control over himself, he lowered his arm and turned his head to confront her.

Her eyes were closed, her lips parted, her cheeks flushed with sleep.

Relief flooded through him, leaving him limp and shaken. There was no need to deal with her now. If he played his cards right, she would never know how deeply her response had moved him.

For she must never know. Once a woman got the upper hand, a man was doomed. Let her but guess how much he desired her, and she would start to trade on it.

Women were all the same. Deep down, they were scheming, manipulative creatures who would twist a man round their fingers, to get what they wanted.

Well, no woman was going to manipulate him. And if Deborah tried it, she would soon find she had picked the wrong target.

Chapter Seven

Bliss. There was no other word for it. Deborah stretched, and yawned, her whole being thrumming with lazy sensuality.

Her sleep had been deep, and completely restful, nestled against the strong body of the man she loved. Sighing, she snuggled closer, daringly placing one hand upon his waist and pressing a kiss against his back.

He rolled over, and looked down at her with a perplexed frown.

He had hoped that last night had been an aberration. He had reasoned that he must have been more worried about his ability to function normally than he had admitted to himself. That was why he had wept. It had been relief on finding he was whole, in that respect. It was not unprecedented. One of the company sergeants, one of the most hard-bitten men he had ever known, had wept with relief when the regimental surgeon had told him they could save his arm.

Last night's outpouring of emotion had nothing to do with the particular woman he was with.

And there was no reason why his heart should seem to be expanding and melting within his chest, just because she was touching him voluntarily this morning.

He was damned if he was going to melt into emotional mush every time his wife reached out to him!

He sat up abruptly, plucking her hand from his body, and flinging it from him.

'We have no time for that. We need to get up, and on the road. Go to your room, now, and get dressed.'

Shaken by the vehemence of his rejection, Deborah slid from the bed, fumbling her arms into the totally inadequate silken wrapper that had lain on the floor all night. He would not even look at her, but lay with his arm flung across his eyes as though the very sight of her made him angry.

Not that she could believe he held her personally in aversion, or he would not have asked her to marry him at all. But she could not forget the stunned look on his face when he had rolled over, and seen that it was her. Just before the shutters had come down, and he had repulsed her, he had looked positively confused.

Then it hit her with blinding clarity.

She was not Susannah.

Head bowed, she fled from the room, shutting the door firmly behind her.

For a few moments, she sat on the edge of her untouched bed, her arms wrapped about her middle, which seemed to be completely hollowed out.

She was glad that Linney would be sharing the

carriage with them today. She did not know how she would have coped being shut up with her husband, not today. She felt he had reduced her to nothing, somehow, by throwing her out of his bed this morning.

And she was nothing, to him.

Last night, she had interpreted his groans of pleasure as a sign that he had felt something for her. But while she had been pulsing with love, all he had wanted was a convenient female body. She understood now, in the clear light of day, why he had spoken of urges, rather than love, when he had insisted they share a bed.

She found it hard work to climb into the carriage later, weighed down as she was by the conviction that not only did he not particularly care which woman he used to satisfy those urges, but that in order for him to be so proficient at it he must have done it with many other women. He had known exactly how to touch her, where to press his lips, to reduce her to a quivering mass of throbbing need.

He did not seem inclined to talk today, either, though she could feel his eyes upon her from time to time. Once, she returned his look, flinching at the ferocious blast of hostility that met her gaze.

Depression settled over her then, like a greasy pall. She felt unloved, and used and so lonely! Why had she ever imagined she could reach him and heal him? He did not want to be healed, least of all by her.

Had she made a terrible mistake, in marrying such a deeply wounded man? She certainly felt way out of her depth with him this morning, and half-convinced that she would not be able to keep her head above water for very much longer, unless he threw her some kind of lifeline.

'We are here,' he said, jolting her out of her silent misery.

They were slowing down to pass through a pair of wrought-iron gates, set between two stone pillars.

'Wh-where is this, exactly?' she plucked up the courage to ask. 'Am I permitted to know, now?'

'There is no harm in telling you now we are here, no,' he grunted. 'You cannot blab to anyone, and it would be too late to do anything about it, anyway. This is The Dovecote. In the county of Berkshire. Our new home.'

He craned his neck to look out of the window, as they swept round a curve in the drive, and a house came into view.

It was not as big as Deborah had imagined it would be from the way he had talked about it. The four-square, three-storey building was not even as big as the vicarage where she had grown up. She would guess it had no more than six or seven bedrooms, and the grounds that surrounded it were more of a large garden than an estate. Had he put her through so much unhappiness for this?

The carriage drew to a halt before a shallow flight of stone steps, leading to a covered entranceway. A group of household staff came pouring out, as though they had been waiting in the hallway for their arrival. When Linney leaned out to open the coach door, they surged forward, gathering around in a semi-circle as he let down the steps. They were all smiling.

Linney helped Captain Fawley out first, then offered Deborah his burly arm. As she emerged from the coach, the entire group of staff burst into a spontaneous round of applause.

'Welcome, welcome to The Dovecote,' a large woman of middle age said, stepping forward, her face wreathed in smiles. 'I am Mrs Farrell, your housekeeper, and right glad we are to see you come home at last, Captain Fawley. And you, Mrs Fawley, of course!'

'Thank you,' said Deborah, when her husband remained mute. One glance in his direction was enough to tell her that he appeared to have been stunned into silence by the enthusiastic reception. 'I am sure we will be very happy here.'

Mrs Farrell's smile, if anything, grew even broader. 'We all hope you will be, and will do all we can to make sure of it. Terrible it would have been, if that Percy Lampton had pushed his way in here.' She shook her head in disapproval. 'My mistress would not have rested easy if he had got his hands on all she had worked so hard to build up.'

She felt her husband's tension flow from him in waves at the mention of Percy Lampton's name. From the swift look he gave her, the anxious frown that drew his brows down, she guessed he must think his housekeeper had betrayed a secret he still wished to keep from her.

'But you won't want to stand about talking after your journey. I'll just introduce all the staff, and then you will want to see your rooms, I don't doubt.'

'Thank you, yes,' Captain Fawley said, taking Deborah's arm as the housekeeper turned to do the honours.

'This is Cherry, the upper housemaid, and Nancy, the lower. We don't have a butler. I do all a butler would do, save order the wine cellar, which there was no call for in Miss Lampton's day. She never drank, nor would she have a male servant in the house.'

It finally hit Deborah what had seemed odd about the group of servants who had come out to greet them. Not a single one of them was male.

'And here is our cook, Susan,' Mrs Farrell continued happily, 'and May the kitchen maid. We have Bessie as the boots, and Betty the under-housemaid. Freda does the garden with her helpers...' a group of women and girls with weatherbeaten faces bobbed curtsies '...and Joan looks after the stables. We did once have a male groom, but he proved unsatisfactory.' She wrinkled her nose in distaste. 'Joan does much better. But then we only have a couple of carriage horses in the stables. Miss Lampton rarely went out, save in the gig to the village. Used to have a couple of hunters, when she was younger, but she had to get rid of them once her joints got too stiff for her to mount.'

'I see,' said Captain Fawley, looking thoroughly discomfited, though whether by the complement of female staff, or the housekeeper's volubility or the fact that Deborah now knew Percy Lampton was the other man in line for this property, she was unable to guess.

'Of course,' the housekeeper remarked, running her eyes assessingly over Linney's burly frame, 'we know things will not be run the same, not now you are here. You will want a man to see to your clothes, and so on.'

'And to stock the wine cellar,' Captain Fawley said firmly. 'And my own horse will be arriving in the next day or so, with the rest of our things.'

The housekeeper nodded again. 'Only natural, a

married man would want to run things different from a single lady, but I assure you that had we not all been prepared to work for you, we would not have stopped on, is that not so?' She turned to the other female staff, who all nodded, or spoke their affirmation.

'Then perhaps you would show us to our rooms, Mrs Farrell?' he said, politely.

Mrs Farrell led them through the front doors, and into a room to the right. 'Sitting room,' she said. 'Miss Lampton would always receive callers here. Office,' she said, flinging open a door to the rear of the guest sitting room. An oak desk squatted with its back to the window, dominating the room. Around the walls stood glass-fronted bookcases, each containing ledgers of a different colour. 'Travers, her factor, will be coming by tomorrow, to discuss Miss Lampton's affairs with you. Only male she had any time for, and that only because he did exactly as he was told.' The housekeeper grinned.

'Kitchens and offices.' She pointed out the green baize door to the back of the hall, but seemed not to expect they would wish to pass through it. 'Your private rooms are over here,' she said, crossing the hall. 'Stairs got too much for her, in latter days, and knowing your particular requirements, we left things as she last had them.' They entered a small, cosy-looking sitting room, crossing through it to reach a bedroom. It contained a large double bed, of japanned pine, with floral chintz valance and curtains, topped by a snowy white quilt and pillows foaming with lace. Next to the door stood an old-fashioned clothes press, painted all over with flowers to match the bed hangings. It was all rather ornate and fussy and so feminine Deborah was sure her husband would want to change it all at the earliest opportunity. To the rear of the bedroom was a door that led to a dressing room, containing a hipbath and towel rail, as well as a traditional marble-topped washstand with a floral china basin and pitcher.

'Upstairs?' Mrs Farrell looked dubiously at Captain Fawley, but he elected to climb, albeit slowly, to the upper floors, where they found six guest bedrooms, two of which, the housekeeper cheerfully suggested, could be made into a nursery and schoolroom, when the time came.

Deborah's insides gave a peculiar lurch. What they had done last night was not unlike what the farm animals did during their mating seasons, which resulted in fresh batches of calves, and lambs and chicks. It was very lowering to think that such a sublimely pleasurable activity was no different, in the long run, from the very basic instinct of all God's creation to procreate.

'The servants' attics are above,' said Mrs Farrell, startling her out of her reverie. 'No need to examine those. I will show your man later, if he wishes?' she finished, darting a brief glance at Linney, who had been shadowing his master closely.

When the tour ended, the housekeeper said she would bring tea to the front parlour.

'How do you like our new quarters, then?' Captain Fawley asked Linney as soon as the housekeeper had left them. 'Think you could cope with promotion to the position of butler?'

Until that moment, Linney's face had stayed impassive, but he broke into a grin as he admitted, 'Dare say I could.'

'Good man. I don't want some stranger coming in, thinking he knows how to run my household. And you'd best cast your eye over the stables too,' Captain Fawley said, settling into a comfortable-looking wing-backed armchair before the fireplace.

Deborah slid into one that was angled so that whoever sat in it could look out of the front window, feeling utterly superfluous. He had not deigned to ask what she thought of the house, or its peculiar set-up, nor whether there were any changes she might wish to make.

When the maid brought the tea in, he dismissed Linney, and the maid, saying, 'My wife can pour for me.'

Perversely, now that she was alone with him, she felt rather shy and very conscious of her limbs as she moved over to the table where the girl had deposited the tray. Her hands shook as she lifted the lid of the pot to see whether the beverage had brewed long enough to pour.

'Do you take milk, or lemon?' she asked, in a rather high-pitched voice. 'And sugar?'

He shrugged. 'Surprise me.'

When she shot him a bewildered look, he explained, 'I don't drink the stuff at all, to tell you the truth. Would much rather have a tankard of ale, but I daren't offend the sensibilities of Mrs Farrell within the first five minutes I am here. Linney knows my tastes. He will arrange it all how I like it, without me having to make a fuss. We'll need to get supplies in, but for the first day or so, we must both just make do with things as they are,' he ended quite sternly, as though daring her to make any complaints.

Linney knew his tastes. Linney would arrange things,

she thought angrily, heaping an extra spoonful of sugar into her cup.

'You did not seem all that surprised to learn that, had we not married, Percy Lampton would have inherited The Dovecote,' he said, an irritable edge to his voice.

Though what had he to feel irritable about? He was the lord and master of this domain, while she was like some slave girl, brought in solely for the purpose of satisfying his animal urges. She felt so brittle, she feared one more unkind word would snap her in two like a twig.

She poured tea into both their cups, adding a splash of milk to hers, and leaving his black and unsweetened. She hoped he found it as unpalatable as she would have done.

'I wondered if he might be the other legatee the lawyers mentioned, yes,' she admitted. 'Having observed your aversion to each other,' she said, carefully placing his cup within reach of his right hand, 'I then wondered if you were attempting to deprive him of something he took for granted belonged to him.'

'And it did not bother you?' he sneered.

'It was only a vague suspicion,' she defended herself, suddenly loathe to admit how comforting it had been to hear Mrs Farrell confirming her hope that the former owner really had wanted her husband to inherit. 'And anyway, why should it bother me, if it did not bother you?'

'My motives were nothing like yours!' he flared. How like a woman to lay the blame for her mercenary actions upon another! She had not cared that she was pushing another claimant out of the way. She just wanted to get her hands on his inheritance. 'Lampton deliberately attempted to prevent me from inheriting when he thought I was about to make a match with Miss Hull-worthy. If he had not acted so despicably, I would not have felt the need to retaliate!'

Deborah flinched, as though from a blow. It was bad enough that she knew he did not care for her, but to have him fling it in her face, the moment they had set foot in their marital home, was the act of a callous beast!

'You married me to get revenge on Mr Lampton…' Because he had stolen the woman Captain Fawley loved.

'And why not? He deserved some punishment. He will drop Miss Hullworthy, now she can be of no further use to him. Do you think he should get away with such cruelty to a woman—your friend, might I add?'

She swallowed down her hurt, clenching her fists in her lap as she reminded herself he did not know how cruel he was being. He did not know she loved him. He firmly believed she had agreed to the marriage for purely financial reasons.

She wondered what he would do if she bawled out, 'I love you, you idiot! That is why I married you!' before flailing out at him with those clenched fists.

She took a deep calming breath. Letting it out, she rose unsteadily to her feet. 'If you will excuse me, I should like to go and lie down for a while.'

He frowned at her. 'You do look pale. Are you ill? Should I ask Mrs Farrell to fetch a doctor?' He lurched to his feet, and tugged on the bell pull. 'Mrs Farrell!' he bellowed, going to the door, and flinging it open, 'My wife is unwell… Ah, you, girl, what is your name?' he snapped at the young maid who had come running in answer to his summons.

'Cherry, sir.' She bobbed a curtsy.

'Help my wife to our room, and get her whatever she needs. She is not well....'

'I am only tired, that is all,' said Deborah. 'If I might just lie down quietly for a space, I am sure I shall recover.'

'If you are sure?' He watched her with a troubled frown as she crossed the hall to their rooms.

'Quite sure,' she said, head lowered so that he would not see the effort it was costing her not to cry. She felt quite disgusted with herself for being so feeble as to want to weep, simply because he had shouted at her. She was pathetic. Quite pathetic.

The maid, however, took one look at her, before huffing, 'Men! Don't know why Miss Lampton thought that one would be any different just because he had a rough start in life.' She hustled Deborah to an upholstered chair by the window and bent to loosen her boots. 'Tyrants, the lot of 'em! Shouting at you like that, and you only just wed! That man of his is no better, either, looking us up and down while he tramps round the place in his noisy boots.'

'Captain Fawley is not a tyrant,' Deborah hastily intervened. 'He was not shouting at me.'

'If you say so, madam,' Cherry said, looking totally unconvinced.

'No, really, he shouted for help because he was concerned for me,' she explained. Though why she should be defending him, she did not know. 'I know he has a loud voice, but he was in the army, and used to giving orders to men. I am sure, after a period of adjustment, he will get used to ordering female staff, just as you will get used to having him about.'

'And was that great lummox of a serving man of his in the army too?' Cherry huffed, going round the back of her chair to loosen Deborah's laces.

It pained her that she did not know. So she said, 'I really would feel better for a lie down. I am not ill, but I was ill, and I seem to get tired very quickly.'

'Country air, that's what you need,' Cherry said firmly. 'Plenty of walks, and good plain cooking and lots of sleep. You'll be right as a trivet in no time. London…' she pulled a face '…that's what you need to recover from. Never went up to town, but what Miss Lampton came back with a white face and a need to sleep for a week,' she said.

'Miss Lampton visited London often?'

'At least three times a year, though we was never to let on.' Cherry went a bit red in the face. 'I don't suppose it will do any harm to tell you, though, especially not now she's gone. It was only her brother that would have put a stop to her doing her business, if he had known about it. But he never found out. Lor!' Her face lit up. 'You should have seen his face when the will was read out, and he found out how much money she had made. And that it weren't to go to his precious son! Madder than a wet hen, he was!'

Deborah was prevented from learning anything more about the previous owner of The Dovecote, when a knock on the door heralded the arrival of the house-keeper, with the tea tray.

'Your husband said as to be sure you drank your tea, and had a morsel to eat.' She beamed. 'And I was to ask if there was anything else you needed. Does a body good,' she said, depositing the tray on a low table next to the chair, 'to see a man actually taking care of his wife. Out you go, Cherry,' she addressed the maid, who bobbed a curtsy and scuttled out. 'I had thought Cherry could serve as your personal maid, if you have no objection. Miss Lampton's woman left after she died, and went to live in Ramsgate on the nice little pension she got for her troubles. Cherry is not exactly trained, but the most suitable for now, since you have not brought your own maid.'

'Everything was rather rushed,' Deborah said weakly, as the woman handed her the same cup of tea she had poured herself earlier. She decided she could not fathom her husband out at all. He would shout at her one minute, then send a servant to see to her welfare the next.

'Well, no need for rush and hurry as though you was in London now. Nice and steady we take things here at The Dovecote. I'll just pull the curtains across, and you can take forty winks. I'll send Cherry to wake you in time to change for dinner.'

Rather overwhelmed by the woman's determined helpfulness, Deborah went to the bed, climbed up and lay down on top of the silky counterpane. She closed her eyes as the woman bustled round the room, needing, more than anything, to be left alone to think. She did not open her eyes after she heard the door close behind the housekeeper. She might as well try to doze. She had not slept properly for the two nights before that dreadful, hastily arranged wedding. That probably explained why she was finding it so hard to cope with her new station in life. In time, she would get used to her husband's abrupt manner, and learn to read his moods to the extent she would not provoke him to anger.

He *was* trying to be kind to her in spite of the fact that she annoyed him. He had sent both the housekeeper and a maid to look after her.

It wasn't his fault that she would rather be in the parlour, discussing the peculiar woman who had arranged the household in such an eccentric manner, or laughing together over Linney's face when he realised he was the only male servant in a house full of women.

That was not the sort of relationship he wanted with her. He had not offered her friendship. Only financial security and children.

Somehow she had to find the strength to bear the limits he set on their relationship. Nor must she yield to the temptation to feel sorry for herself. It would only make him dislike her even more.

Wearily, she turned on to her side, laying her cheek upon her open palm. And before she knew it, she had fallen asleep.

She was not sure what woke her, but when she opened her eyes it was to see her husband leaning on the bedpost, gazing down at her with a pensive frown.

'How are you?' he asked, running one finger along the bevelled edge of the footboard. 'Better, I trust, after your rest?'

Her heart went out to him. It was not his fault he was not in love with her. Nor that he had not a glib tongue, to soothe over any awkward moments. He had warned her he would speak bluntly. In truth, it was one of the things she had liked so much about him, that slightly gruff manner, which made him stand out from the other men who had swarmed about Susannah. It had made him seem so much more manly than the others. She could easily imagine him barking out orders to a troop of battle-hardened soldiers, and them respectfully obeying him.

She smiled at him, sleepily. 'I am sure I will feel much better, when I am properly awake. Just at the moment, I still feel a little drowsy.' She yawned, and stretched, raising her arms above her head. He watched her sinuous movements with a dark, hungry look. She stilled, pierced by the force of desire she read in his stance. She couldn't help remembering how it had felt to be the recipient of all that pent-up longing the night before. Unwittingly, she shifted on the bed, revelling in the way his fingers clenched on the footboard as his eyes focused on her body. Her dress, which Cherry had loosened so she would be more comfortable, had partially slipped from her shoulders while she slept. She had kicked her shoes off, so her feet were bare, and she could feel that her skirts no longer covered her ankles, or calves. As he ran his eyes over her recumbent frame, she felt as though he was touching her all over.

'We need to wash and change for dinner,' he said abruptly, straightening up. 'I will use the facilities first, since you look as though you are still half-asleep.' Swinging away from her, he marched into their dressing room.

She watched him go, not sure whether to be glad or sorry. He did not want to want her so much, that was obvious, even to a woman of her inexperience. But want her, he did. There was no mistaking the hunger she had seen in his eyes as they had roamed over her recumbent form. She hugged the knowledge to herself as she sat up, and lowered her legs to the floor.

It was a start.

As she got to her feet, she felt a rush of feminine satisfaction surge through her. She caught her lower lip between her teeth. He wanted her, in spite of himself. And, oh, how she wanted him! Her body tingled in all the places he had paid the most attention to the night before. And her stomach gave a lurch at the prospect of receiving his attentions all over again.

In the dressing room, Captain Fawley grinned to himself as Linney helped him out of his jacket. He need not have worried that he was growing sentimental, after all. The jolt of lust he had felt, upon looking down at her, had been reassuringly carnal. All he had wanted was to lift her skirts and sink himself into the warm wet welcome, he could tell from the wanton wiggles she made, that he would find in his wife's sleepily pliant body.

There had been, apparently, no need to worry that she might find him repulsive, because of his scarring. As Linney helped him pull his shirt off over his head, he wondered if that had been because he had been so careful to shield her from the full horror of his injuries. He had kept the room dark, making sure what little light there was illuminated his good side.

Though, just now, she had looked up at him, in broad daylight, and given him clear signals that she felt aroused just by sensing the need in him. That was what she had been thinking of, as she had lain on the bed just now, watching him. Not how ugly his face was, but the way he had made her feel.

He frowned as he worked a soaped washcloth over his face and neck. It was surprising to think that a properly brought-up young lady like she should find such pleasure in the marriage bed. Although, he huffed, splashing away the soap with clean water from the basin, perhaps that was entirely due to the fact that her mother had not had time to warn her she ought not to enjoy it. She had, in effect, been surprised into her sexual awakening.

It felt good, he reflected, drying himself on the towel Linney handed him, to know that, in the dark of their bedroom, it had not mattered what he looked like. He had raised Deborah to heights of rapture, with his one good hand, his mouth and his own manhood. She was too innocent to have faked her response.

It felt good.

It evened things out, somewhat, to know that while she had made it possible for him to live in comfort, and independence, he had introduced her to pleasure she had never guessed at.

His chest swelled; he walked a little taller as he went to the upstairs salon to await the serving of the evening meal. In one department, at least, as a man, he had no lack.

Deborah sidled into the salon some time later, feeling completely exasperated. She had made the mistake of lying down in the only dress she had with her. It had not withstood the abuse well. She had agreed with Cherry that there was nothing for it but to borrow one of the late

Miss Lampton's gowns until her own could be brushed and pressed into some semblance of respectability.

Miss Lampton had clearly been somewhat shorter, and a great deal more plump, than she was.

'What,' her husband said, his eyes lighting with amusement, 'are you wearing now?'

'Another borrowed garment,' she flashed, 'since you did not give me time to pack anything of my own.'

His amusement faded, to be replaced by a look that in another man she might have described as contrition.

'Now, Deborah, you surely understand by now the reason for my haste in getting you to the altar. I could not risk Lampton getting wind of my plans, or he would have done his utmost to overset them. He had tried such a trick before, don't forget.'

She nodded, her hands tugging ineffectually at the voluminous skirts that left her legs bare almost to the calves.

'No, do not try to pull your skirts lower. You have very pretty ankles. I like looking at them.'

'It is hardly proper to be talking about my ankles,' she snapped, although she knew it was not talking about her ankles that had annoyed her, so much as hearing once again of his reluctance to confide in her.

'Deborah,' he said, holding out his hand towards her, 'I know I must have taxed your patience to the limit. I whisked you away from your home without giving you time to prepare, and I have been so anxious that something would prevent our marriage I fear I have been less than polite to you at times.'

'Well, yes, I have to confess your manner has been a little…abrupt,' she conceded.

He smiled his lopsided smile, the one that always tugged at her heartstrings.

'I do regret the necessity for keeping you so much in the dark,' he said, removing her excuse for maintaining any anger with him. 'But given your close friendship with Miss Hullworthy, and her own infatuation with that boor, how else could I have acted?'

You could have trusted me... She sighed, settling on to a chair and taking the glass of lemonade someone had placed on the table beside it.

'If I had laid my cards on the table,' he continued, 'would it not have been a burden on you?'

She bit at her lower lip, watching a pip bobbing about near the bottom of the cloudy liquid. Yes, she admitted, she would have found it hard not to have gone to Susannah and warned her about Lampton's duplicity. She supposed it was just possible that he had been trying to shield her from anxiety, just as Lady Walton had suggested.

However, she reflected bitterly, taking a tentative sip of the drink and finding it surprisingly pleasant, it was more likely that her husband was so used to barking orders at inferiors, and never having to explain himself, that he had just not considered her feelings at all.

Although to be fair to him, she sighed, taking a large, unladylike gulp of the refreshing beverage, he was not a man given to trusting anyone. Why should he? He had been surrounded by treachery and betrayal since before he had been born.

Mrs Farrell came in to announce dinner was served, and they both rose and went to the door.

'Oh, how lovely!' Deborah exclaimed on passing

through the double doors of the dining room. Crystal glasses sparkled in the rays of the setting sun that slanted in through the mullioned windows. Silverware glittered at the place settings laid out on a heavy damasked table-cloth, and the whole room was scented by masses of fresh roses prettily arranged in bowls along the table.

Her reaction brought a delighted smile to Mrs Farrell's face.

That look faded to one of affront, as Linney helped her into her chair, saying, 'Thank you, Mrs Farrell. I will take over from here.'

He had arranged things so that the food came from the kitchen to a sideboard just inside the door. He brought it to table, served his master and mistress, and removed the empty plates and dishes when they were finished with.

She would have to have a word with Mrs Farrell, and explain her husband's aversion to having strangers watching him eat, so that she did not take offence at Linney's peremptory dismissal. Thankfully the servants were used to serving an eccentric employer. They would grow used to her husband's foibles far more readily than some.

'Your things should be arriving in a day or so,' Captain Fawley remarked, as Linney brought out a dish of quince jelly.

'I shall be glad of it,' she admitted, shifting uncomfortably in the dress that, in spite of all she could do, would keep slipping off one shoulder.

'Yes, the sooner we can get you out of that dreadful gown, the better pleased I shall be.'

Deborah felt a flame of heat engulf her at the prospect of her husband taking off her gown. Guiltily she lowered her head, concentrating fiercely on her pudding. She was sure Robert would not have deliberately said something so indelicate in front of Linney. But when she eventually regained her composure, and lifted her head, he shot her a quite unrepentant grin.

She felt her cheeks heat to an unbecoming degree.

'You are looking a little flushed, my dear,' he said, leaning back and contemplating her thoughtfully. 'Are you feeling unwell again?'

'N-no, that is…'

He nodded, his face solemn, as he lay his napkin down beside his place setting. 'You probably just need another lie down. An early night would do us both good, I think. Linney!'

'Yes, Captain?'

'Get someone else to finish clearing away in here. My wife needs to get to her bed. I do not want to keep her waiting.'

Deborah wished she could sink through the floor. How obvious could he be making it that going to sleep was the last thing on his mind? She found herself exerting a vice-like grip on her dessert spoon, as he rose and limped past her to the door.

'As soon as I am ready, I shall send Linney to fetch you,' he shot at her over his shoulder, as he went out.

She looked at her dessert. She measured the distance to the door that had just closed on her insufferably insensitive husband. She picked up the bowl…and thought of Miss Lampton's staff. It would not be fair to indulge in a childish tantrum on her very first night here. Why should they have to clean up the mess she had made of her life?

She slammed the bowl down on the table, slinging the spoon in with a little cry of vexation. He had warned her how it would be, yet somehow, she had not believed he could be so…crude.

Well, she was not going to put up with being ordered to his bed, in front of a servant, as though she were a woman of easy virtue.

Getting to her feet so abruptly her chair overturned, she left the dining room and went down the stairs in pursuit of her husband.

She hesitated on the threshold of their bedroom, knowing he was probably in the process of having Linney remove his false limbs. Even though he had just humiliated her, she did not think it right to descend to the same level. She just needed to draw a line, across which she refused to let him go!

Raising her fist, she banged on the door.

When Linney opened it, she drew herself up to her full height. 'I do not care what your master asks of you. I will not have you marching into my dressing room, while I am in a state of undress! Send a message to my maid, when it is appropriate for me to come to bed, and she can relay the information to me.'

'Yes, miss—madam,' he corrected himself. 'Will that be all?'

Would that be all? As though she had requested he bring her a cup of tea, rather than touch upon a subject that was so delicate she wondered at herself in broaching it!

'Yes. That will be all,' she said, with as much dignity as she could muster, before turning with a twitch of her voluminous, borrowed skirts, and heading down the corridor to the other door that opened on to her dressing room.

Chapter Eight

She reminded him of a bristling alley cat when she finally stalked into his bedroom. Her eyes were snapping, her fists were clenched at her sides, and if she'd had a tail, it would have been twitching.

She had never looked more beautiful.

Wondering what it would take to goad his very correct young wife into losing her tenuous grip on her temper, he eyed her ill-fitting nightwear, and said, 'Take it off.'

She did not mistake his meaning, and, though her eyes narrowed, she just tugged the ties of her wrapper open, flung the garment to the floor and kicked it away from her feet.

And stood before him gloriously, furiously naked.

'Satisfied?' she demanded, planting her hands on her hips.

'Not yet,' he growled, though he knew satisfaction was not far off. It had not escaped his notice that tonight she had left her hair loose. Anticipating his demands. 'Get into bed now.'

The smouldering look that went with that peremptory command scythed right through her anger. Dropping her gaze to the folded-back edges of the bedcovers, she clambered in beside him.

Immediately, he hooked his arm round her waist and pulled her close. His weight pressed her back into the pillows as he kissed her forcefully.

'Ohh…' She shuddered when, eventually, he paused to draw breath. She wondered whether it was silly of her to feel flattered that he had not hesitated, as he had done the night before. She must have pleased him, though she was so inexperienced, for him to have set to work so swiftly.

'Oh, indeed,' he murmured thickly against her throat.

As his mouth worked hungrily against her neck, she felt as though she was melting. He raised himself slightly, just far enough so that he could run his tongue around the delicate whorls of her ear, and she found that she was running her hands up and down his flanks. He nipped the lobe gently with his teeth. She hooked her leg over his, so that she could run her foot over the calf muscles.

And they went up in flames, just as they had done the night before.

Deborah was amazed that he could want her with such ferocity, in the darkness of their bed, when by daylight, he did not seem to want her anywhere near him. But her awareness of how little she meant to him did not stop her from responding with her own fierce delight. And marvelling that this time, when he finally entered her, there was no pain, only an intensifying of her own pleasure.

Afterwards, they sank back into the soft feather

mattress, side by side, not quite touching, though she was aware of every breath he took. She felt as though she was waiting for something for him. Some sign. And wondered why she should suddenly feel wary, when they had just been so closely engaged.

It was a bit like a truce after a bloody battle, she mused, when each side gave the other time to collect their wounded from the field of combat, each aware of the other, but in no fit state to engage in further action. They had even communicated their passion through their sighs and moans, neither of them quite daring to shatter their tenuous bubble of harmony by putting anything into words.

As Deborah slipped into an exhausted sleep, she wondered if she would always feel as sad as this after they had been together.

The bedchamber was still shrouded in darkness, the heavy curtains firmly shutting out the feeble rays of early daylight, when she woke, to hear Linney moving about the room.

All the previous night's anger surged back. It was one thing having her husband see her naked, though that had been embarrassing enough. But she drew the line at having his servant wandering about the room while she had no clothes on!

Sitting up, having first made sure that the sheet was decorously clutched over her breasts, she turned a furious face to the manservant.

'Get out!' she yelled at him.

He paused in the act of settling a tray on a small table under the window.

'Begging your pardon, miss…madam, but I always bring the Captain's breakfast to—'

'Not any more you don't! Not while I am in his bed. If the Captain wants you, he can ring for you.'

Linney straightened up, his face blank. 'He did ring for me.'

She turned to look at her husband, who was regarding her with a look of barely concealed impatience.

Mortified, she slumped back on to the pillows, her only recourse to pull the covers completely over her head. Only once she had deduced, from the noises of crockery clattering, floorboards creaking, and the door squeaking open and shut, that Linney had left the room, did she emerge from under the covers.

'Good morning, to you too,' he growled.

'I don't know what kind of women you usually associate with,' she replied, resorting to frosty haughtiness to overcome her sense of humiliation, 'but I am not in the habit of displaying my naked body to anyone, let alone male servants!'

'Linney is more than just a servant to me,' he replied darkly.

Deborah gasped. He really put the dignity of his servant before her own discomfort. But then he added, 'Though, of course, I can see we cannot continue in quite the same habits we used to have. It's merely a question of logistics.'

'L-logistics?' she squeaked, increasingly outraged by the way he was treating her.

'Yes, you see, Linney and I have got into a routine that has worked for us both for several months now. It is not a simple matter to get me prepared to face the day. I warned you that you would have to get used to him being an integral part of our life. He is not just a valet, who lays out my clothes, pours my washing water and shaves me.' He speared his fingers through his fringe, pushing it out of his eyes. 'Damn it, Deborah, have you no sensitivity at all? Do I have to spell it out for you? I need help just to piss in the mornings! And if you don't get your carcass out of this bed, and ring for him to come back, you are going to have to be the one to hold the bottle to my…'

'I'm sorry, I'm sorry,' she stammered, sliding out of the bed and groping on the floor for her wrap. 'I'll ring for him to come back, and get out of your way.' Her cheeks flaming, she did as she had said, then hastily made for the door to her dressing room.

Once again, she had only looked at things from her own point of view. Her husband had told her he did not want her in the room while Linney undressed and put him to bed at night. She pressed her hands to her flaming cheeks, recalling the crude way he had spoken of having the man carry him back to his own bed, if she insisted on having her own room. Why had she not taken in the significance of what he had been trying to tell her? He could not get about with any ease, once he had removed his false leg, without the help of his burly serving man.

She sank to the floor by the washstand, bowing her head in her hands. She had not really comprehended just how awkward things that she took for granted were to him. And with her clumsy insistence on her own rights, she had forced him to speak of the weakness he managed to conceal from the rest of the world with such resounding success.

She felt thoroughly ashamed of herself.

And, worse, experienced a sinking feeling that she had given her rather touchy husband yet another reason to dislike her.

Captain Fawley lifted his eyes from the balance sheets, to see if Travers was trying to make fun of him.

There was nothing in the factor's pale eyes to show he was anything but a diligent employee.

'Are you quite sure?' he eventually brought himself to ask.

'Well, of course, the figures are only to the end of last quarter. Bound to be some fluctuations in the overall value since then. But not to any significant extent.'

'I had no idea.'

Travers smiled for the first time since he had walked into the office, as arranged, to go over the books with the new owner of The Dovecote.

'Nobody did, save Miss Lampton and myself,' said Travers, a gleam of enthusiasm lighting his formerly colourless demeanour. 'A very astute mind, had Miss Lampton. Invested very wisely.'

Captain Fawley suddenly found himself assailed by a wave of curiosity towards his benefactress.

'Explain,' he barked, inadvertently reverting to the attitude of commanding officer towards a subordinate up on a charge. Travers automatically sat a little straighter in his chair.

'Well, Miss Lampton, you see, sir, did have a little

money of her own, when she initially came to live here. Her father had banished her from the parental home when she refused to enter the marriage he had arranged for her. But instead of begging his forgiveness, Miss Lampton found that his harshness had stiffened her resolve to become independent of any man. And so, secretly, she began to, umm, speculate in various ventures….'

'On your advice?'

'Oh, no, sir. She had her own ideas about how she wanted to invest her money. Very forceful, she was. Would have dealt with the city traders herself, but for the fact such activity is forbidden a lady. Disliked having to use me at all, to tell you the truth, at least at first. After a few years, though…' he smiled as though indulging in fond memories '…well, we got used to each other.'

'A very successful partnership, in effect.'

'Yes sir, as you can see.' Travers indicated the ledgers which lay open on the desk.

Almost every single venture Miss Lampton had decided to dabble in had paid huge dividends. The wealth she had bequeathed to Captain Fawley was stupendous. He could live like a lord for the rest of his days. He frowned. His own modest requirements would scarcely make a dent in such an enormous fortune. He was too disfigured to try to cut a dash in society. At one time, he would have been delighted at the prospect of being able to indulge in his love of horseflesh. Now he could scarcely control the gentle mare Lensborough had trained and sold to him on terms that were akin to giving the creature away.

'I cannot continue on the path she trod,' he admitted to his factor, after a moment or two of reflection. 'I have always been a soldier. I have no head for business.'

'She foresaw that eventuality,' Travers said just a shade too quickly. 'She suggested you might like to simply sell up, invest in the funds and live a life of indolence.'

From the expression on his factor's face, Captain Fawley judged that Miss Lampton had not held very high expectations of his capabilities. Yet that had not prevented her from leaving everything she owned to him. He ran a rather shaky hand over the stack of ledgers on the desk.

He had a sudden vision of the woman who had lived in this house, scheming and plotting to make a fortune that she would leave to a complete stranger. She had not done it because she had any personal feelings for him. From what he had been able to tell so far, she disliked all males, on principle.

'Why me?' he grated. 'I am no relation to her at all.'

Travers stuck his chin out a little as he said, 'That was to your advantage, sir. Her family washed their hands of her when she became, as they termed it, difficult. Either of her brothers could have defended her when her father ousted her from the family home. Or even when the old man died. But they did nothing. The only person who tried to intercede on her behalf was your mother. She went to the old man and begged him to let Euphemia choose a husband she could love. It was perhaps inevitable that when Algernon became head of the family, he began to persecute your mother. He blamed her, you see, for encouraging his sister to defy their father. By the time Miss Lampton discovered what was afoot, there was nothing she could do for the unfortunate lady. But she felt she could partially redress the injustice by making you her heir. Shall I proceed with the sale for you, sir?' asked Travers, when Captain Fawley remained broodingly silent.

'I suppose that would be for the best,' he conceded. He could settle up his payment plan with Lensborough. It would be the first thing he would do. 'See to it, would you?'

Travers smiled as he got to his feet. 'With pleasure, sir. And may I say how glad I am you have fulfilled the terms necessary to inherit the fortune Miss Lampton worked all her life to bequeath to you. I would have been sorry to see that scapegrace nephew of hers get his hands on it.' His smile dimmed. 'Not once did he ever try to so much as visit her, when he thought she was just an eccentric old lady, eking out her existence in rural fastness!'

'To be fair, nor did I.'

'Ah, but you never even knew of her existence, did you, sir? It amused her, to think of herself as a sort of fairy godmother, weaving her magic behind the scenes…' He ground to a halt at the appalled look on Captain Fawley's features.

'Well, I don't deny she was a little eccentric,' he said uncomfortably. 'Just one more question,' said Captain Fawley. The factor schooled his face into that of bland servitor, awaiting his pleasure. 'If she disliked her brother, and her brother's son, so much, how did Percy Lampton manage to get himself a mention in her will at all?'

'A bad business, that.' Travers' face darkened. 'In

her latter years, when she became less mobile, Algernon took to visiting her occasionally. He would stride about the place, assessing its value, assuming she must bequeath it to another member of the family. He wanted his younger son, Percy, to inherit it, since the major part of his own estate went to his own heir. When he discovered that not only had she already made a will, but that it was in your favour, he became…well, I think *vicious* is the only word to describe it. He bullied and hounded her until she made that codicil, for writing you out altogether, he could not make her do!' Pulling himself together, he finished, 'Will that be all?'

Captain Fawley felt faint stirrings of a strange sense of kinship with the woman he had never personally known. She seemed to have disliked her brother almost as much as he did. She must have done, to have taken such pains to make sure that the boy he had set out to oppress became wealthy.

When the factor had left, Captain Fawley remained seated at the desk, marvelling at the extent of his good fortune. A feeling of exaltation rose within his chest and burst from his lips in the form of laughter. He had hoped he would never have to worry about a bill again. Buy a fresh set of linen whenever he felt like it. Play a hand of cards without having to consider how much change he had in his pocket first. Not this!

He had to find Deborah and tell her. Striding to the chimneybreast, he rang for the housekeeper.

'Tell my wife I want a few words with her,' he barked.

Mrs Farrell raised her brows in an expression of disapproval, but said nothing as she turned to obey his command. It was only when, some minutes later, a very timid knock on the door presaged his wife's arrival that it occurred to him it might have seemed a little autocratic to send for her as though she was one of his subordinates.

The look of trepidation on her face as she approached the desk behind which he sat only confirmed his sense of having treated her with less than the respect due to a wife. He recalled the way she had fled from his fit of temper that morning. He had not seen her since. She looked as though she wished she was not seeing him now.

'I only asked you in here to share the news that the factor has just given me,' he said. 'Do sit down! You look like a nervous subaltern up on a charge!' he snapped, his conscience provoking him to lash out, quite unfairly, in completely the wrong direction. It was with himself he was annoyed. He felt even more angry with himself when she sank into the seat, her head down, hands clasped in her lap as though expecting a scold.

Rapidly reviewing the few words they had exchanged since making their vows, he could hardly blame her. With a heavy sigh, he said, 'It cannot have been easy for you, the last few days. I apologise.'

'You apologise?' She looked up at him with swift enquiry. Then shook her head. 'It has occurred to me, during this morning, that I have some things to apologise for too.'

'You do?' he sat bolt upright, completely astonished. 'Why, what have you done?'

'Well, I have been angry with you on more than one occasion…'

'Which I thoroughly deserved, I dare say. Look,' he

said, when she opened her mouth as if she would have protested, 'it is clearly not such a simple task to merge two lives together as I had thought it would be. We will have to come to some accommodation regarding Linney's presence in our room. I cannot do without his aid, you know, but—'

'If you would just tell me before you sent for him, so that I could cover myself up. Or leave altogether if your need for help is of a delicate nature.'

Her cheeks went bright red. It reminded him how delightfully tousled she had looked that morning, after having spent some minutes hiding under the blankets. He made an effort to soften his voice as he said, 'I should not have used such coarse language this morning, Deborah. It was inexcusable.'

She smiled shyly up at him. 'As you say, we both have adjustments to make, being married. I dare say it will take us some time to get used to each other's ways.'

What a generous nature she had! And how reasonably she was dealing with their earlier quarrel. He recalled some of the scenes that had gone on in Walton House when his half-brother had first brought home his French wife. Doors slamming, crockery being thrown, sulks and tantrums. Heloise had gone about town, acting as outrageously as she dared, to try to punish her husband for his cold and autocratic treatment of her. They had settled down eventually, but for a while, they had made each other miserable.

Of course, he had known from the outset Deborah would never treat him to such tantrums. He had never seen her make a fuss about the difficulties life threw in her way. She just got on with whatever she had to do, with good grace.

'We have a lifetime.' He smiled, congratulating himself on choosing such a levelheaded girl to wife. 'And if we can both be as reasonable as you are being this morning, then it will be a pleasure to get used to your ways.'

'Oh,' she said, her smile growing broader. What a lovely thing it had been to say. Especially since she knew he meant it. Had he not promised never to offer her Spanish coin? She ducked her head, fidgeting with a stray thread that was working its way from her cuff.

Watching her nervous gesture, he suddenly knew what he wanted to spend his money on. It was not just that she had not brought many clothes with her. She had never had many clothes. She had worn the same ball gown, with different trimmings, for the entire Season, until the night of Lensborough's ball. She had only three or four bonnets, to his knowledge, and she had always worn her gloves until the seams started to split.

'When we go back to London, I want you to buy an entirely new wardrobe,' he said decisively.

She looked up at him in alarm. 'You do not like my clothes?'

'That is immaterial. You need new ones. I want you looking extremely fashionable.' He wanted to see her enjoying herself. Women enjoyed shopping for clothes. And then showing them off.

'We will have to get a barouche, so you can drive round Hyde Park in it.' He frowned. 'And a house, a fine house, in the very best address.'

Deborah's heart sank. She was not the kind of woman he should have married at all. While her head had been full of dreams of a house in the country, filled with children, it seemed that, all along, he had wanted to live in town and cut a fashionable figure. With a pang, she realised that they had never discussed what they wanted out of marriage. Robert had mentioned children, and security, but not any details of where or how he antici-pated they might live out their lives.

She pasted a brave smile on her lips as she forced herself to say, 'That sounds lovely.'

He frowned. 'It cannot be done all at once. It may take Travers some time to raise the capital.' He indicated the pile of ledgers on the desk that separated them.

'Oh, I shan't mind staying here for a while,' she put in quickly. If he intended to return to London, she had best make the most of what little time she had here. From the window seat of an empty upstairs bedroom, where she had taken refuge that morning, she had noticed, not an oak tree, but a massive yew in the centre of a velvety smooth lawn. Beyond that was a walled garden, over which peeped the boughs of what looked like a productive orchard. The housewife in her wanted to explore the orchard, the vegetable gardens and the stillroom. The mother in her wanted to see if it would ever be possible to build a tree house in that yew. Or, if not, at least hang a swing from its lower branches. From her recollection of the journey, the house itself stood not far from the village. She wanted to walk to it, and explore it and find out if there were other walks in the area. She wanted to attend the church with its squat,

Norman tower, and make friends with the local ladies. In short, she wanted to make The Dovecote her home.

She would not care all that much if she never set foot in London again. Life there had seemed shallow, and brittle and not the least bit comfortable.

'I am sorry I did not give you the chance to bring a change of clothing with you,' he broke into her reverie. 'But you won't be needing much anyway, for the next few days.'

No, he would not wish to entertain, she thought, entirely missing the wicked grin that lit his face.

'No, I suppose not,' she said, trying to be as amenable to his wishes as she could. He could barely tolerate having his own wife in the room while he was eating, let alone strangers. She could make this one gown do until her trunks arrived, since she would only be pottering about the gardens and house. She would put off visiting the neighbours until the next time they came down here. Whenever that might be.

'Then you agree?' he said, getting to his feet and coming round the desk.

'Agree?' She was not aware he had asked her a question. With a puzzled frown, she swiftly reviewed their conversation.

'That we should spend these next few days getting to know each other better,' he said, coming to stand over her. She looked up at him in bewilderment. He reached down and ran one finger along the curve of her cheekbone.

'I want to take you back to bed, Deborah. Now. In broad daylight. Does that shock you?' His face took on a shuttered expression. 'Disgust you?'

Her heart leapt at the look of longing she had read before the shutters came down. She had thought he could barely tolerate having her in bed, because she was not the woman he wanted. Now she saw that part of his insistence on complete darkness stemmed from his fear *she* would find *him* repulsive. She wanted to cry. How could he think she might feel disgust, just because he had a few scars?

Slowly, she got to her feet. Then reached out her own hand, mirroring the way he had just caressed her face. Deliberately, she ran one finger down the unblemished side of his face. Then she reached up on tiptoe, to kiss the cheek that was puckered, and reddened, before saying, 'Not disgusted. But perhaps more than a little shocked. Oh, not at your suggestion, but at my reaction to it. I find that when you speak of wanting to return to our bed, my heart has started to beat faster. I believe it is quite improper, and yet…'

He caught her hand to his cheek, on a ragged gasp, his eyes darkening. 'You want me,' he growled, before sliding his hand round to the nape of her neck, and kissing her soundly.

'Yes.' She sighed, when he finally broke the kiss. 'I should not, but—'

'Why not? We are married. There is no sin in this, Deborah.' Grabbing her hand, he made for the door.

Now her heart was really beating fast. The thought of retreating to the seclusion of their room, in broad daylight, was incredibly exciting.

'Damn it,' he cursed, coming to an abrupt halt. 'I am going to have to get Linney to get me out of this leg first.'

She made a little mew of disappointment as she pictured the scene. He would ring for his serving man, and go through all the rigmarole of getting ready for bed, having first ensured her absence from whatever ritual he was so unwilling for her to witness. Then he would send for her. And then, when he had finished with her, send her away so that Linney could help him wash and restore him to an appearance of wholeness. The whole procedure would be cumbersome, and awkward, and embarrassing for all concerned.

'It will not be very romantic,' she acknowledged ruefully.

'We agreed, when I proposed to you, we would not try to cozen each other with romantic nonsense,' he spat at her irritably.

'Romantic nonsense…' She sighed, recalling she had gone along with everything he had demanded, so thrilled had she been he was proposing at all. 'No, we would not want that.' She looked at her husband, tense, frustrated and growing angrier by the second, and wondered what she could do to help him.

'I know what I do want, though,' she said carefully, drawing his gaze from the door at which he had been glaring balefully for the past few seconds.

'What is that?'

'The same thing as you.' And then she blushed, though she managed to hold his gaze. 'When you spoke about returning to bed…well, do we really need a bed? I do not know very much about it, but it seems to me that, umm…' And then she lost the ability to look at anything other than her hands, which she found she was twisting at her waist.

Without saying a word, Robert reached past her, and turned the key in the lock. Then, quite calmly, he went to the windows and very deliberately drew the curtains.

'Are you quite certain about this?' he husked, turning to look at her. Even in the shadowed room she could read intense hunger in his face. Her own blood was pounding through her veins. She could not speak. She only nodded.

'Then come here,' he urged her, holding out his hand.

She flew to him, and he caught her, claiming her mouth in a kiss that had nothing of tenderness in it. Yet her spirit still soared. She did not care how unseemly this was, she only knew she would let nothing stop her from expressing her love in the only way he seemed able to accept it from her.

'I wish we could be naked,' he growled against her neck, while his hand kneaded at her breast. 'I wish I had the agility to take you standing up, against the door, or that you were not a lady, and I could bend you over the desk…'

The images his words conjured up should have shocked her. Instead, she found that she was growing even more excited. And eager to accede to his every demand.

'Do it, then,' she heard herself say, in a voice roughened with need.

His head flew up in astonishment. 'Do what?'

'Whatever you want,' she said, reaching round his waist to yank his shirt from the waistband of his breeches. She sighed at the satin texture of his body under her fingers. 'I need to feel your skin too,' she confessed, looking up at him with trepidation at her boldness. 'I want you now. I don't want to leave this room.' Her breath hitched on a sob. 'I don't want to have to wait for Linney, and for it to become cold and businesslike.'

'I won't let it be cold then,' he husked, 'nor make you wait. But if you want it now,' he warned her, 'you are going to have to help me.'

'I know,' she whispered. 'Show me what to do.'

With a fierce growl, he sought her mouth again, kissing her greedily. For the first time, he flung his injured arm about her waist, holding her close to him. She could feel how strong it was, holding her to his chest. It felt a little strange, ending just below the elbow. But that was just a fleeting thought. It was what his other hand was doing that dominated her mind. He had bunched up the material of her skirts and reached underneath until he found the soft skin of her thighs above her stocking tops. He only paused there briefly. Soon she began to moan, clinging to his shoulders for support when her knees became so weak under the ministration of his clever fingers, she thought her legs would give way.

'The wall, the wall,' he grunted, pushing her backwards until she was leaning against a space between two glass fronted bookcases. 'Lift your skirts,' he ordered, as he let them go, to unbutton the fall of his breeches.

'This won't be very decorous,' he warned her, as she swiftly obeyed, granting him the access he sought.

No, she gasped. It wasn't in the least bit decorous. Nor was it cold or businesslike. It was frenzied, and exciting and…necessary. Oh, so necessary, for her to have this—this proof that he could not wait for the night, but needed her now.

'Robert,' she gasped, winding her arms about his neck. 'Robert, I…I…'

I love you, she wanted to cry.

His mouth found hers, and the words were never uttered. He kissed her as though his life depended on it, pounding into her while she clung to him, her anchor through the storm of passion that swept them away.

This time, they drifted to shore together, clinging to each other like survivors of a shipwreck. Their limbs tangled, they sank to the floor, gasping and shaking with the force of what they had shared.

'My goodness,' Deborah panted, her face pressed into the worn cloth of his jacket.

'Goodness had nothing to do with it.' He chuckled, rolling on to his side to look down at her. Her cheeks were flushed, her eyelids still heavy with passion. He leaned down to kiss each one in turn.

She flung her arms about his neck, arching up against him. She wanted this interlude never to end. She had hated it when he rolled away from her at night, silent and brooding. If only she knew how to prolong this sense of closeness!

'Have mercy, woman,' he groaned, rolling over so that he was partially on top of her. 'At least wait until after luncheon, when I have had a chance to recover, and we may retreat to the privacy of our bedroom.'

'What?' She gazed up at him in bewilderment for a few seconds before the penny dropped. He thought she wanted more of what they had just been doing! There was no tenderness in his look, just a sort of smug pride. The sort of look she guessed a man would give a woman he had just thoroughly seduced in his office.

She felt confused, cheapened somehow by the realisation that as far as he was concerned, their joining had nothing to do with love.

She sat up, twitching her skirts down over her knees. He rolled on to his back, his arms splayed out at his sides.

'Look at what you have done to me, woman,' he groaned in mock despair. 'You will have to help me to my feet, tuck in my shirt, do up my breeches…'

She wanted to slap him. It had been as much his doing as hers. More, in fact. He was the one who had suggested going back to bed in the first place! Briskly, she knelt up, then bent to the task of tidying his clothing. He caught her hand.

'What have I done now to make you angry?'

'Nothing!' she snapped.

And all the light died from his eyes.

He rolled on to his side, and pushed himself up on to his good knee, supporting his weight on his hand.

'I can manage without you!' he said, when she went to help him to his feet. And then, with an agility she had not suspected, after the way he had gone on and on about needing Linney all the time, he got to a standing position, using the leg of the desk, the back of the chair and sheer determination.

'I will leave you alone, then,' she said, as he slumped into the chair behind the desk.

'Deborah, wait!' she heard him say as she whirled

away to the door. It took her a few minutes tugging on the handle before she remembered he had locked it.

'Deborah, for God's sake…'

She did not hear whatever else he had to say. Flinging the door open, she dashed out into the hall, making blindly for the front door, which stood ajar. Once outside, she lifted her face to the sun that streamed down from a cloudless blue sky. It seemed all wrong. How could it be such a gloriously beautiful day, when she felt so churned up and…muddied inside?

It made no difference though. She had to put some distance between herself and the man who could make her melt into a puddle of surrender at one moment, then shatter her with his coldness the next.

Stepping off the porch, she made her way out into the grounds.

Chapter Nine

'Would you tell my husband I have gone to our room for a rest?' Deborah asked Mrs Farrell.

She had walked for what felt like hours. She was footsore, and heartsore, and had the beginnings of a headache nagging at the base of her skull. It was her own fault, for dashing off without a bonnet. She could not quite understand what had happened to the sensible, practical girl who had weathered so much in the wake of her father's death. The slightest thing had her flying off the handle these days.

She had not even got across the lawn before seeing that the scene in the office had not been Robert's fault at all. She had been feeling ashamed of her wanton behaviour, and, when he had teased her about it, had lashed out at him. Turning towards the orchard wall, she harboured the mutinous thought that if only he had whispered words of affection, and reassurance, she would have been able to carry off the whole thing with aplomb.

But her innate honesty soon had her rejecting that

scenario. As she pushed open the door to the orchard, she realised that it was the fact that she loved him enough to abandon all her principles that had left her feeling so prickly. Whatever he had said would have been wrong. Even if he had murmured those lover-like words she so longed to hear, she would only have accused him of being dishonest.

No, none of this was Robert's fault. He had been scrupulously honest with her. She was the one who was living a lie, by letting him think she had married him for financial security.

Mrs Farrell gave her a strange look.

'Well, since you missed your lunch, would you like me to bring you a tray too?'

'Thank you, yes,' she said, fumbling for the handle to the door to her rooms. 'If you will excuse me?' She crossed the sitting room swiftly, but paused on the threshold to the bedroom. Somebody had already been in, and drawn the curtains, as if they had known she would return with a headache.

'Where the hell have you been?'

The voice, emanating from the bed, made her jump out of her skin. Through the gloom she could make out Robert, reclining on top of the quilt. He looked incongruously dark and menacing, lounging against the froth of lace pillows banked against the headboard.

Her hand flew to her throat. 'I have been walking about the grounds,' she gasped, her heart still pounding with shock at the hostility in his voice. Though why should she be surprised he was angry with her? She had behaved extremely badly.

'Robert,' she said, hastening to the foot of the bed before he had a chance to say another word, 'I am so sorry for the way I ran off, after we—after, umm, well, you know.'

'Had marital relations up against the wall of my study?' he said coldly.

'Please don't make this more difficult for me,' she begged, her fingers gripping the footboard until her knuckles went white. 'I don't want to fight with you all the time. But I cannot…quite cope with…'

'The practical reality of being married to a cripple?'

Her head flew up, a stunned expression on her face.

'It is not that! You must never think that!'

She had thought once before that Robert's wounds were not just physical. His hurts went deep, and, in typical male fashion, he lashed out at anyone who touched on them.

Ruefully, she reflected she was guilty of doing exactly the same thing. Every time she became aware of just how little he valued her, her wounded pride made her lash out at him.

If they were ever to get beyond this dreadful sniping at each other, one of them was going to have to be willing to abandon their pride, and simply absorb the hurts the other dealt them. She did not suppose for a minute that person would be Robert.

She went round to the side of the bed and perched on the edge of the mattress.

'The practical reality of just being married at all is quite enough for me to cope with,' she confessed, linking her hands in her lap, and regarding them solemnly. 'I had little idea of what went on in the marriage bed before our wedding night. It was such a revelation. And when you began to speak of it…' She faltered, searching in vain for the words to describe what she had felt. 'My heart began to pound,' she said, her cheeks flushing as she admitted, 'and it suddenly struck me that we could do *that* again, and I…well, I know I lost my head. And afterwards, when you began to make a joke of what we had just done, I…well, I felt humiliated, if you must know. I had done something of which I felt quite ash…shamed.' Her voice hitched on a suppressed sob. She paused, sucking in a breath, turning reproachful eyes on him as she said, 'And then you mocked me.'

'That was not my intent,' he grated, reaching out to place his hand over hers.

'No, I…I worked that out for myself, as I walked round the orchard. You were just trying to make light of the difficulties you would have getting up off the floor.' She shot him another look, this one full of trepidation.

'In future, I think it would be better if we restricted our activities of that nature to the bedroom,' he growled. 'You may remember it was my first choice. I just wanted to get you naked and into bed and keep you there until it is time to return to town.'

She had completely forgotten the earlier part of their conversation, until this reminder. Her mind flew back to his stated determination to get to know her, and his puzzling reference to not needing clothing. Why had she not understood at the time that he had meant in a carnal way?

At that moment, Mrs Farrell returned with the promised tray. Deborah was glad of the interruption.

She was feeling quite flustered by the blunt way Robert spoke of what she considered a very delicate topic.

'There, now,' said Mrs Farrell, placing the tea tray on the small table under the window, 'you have a nice cup of tea, and a bite to eat, and you'll soon be feeling much better.'

Smiling wanly, Deborah went to the table, allowing the housekeeper to pour for her.

'You too, sir, if you don't mind me saying so. Hardly touched his lunch,' she informed Deborah, with a sorrowful shake of her head. 'I can see the news Mr Travers brought you came as quite a shock.'

After only a moment's hesitation, Robert swung his legs off the bed and joined Deborah at the table.

She noticed that all the food which had been brought had been prepared so that her husband could eat it without assistance. Even the cold mutton pie had been cut into tiny squares. There would be no need to ring for Linney and have him hovering over them while they ate. She felt some of the tension ease from her shoulders.

Mrs Farrell only departed when she saw they were both making inroads into their light meal.

'She seems quite determined to mother us,' said Robert, jerking his head in the direction of the doorway through which their housekeeper had just gone.

Instead of making the riposte that his own manservant was not exactly a typical valet, she pondered over something Mrs Farrell had said, which had puzzled her.

'Did Mr Travers not bring the news you expected? Are you very disappointed?' She was not surprised the supposed fortune was not what Robert had hoped for.

The house was modest in its dimensions. And from what she had seen, the grounds were only capable of providing the kitchen with the barest essentials. 'I beg your pardon,' she added hastily, at the stony expression on her husband's face. 'I did not mean to pry....'

'No, not at all,' he said, eyeing her keenly. It had not occurred to him, until this very moment, that she had no idea of the size of the fortune that would transform their lives for ever.

He could no longer attribute her enthusiastic participation in their sexual athletics in his study to a desire to pander to her suddenly wealthy husband, in anticipation of the rewards he would shower on her for showing him such generosity.

'I never did get round to telling you what Travers told me, did I?' he mused.

If he had been thinking logically, he would have known that if avarice had prompted her spectacular departure from propriety, she would not have flounced off in such a huff afterwards. He might have been able to eat his lunch, instead of pushing the food around the plate morosely, wondering why he was so disappointed at receiving further proof Deborah was no different from any other woman.

'When that was the whole purpose of asking you to join me in the office. We got...distracted, did we not?'

She looked away, quickly, rolling a piece of bread and butter between her fingers into a doughy ball.

He popped a piece of mutton pie into his mouth, recognising her action as a symptom of acute embarrassment.

Though she had shown no embarrassment in his

office. She had been just as keen to lift her skirts as he had been to get underneath them.

Until that morning, he had always thought she was a rather shy, retiring girl. And her stammered confession earlier had confirmed his belief she was also rather naïve. What on earth had come over her, then? Not two days ago she had been a virgin. This morning, she had practically ripped off his shirt in her eagerness to press herself against his naked skin.

Had she truly enjoyed her first sexual experience so much that she could not wait to repeat it? She *had* admitted to losing her head. It was only afterwards that she had felt ashamed.

Having a vicar for a father, she was bound to have had a rigidly moralistic upbringing. Did she believe that enjoying sex was sinful? Was that what it had all been about? Not money, but morals? It certainly fit with his initial assessment of his wife's character.

'Deborah,' he said gently, 'there is nothing wrong with enjoying marital relations. Don't you remember the words of the marriage service? Yes, celibacy is an honourable estate, but there are some people who just have passionate natures. You are one of them.'

She dropped the sticky ball of dough on to her plate, wishing she had the courage to tell him how wrong he was. She did not have a passionate nature. Until she had met him, she had never hankered after male attention. She could have lived her whole life without ever marrying, and been content. It was meeting Robert that had changed everything. Because she had fallen in love with him!

When he was not with her, she had only to think of

him to turn shivery with longing. When she saw him, she always yearned for his touch. And when he did touch her, she stopped thinking of herself as a practical, plain spinster, whom no man would look at twice. She became Captain Fawley's woman, her heart beating with such passion it swept everything away but her body's insistent clamour to merge completely with him.

But he did not want to hear her speak about anything to do with the emotions. No romantic nonsense for him! She turned to stare bleakly out of the bedroom window.

'You don't need to be ashamed of the way you are,' he persisted. 'I, for one, am very glad of it.'

She was shocked when a little dart of pleasure shot through her.

He reached across the table, capturing her chin in his hand, and turned her face towards his. Looking deep into her eyes, he said, 'Do you have any idea what it did for me, to have you clawing at my back, urging me on, while I pushed up your skirts?'

'Robert, please, don't…' How could he like the idea she could behave like that, without knowing it was because she loved him? She tried to avert her head, but his grip on her chin was too strong.

'No, Deborah, it is too late to pretend you don't enjoy my attentions. Why should you even wish to?' He relaxed his hold, so that his fingers only framed her face. 'We are man and wife, now. I never thought,' he said, his hand stroking her face gently, now that she had ceased trying to avert her gaze, 'that I could…' He halted, on the brink of confessing he had once feared he would never fully recover his manhood. He had accepted the fact that even if he ever did regain his natural urges, any encounters would be brutish, brief, and confined to the kind of dark dens where money exchanged hands. To have this lovely woman kissing his face as though there were nothing wrong with it, exploding into rapture while he took his pleasure in her, was more than he could ever have dreamed of. That, he suddenly saw, was why he had been so disappointed to think she had been motivated by avarice, had perhaps even faked her response.

He shook his head. He had met this woman only a few weeks ago, had been intimate with her for a matter of days. He was not about to bare his soul when he had not the least idea what motivated her.

So he leaned across the table and kissed her instead.

For a fleeting moment, she wondered if she ought to put up some resistance. But it was only the last dying gasp of her rapidly withering pride. He wanted her, and even if it was only in a physical sense, even if this was the only way he would ever want her, she would not deny him. Besides, she wanted him too. She would be a hypocrite to pretend otherwise when just the merest brush of his lips on hers reduced her to a quivering mass of longing.

She sighed into his mouth, winding her arms round his neck. It was all the encouragement he needed. Getting to his feet, he dragged her upright, and pulled her hard against him. He wondered, after what had happened this morning, if her conscience would make her fight her own inclinations. But far from struggling away, she pressed herself up against him, her breath coming in needy little gasps.

'Bed,' he said firmly, in between kisses. He did not break contact with her for more than the second necessary to grate that one word as he backed her away from the table.

She felt her knees hit the edge of the mattress, and then they fell together in an ungainly tangle of limbs. Clinging to her resolve to concentrate on his needs, she asked, 'Don't you need Linney?'

'Not until later,' he growled, raising himself to tug at the laces to her gown. He pulled her bodice down, growled, 'Much later,' and lowered his head to suckle at her breasts through the material of her chemise.

'These buttons would not dig into you so if you were to undo them,' he said, a little later.

She felt a sense of jubilation at this invitation to remove his jacket. She knelt up on the bed beside him when he sat up to facilitate the procedure. It would not have been at all hard to push the sleeves down his arms, since he was not in the habit of wearing his false hand when they were at home, if he had not been kissing her neck all the while.

'Now your shirt?' she asked, still hesitant to proceed without his full agreement. Once she had bared his upper body, he would not be able to hide the scarring she had glimpsed down the left side of his chest. When he nodded, she felt honoured that he was permitting her to do something so intimate for him. It was a simple matter to unlace his shirt, and pull it over his head. But, terrified of shattering his trust at such a crucial moment, she kept her eyes averted from the stump of his left arm, bending swiftly to kiss his mouth, as soon as she had flung the shirt to the floor.

Freed of this barrier of clothing, Robert rolled her beneath him, taking back control. Gripping the neckline of her chemise between his teeth, he bunched the delicate fabric in his fingers, and ripped it away from her breasts. It may have been his inability to deal with tricky fastenings that had him tearing her clothing, but oh, it felt wickedly exciting! She writhed ecstatically beneath him as he licked, and nipped with his teeth, and suckled at her, her hands sweeping the breadth of his back.

Her legs felt trapped by her skirts. She wanted to be able to spread her thighs, so that he could settle between them. As though he had read her mind, he solved their mutual difficulty by reaching down and ripping the flimsy muslin from ankle to her waist. For a split second, she regretted the ruination of the one gown she had brought with her, but then she recalled his stated intention to keep her naked, in bed, for an unspecified amount of time, and a sensuous thrill swept all her practical concerns away.

He could not fully remove his breeches. He had been lying on the covers fully clothed when she had come in. His boots, she thought fleetingly, as between them they frantically tore away the last barriers of fabric, were going to ruin the quilt. But then they were one, and her capacity for rational thought ceased. She loved him, oh, how she loved him. And to feel him filling her, embracing her, needing her in this way, stoked her own need to fever pitch.

But afterwards, as they lay side by side, amidst the tangle of ruined clothing, the doubts and fears crept slowly back. He had only to kiss her, and she lost her head.

How was she going to explain to Mrs Farrell just how they had managed to get boot blacking all over the beautiful white quilt? And it was all very well saying she did not need clothes, but that was nonsense. She supposed she could borrow one of her husband's shirts, she reflected, chewing at her lower lip. Or send a maid to fetch one of Miss Lampton's shapeless gowns for the moments when she simply would have to leave the bedroom....

'Stop it,' Robert growled.

'What? Stop what?'

'Thinking. You are growing as tense as a board.'

He tugged her up against his side, dropping a kiss on to the crown of her head.

Bother the quilt, she thought, snuggling into his side and draping her arm about his waist. And bother the servants too. They can think what they like. *So long as Robert wants me here in bed, he shall have me.*

And with a smile playing about her lips, she slipped into a deliciously restful sleep.

Robert shifted slightly, so that he could look down at her. Her head rested upon his scarred shoulder, her hair flowing over his mangled arm like a sheet of softest silk. Something stirred in his chest at the sight of her gleaming perfection curled up trustingly against his battered body.

It was not tenderness.

It was not!

It was the warm glow that sometimes came over a man after such a satisfying sexual encounter. And— naturally he felt particularly pleased at the way things were working out. He had feared he might never have a willing woman in his bed again. Not only was Deborah willing, but she could rouse him to a state where he could perform twice in one day!

Naturally he got a warm feeling when he looked down at her lying in his arms. She had given him much to be thankful for.

And over the next two weeks, he decided that asking Deborah to be his wife had been an inspired choice. She seemed to have taken on board his assurance that it was not a sin for married people to enjoy sex. Though she never instigated it, she always responded enthusiastically to his overtures. Once, she had even made him laugh, tilting her head to one side, tapping her finger thoughtfully against her chin, saying, 'It is as well I am of such a practical nature. And that I care little what becomes of my clothing.' For despite him saying they had best restrict any amorous interludes to the bedroom, he soon discovered there was nowhere they could not make love, in spite of his disability, if she put her mind to it.

She was a marvel.

He looked at her across the width of the dining table, admiring the way the candle-light brought out the rich chestnut tones in her hair, and wondered how he had ever existed before she came into his life.

The thought was like being doused with a bucket of cold water. He had only planned to spend a week at The Dovecote, at the most, just long enough to take possession and look over the place. His one driving ambition had been to return to London, and flaunt his wealth in Percy Lampton's face. But she had put all his plans out of his head. They had been here over a fortnight, and all he had done was establish that there was nowhere a disabled man could not have sex, if his partner was determined enough.

Laying down his wineglass with a snap, he glared at her.

'We have dallied here long enough. Tomorrow, we must return to London.'

His grim face and curt tone cut Deborah to the quick. She had, she suddenly saw, allowed herself to hope that his attentions over the past two weeks had meant he was growing fond of her. But that one word, dallied, was like a sharp frost, blighting tender shoots that had been fooled into premature growth by a few unseasonably warm days. Dallying was what a man did with a kitchen maid. Not their own May, of course, since any man foolish enough to try dallying with her would likely receive a frying pan to the skull for his temerity.

She bowed her head over her plate, forcing herself to continue cutting up her pigeon as though his remark had not just shrivelled her burgeoning happiness to a stalk.

Carefully wiping the meat through the sauce, she placed it in her mouth, chewing slowly while she tried to muster some response that would not sound as though she were a petulant child. Robert had never offered her affection. It would be foolish of her to distance him by complaining that he hurt her when he dismissed their physical intimacy as exactly that. Merely physical. She would always treasure the memory of the two weeks they had spent here. They had acted just like real lovers, unable to keep their hands off each other. Even if it had meant so little to her husband, to her it had been a real honeymoon. She would allow no cross words, no petty accusations to taint this magical time.

'I shall be glad to see my mother again,' she eventually managed. 'I have been a little concerned that she has not written to me. Nor has Susannah. They must have the address,' she continued, 'because they sent my trunk here.' Her brief fears that she would have to wander about the house clad in only her husband's shirt had proved groundless. The very day after they had ruined Miss Lampton's pristine white quilt, a carrier had turned up at the door with her possessions.

Captain Fawley's frown deepened. He suspected that if Lampton was running true to form, he would have ditched Miss Hullworthy the minute he heard about Deborah's wedding, leaving her prey to malicious gossip. Mrs Gillies would not wish to blight her daughter's honeymoon with that kind of news. He was only surprised Miss Hullworthy had not written to tell her supposed best friend of that misfortune herself.

'I expect they had their reasons.'

'Well, I shall be able to see them both, soon, and speak to them, which will be better than getting a letter, will it not?'

It comforted her to speak of her mother and her friend, she reflected. She really would be glad to see them both again. Perhaps her mother would be able to offer her some words of wisdom, even if all she did was listen while Deborah poured out her heart. It would help her to cope with this unequal marriage.

'I should like to make an early start,' said Robert, his eyes snapping a challenge.

He expected her to make a fuss, she could see. Complain that he had not given her enough notice, and that she needed time to pack. Laying her napkin down beside her plate, she rose to her feet with a sad smile.

'Then we should have an early night.'

Their last night in the house where she had been so blindly happy. Tomorrow, they would return to London, and she had the horrible feeling that it would be a return to real life. In London, she would discover what marriage to her really meant to her husband.

If it meant anything at all.

Their coach drew up outside the front steps of Walton House late the following afternoon.

'We will live in the rooms my brother set aside for my use to begin with,' Robert had explained on the journey up from Berkshire. 'Though I should like to begin searching for our own house at once. Do you have any preferences?'

'I?' Deborah had been startled when he had asked for her input. She had assumed he would just do as he pleased, and ride roughshod over any objections she might raise.

'Yes, you. It will be your home too. And don't forget, money is no longer an object. Miss Lampton left me an enormous fortune.' Then he frowned, remembering they had still not discussed anything that really mattered. Whenever they had been alone, talking had been the last thing on either of their minds. He had no more idea of what went on behind those languorous brown eyes than he had on their wedding day. She had fascinated him, dazzled and distracted him with her eagerness to participate in lovemaking. Physically, yes, they were as intimate as it was possible for two people to be.

But he did not really know her.

'My wealth exists in the form of shares in various enterprises. You may reside at as fashionable an address as you wish.'

'I…I had not given it any thought,' she admitted.

Robert had scowled at her, as though her remark displeased him. But all he had said was, 'Perhaps we should get an agent to scout about for us and let us know what is on the market before making any decisions.'

'Very well.'

'And in the meantime, you will open accounts at dressmakers, milliners and so forth. Lady Walton will be only too pleased to guide you, I dare say. She always looks bang up to the knocker.'

And I do not, she thought, battling yet another wave of hurt. He had told her once before that he wanted her to look fashionable. Like Lady Walton. His dear friend, she thought, her lips compressing in irritation. The woman he had confided so much in, when he did not trust her as far as he could throw her. He did not even trust her enough to purchase her own clothes. He wanted another woman to watch over her, and make sure she did not go about looking like a provincial dowdy any more.

An impressive-looking footman, in blue-and-silver livery, bowed them into the house when Linney knocked on the door. Robert just stalked across the hall, opened an inner door, and said, over his shoulder, 'If you have any complaints about the accommodations, I don't want to hear them. We will only be here until you choose our new address.' With that, he just disappeared through the doorway, leaving her floundering in the hall.

To her surprise, it was Linney who came to her rescue.

'Don't pay no attention, madam. He's always like this when his leg's giving him pain. And long journeys in a carriage near always jolt him up. I hope one of the first things you will persuade him to buy, now he's got so much money, is a really well-sprung coach. So he won't go hiring no more of them bone-rattlers no more.'

'Thank you, Linney,' she said, though she did not know why on earth he would think she might have any influence over her irascible spouse.

She trailed across the hall, pausing on the threshold to her husband's domain to see why he should think she might not like the rooms.

She was looking at a sitting room. A very masculine room, she had to admit, with large, leather sofas and chairs dotted about a floor that had not seen polish for some time. Robert was sprawled upon one of the sofas that flanked an empty fireplace, a crystal tumbler of spirits already clutched in his hand, leading her to suppose that Linney's assumption had been correct.

'Through here is the bedroom, madam,' Linney said, opening a door to the right of the fireplace. She peeped inside. Again, it was a very masculine room, with a solid-looking oak bed, heavy furniture and bare floor-boards throughout. The washstand, she noted with some misgiving, was placed beside the wardrobe. She would have no privacy, unless she evicted her husband from his own bed every morning. The logistics, as Robert had once put it, would be somewhat tricky. There was a truckle bed just protruding from under the main bed, upon which she guessed Linney had used to sleep. Eyeing it, he leaned towards her, murmuring, 'I will move to rooms along with the rest of the staff here, madam. He won't be needing me the same, not now he's got you. And if he gets into any difficulties, you will only have to ring, and I can be down here in a trice.

'This here is the door that leads to the mews,' he continued, in a louder voice, indicating a door tucked into a far corner of the sitting room.

'My wife will use the front door of Walton House, not skulk in at the back as though she were some kind of miscreant,' Robert growled from the sofa.

'Do many miscreants come in at the back, then?' she asked, taking a seat on the sofa opposite her husband and pulling off her gloves. If she did not manage to lighten the atmosphere, she was afraid she might burst into tears.

'One or two,' he growled, draining the glass and letting his head fall against the sofa back, though he kept his eyes fixed on her.

'What a very interesting life you must have led before you married me. I hope I am not cramping your style?'

'We had best keep that door locked, now you are in residence,' he said, ignoring her attempt at humour. 'All the miscreants I know must come in through the front door, from now on. See to it, Linney, would you?'

She untied her bonnet, and laid it upon the cushion beside her.

'May I fetch you some refreshment?' said Linney.

While Linney played the host, her husband simply lay there glaring at her.

'Thank you. What is there?'

'Only strong liquor or ale down here. But I dare say that, if I was to ask, Lord Walton's staff could rustle you up some tea and such.'

'Thank you, Linney. That would be welcome.'

With a nod, and an affable smile, the manservant left the room.

She fiddled with the ribbons of her bonnet, wondering if there was any topic she might safely broach without getting her head bitten off.

'Well?' he snapped. 'Can you live in two rooms that have been set up for the purpose of making life easy for a cripple?'

And then it hit her why the floorboards were bare, and unpolished. No rugs, or slippery surfaces to trip him while he had been learning to walk first with a crutch, and, later, his false leg. No need to climb the front steps, should he wish to go out. The way to the mews was probably all on a level. No little tables, that he might bump into in here, either, she noticed for the first time. Only a sturdy desk, under the window, with two upright chairs beside it that informed her it doubled as a dining table. She remembered the handrail beside the bed, where she would have expected a night table to stand. The extra-broad steps placed to make it easy to get into, and out of, that bed. Nothing in itself had been remarkable enough to draw notice, but, put together, they clearly spoke of his disability. And he hated her seeing it.

'It looks like any other set of bachelor's rooms, I

would imagine,' she said, with a slight shrug. 'Why should I object to any of it? After all...' she shot him a look from under her lashes '...I never heard you complain about all those feminine frills that dominated the decorations at The Dovecote.'

'Hmm,' he said, looking at her through narrowed eyes. 'You have a knack of making the best of things, haven't you?' His lips twisted into a sneer. 'You would no doubt have resorted to quoting some uplifting portion of scripture to get you through the days if you had become a teacher.'

She flinched at the bitterness in his tone. And felt heartily relieved when Linney returned, saving her the necessity of having to make any reply.

'Lady Walton has heard you have returned, and wonders if you would like to take refreshments in her sitting room? She wants to discuss the ball.'

'Ball?' said Deborah.

'Hell and damnation!' said Robert. 'I had forgotten all about the wretched ball.' Sitting up, he wearily rubbed his hand across his face. How could he have forgotten the ball he had arranged to hold here, in Walton House? It had all been part of his plan to flaunt his victory in Percy Lampton's face. And his brother had been equally as keen to do his part.

'It will be a public demonstration of our family solidarity,' Charles had said. 'A way of silencing the disgraceful rumours regarding your birth once and for all. Though how they got away with it for so long beats me. Anyone who has ever been in the portrait gallery at Wycke would see at once you are more of a Fawley than I am!'

'I suspect the circumstances surrounding my marriage will cause far more gossip than will be silenced by one ball,' he had countered.

The Earl had smiled coldly. 'But it will serve to separate the sheep from the goats.'

Society would be polarised between those who wished to retain the Earl's good graces, and those who supported the Lamptons. Lord Lensborough would stand buff, he was sure, and he was not without influence. His presence would assure his and his wife's acceptance amongst his own coterie. His true friends, comrades from his regiment, would stick by him no matter what. And as for what the rest of society thought, well, he did not give a rap! The Lamptons would no doubt spread tales of him being a usurper, who had gained his fortune by deceit and trickery. But he was used to their malice. So far as they were concerned, he had always been the cuckoo in the nest.

He had been looking forward to launching himself into the polite society that had always excluded him, thanks to the Lamptons' lies. Yet one night in Deborah's bed had put all thought of it clean out of his head.

He glared at her. 'The ball to celebrate our marriage is to be held two weeks' Friday. You had better go and find out what arrangements Lady Walton has made. And offer what belated help you can. She should not have to do all the work, not in her condition.'

She felt a peculiar shrinking sensation in her stomach. He was chastising her for not organising a ball she'd had no idea was being held.

'Well, get on with it!' Robert barked, when she had

sat frozen on the sofa staring at him in silence for several seconds. 'But don't expect tea up there. Heloise won't touch the stuff.'

'Are you not coming?'

'Absolutely not!' What did he know about arranging a ball? It was women's business. They would enjoy it, no doubt—women seemed to. And it would be a good opportunity for Deborah to get to know Heloise better. The countess had few close friends, but she had already taken to his wife, for some reason that eluded him.

'All I want is my bed. And some peace.' He needed to remove his false leg. He had been wearing it for longer and longer periods, and it was chafing almost un-bearably. This was the price he had to pay for indulg-ing in vanity. He had not wanted his wife to see him hobbling about the place on his crutches. And he had left off having Linney in each night, to rub on the ointment that might have soothed the stump, because Deborah did not like having a servant intrude in their bedroom.

Rather stiffly, Deborah got to her feet and stumbled to the door. He wanted some peace. In other words, she was irritating him. This was why he had suddenly decided to come back to London. Not only was he was tired of the dalliance, but he wanted his life to go back to the way it had been. He could not have told her more clearly that, if it had not been for the inheritance, he would as soon have not married her at all.

Chapter Ten

Susannah had been quite right. The Countess of Walton was a useful person to know. Modistes, milliners, haberdashers—they all fell over themselves to serve such an exalted personage. Even with the Season being in full swing, and all the best dressmakers working flat out to meet the demands of their fashionable customers, they assured the Countess that her friend would have a fabulous creation ready in time for her ball.

The Countess picked out an underskirt of pink. Since it suited Deborah's dark colouring, she saw no sense in raising any objections, especially since she was sure that, had she come alone, this particular modiste would have shown her the door. She did demur over the level of the neckline, but both the modiste and the Countess insisted she would not look fashionable if she had an extra inch of lace added to preserve her modesty. Since Robert had stipulated he wanted her to look fashionable, she ended up agreeing to purchase a garment that she felt was little more than a strip of ribbon bound round her nipples, from which quantities of spangled gauze cascaded as insubstantially as a waterfall.

While the seamstresses set to work on it, Robert accepted an invitation to an informal card party at the house of one Captain Samuels, and an evening at the opera with the Earl and Countess.

'My friends won't care what you look like,' he bluntly informed her. 'So it won't matter if none of your new gowns are ready. And I thought that sparkly thing you had on at Lensborough's ball would do nicely for the opera. Just be sure to get a cloak to wear over it. That should not be too difficult, should it?'

'Not at all,' she had replied, baring her teeth in a polite smile. Not even a clueless, provincial vicar's daughter could fail to get her hands on an opera cloak with two full days' warning. She could borrow Susannah's, at a pinch.

She managed to enjoy herself eventually, at Captain Samuels's party, though the angular, sandy-haired officer greeted her with a sort of bluff camaraderie that was quite outside her experience. It took her a little while to work out that all the gentlemen present now regarded her as a fellow officer's wife and accepted her into their midst as an extension of Robert.

The evening at the opera was more unsettling still. Whenever the Earl introduced her to anyone as his sister-in-law, they began looking at her as though she was someone worthy of respect. Not at all as people had looked on plain Miss Deborah Gillies. Of course, she was not Miss Gillies any more. Not now she was married. Though just who she was, she was not yet quite sure.

It dawned on her that it was a miracle she had ever met Robert at all. He moved in completely different social circles from what she was used to. In fact, if he had not been so doggedly determined in his pursuit of Susannah…

No, she would not allow her thoughts to stray in that direction. She would *not* allow jealousy to rear its ugly head.

Besides, nobody could feel jealous of poor Susannah at the moment. She was quite wretchedly miserable.

For Percy Lampton had not been near her since the day the notice of Captain Fawley's marriage had appeared in the *Morning Post*.

'I was not unduly concerned at first,' Mrs Gillies had confided in her, when Deborah called, the morning after her return to London. 'Any number of matters could have prevented him from taking Susannah on those daily outings to Hyde Park. But then I began to hear whispers that he was actively avoiding any gatherings where he might run the risk of meeting her again. There is always someone malicious enough to relay that kind of rumour! I do not know what to do with her.' She sighed, then continued, 'If it was you, I could tell you to hold your head up, and weather it out. But Susannah does not have so much backbone. She will *droop* around the ballrooms once she discovers Mr Lampton is not there. Which, of course, is *fatal*.'

For a moment or two, Deborah had wondered if she should explain exactly what Percy Lampton had been up to. Only, she wasn't sure if knowing he had only toyed with her to lure her away from Robert because of their long-standing feud, would make everything worse. Believing he had just been indulging in a casual flirtation was hurting her badly enough. Oh, it made her blood boil to think of the way he had led her friend on!

'A lady should *never* wear her heart on her sleeve.' Her mother had shaken her head disapprovingly. 'Why, you would not let the world see your heart was broken, if you loved some man who did not return your regard, would you? She has ruined any chances she might have had amongst my own acquaintance. I do not know what to do with her. If she cannot pull herself together, I shall have to take her home. And then it will be even worse for her next Season. She will have destroyed any illusion that she could pass for a lady of quality! But anyway, enough of that.' She had folded her hands in her lap, as though closing the topic.

'I must say it is good to see you looking so well, my dear. The break in the country has done you the world of good.'

Deborah bade farewell to any hope of confiding in her mother then, for Susannah came drifting into the drawing room. With a determined smile, she launched into a description of The Dovecote. By the time she had recounted the peculiarities of the staffing, Susannah was beginning to look interested. Though she flinched the first time Deborah mentioned the name of Lampton, she did seem to find that lady's history and eccentricities quite diverting. Deborah felt that, on the whole, her visit had lifted her friend's spirits, though she wished she could have done more.

It had been several nights later that she realised there

was one way, at least, in which she could help her friend. And it was Mrs Samuels who showed her the way.

'We are going on a picnic on Wednesday,' she said over her shoulder, while leaning over the edge of the box where they were taking supper at Vauxhall Gardens. 'The lads are going to row us upriver till we get to green fields. We will be taking two boats, at least. I expect it will degenerate into a race, with neither team wanting to concede until we end up at Windsor!' She laughed. 'Do say you will come. It will be tremendous fun. The Countess used to come on some of our jaunts, before that Friday-faced husband of hers put his foot down. She always used to enjoy herself immensely!'

Score one more point to the Countess of Walton, thought Deborah resentfully.

Mrs Samuels, seeing Deborah's reluctance, gave up trying to attract the attention of a particular friend she had seen disappearing down one of the dimly lit paths, and sat back down next to her.

'I realise you might find our set a little overwhelming at first, without your husband,' she said in a reassuring tone. 'Look, why don't you bring a friend along, to help you keep that pack of ruffians at bay?'

She tilted her head to where several of their party were frisking about a pair of strolling beauties across the lamplit lawn, like a pack of springer spaniels. She would have been mortified to have been the focus of such boisterous attention, but the beauties were lapping it up. And when one of them dropped her haughty pose of indifference to giggle, causing the young officers to set up a rousing chorus of cheers, it came to her in a flash that this was exactly the kind of diversion Susannah needed. Oh, not that she would get over Lampton's defection all at once. But receiving the adulation of a fresh set of admirers might at least halt her downward slide.

'Thank you,' she smiled. 'I should like that.'

It was only as she was on her way home that she wondered why the woman had assumed Robert would not come with her. Had he asked Mrs Samuels to take her off his hands? Though it was not as if they saw all that much of each other these days. Life in London was such a whirl. With her having a ball to organise, and Robert being tied up with all sorts of business men in connection with the settling of his new fortune, as well as visits to his tailors and so forth, they only seemed to meet up at mealtimes. Their conversation consisted of relaying their daily schedule, and discussing which invitations to accept.

'Though before long, I don't expect our social lives will coincide much at all,' he had once said, sending a chill down her spine.

Had that been his subtle way of saying he did not want her hanging on his sleeve in public all the time? Until Mrs Samuels's invitation, she had been trying to laugh off her ridiculous sense of foreboding. Why, Robert did not know how to be subtle. If he had anything to say, he would say it straight out!

Surely?

She shook her head. She knew she was unbearably sensitive where her husband's moods were concerned. She was probably reading too much into his words.

But as to this picnic…oh, she would love to get

beyond the noisy, crowded city streets for one day, and breathe fresh country air for a while.

And she *would* invite Susannah to come along. Especially since Robert was not, apparently, going to form one of the party. She did not suppose for a minute that Susannah would find it awkward to run into Robert again, but he certainly would.

Her shoulders slumped as she climbed the front steps to Walton House. She couldn't help feeling that if it were Susannah who had married him, he would have escorted her everywhere, proudly showing her off. As it was, he stood stiffly beside Deborah, at the few events they had so far attended as a couple, snapping curt responses to the fulsome congratulations he had received from his military friends. While she did not expect him to look at her with pride, or affection, like some of the other officers did at their wives, could he not at the very least try to look as though he was content with her? That was not too much to ask, when in public, was it?

She went to the multi-purpose table under the window and pulled open a drawer to extract some writing paper. She would invite Susannah to the picnic, and send the letter via one of Lord Walton's footmen. Lady Walton had airily told her she must consider them all at her disposal, until Robert hired more servants of their own. She grinned, flicking the end of the quill under her chin as she envisioned Susannah's face lighting up when a liveried footman of a belted earl delivered a note to her door. And the vicarious thrill her parents would get, when she wrote to tell them that little snippet of news.

From the shadowy bed, where Robert had been re-clining, he saw the mischievous smile that lit her face with a feeling of deep unease. She had looked dispir-ited on entering. He had always known marrying him would not be a sinecure for any woman. But Deborah normally bore it with the fortitude that carried her through whatever life threw in her path. That grin though, as she penned a letter…

He grimaced in pain, though for the first time since returning from Berkshire, it was not on account of his leg. He had paid a heavy price for the bliss he had known in Deborah's arms, for the first few days of his return to London. The devil of it was that it was usually his foot that hurt the most. It was an eerie feeling, to wake with the burning need to fling off the agonising weight of the bedcovers, only to remember that the foot which hurt so abominably was actually lying on some dung heap in Spain.

No, the spasm of pain that had him rearing up off the bed was not a physical one. It was jealousy. Raw and scalding. He felt its sting every time some fellow con-gratulated him on his marriage, running appreciative eyes over his lovely young bride. For she was lovely. She had a healthy glow about her that had been lacking when they first met. Two weeks in the country had put flesh on her bones, and brought colour to her cheeks.

But the sparkle in her eye, as she received the com-pliments of his fellow officers, chilled him. She would lower her head, and look up coyly through her lashes at men he had considered his friends, and blush receptively at their frankly lecherous looks. He wished he had not taken such pains to ensure her pleasure in the marriage bed. He wished he had been brutish, and swift and made it such an ordeal she would shudder with revulsion at the prospect of a man's touch. He had thought sexual pleasure was the one thing he could give her, in return for all she had given him. But it had been a grave error. Now he had awoken that side of her nature, there would evidently be no stopping her.

She must have heard him moving about in the bedroom, for she looked up from her missive, a troubled frown appearing on her face. It did not escape his notice that she shoved the half-finished letter furtively into a drawer.

He leaned against the doorjamb, feeling unutterably weary. What did a man do in such situations? Demand she tell him who she was writing to? Forbid her to have anything to do with any other man?

Why should it bother him, anyway? he thought, slouching across to the well-stocked sideboard. He had gone into marriage knowing no woman could stand him. Deborah had tried, he had to give her that. But when it came down to it, of course she would prefer the company of a man who was whole, and handsome and given to dishing out the kind of complimentary claptrap all females lapped up like cats at the cream.

She frowned when she saw him slump on to the sofa, a large tumbler of brandy in his hand.

'Is your leg giving you pain?'

'No,' he snarled, tossing back half the drink in one go.

From the way he was glaring at her, Deborah suspected he wanted to say that she was the one driving him to drink. Suddenly, she decided she would go and visit

Susannah in person. Reaching into the drawer, she took the crumpled letter and stuffed it into her reticule. She did not want to leave it lying around for Robert to find.

'Where are you going?' Robert asked as she set her hand to the door.

She did not wish to hurt him any further, when he was already in such low spirits, by mentioning the woman he had wanted to marry.

'To visit a friend,' she replied, hastily escaping through the door.

A friend. He downed the rest of the drink in one great gulp, and tossed the empty glass among the cushions.

If he were a whole man, he could scotch her schemes by offering to escort her. Or maybe even follow her. Though what good would that do? If he prevented her from embarking on an affair now, it would only postpone the inevitable. Women were fickle creatures. No constancy in them. He had always known that.

So why did it hurt so damn much, knowing Deborah was just like all the rest?

Deborah had sent one of the footmen to procure a cab. She planned to go and collect Susannah in it, rather than have her come to Walton House, and risk her running into Robert. Then they would go down to the landing stage to join up with the rest of the party.

'You are looking decidedly fetching this morning,' Robert remarked gravely as she tied the ribbons of a new chip straw bonnet in a jaunty bow under her left ear.

'Why, thank you!' She felt ridiculously pleased by this compliment. He gave her so few. It made them all the more precious, because she knew that when he uttered one, he meant it, not like some men who spouted such stuff almost out of habit.

'Going somewhere special?'

'For a picnic, with Mrs Samuels, Captain Samuel's wife, and some of his friends. We are taking a couple of launches up the river.'

'It is a fine day for it,' he remarked, glancing out of the window. 'Perhaps I shall come with you.' There was no mistaking the consternation his statement created in Deborah's breast. And it decided him. He jolly well would go with her, and find out which one of his so-called friends was sniffing round her skirts. 'An outing with Sammy's crowd may be just what I need to shake off these blue-devils.'

Deborah's heart sank. But while she struggled to find a way to gently explain that he might rather not come, because of Susannah, he had turned on his heel, saying curtly, 'I shall fetch my hat.'

Linney sat bolt upright, a concerned expression on his face.

'Should I—?'

'No! No need for you to tag along,' he snapped. 'Take the day off. I shall be among friends.' He did not want Linney to know, quite yet, what Deborah was up to.

'If you are sure…?' he began doubtfully, glancing at Deborah.

Deborah gave him an encouraging nod, as her husband disappeared into his room to fetch his hat, and a brand-new ebony cane with a chased silver handle.

'For getting into and out of the boat,' he explained.

'I told you I would not need you, Linney. For even if I should slip and fall into the water, there will be half a dozen muscular young chaps ready to haul me out.'

Suddenly, Deborah understood why Mrs Samuels had assumed he would not be going on such an excursion. Why could she never remember he was not in top physical form?

It was not until they had got into the cab that she rather haltingly confessed she was going to collect Susannah.

He made no verbal response, but she could tell by the tightening of his lips that he was not looking forward to coming face to face with the woman he had loved and lost.

'I will come in and pay my respects to your mother,' he said when the cab drew to a halt outside the rented house. 'It was remiss of me not to have performed that duty sooner.'

'I am sure she understands completely,' said Deborah sympathetically, when his frown deepened. Her mother had felt so sorry for him when Susannah had turned to Percy Lampton.

'She could have called on us,' he reflected, as he descended from the cab. 'Have you said anything to make her suspect she might not be welcome?'

Rather taken aback, Deborah said, 'Of course not! If you must know…' she took a deep breath, steeling herself to be the one to break it to him '…Susannah is taking Mr Lampton's defection extremely hard. She barely goes out, and, when she does, she *droops* apparently. And my mother does not like to leave her in the house on her own.'

Captain Fawley flinched. 'I should have thought she would think herself well rid of that toad.'

'Well, she does not. I think she really l—'

She could not tell her husband Susannah had fallen in love with his worst enemy. He already had quite enough to contend with.

She tried to keep a smile pasted to her face while her husband paid the formalities to her mother. She wished now she had warned him exactly what her plans had been at the outset, so that he need not have come. He could hardly withdraw now.

She felt so guilty for having put him in such an awkward position. He was plainly so uncomfortable at being cooped up in the hired cab with both the woman he loved and the woman he had married, that her own insides began to churn in sympathy.

By the time they reached the wharf, though, it had become plain that he had mastered his own roiling emotions, and compressed them into an iron-hard resentment, which he aimed directly at her. And then, later, at the young officers who dared to flirt with Susannah.

Deborah had no defence against the piercingly sharp glances he continually darted in her direction. She did not even try. She felt she deserved his contempt for forcing him into this excruciatingly painful position. From the moment a pair of his robustly healthy comrades handed him into the boat with the same tender concern they had shown the ladies, she wanted to curl up and weep.

Susannah sat across the thwarts from him, twirling her parasol, completely oblivious to the pain that racked him every time one of the shirt-sleeved oarsmen coaxed a smile to her lips, while Deborah's conscience smote her afresh, every time she glimpsed him moodily repelling all attempts to draw him away from the fringes of the rest of the day's activities.

She was relieved when at long last, they deposited Susannah back at her house, and his ordeal was at an end. She was not surprised that he did not speak a single word to her in the carriage home. His embittered look said it all. By keeping him in the dark about her plans to help Susannah get over her heartbreak, she had caused more for him. He had been obliged to watch her gradually unfurl and blossom like a bud under the adulation of his peers, while Susannah had not spared him one glance.

He slammed the door of their rooms shut with unnecessary force, striding across to where she was removing her bonnet and spinning her round by her upper arm.

'You are my wife, damn it!' he growled.

Oh, yes, and how he must wish she was not. Especially when he'd had all day to compare what he had wanted, with what he had ended up with. Tears sprang to her eyes, even though she knew the last thing he wanted from her was sympathy. Indeed, even as she opened her mouth to speak her heartfelt apology for making this day such hell for him, he brought his lips crashing down on hers, silencing her in a kiss that spoke of loss and anger.

Though she fully accepted he could not help being angry, at length she had to try to break away from his determined possession of her mouth. She could hardly breathe. Her head was beginning to spin.

It took him a moment or two to realise she was struggling, but as soon as he did, he broke away, to glare down at her with all the resentment that had been growing steadily throughout the day, blazing from his eyes.

'Oh, Robert,' she gasped, raising her hand to his cheek.

He caught it before it reached the puckered skin, his grip on her wrist bruising.

And before she knew it, he had tugged her into the bedroom and pulled her down on to the bed beside him.

Her heart soared as he kissed her more passionately than he had ever done before.

But then he closed his eyes as he pushed up her skirts. Buried his face in her neck as he freed himself from his breeches. And as he entered her with no further preliminaries, he gave a groan that reminded her it was not passion driving him, but pain. Pain that Susannah had caused. Oh, he might be seeking solace in her body, but *she* was not the one who had wrought him to this pitch.

A sob welled up and shook its passage through her throat as she did the only thing she could do for him. She wound her arms round his neck, her legs round his waist and let him pour all his grief and suffering into her, absorbing it with a shuddering desperation of her own. For even though she was convinced he was only using her, she could not stop her body responding to his wild mating as it always did. Need was soon driving them both, raw and agonising in its intensity. She pulsed around him the very second he emptied himself into her, tears flowing unchecked down her face and into her hair.

'I am not sorry,' he panted hoarsely into her ear. 'I do not care if I hurt you.'

'I know,' she whispered, letting her arms fall limp against her sides. 'But you did not hurt me.'

'No, you liked it, didn't you?' He raised himself up, looking down at her with searing contempt. 'You like it hard, and fast, like the cheap slut you are.'

He rolled off her then, flinging his arm over his face, as though he could not bear the sight of her.

She felt something inside her die. Hadn't he always assured her that he liked the fact she always responded to his advances with a passion to match? Now he was telling her it was no such thing. And it was too late to try to explain that she could not help it if she responded the way she did. He would think she was making up excuses to try to justify her behaviour, if she told him she loved him after what had just taken place.

He had taken her loving, free offering of herself, twisted it into something nasty and sordid, then flung it back in her face. She slid off the bed and staggered from the room.

But it was not far enough. She could not stay in the same house as him—no, not for one second longer.

Picking up her bonnet from the side table by the door, she let herself out quietly, and stood irresolutely on the front step for some minutes. A cab swept round the corner, disgorging its passengers outside a house three doors down.

She hurried along the pavement, intent on seeking the only sanctuary she could think of.

'Could you take me to Half Moon Street, please?' she asked the driver.

She needed her mother.

* * *

It was ridiculous to be holding this ball, thought Deborah some ten days later, to celebrate the marriage of two people who barely spoke to one another any more. She stood pale and trembling to receive her guests, beside Robert's stiff and taciturn form, though only Lady Walton seemed to have noticed anything was amiss. She had taken one look at their set faces at the dinner preceding the ball, and leaned across to whisper to her,

'The first few weeks of marriage are horrid, are they not? But once you get past all that silliness, I am sure you will be as happy as Charles and me.'

Deborah very much doubted it. Though given to extreme formality in his dealings with most people, the Earl of Walton was clearly very much in love with his wife. He revealed it in a dozen little ways. A touch of his hand to the back of her waist as he escorted her into a room, or a glance and a smile that spoke of shared thoughts.

Robert never smiled at her. Nor could he bear to touch her any more. Not since the day of the picnic, when he had expressed his contempt for her in such a way that even she could no longer cling to any hope that he might one day grow fond of her.

He had even argued with his brother upon the subject of this ball. Though it was to be held in honour of his marriage, he saw no reason why he should be obliged to dance at it.

'Do you think I want to make a spectacle of myself capering about a slippery floor while the guests are laying side bets as to how long it will take for me to fall over?' he had snarled.

Deborah had wanted to curl up and die. He would not be raising any objection if he had married Susannah. He had begged and pleaded for a dance with her, pursuing her from one event to another. And he had not looked as though he cared in the least what Lord Lensborough's guests had said or thought, when she had finally capitulated.

'Why do you not open the ball with a waltz?' Heloise had suggested. 'Rather than a really long set of country dances?'

'Not exactly the traditional opening to a ball, but I think it would serve,' replied the Earl, looking proud of his wife's suggestion.

Robert had simmered down, his grudging agreement twisting the knife a little deeper. 'I will dance part of one waltz with my wife, and that is my limit.'

He would have walked across hot coals for Susannah, but he did not even want to perform one sedate waltz with his plain, despised wife.

Yet dancing a waltz required that she take hold of his left hand, the false hand, the very prospect of which had made Susannah squeal with disgust.

Saddened, she looked over his left shoulder as the musicians struck up the first chord, remembering the defiant tilt of his chin when Linney had buckled it on earlier before helping him on with his shirt. Like a knight, being armoured by his squire, ready to go into battle. She felt that it would have been an honour to take that hand now, and demonstrate to the world that nothing could ever come between them, if only he was not so reluctant to have her in his arms.

A fine sweat broke out on Robert's brow. Damn it, perhaps he should have just gone along with the set of country dances, and put up with the pain all that capering about would have brought to his severed limb. It could not have been worse than the agony of having so many people watching him stumbling about the floor with a woman whose face was rigid with distaste. He could hardly blame her. What they were doing was not so much dancing, as walking very carefully in time to the music. Once upon a time, he would have relished sweeping his dance partner into a spin turn at the corner of the dance floor, taking the opportunity to pull a pretty woman a little closer to his body than was strictly allowed. Now, he dreaded coming across any kind of obstacle that would require him to attempt anything more than the most basic step. Thankfully, after a few bars of excruciating embarrassment, the Earl led his wife on to the floor, Lord Lensborough followed with his, and soon, so many partners were twirling around him that he felt safe to abandon the pretext of dancing at all, and headed straight for the nearest open door.

'Thank God that's over with,' he said, letting go of Deborah's arm.

'I suppose you will be spending the rest of the evening in the card room?' she said stiffly, as he subsided on to the nearest chair. Since the picnic, this had become the pattern of the few events they had attended together. He had escorted her, introduced her to a few of his friends, then abandoned her to their care while he strolled off to watch the play.

He got to his feet, and gave her an icily polite bow

before stalking away, leaving her entirely alone. On other evenings, it might have been excusable. But could he not have pretended just this once, on the night they were supposed to be celebrating their marriage, that he did not regret having done so, quite so much?

Was he deliberately trying to humiliate her?

She squared her shoulders, and raised her chin before stepping back into the ballroom. She would not let anyone know that she cared. She would not become the object of anyone's pity. And so she acted as though she was perfectly happy to dance with other gentlemen, and that she did not feel acutely distressed by the way her husband publicly shunned her. Her dance card was soon filled by Robert's friends, who jokingly commiserated with her for being shackled to such a dull dog of a husband. One or two of the Earl's political cronies, who would not have deigned to so much as nod to her when she had been Miss Gillies, seemed to feel it was appropriate to notice her at her own ball, as well.

At length, she calmed down enough to stop thinking only of herself. She knew she ought at least to make sure Susannah was coping. She had noticed her dancing with the Earl at one point, but not looking all that happy to be doing so. Now, she was nowhere in sight.

She went to the chaperons' benches, to ask her mother if she knew where she was.

'She went out on to the terrace to try to compose herself,' said her mother, ominously.

'Oh, dear. Perhaps I had better go after her, and keep her company for a while.'

'Oh, yes, dear, would you? I must confess, I am at

my wits' end with her. Why, at one time, just being at an event like this would have…' She trailed away, shaking her head.

Deborah knew exactly what it would have meant, at one time, to her ambitious friend to be moving in such exalted circles and dancing with an earl.

She got right to the end of the terrace before she detected the faint sound of sobbing coming from beyond the flight of steps that led into a sunken garden. As she got further from the house, and the music from the ballroom grew fainter, she became increasingly concerned by the way her friend seemed to have finally broken under the strain, even hiccupping out the odd words between sobs. But when she finally found her, rather than hurrying to her side and wrapping her arms about her, she froze.

For Susannah was not alone.

And the man who was with her, who had just pulled her into his arms so that her sobs were muffled against his chest, was Robert.

'Hush, now,' he said as Deborah skidded to a halt, not five feet away from them.

It was not seeing her husband put his arm about Susannah's shoulders that shocked her so much. It was the fact that *she* had overcome her revulsion enough to let him hold her. That she was clutching at his shirt front, raising her tear-stained face to his, and confessing,

'I have made such a terrible mistake!'

'Not so great a one as I have,' replied Robert, looking ruefully down into her beautiful face.

Chapter Eleven

Deborah walked back into the ballroom, feeling as though she was encased in ice. She never could remember the rest of that evening's events. She supposed she must have mechanically executed the steps of the dances she had promised to all those faceless men who came to claim her, but all she could see was her husband, telling the woman he loved that he had made a terrible mistake.

He meant in not asking Susannah to marry him, of course. If only he had gone to her, and explained that a great fortune could be hers, this ball could have been given in her honour. She would have become a member of the Earl of Walton's family, and gone shopping in Bond Street with a countess.

For such compensation, Susannah would have been well able to overcome her revulsion at Robert's injuries. She must be sorry now she had ever let that revulsion show. Yes, her mistake had been spurning Robert's devotion.

She did not like to think what the next step would be for the ill-fated lovers now they had reached an understanding. Whatever they chose to do, there would be an almighty scandal. Robert would come out of it none the worse, of course. He had married for convenience. Nobody would expect him to stay faithful to his wife. And if the most beautiful débutante of the Season chose to throw herself at him, who would blame him for taking what was on offer? Other men would just chuckle, and call him a sly dog, but all doors would remain open to him.

But Susannah would be ruined. Even if Robert did not go so far as to make her his mistress, there were enough beady eyes trained on Miss Hullworthy to ensure any clandestine encounters, such as the one Deborah had witnessed, would be shouted from the rooftops. Social ruin was as painful as ruination in fact, with none of the attendant pleasures.

Once all the guests had gone, she returned to their rooms on the ground floor. Deborah stood stock still in the sitting room when Robert stalked past her into the bedroom, finally realising that there was a point beyond which even the strength of her love could not take her. It would be like a knife thrusting into her heart every time he sneaked off for snatched moments of intimacy with Susannah, expecting her to turn a blind eye. And if he ever took her with his eyes shut again, slaking the lust that another woman had aroused, her very soul would shrivel away to dust.

She rather thought she might go back to The Dovecote, before the storm broke. If she left it until the affair became public knowledge, people would see how she felt. No lady, surely, could conceal that amount of anguish behind society manners? She knew such a feat was beyond her. She would feel humiliated every time she went out of doors, conscious of people eyeing her and talking about her. Eventually, it would prove too much for her, and she would have to flee from town.

She might as well get the fleeing part over with, then, right now, and avoid the humiliation.

She rose early the morning after the ball, having spent a sleepless night shivering on the sitting-room sofa. She had not been able to bring herself to enter the bedroom, not even to get herself a blanket. It was only when she realised she could not leave the house wearing her ball gown that she summoned up the courage to tiptoe in, and sneak a walking dress, coat and bonnet from the clothes press. She could not prevent herself from stealing one last look at her husband, who was, she discovered resentfully, sleeping soundly, with his arm flung out across the space where she usually lay.

She would go to her mother first, she decided, as she tossed the flimsy ball gown over the back of the sofa, and wriggled into her sensible, cambric walking dress. It would not be fair of her to leave London without warning her the affair was likely to commence as soon as she was out of the way.

A sleepy footman unbolted the front door for her, asking if she needed his escort.

'No, thank you. I plan to take a cab straight to my mother's. Oh, see! There is one just at the corner.'

Having given her address to the driver, she climbed

inside, and sank gratefully on to the cushions. She hoped it was not too early to be making such a call. She was sure her mother would not mind getting up. Or perhaps she would just go straight up to her mother's room and speak to her there. What she had to relate was not for anyone else's ears.

She wondered that she had not yet felt the urge to cry. She knew she loved Robert more than life itself. Yet, since the moment she had seen Susannah in his arms, she had felt strangely frozen.

She had heard people talking about being numb with grief. She supposed that was why she was outwardly maintaining an appearance of calm, whilst inside she felt so terribly cold. She had been just like this after her father had died, mechanically seeing to all the necessary details. It had only been after the funeral was over, when she had been folding away one of his coats, and caught his dear, familiar scent lingering about the cloth, that it had hit her that she would never see him again. That was when the tears had begun to flow.

She would mourn Robert when this chilling numbness wore off, she expected. Wearily, she turned to look out of the window. And sat up with a sharp frown upon seeing the cab was passing through a shabby street she was sure she had never been down before.

She pulled the window down, and shouted up to the driver, 'Excuse me, I think you may have mistook my direction. I asked you to take me to Half Moon Street.'

The driver pulled the cab to a halt at once. Another man, one who had been sitting on the box with the driver, got down, and came to the window from which she was leaning.

Instead of apologising for his error, to Deborah's complete astonishment, he opened the cab door.

'What do you think you're doing?' she squeaked as he pushed her roughly back into her seat, and got in, sitting down opposite her.

'Making sure you don't slip through our fingers,' he said laconically.

'Slip through…what are you saying?' Her heart began to pound against her breastbone. 'Stop this cab and let me out at once!' she demanded, in as authoritative tone as she could muster. 'Or you will be sorry!'

'Threats, is it, now?' He grinned. 'No, you should not be making any threats to me, Mrs Fawley. What you should be doing is begging for mercy.'

The dim hope that he must have mistaken her for someone else fled when he addressed her by name. Nevertheless, she put on a brave face, forcing herself to look directly into his puffy eyes, as she said, 'Begging for mercy? Oh, no. You are the one who should beg my forgiveness for being so ill mannered as to try to frighten me.'

The man chuckled as he dealt her an open-handed slap across the face. She could not believe it. He seemed to have hardly put any effort into the blow at all, and yet it had sent her reeling into the corner of the carriage. She pulled herself upright, her hand instinctively going to her stinging lip. The man's grin broadened, as though well pleased with his little demonstration of brute strength.

'That was just a hint, Mrs Fawley, to show you we mean business. If you have any sense, you won't try to argue with me again. Just behave yourself, and there'll be no need to give you another lesson, see?'

He spoke so calmly that Deborah could hardly believe he had just hit her. But then she looked down at her glove and saw a red stain upon it. The force of his blow had split her lip. The feeling of wetness on her chin was her own blood, trickling from the stinging wound.

The disbelief on her face seemed to amuse her captor, for he chuckled, before folding his arms across his chest and settling down to watch her with lazy contempt.

He thought he had cowed her. Well, she would show him how wrong he was. If he thought she was so feeble-spirited that she would meekly let him carry her off without putting up a struggle, he was fair and far out!

As soon as the cab stopped, and her captor leaned forward to open the door, Deborah sprang to the opposite door, flung it open and dived out into the street. She had no idea where she was, but if she ran, shouting for help, someone was bound to come to her aid.

Her feet had barely hit the muddy surface, when a large hand descended on her shoulder. The man who had hit her had lunged through the coach the moment she had leapt out and grabbed for her.

'Help!' cried Deborah, struggling against his grip. She felt her coat rip along the shoulder seam, as she pulled from him with all her might. But then the driver, about whom she had forgotten, came to his partner's aid, jumping down from the box and landing in the street before her. With a scowl, he put his open, gloved hand against her face, and shoved her, sending her sprawling backwards into the coach, where she landed on the floor at the other man's feet.

Her skirt tore as he dragged her, kicking and struggling, through the carriage and out the other side, where she landed on all fours in the mud. He grabbed the collar of her coat, yanking her roughly to her feet and, not content with having recaptured her, he swung her round, smashing her face into the side of the cab. She reeled back from the explosion of pain, half-stunned. As her knees buckled, her assailant grasped her round the waist and swung her over his shoulder, as though she weighed no more than a sack of hops.

A series of impressions flitted across Deborah's dazed mind. A weary-looking woman, her eyes sliding away as though the sight of a kidnap in broad daylight was none of her business. Blood dripping down the back of the man's coat from her own face and splashing on to a flight of rough-hewn steps. Increasing darkness, and with it a strong smell of damp as her captor carried her ever deeper into his lair.

Finally, he stooped to pass through a low arch, then dropped her on to a mattress stuffed with straw. He stood looking down at her prostrate form with complete composure, while her dazed state crystallized into ice-cold fear.

'I warned you to mind your manners,' her captor said coolly. He squatted down on his haunches beside her bed. 'You ain't going to make any more trouble now, are you, pretty lady?' For good measure, he laid one meaty paw upon her ankle, running his hand under her skirts a way.

Deborah had thought she was levelheaded enough to

cope with anything. But the slide of that man's hand filled her with such sick loathing, she couldn't prevent herself from uttering a shriek of terror and drawing her leg away. She was completely in his power. The violence he had used to subdue her had been meant as a demonstration of what she might expect should she offer any further resistance. He could do anything to her, and there was nobody who would stop him.

She felt as though she had stumbled into another world. A world where the rules that had governed her sheltered existence until that point no longer applied. In this world, men could strike women in the street, and anyone who saw it would pretend they had not, lest they suffer the same fate.

'Pity, almost, you've broke so soon,' he mused. 'I would have enjoyed making you mind me.' He reached out, as though intending to take hold of her again. And Deborah scuttled backwards along the bed until she was curled into a ball, pressed up against the wall. He leaned over her, his eyes boring into hers as he took firm hold of her arm. When he snapped the strings of her reticule, as he pulled it from her wrist, she almost fainted with relief. He tore it open, tipping the contents on to the rough brick floor.

'You don't carry much money for a woman as has married such a wealthy man,' he complained as he picked out the coins from amongst her clutter of personal effects. 'Still, it will pay for the cab fare, and your board for as long as you're with us.'

With that, he left the room, bolting the door behind him.

She was ashamed to find she was shaking like a leaf,

little whimpers of distress escaping her lips with every ragged breath. She had not thought she was a coward, but that man's casual attitude to violence, his clear enjoyment of inflicting injury on her, had been inhuman. He had even indicated he wanted her to resist, so that he would have an excuse to hurt her even more. What kind of a monster was he?

And why had these men taken her? She simply could not understand why anyone should want to kidnap her. Though she was definitely their intended victim. They had called her by name.

Her face and hair felt sticky, her left eyebrow throbbing from where her kidnapper had slammed her face against the coach door. She knew she was bleeding, but had no way of attending to her hurt, other than pressing her already-stained glove to the cut, hoping pressure might stem the flow. There was nothing in her prison, save the mattress she cowered on and a bucket by the door, which she assumed was for her convenience.

The room itself she guessed must be a part of a cellar, since it was so dark. As her eyes became accustomed to the gloom, she saw that it was shaped in the form of an arch, made of brick. There was no window, and what little light there was filtered in through a small grille set into the stout oak door, which she had heard her captor bolt on the outside.

She did not know how long she crouched there. It seemed like a very long time, yet it was not long enough for her to stop shaking. But at length she heard footsteps approaching, and the sound of a chair scraping back. Was her captor sitting on the other side of the door then, guarding her? Though why should he, when there was no way she could escape such a secure prison?

She heard the bolts grate and then the door swung open.

She found she was panting with renewed fear. Why had they opened the door? What new cruelty did they mean to inflict on her? She felt so vulnerable, huddled on the floor, that she pushed herself shakily to her feet, leaning against the wall when her legs proved to have the consistency of jelly on a summer's day.

A neatly dressed, thin man walked in, and stood regarding her with his head tilted to one side for several minutes.

'I expect, Mrs Fawley,' he said eventually, 'you are wondering why I have had you brought here?'

She nodded, her mouth so dry with fear she was incapable of speech.

'I need to get your husband's attention. He owes me, you see, and needs to understand he must pay me back.'

'R…Robert does not have any debts!'

'Well, now, that is where we have to differ. When he cheated a man who does owe me, leaving him without the means to repay me, that man's debts became his.'

Robert would not cheat anyone!

The only person who could even come close to making such an accusation against him would be… Percy Lampton.

Had the fool borrowed against his expectations?

From this man?

She looked upon the thin man with dawning comprehension. Lampton had no means of repaying anyone anything now. Robert had all the money he had assumed would be his.

'I see you know exactly what I mean,' the man sneered. 'So glad you have dropped the pretence of innocence. People like you need to learn you cannot get away with cheating men like me. You must pay. One way or another,' he said, taking a step towards her, 'I always make 'em pay.'

As he moved, she saw the dull gleam of a knife blade in his hand.

'No!' she cried, feeling the blood draining from her face.

'I would advise you to hold still, Mrs Fawley, if you don't want to get hurt any further,' the thin man said menacingly. 'It will all be over before you know it.'

Mad panic gripped her. She darted towards the open door, running full tilt into the burly man, who appeared out of nowhere. He flung her back into the cell so forcefully that the back of her head cracked against the rough brickwork on the wall opposite the door. He stalked in after her, closing one meaty great hand round her throat, whilst deftly untying the ribbons of her bonnet with the other. Deborah's senses swam. The stench of him filled her nostrils, choking her as effectively as the stranglehold he had round her neck. Spots danced before her eyes while pain blossomed and spread its tentacles from the initial point of impact at the back of her head. She only dimly registered him tossing her bonnet aside, for she had seen the thin man approaching, the knife stretched out towards her.

With one swift flick, he cut off a lock of her hair, the

burly man left off his stranglehold, and Deborah fell to her knees on the floor between them.

'Tsk, tsk.' The thin man shook his head at her. 'Such a lot of fuss over one lock of hair. Anyone would think we meant to murder you.'

As she dragged in a painful breath through her bruised throat, she knew that was exactly what they had meant her to think. They wanted to keep her in a state of terrified submission. They both laughed mockingly as she cowered on the floor at her feet. And she felt a fresh wave of humiliation that they were succeeding so well. She *was* terrified.

'Now give me your hand,' the thin man ordered.

Well beyond the point of daring to display any defiance, Deborah held up her hand. At a nod from his master, the burly man knelt on the floor beside her, took her outstretched hand between his and slowly unbuttoned her glove. He then stroked it from her hand, finger by finger, his gloating, puffy eyes never leaving her face.

She felt violated.

She did not stop shivering, her stomach heaving, until long after the door had been shut on her again, leaving her in darkness.

But she would not cry. The burly man was out there, sitting on a chair, guarding her. He would hear if she began to cry. She would not give him the satisfaction!

It was quite late in the evening when Robert received the packet. He was in no mood to receive any kind of post. It was probably a sample from a tailor, he thought moodily. He was past caring about such trivialities, though once the prospect of having silk shirts and natty waistcoats had filled him with pleasurable anticipation.

'Here, deal with this, would you?' he said, tossing it to Linney.

Deborah had shunned him last night. She had finally given up the pretence she could bear sharing a bed with him. And this morning, before the rest of the household had begun to stir, she had run off to her mother's house. She had not returned since, not even to keep the various social engagements she had previously arranged.

'Captain!'

The tone of Linney's voice had him turning from the sideboard where he was pouring himself a brandy.

Linney's face was white.

'What is it?' Robert demanded sharply.

In reply, the man held out the contents of the package. A bloodstained glove and a lock of dark hair. He recognised that glove. He knew that hair.

'Deborah!'

In two strides he was taking the note that had come in the package from Linney's hand: *You stole from my client. I reckon his debts now belong to you, along with all the rest you took from him. Settle them if you want to see your wife again.*

There was no signature on the letter, and no direction on the packet.

He went cold inside. How could he pay a ransom, when he did not know who to pay it to?

'This will be the first of a series of notes, I expect,' said Linney darkly as Robert sank to the sofa, Deborah's bloodstained glove lying limply on his open palm. 'This was just to get your attention. He'll send instructions as to how to pay, and how much, once he's let you stew a while.'

'I cannot!' Robert lurched unsteadily to his feet. 'I cannot sit here and wait for further messages, while Deborah may be suffering God alone knows what!' He looked at the bloodstained glove, his cheeks going chalk white. 'They have already hurt her.'

'Might just have been done for effect. Might not be her blood, sir.'

'By heaven, it had better not be.' His expression hardened. 'This is Lampton's doing. There is no one else that could accuse me of stealing from him. Though I had every right to claim that inheritance! It is his lying tongue that has exposed Deborah to danger! It must be!'

'Sir, Captain sir, just think for a minute—'

'No, I've done with thinking, and behaving and pretending to be a gentleman! I am a soldier. And I will take a soldier's solution.'

Linney swore under his breath as his master pulled open the sideboard drawers and pulled out a pair of heavy military pistols.

While he clumsily loaded them, Linney fetched a wicked-looking blade, which he hid under the folds of his coat. He helped his master into his old army greatcoat, clapped a battered forage cap upon his head, then both men plunged out into the night, side by side.

The man who opened the doors of Lampton's rooms in Albany Chambers soon lost the haughty expression he habitually wore when denying access to unwelcome visitors. But then, nobody had ever requested entrance at gunpoint before.

'Is your master in?' said the scar-faced ruffian on the doorstep. 'Don't tell me any lies now.'

'I wouldn't dream of it, sir,' he replied, nervously swallowing as he caught sight of a second, broad-shouldered man standing on the step, his back to the building as he scanned the street.

'Show me to him, then!'

Any hope the valet had of summoning assistance for his master, who he was convinced was about to be murdered, faded when the second intruder bounded up the steps, slammed the front door behind him, and bore down upon him with grim purpose.

'He…he's in there,' said the valet, turning white as he indicated the sitting-room door. He could not stand the sight of blood. It had been bad enough the last time, but those men had not used pistols. He really would have to think about handing in his notice. Staving off criminals was not part of his job description. Though after tonight, he would probably not have a job any longer. Resentment swelled his emaciated chest. What kind of person would employ a valet whose former master had been brutally murdered? Only the kind who sought notoriety. He had no wish to work for that sort of person. With an affronted sniff, he sat down on a settle in the narrow hall, glaring waspishly up at the thickset man who stood, arms folded, with his back to the front door.

Captain Fawley strode into the sitting room, training one of his pistols on the young man who was sprawled on an armchair in front of the fire. He checked at the sight of Percy Lampton's face. It was covered with fading bruises and crusted scabs. The once elegant fop was bundled up in a disreputably shabby dressing gown, a bowl of what smelled like punch at his elbow, a great deal of which, judging by his heightened complexion, he had already imbibed.

'Come to finish me off, have you, Fawley?' Lampton drawled, eyeing the pistol with weary, bloodshot eyes. 'Don't suppose you want to hear it, but in fact, you would be doing me a favour.'

'It would be only what you deserve,' Robert bit out coldly. 'But I am no murderer. It is answers I want, not your blood.'

'Just as well. Don't think there's all that much left,' Percy said, his fingers tracing over the patchwork of bruises. 'Though I don't know what kind of answers you might want from me.'

'I want to know who has taken my wife!'

'Taken your wife? In what way?' he sneered. 'Cuckolded you already, has she? Not that anyone could blame her.'

The pistol went off, shattering the punch bowl and showering shards of glass everywhere.

'Your aim is off,' Percy taunted, flicking rum punch nonchalantly from one elegant hand, though his lips had gone white.

'My aim is perfect,' Robert replied, pulling the second pistol from his pocket. 'The next ball will go straight through your black heart unless you tell me what I want to know.'

'I have no idea who your wife may have taken as her lover, nor why you should suppose it was me,' he protested. 'I am no adulterer!'

'No, just a seducer of innocent young girls!'

'I have never seduced an innocent young girl!'

'Have you forgotten Miss Hullworthy already, you rogue?'

'I did not seduce her! I just—'

'Led her to believe you would marry her. Toyed with her affections and broke her heart! You villain. Are there no depths to which you Lamptons will not sink? You would destroy a woman for sport—'

'Now hang on a minute!' Percy sat forward, his brow knotting angrily. 'A little light flirtation is hardly a crime. I gave Miss Hullworthy no assurances. If she imagined I would ever propose marriage to a woman of her class, that was entirely her own fault! And as for accusing any Lampton of acting dishonourably towards a female…'

'Your father did! Claiming I was not my father's child was tantamount to branding my mother a whore! It destroyed her! Can you deny it?'

'Th…that's ancient history,' Percy countered, his face darkening. 'I had no part in that.'

'But you are just like him! Claiming a woman is not fit to marry because of her background. No woman should be treated as you have treated Miss Hullworthy. Or as your father treated my mother. Women should be protected, cared for, not abused as though they are of no account!'

As he said it, Captain Fawley realised he meant every word. This was the creed by which he had grown up.

When had he lost that belief? When had he begun to treat women with the cynical contempt that had made him ruthlessly exploit Deborah's vulnerability so that he could exact revenge on his enemies?

It was not just his body that had been crippled at Salamanca, he suddenly saw. His mind had been warped too.

Shakily, he sank into the chair opposite Percy, his fingers clutching convulsively on the grip of his pistol. When he had first seen his face in the mirror in that makeshift hospital outside Salamanca, he had been appalled. As a youth, he had been handsome. Nobody could have looked at the mass of blistered, suppurating skin and felt anything but disgust.

In the long months of his recovery, he had seen the way women reacted to the sight of his broken body and scarred face. Where once they had smiled at him, flirted with him, now they twitched their skirts away in disgust.

So he had branded them all shallow, calculating bitches when the truth was, he hurt so much, whenever one of them wrinkled up her pretty little nose, he could scarcely breathe.

Driven by a sense of the injustice done him, he had used Deborah as ruthlessly as Lampton had treated Miss Hullworthy, as Lampton's father had treated his mother. He looked at Percy Lampton with growing horror. He had allowed bitterness and resentment to eat away at his soul until now there was nothing to choose between them.

'Somebody has kidnapped my wife,' he said bleakly. 'The note I received this evening, along with this…' he laid the pistol across his knee as he drew the blood-stained glove from his pocket '…led me to assume it was connected to our long-standing feud. It demanded repayment of debts that somebody seems to think I ought to pay, though I suspect it was you that racked them up.'

'Hincksey,' said Percy, his eyes fixed on the bloodied glove. 'My God, Fawley, I never meant it to come to this. I just thought he would send some of his men to dish out more of the same...' he fingered his bruised face '...to you.'

'You expect me to care what you think?'

Lampton's eyes narrowed. 'Look, I know your view of me is coloured by what my father did, but I am not like him. I would never deliberately put a woman in harm's way.'

'What of Miss Hullworthy? Or Lady Walton? Last year, you—'

'I did not cause that French woman any real harm! I just saw the opportunity to make Walton a little uncomfortable. And after the way he did me out of Aunt Euphemia's property, that was the least he deserved! And it wasn't as if she lost all that much money at cards. Chicken feed, to a man of his wealth!

'And as for Miss Hullworthy, she'll soon get over me when someone with a title decides to drop her the handkerchief, you mark my words! But that...' he pointed to the bloodied glove lying in Captain Fawley's lap '...that is not something I would ever wish to happen to a lady.' He grimaced. 'It's all Walton's fault anyway that I fell into Hincksey's clutches in the first place,' he whined. 'If he had not contested that will...if I'd had the money my father swore was coming to me...'

'That was not how it was at all!' Captain Fawley

thundered. 'It was your family that contested the will. Your aunt left everything to me!'

'Well, she shouldn't have done! *You* ain't her nephew!'

'And you think that is justification for telling your money-lender he could apply to me for restitution of debts you had run up?'

'He was threatening to break my legs. Good God, man, have you not seen the state of my face? Haven't been able to go anywhere for days. And I did not say he could apply to you. I just explained about the legacy— how I had thought it as good as mine, but that, in the end, you managed to snaffle it by marrying Miss Gillies.'

His eyes widened in horror. 'My God, I gave him her name. I might as well have handed her to him on a plate. I shall never forgive myself if…'

Captain Fawley could see his rival's remorse was genuine. While Percy Lampton was not the most honourable man he had ever known, the thought that any action of his might have exposed a lady to real danger clearly appalled him.

'Help me find her, then.'

'I shall.' Lampton sat up, looking Robert straight in the eye. 'And while we are about it, I want to say that I deplore what my father did. Even—' his face flushed '—the way he acted over my aunt's will. I wanted the money, I don't deny it. But not that much…' He eyed Deborah's bloodstained glove, his fists clenching. 'If there were anything I could do to settle this stupid feud, once and for all, then believe me, I would do it.'

'Would you, now?' replied Robert, eyeing him with a cynical sneer. 'Forgive me for finding that hard to believe.'

'Try me!' said Percy, leaping to his feet, showering the hearthrug with shards of crystal punch bowl. 'I would do anything to atone for any harm that may have come to poor Miss Gillies through any careless word I may have spoken. Anything!'

Chapter Twelve

Deborah lost all sense of time in that uniformly dark prison. Three times after the thin man had cut off a lock of her hair, the door opened, and the burly man who had hit her came in with a plate of bread and cheese, and a mug of what looked and smelled like ale.

The first time, though her throat still ached from when he had half-choked her, she had disdained drinking the ale. The prospect of having to use that bucket later on, and either have him empty it with a smirk, or leave it to add its pungency to the already nasty smell of the place, were both too horrible to contemplate. She had torn a strip off her petticoat, dipped it in the ale jug, and pressed it against her brow, though, hoping the alcohol might cleanse the cut, which simply would not stop bleeding. It only made her feel worse. Not only did it sting rather badly, but now she stank of ale too.

Not long after that, she began to scratch. And she discovered that the mattress, upon which she had been sitting, was hopping with fleas. Horrified, she leapt to her feet, and made for the furthest corner of her cell. She could not stand still for ever, though. The blood seemed to pool in her feet, making her feel faint. She tried pacing up and down, which helped a little, but she could not keep going indefinitely. Eventually, when exhaustion overcame her, she crouched in a corner, as far from the verminous mattress as she could.

When, at length, the door opened, and the burly man brought in fresh food and ale, she felt too weary, her legs too stiff and her back too sore to wish to reach for it. And the darkness, which had seeped into her soul, as dampness soaked into her clothes, made her wonder whether it was worth trying to keep her strength up anyway. She dared not hope Robert would part with any money to rescue her. It was the money he cared about, not her. But her captors had said 'someone' would pay. It was increasingly obvious that 'someone' would be her.

A shudder racked her body. She would never be strong enough to fight them. They would do what they wanted with her. They would make her suffer. Her only hope was that she might be too weak to survive her punishment for long. In a spurt of defiance, she kicked over the ale jug, and ground the stale piece of bread into the floor, the crumbs mingling with the mildewed mortar that held the bricks in place.

The last time her enemy had come in, she had felt too weak to even reach for the dishes he dropped on to the floor next to her. Her very frailty caused a brief flare of triumph to loosen the despair that had closed round her, like an iron fist, as the unremitting darkness had gone on, and on. It might not be so very much longer, she smiled to herself, before she was out of here.

She could hear her jailor moving about on the other side of her door. She heard another man join him. She heard the low murmur of male voices, a chair rasping across the brick floor, and then periods of quiet, interspersed with terse outbursts of profanities. From the occasional recognisable word that filtered in through the grille, she deduced that they were playing cards.

Then there came a clatter of booted feet on the cellar steps. The beginning of a shout was choked off into a grunt of pain, and then it sounded as though somebody was throwing furniture about.

There was a fight going on.

'Deborah!'

She lifted her head from where she had been resting it on her bent knees.

'Robert?'

She could hardly believe her ears.

'Deborah, where are you?'

From some hidden inner reserve, she gathered the last of her strength and crawled to the door. 'In here!' she croaked hoarsely, straining upwards to try and reach the grille. 'Robert!' Her voice was rusty from disuse. He would never be able to hear her. In desperation, she raised her fists, and pounded ineffectually against the stout door.

She heard the sound of the bolts being drawn; before she could get out of the way, the door swung inwards, pushing her aside so that she sprawled inelegantly in the middle of the floor.

And Robert stood there, a dark silhouette against the dim light from the outer cellar.

Her arms shook with the effort it took to raise herself to a sitting position. She felt as though she had expended the last of her strength in making him hear her. But he just stood there, in stony silence, and somehow she knew she was going to have to get up on her own.

He did not want to be here. He could not have made it more obvious if he had shouted it. The very way he drew to one side, as she finally managed to stagger towards the open door, spoke of his reluctance to so much as touch her.

But he had come. She would live.

And that knowledge gave her the strength to reach the doorway, where she leaned for a moment or two, her head spinning.

In the outer room four men were fighting like demons. Her jaw dropped at recognising one of them was the Marquis of Lensborough. The first time she had met him, she had thought he was an ugly customer, and he certainly had an ugly expression on his face now. But it was magnificent to behold, for the man he was pounding, as though he were a punch bag in a boxing school, was the man who had taken such pleasure in hurting her.

Her hand flew to her mouth as the other villain, the one who had been driving the cab, raised a chair to smash over her other rescuer's head. To her shock, she recognised the gleaming golden brown hair of the Earl of Walton. But the Earl surprised both her and his assailant with the agility of his next manoeuvre. He sprang aside, dodging the chair and simultaneously raising his knee to jam it into his assailant's stomach. As the cab driver doubled over, the chair somehow ended up in the Earl's capable hands. He brought it smashing down over the kidnapper's head, a split second after the Marquis dealt a massive knockout punch to the burly villain's jaw.

The kidnappers lay sprawled amongst the smashed furniture. The Earl and the Marquis stood there panting, then grinned at each other like a pair of mischievous schoolboys as they reached over the bodies to shake one another's hands.

'This way,' said Robert, extending his arm to indicate a stairway, snaking up out of the cellar. 'And be quick about it.'

Flinching at the curtness of his tone, Deborah tottered towards the stairs. She had not gone more than a few steps, before the Marquis took one arm, the Earl her other, and they half-dragged, half-carried her up the stairs, while Robert followed behind. The four of them emerged into a dank courtyard in which stood a plain black cab. Linney was sitting on the box, a brace of pistols sweeping the few people who dared to poke their noses out of the doorways or windows.

'How did you find me?' asked Deborah, once they had all got into the cab. 'Did you have to pay a ransom? That man said you owed him money—'

'Lampton owed him money,' said Robert curtly as the Earl and the Marquis settled on the seats opposite them. 'And it was Lampton who told me where I might find you.'

The coach set off with a jolt that flung Deborah back into the cushions. Robert steadied her, then moved away swiftly. So swiftly that she had to turn her head away from him to hide her hurt.

'Your man may be handy to have about in a tight spot, but he is no coachman,' observed the Marquis, grabbing hold of the strap.

'You are a handy man to have in a tight spot too,' said Deborah, turning wide eyes upon his saturnine features. 'I must thank you for what you have done today. Both of you,' she added, addressing the Earl.

'I am merely returning a favour Captain Fawley did, not so very long ago, for my own wife,' the Marquis replied coolly.

'Think nothing of it,' added the Earl. Then, turning to Robert, he drawled, 'I had no idea taking you into my home would provide me with such adventures.'

They kept up a constant barrage of inane observations, reminding her again of a pair of naughty schoolboys who had just got away with some prank. It didn't take her long to work out that much of the badinage was intended to distract her, for which she was grateful. The last thing she wanted to do was break down in front of two such aristocratic males and, judging from the way neither of them could quite meet her eye, the sight of a female in tears would make them extremely uncomfortable too. And she had felt very inclined to burst into tears when the cab had set off, signalling her ordeal was at an end.

The Earl and the Marquis helped her out of the cab when it stopped in an alley at the back of Walton House. Contrary to her expectations, there was a flight of steps leading to Robert's back door, which they reached by crossing a paved yard. There was even a sign on the door, bearing his name, and a doorknocker in the shape of a lion's head, as though this were a private, rented apartment, rather than an integral part of Walton House.

The Countess was waiting for them. The moment she saw them, she leapt to her feet, her eyes widening in horror at Deborah's appearance. Her next action was to snatch up a blanket from the sofa on which she had been sitting, hurry to her side, and drape it round her, shooting just one reproachful look at Robert as she did so.

'Nobody must see her looking like this,' she exclaimed. 'What were you thinking?'

'Of getting her out of that place, primarily,' Robert snapped back. 'But at least I took the precaution of smuggling her in by the back door. Nobody knows about this dreadful business,' he said to Deborah. 'We have managed to hush it up. I was sure you would not want to distress your mother. So whenever enquiries were made as to your whereabouts, I said either you were indisposed, or out shopping, depending on who was doing the asking. Now I suggest you go upstairs with Lady Walton, who will see to your immediate needs.'

It was as if he could not wait to be rid of her, she thought, glancing at his set features.

Strangely, her earlier desire to weep had frozen solid under the blast of his coldness. She could feel it, a tangible presence, just under her breastbone, as though she had swallowed a lump of ice. It was amazing, she reflected as Lady Walton led her up the stairs, just how much strength pride could lend to legs that she had thought too weak to carry her one step further.

'You will feel better for a bath and something to eat,' said the Countess, ushering her into her pretty, feminine sitting room.

'Will I?' She shook her head, wearily. She had not been able to forget for one second, even through all her other terrors, that her husband was about to embark on an affair with another woman. So far as he was concerned, she could not have got herself kidnapped at a more inconvenient moment. He must have had to go to a great deal of trouble to effect her rescue, when he would much rather have been planning…

Feeling a wave of faintness overcome her, Deborah dropped on to the nearest sofa, bowing her head over her knees.

'Here, here!' The Countess knelt at her feet, holding up a teacup and saucer.

'I thought you never took tea,' Deborah attempted to joke weakly, as she gratefully took the hot, sweet drink.

'Oh, no, I hate it. But you English love it, and say it is restorative, and you look as though you need to be restored. Did they not feed you? Oh, pardon! I am not supposed to pester you with questions. Robert said you would not want to talk about it.'

Getting to her feet, the Countess went to the fireplace and tugged on the bell rope.

'Please to come into my bedroom, Deborah. The maids will bring up water for a bath, but I am sure you will not want them to see you…' She trailed off, her eyes darting to her face, and then flinching away.

For the first time, Deborah wondered what her face looked like. It ached all over, so she supposed it must be bruised. Draining her cup to the dregs, she followed the Countess through into an opulent bedchamber. The bed was hung with velvet curtains, the carpet was a soft swathe of blue that invited a woman to sink her bare feet into it, and there were bowls of fresh flowers upon several of the little tables that dotted the room. She could smell them, above the stench of imprisonment that clung to her clothes. Everything looked so clean, and so delicately feminine, that Deborah felt as though she were polluting the place just by standing there in all her grime and disorder.

The Countess darted out, upon hearing the maids clanking about with cans of water in the dressing room, and Deborah took a moment to go to the dressing table and peer at her reflection in the mirror. Her face was swollen almost out of recognition. She had a black eye that would not have looked out of place on a professional boxer, and a crusted scab over her eyebrow. Her hair on that side of her face was matted with blood from that cut, and her mouth… She touched it gingerly with the tips of her fingers. Her lower lip was puffy and scabbed from that initial, casual cuff.

Absently, she reached under the sleeve of her dress, to scratch at one of the fleabites on her wrist, then suddenly she was tearing off her filthy clothes. By the time the Countess returned to tell her the bath was ready, Deborah was crouching naked before the fire, holding her petticoat in the flames with a poker.

'It has to be burned,' she explained, when Lady Walton looked at her in amazement. 'All of it. Right down to my shoes.' It was the only way to stop the fleas from getting into the carpets and curtains. When the Countess made an involuntary movement towards her, she held up her hand to ward her off. 'No, I must do this myself!' She did not think she carried any fleas on her person, but she did not want to take the chance of passing them on, if she had.

As she stood up, she noticed that her knees were badly grazed, though she could not remember exactly when that had happened. It could have been when she had fallen to the cobbles, when the burly man hauled her out of the cab. Or later, when she had been forced to her knees in the cell after they cut off her hair. By the way the Countess had been glancing at her back, then looking hastily away, as though something distressed her, she guessed she had bruises all over her.

The Countess proffered a large towel. 'Your bath is ready,' she said, her eyes full of tears.

'Oh, yes, how I need one,' Deborah agreed. She had been in the same clothes for she knew not how many hours. Fear had made her sweat profusely during several thoroughly unpleasant incidents. That cell had been filthy, the men who had manhandled her had left their rank odour in her nostrils… Was she just imagining it, or was it really there? And then, of course, she had attempted to wash her cut in ale. She must smell like something out of a tavern.

Though a bath in water, no matter how deliciously scented, would never erase the imprint of ugliness and evil from her mind. She had seen another face of human nature these past few days, and she already sensed the experience had left an indelible stain on her soul. As she sank gratefully into the perfumed water, she murmured, 'I wonder if I will ever feel completely clean again.' Then, concerned lest any of the fleas should have taken up lodging in her hair, she slid beneath the surface of the water, immersing herself in the hope she might drown them.

Robert sat on the sofa, an untouched tumbler of brandy in his hand, staring blindly at the floor between his boots. He did not think he would ever get the image of Deborah, cowering on that filthy straw mattress, her face all over bruises, her dress soiled and torn, out of his mind. He had wanted to go to her and carry her out of that foul cell, wrap her in his arms and tell her he would never let anyone hurt her ever again.

Instead, he had to endure the humiliation of letting others fight for her freedom, and accept that he would never be able to lift her in his arms and carry her anywhere. When she had got into the coach, and he had seen the bruises on her neck, it had been all he could do to restrain himself from marching straight back into that warehouse and shooting the brutes where they lay on the floor.

He had been angry enough at the thought of Deborah being taken, imprisoned, and perhaps frightened. But to see what they had done to her…blacked her eye, split her lip, half-strangled her…to have left such marks on her body attested to a level of violence that told its own story. There was only one reason why men held a woman by the throat, punched her in the face and tore her gown.

How many of them had raped her? How often? She

had been in their clutches for a night and the best part of two days. He groaned, leaning his forehead on his hand to hide the tears, which were stinging his eyes, from Linney's notice.

It was all his fault. He had never considered what repercussions might rebound upon her when he had been making his plans to best Percy Lampton. Not that he could have foreseen she might have suffered this level of brutality. But nor had he taken any steps to ensure her safety, when he should have known… He thumped his thigh with his clenched fist.

It had all got completely out of hand. This feud with the Lamptons had gone too far! Because of his obsession with them, Deborah had suffered the most terrible fate that could befall a woman.

It was not the men who had raped her that should be shot, it was he. He had brought her to this.

He had crept in to her bedroom, and stood over her, just filling his eyes with the sight of her, once Heloise had come to tell him she had fallen asleep.

'She must have been exhausted,' Heloise had said, as they had climbed the stairs, side by side. 'I wondered, after all she had suffered, and considering the pain she must feel, if I would need to give her something to help her sleep, but almost before she had finished her bath, she was struggling to keep her eyes open. And she told me she had hardly slept at all…nor does she seem to know what day it is, for it was so dark in the cell….'

He had not been surprised to hear she had fallen asleep so quickly. She had obviously exhausted her meagre reserves of strength trying to fight off those men. Her whole body had been trembling with the effort it had taken her just to get up off that filthy floor.

Heloise had gone on to tell him how Deborah had burned her clothes, saying she would never feel clean again, and his heart had sunk to his boots.

She had begun to tactfully withdraw from the bedroom, intending to leave him alone with his wife. But he prevented her. Their marriage had faltered to the degree where the last thing she would want, if she should wake, was to see him looming over her. It would be like waking from one nightmare into another. He stood, ramrod straight, cursing himself as he looked down at her battered face.

She had not bothered to plait her hair neatly for bed. It spread in damp tendrils all over her pillow, making her look very young and vulnerable.

He longed to reach down and take one of those locks of damp hair in his fingers, raise it to his lips and kiss it. He had dreamed of her hair, the night she had been away from him, the few times he had managed to doze off. He had dreamed he was running his fingers through it, as she lay beside him, smiling up at him with the sleepy satisfaction he had sometimes had the privilege of imparting to her face. But then her image had shimmered, and dissipated like mist on a breeze. He had leapt out of bed, run to the door, and, shouting her name, run out into the street to search for her. But that mist closed in, blinding him, and as he batted it from his face with his hands, he would wake, sweating and shaking, to the harsh reality of his life. He had lost the hand, the one he had dreamed was filled with the silken texture of his wife's hair, in a makeshift hospital tent outside Salamanca. Nor would he ever leap, or run anywhere, ever again. But that loss was as nothing compared with the pain of knowing his Deborah was gone, and he did not know how to get her back.

She should have a decent husband, one who could protect her, not a useless cripple, who drew danger down on himself and those around him!

Most of all, she should have someone she could turn to, someone who could hold her in his arms and comfort her, not a man whose touch could only add to her distress.

He ached for her isolation. Yet he knew there was nobody she could talk to about her ordeal. It would be like living it all over again. As a soldier, he had encountered women who had been brutalised by French troops, and the last thing any of them had wanted was to have anyone so much as mention their violation.

Eventually he had retreated to his rooms, though he knew he would not sleep tonight. Knowing she was upstairs, and safe, should have brought relief. Instead his agony was redoubled by the knowledge that, if she had not hated him before this, she surely would do now. She was more lost to him than ever.

Bone weary, he sank on to a sofa with a glass of brandy. It had taken hours of painstaking searching through Hincksey's known haunts before a handful of guineas had brought them the information he needed.

'Want to know where Hincksey would hold a woman?' the denizen of Tothill Fields had leered. 'Same place as he always takes them, to break them in, I'd wager.'

When Robert had seen her in that place, he had

wanted to howl with rage and pain. His Deborah, his beautiful wife, defiled by those brutes! And all he could do was stand there, and look at her, knowing that if he once knelt down on that floor, and took her in his arms, he would have broken down completely. But there was no time for such self-indulgence. Hincksey had left only two men to guard her, but he was the head of a criminal gang, whose members ruled the area they had infiltrated. All they had on their side was the element of surprise. They had to swoop in and get her out, fast.

Walton and Lensborough had both agreed, having seen the state of her, that there should be no trial. Though kidnapping alone was a hanging offence, bringing the villains to trial would mean Deborah would have to give evidence. She would have to relate all that had happened.

All of it.

And though if ever two men deserved to hang, it was those brutes, he could not expose Deborah to the shame of having all society knowing what they had done to her.

Once she had recovered enough to travel, he would send her out of London.

She was too straightforward a person to want to have to make up some tale about how she had come by her facial injuries. So she could not go to The Dovecote, where the servants, who had no idea how they ought to behave towards their betters, would all expect some kind of explanation. No, it was better that she stay among people who knew what had happened, and could help her to come to terms with it.

He knew Walton wanted Heloise to travel down to

Wycke for the birth of their child. Nobody would question it if Deborah went with them. What could be more natural than for a lady to want her sister-in-law to be with her for the lying-in? Everyone knew Heloise had no other female relatives in England.

Deborah could avoid having to answer any questions that might arise from her inability to go out of doors until the bruises healed. He had his own suite of rooms at Wycke, to which she could retreat should she wish for privacy. And female company, in the form of Lady Walton, should she need to confide in someone.

It was the best he could do for her.

'How are you feeling today?' Heloise chirruped brightly, coming in behind the maid who bore her breakfast tray.

Numb. She felt numb. She just could not dredge up any sort of emotion at all. It was as if all her capacity to feel had frozen solid.

She assayed a polite smile and replied, 'Oh, much better, thank you. I slept so well.'

It had seemed unreal, when she had woken earlier, to find herself in this beautifully soft bed, with its crisp, clean sheets and velvet hangings, in a room that smelled of flowers. And to be wearing another of the Countess's scandalous nightgowns.

She had reached out for Robert, during the night, but of course, he wasn't there. And then she remembered that she would never wake up next to him again. For a while, she had found it hard to breathe. It felt as though a great weight was crushing her. But slowly, slowly, as she had lain on her back, gazing up at the pleated velvet canopy, listening to her breath going in and out, in and out, the numbness returned. And she welcomed it.

She endured the day as well as she could, replying with politeness to all the Countess's attempts to draw her into conversation, meekly eating what food was set before her and then getting dressed, when a selection of clothing was brought upstairs for her from Robert's rooms. She refused the offer of a visit from a doctor. She was sure her physical injuries were only superficial. Bruises always faded in a day or so.

The Countess finally left her alone when she claimed she still felt exhausted, but, though she lay down on the bed, sleep was far from her.

Why had Robert not come? She knew he did not care for her, but could he not at least have pretended? Just this once?

Though why should he, when he had warned her, from the very start, that he would not pretend anything he did not feel, or use soft words when blunt ones would serve his purpose much better?

The day dragged interminably on, the one maid who had been granted the task of caring for her tiptoeing around her, wide-eyed, as though she was some sort of bomb that might explode upon the least provocation.

And Robert did not come to see how she was.

She ate, and slept another night, in her own nightgown this time. One that she'd brought up to London with her, which had remained among her things during the moves from The Dovecote to Robert's rooms. It had worn almost transparent from washing, and had a patch near the hem where she'd put her foot through.

As she lay in the solitary comfort of the Countess of Walton's bed, it seemed symbolic of her state. Once, she had slept naked in her husband's arms. Now, she slept alone, in the nightgown she had worn as a single woman.

Single.

Alone.

She found it harder to rouse herself from bed the next morning. She had tossed and turned all night, replaying every single minute of her relationship with Robert, trying to see if there was anything she could have done differently, any way she could have made him love her, just a little.

And the harder she thought about it, the more she began to see that she had made excuses for him every time he had been rude or unkind. She had built him up in her imagination into something he was not, then clung to this image of him, when all the evidence was to the contrary.

The imaginary Captain Fawley, the hero of the Peninsula War with whom she had fallen in love, would have come to her, sat with her holding her hand lest she have nightmares, kissed her bruises and told her she was beautiful in his eyes, not flinched from her appearance as though it turned his stomach.

The real Captain Fawley was a hypocrite. He knew what it felt like to have people turn their eyes from his injuries, and yet he had done just that, to her!

He had only married her to spite Percy Lampton. He had wanted to hurt the other man, and did not care whom he used to achieve his aims. He had urges, and had used her to satisfy them. And because she had been a romantic fool, and had responded with love, he had called her a slut. And had then carried on pursuing Susannah.

She had been such a fool! She had fallen headlong in love with a schoolgirl's vision of a wounded hero, not the real man at all.

By the time he did come up to the Countess's sitting room, after dinner on the second day, she was having trouble remembering what she had ever seen in him. And it was all she could do to keep her resentment reined back when he walked in. How could he have done this to her? Made her love him, then made her fall out of love just as fast?

She could feel the ice round her heart melting under a scorching blast of anger. Which was swiftly followed by the most agonising pain. Oh, how she wished she were still frozen in shock. Falling out of love hurt far, far worse than falling into it. For when she had fallen, she had at least had hope. Now there was none.

'What do you want?' she shot at him, as he hesitated upon the threshold.

'I have only come to inform you that arrangements have been made for you to accompany Lord and Lady Walton to Wycke, when they remove there at the end of the week. I will not be going with you. I thought it would be for the best.'

Yes, he would want to stay in London with Susannah while the Season lasted. Sending her to the family estate, to be a companion to the Countess during her lying-in, would cause no undue comment in society at all. He would be rid of her, well rid of her.

And she of him!

Lifting her chin a notch, she said, 'I could not agree more. Is that all?'

'No. I thought you would wish to know there will not be a trial, as a result of your...ordeal. Nobody need know if you do not tell them.'

So, he did not think it worth prosecuting the men who had dragged her off the street, beaten and starved her and held her captive? What further proof did she need of his total lack of compassion? He just wanted the whole incident swept under the carpet.

Just as he wanted her to disappear from his life.

She was only surprised he had bothered to come and rescue her at all. If he had left her, he would probably be without a wife at all now. The will only said he had to marry, after all, not that he had to stay married for any specific length of time. As a widower, he would have been free....

No, she could not pursue that line of thought. It was one thing to accept his nature for what it was, quite another to think he would connive at her death. Shakily she raised one hand to her brow, waving the other towards him in a dismissive gesture. She was not thinking clearly. She was still overwrought, that was what her mother would say.

When she raised her head, to give him some kind of reply, she found she was alone in the room once more.

Well, what had she expected?

He had come to tell her what his plans were for her

future. He had no reason to stay once he had delivered that message.

No reason at all.

Quite suddenly, it felt as though a black pit had opened up before her. She was falling, falling into it, and there was nobody to help her, nothing to cling to. She reached out and grabbed at the arms of the chair, reminding herself that she was in a pretty sitting room, on a comfortably upholstered chair, and soon she would be travelling into the country to stay at what was, by all accounts, a magnificent estate.

Her world was not really coming to an end.

So why did she start to weep? Why did the sobs rack her body, driving her to her knees on that soft, blue carpet? Why did she curl up into a tight ball, her fists clenched?

She did not know.

She did not love Robert any more, so it was foolish to cry because they were going their separate ways.

She thanked God she had fallen out of love with him, she really did.

Or being sent away from him would have broken her heart.

Chapter Thirteen

They were going to travel to Wycke on Friday. She would be glad to go. She was beginning to feel as much a prisoner in this pretty suite of rooms in Walton House as she had been in that filthy cell. After the first couple of days, when she had felt too weak and battered to do more than eat and sleep by turns, she spent longer and longer pacing up and down like a caged tiger she had once seen in the Tower menagerie.

At least at Wycke, she could take long walks in the grounds and burn off some of her anger in the exercise. Or ride. The Earl had come in, and spoken to her quite kindly one evening, telling her he would make sure there would be a suitable horse for her use in his stables.

But Robert had not come with him.

She'd had enough! Turning on her heel, she marched to the fireplace, and tugged on the bell pull.

When Sukey came in answer to her summons, she said, 'Can you please send one of the footmen to summon a cab for me?' She wished she had taken that precaution the last time she had decided to go out. Those men, she had realised, a shiver sliding down her spine, must have been watching her movements for some time, looking for an opportunity to take her. She had frequently hailed cabs to take her to visit her mother. She would never be so careless again.

If Lord Walton did not mind, she thought she might even take one of the footmen with her.

She went to the armoire Lady Walton had given over to her use, and took out her blue merino spencer and the bonnet that went with it. It took a matter of seconds to attach a veil to its brim. For some reason, Robert did not want anyone to see her face, though she did not see why he was making such a fuss. Her bruises were fading now, and much of the swelling had gone down. Arnica was wonderfully soothing—much more effective than ale, she grimaced as she twitched the veil into position.

A few minutes later, Sukey came to tell her a cab was waiting. She had got part way down the stairs, before noticing Robert bristling at the foot of them.

'Where are you going?'

She lifted her chin.

'To visit my mother.'

'That would be ill advised.' The expression on his face was forbidding.

But she had had enough of his high-handed edicts. 'I am not going to leave town without bidding her farewell. She will think it most odd.' Deborah descended the last stair and made as though she would have stalked past him. But he reached out, taking her arm, saying,

'If you insist on going, I will go with you.'

'There is no need.'

'There is every need!'

She locked glares with him for a few seconds, puzzled as to why he would want to go with her, when he had made it so plain that he was sick and tired of the very thought of her. It only took a few moments' reflection to work it out. He would not want her to say anything that might upset his precious Susannah, who was still living with her mother. The only reason he was insisting on going with her was to make sure she behaved herself.

She felt the insult keenly.

'If you insist, I suppose I cannot stop you.' She sighed, turning her head away from him, to gaze longingly at the open door.

It took him only a minute or two to fetch his own hat and coat. Then they walked to the cab together, he handing her in as correctly as though they were any normal married couple, going visiting together.

But his face was grim, and neither of them spoke for the duration of the short journey.

Mrs Gillies was delighted to see them. She rose to embrace her daughter as the butler showed them into the sitting room, where she had been writing some letters. Though her face puckered with concern the moment Deborah lifted her veil to return her kiss.

'Oh, my word! Whatever has happened to your face?'

'I…'

She had not thought of an excuse. She had not thought beyond getting out and seeing her mother. All she had wanted was to kneel at her feet, lay her head in her lap and sob her heart out.

But at that moment, Susannah bounced into the room.

'Debs!' she cried, going to hug her. 'I have missed you so much these last few days. I am so glad you are come, for I have such news! Oh, good morning, Captain Fawley,' she checked herself, dropping a polite curtsy, before turning back to Deborah.

Robert glowered at her before crossing the room to take a seat beside Mrs Gillies, who had subsided on to a sofa, anxiously plucking at the strings to her lace cap.

It was then that Susannah looked at Deborah properly.

'Whatever has happened?' Impulsively, she reached out to touch the bruises that were leaking from Deborah's eyebrow, down the left side of her face.

'I fell out of a coach,' Deborah said. It was almost the truth—the only part that she felt ready to share on this occasion. 'So silly of me,' she said, settling on to a chair by the fireplace and smoothing down her skirts. 'I would really rather not speak of it.' She raised her head to look directly at Susannah. 'Let me hear your news, instead.'

While Susannah went to her favourite chair by the window, Deborah caught her mother's eye, and gave a tiny shake of her head. Then she shot a meaningful look towards Susannah, who was positioning her chair in the exact spot where the early morning sun would paint highlights in her hair.

'I can quite see why you have claimed to be indisposed for the last few days,' her mother said.

She cleared her throat. 'Naturally, I could not go out while the bruises were at their worst. And I was a little shaken up, to be honest. I would not have come today, were it not for the fact that I shall be travelling down to Wycke tomorrow, and wished to take my leave of you both. I will write, of course, from there.'

Mrs Gillies relaxed immediately, understanding the silent message that her daughter would tell her everything in due course.

'Well, I am glad you came in person. For I should not have liked you to find out my news by means of a letter. I am engaged to be married!' Susannah beamed. 'To Mr Percy Lampton!'

Deborah felt the world tilt on its axis. She dared not look in her husband's direction. What a blow it must be to him, just when he had believed he was on the verge of winning his heart's desire.

'H-how came this about? I thought you had quite despaired of him.'

'Yes, I had,' she admitted, her eyes growing soulful. 'And despair…yes, yes, that is exactly what I suffered. I did not know how I could bear it. But only yesterday he came here, begging leave to speak with me in private. I did not know that I should receive him, but in the end, your mother persuaded me to take a turn about the garden with him.'

Deborah's heart jolted. Could he have proposed, in the garden, in the very spot where Robert had proposed to her?

'Firstly, he begged that I would forgive him for neglecting me for such a long time, after having paid me such particular attention. He explained that, at first, he had only meant to pass some time flirting with the prettiest débutante of the Season. But as time went on, his attraction to me grew so strong that he felt impelled to break off all contact with me, before things went too far. For his family would never agree to him marrying a woman from my background. He knew that he would have to choose between me and his family, should he propose marriage. But in the end, he could stay away no longer. He cannot live without me. There!' she finished, her hands clasped together, her eyes bright with wonder. 'Is that not wonderful?'

'Amazing,' said Deborah weakly, finally darting a concerned look in her husband's direction. His face expressed all the contempt she had known he must feel on hearing such an ingenuous declaration. They both knew why Lampton had begun to flirt with Susannah. And could both guess what he was playing at now.

Hincksey was a dangerous man to cross. He was obviously not going to rest until he recouped Lampton's debts one way or another. He must have realised he had made a grave error in supposing Robert would be a soft target, and decided to lean on Lampton again.

Desperate to find the money to pay the villain off, Lampton must have seen he had no choice but to take advantage of Susannah's infatuation with him. It might mean breaking with his family, but, by the sound of it, the threats Hincksey had used on him had made him fear for his very life. He probably believed he would not live if he could not persuade Susannah to marry him, and thereby gain control of her dowry. It would have given his lying words the very ring of sincerity needed to convince Susannah he was in earnest, especially when he was telling her exactly what she most wanted to hear.

'I do hope you will be happy,' she managed to say, when she could not in all conscience offer very fulsome congratulations.

'Oh, I shall be…' she sighed, a faraway look in her eyes '…for I love Percy so much! We will be married as soon as the banns can be called,' she went on, sitting forward. 'I do hope you will be my maid of honour. Even though you never asked me to be yours,' she added with a touch of reproof.

'I am sure Deborah would be delighted,' Robert put in, rather shocking her. 'You must let us know when and where the wedding is to take place, and she will attend you.'

The rest of the visit was taken up in discussing Susannah's bride clothes, how delighted her parents would be that she had made such a satisfactory match in her very first Season, and whether she should marry in the fashionable St George's Chapel, or in their own parish church at Lower Wakering.

Robert, unsurprisingly, had made no contribution to the conversation. When the time came for them to leave, he could not disguise his relief.

He sank into the seat opposite her in the cab that they hired to take them back to Walton House, looking drained.

In spite of the fact that Deborah had decided she no longer loved him, he looked such a picture of abject misery that her tender heart went out to him.

'I am so sorry,' she said softly, barely restraining herself from reaching out to touch him comfortingly upon his sleeve.

His eyes flew open, catching her in the very act of withdrawing her hand and curling it in her lap.

'What have you to be sorry for?'

'That Percy Lampton is going to marry Susannah after all.'

He frowned at her for a few seconds before saying slowly, 'I do not know why you should think I might be sorry Lampton is marrying her. It was at my suggestion, after all!'

'Y-your suggestion? But you could not want him to…not any man to…' She faltered to a close, completely bewildered by his statement.

'Of course I wanted Lampton to marry Susannah. They deserve each other!' he snapped. 'She is a silly, selfish, shallow creature who only looks upon the outward man, and all he wants is enough money to live in style. He does not care how he acquires it, even to marrying a girl he feels is so far beneath him on the social scale that she is fit only to be his mistress.'

Deborah shook her head. 'I cannot believe…' but suddenly, she saw what had happened. He had fallen out of love with Susannah, just as painfully as she had fallen out of love with him. It seemed that unrequited love was doomed to wither away. It certainly explained the bitterness of the words he had chosen to describe Susannah's character. Had she not cursed him soundly, during her long, lonely, sleepless nights? And as she turned to look out of the window she noticed how many people's faces, as they hurried along the streets, looked strained or downcast. Life, she decided, was a depressing business.

'Can you not believe that I would do anything to keep you safe, Deborah?' he said urgently, leaning towards her.

She turned to him with a start. This was the very last thing she would have expected him to say. Her astonishment must have shown on her face, because he sat back, his own face taking on a sardonic cast.

'No, you cannot believe anything good of me. I do not blame you, I suppose, but this I will tell you. I warned Lampton that if he did not marry Susannah, I would make him pay for putting your life in danger. I only had to discharge my pistol the once, to make him see that it was high time he swallowed his pride. He soon decided he could marry a girl whose money comes from trade, once he understood he had to pay Hincksey what he owed, else face my vengeance. Why should I care how miserable either of them are, so long as I know Hincksey will never have cause to go near you again?'

'Y-you threatened him with a pistol?' Her heart had begun to beat in a strange and irregular rhythm.

'I took Linney with me, naturally,' he sneered. 'I am not up to doing much in the way of intimidation on my own. Even with a brace of pistols. But then, Lampton is not much of a match,' he said bitterly. 'He is only up to bullying and cheating women. Faced with a man, even half a man like myself, he soon showed his true colours.'

'Why, Robert? Why did you insist he marry Susannah? When you could have… Oh!' It would be easier to conduct an affair with a married woman. If they were discreet, Susannah's reputation would not suffer.

'Robert, I am sorry, but I do not think it will work

out for you. Susannah loves Lampton. And she never…that is, she could not…' She shook her head again, unable to tell him, even now, that her friend found him physically repulsive.

Though she had turned to him that night by the fountain. Perhaps that one incident had given him hope that, once she had seen through Lampton, Susannah might be desperate enough to turn to him again.

The cab drew up outside Walton House and a footman hurried to open the door and help her, and her husband, to alight.

They went inside, side by side, to all appearances as though they were any married couple, returning from paying a morning call. Though he looked as though his world was coming to an end, and she felt as though she was bleeding inside.

When they reached the foot of the stairs, he cleared his throat.

'Would you spare me a few moments before you return to your rooms?' he said in a clipped voice. 'There is a matter we need to discuss.'

Her heart sank. There could surely not be anything more to say, could there? Their marriage was over. Did he really think she could sit and discuss it, rationally? Yes, she thought, turning to him with a resigned expression on her face. He still thought this had been just a business arrangement on her part. He still had no idea how she had felt when she had agreed to be his convenient wife.

'Please?'

Her eyes came to rest on his face, flinching at the

look that struck such a chord with her own misery. There was nobody who could understand, better than she, what he was suffering right now at the thought of his beloved giving her heart and her life to another. With a sigh, she nodded her acquiescence.

She took her place on one of the sofas before the empty fireplace, mechanically removing her bonnet and veil, laying them on the cushions beside her, while Robert took the sofa opposite. For some while, he said nothing, though he never took his eyes off her. She had the peculiar impression that he was memorising every facet of her, from the tips of her pale blue kid half-boots to the crown of her head.

When Linney came to ask if she would like some tea, Robert's expression turned downright ferocious.

'I have no wish to discuss the breakdown of my marriage over the teacups as though it was a mere formality!' he roared. 'Make yourself scarce!'

Deborah clasped her hands in her lap, focusing on them through a film of tears as Linney beat a hasty retreat.

Funny, but though she had known he wanted an end to their marriage for days, accepted that it was for the best, because she hated him anyway, she really did....

She sniffed, appalled to find the mist clearing as a single tear brimmed over and rolled down her cheek.

Angrily, she wiped it away with her gloved hand. She was not going to cry in front of him! He was not worth it! If he could toss her aside, and still hanker after Susannah...

To her shock, Robert got up and came to sit beside her. He pressed a handkerchief into her hand.

'Please, do not cry, Deborah. You will be free of me soon, I swear.'

He got up then, and moved away abruptly. 'Forgive me. I know you would not wish to have me anywhere near you.' He paused before the sideboard, pulling the stopper from one of the decanters and twirling it between his fingers, before turning to her with a grave expression on his face.

'You must see that we have things to discuss, before you leave me for ever.'

Deborah put her hand to her temple, where a dull throbbing had begun. Was he talking nonsense, or was she in too much of a state to understand what he was saying?

'I don't see,' she admitted, shaking her head in confusion. 'What are you talking about, Robert? What things must we discuss?'

'Have you not thought that you might be with child?' he blurted out, his face going so pale she thought he might pass out. Indeed, having said the words, he came back to the sofa opposite hers, and sat down rather heavily.

Deborah felt as though he had struck her. He had used her, lied to her, thrown her love back in her face and trampled it underfoot, and now he was turning white about the mouth at the prospect he might have accidentally impregnated her?

She had always borne whatever life had thrown at her with the grace she had been taught a lady should always display. On the very few occasions she had felt her self-control waver, she had walked away from the prospect of confrontation.

But now she felt something inside her snap. She surged to her feet, crossed the narrow space between the two sofas and slapped him hard across the face. Tears were streaming unchecked down her face now, but she was past caring. She stood over him, breathing hard as she struggled to find words to tell him what she thought.

But there were none sufficiently strong to express the scope of her anger, or the depths of her anguish.

She watched as the marks of her fingers blossomed red across his pale features, a stunningly satisfying testament to her physical outburst. And she drew back her arm to hit him again.

This time, he caught her hand in mid-air, the crystal stopper flying from his fingers and shattering against the marble lip of the hearthstone.

So she raised her other hand, clenched it into a fist and flailed out at him wildly. He raised his injured left arm to ward off the blows she rained down on his face and shoulders. But all the while, he was twisting her other arm until he managed to bring her whole body down beside his on the sofa. She slithered across the leather seat in her effort to pull herself away, but he was too strong for her. Catching her round the waist with his left arm, he hauled her up against his chest, and somehow she found she was sitting on his lap, sobbing into his neck, while he held her tightly against his body, her arms clamped to her sides.

Eventually she stopped struggling, and just let the tempest of tears flood out. When the storm passed, she sagged into him, her eyes closed, waiting for his hold on her to slacken, for him to put her away from him.

But he just kept on holding her tightly, his own face pressed to the crown of her head.

Finally, though she kept her eyes closed, her face

pressed into his neck, she drew enough strength from some source deep within herself to say, in a voice that quivered with defiance, 'If I am with child, I at least, shall love it. Even if you won't want to have anything to do with it, or with me....'

'No!' He sat up, and, taking her chin in his hand, so that she had to look into his eyes, said, 'If you are with child, I shall support you through the ordeal of bearing it. In any way I can! You only have to send me word, and I swear, I will do whatever you request of me!'

She frowned, once more puzzled by his words. But she seized on the tiny grain of hope she had gleaned from them.

'If I find out I am pregnant, would you come down to Wycke, then?'

'Of course, if you are sure that is what you want.'

Before she had time to think, she blurted, 'Oh, then I hope I am pregnant.'

He reeled back, an expression of horror on his face.

'You cannot wish that! Deborah, you cannot mean it.'

'Why not?' She sat up straight on his lap, glaring at him. 'What is so bad about wanting to have a baby? Even though you don't love me, surely you want to have children? When you proposed, you promised me—'

'This has nothing to do with love!'

'I know...' she sighed '...I know you only married me to get the money. I have always known that you are in love with Susannah. And, indeed, I—'

'In love with Susannah? Have you run mad? Where on earth did you get such a ridiculous notion?'

Her heart was beating very fast. 'B-but you pursued

her. You kept on begging her to dance with you. You even got her an invitation to Lord Lensborough's ball so she would finally agree….'

His face darkened. 'That was what Lampton assumed too. That was what started this whole cursed train of events. Oh my God,' he breathed, shutting his eyes, and letting his head fall against the back of the sofa. 'How I wish I had not been such a damned fool. Though if I had not…' He stilled, opened his eyes and looked at her with such sorrow she wanted to weep for him.

'I know,' she said, disentangling her hand from his so that she could run her fingers over the weals she had raised on his face, 'you would not have had to watch her fall in love with Lampton….'

He drew in a sharp breath, catching her hand in his own and holding it so tightly it almost hurt.

'I can see the only way I am going to make you believe I care nothing for Miss Hullworthy is to confess the whole. Though it makes me ashamed to admit how low I sank.' He bowed his head, pressing his mouth to her palm, the slightest quiver going through his shoulders as he breathed in deeply.

'Though what have I got to lose?' he said bitterly, lowering her hand to her lap. 'You already hate me.'

She halted on the verge of agreeing with him. Could she really sit on the lap of a man she hated, her arm about his neck, hoping and praying he would not tell her to get to her own sofa, and leave him in peace? She had told herself she hated him, had even physically attacked him, and yet, when she had glimpsed one way of avoiding a separation, she had begged him to go to

Wycke with her. That was not hatred. Her stomach seemed to turn over. It was very far from being hatred.

'I first ran across Miss Hullworthy when I was searching for a man who was causing trouble for Lensborough's fiancée. I had picked up his trail, and was looking for someone who could help me run him to ground. The first time she caught sight of me, she…' he grimaced '…shuddered. By that time, I thought I had grown hardened to causing pretty women to feel nauseous. Indeed, Heloise had assured me that my scarring was so much less than when she had first met me…but then Miss Hullworthy turned up her pretty little nose at me, and I…I am ashamed to admit this, I decided to teach her a lesson.'

Deborah cast her mind back to the way he had behaved in those days, her brow furrowing in perplexity.

'I could see how uncomfortable my presence made her feel. And so I made it my business to leap out at her, at every event I could find out she attended, just to spoil her evening! She sank even lower in my esteem when I perceived that if I had a title, or money, she would have overcome her disgust at my appearance, and positively fawned over me.'

Deborah could not argue with that statement. It was an aspect to Susannah's character she had disliked very much herself.

'So I held out the lure of an invitation to the most exclusive event of the season thus far. Lensborough's ball. And she behaved exactly as I had known she would. With the soul of a whore, she put aside her natural inclination and sold herself to me for the space of a half an hour.'

'No…you have misjudged her!' She could perhaps understand why Robert felt so bitter, but he was wrong about Susannah. 'She is just a bit spoilt, and rather silly, that is all. She got carried away with the idea of marrying well, at first, but she soon saw it was wrong to pursue a man only for his title. Lampton has no title. And she has agreed to marry him. She loves him!'

Robert made a sound that expressed his disgust at that statement. 'She does not know the meaning of the word. She is just dazzled by his looks and superficial charm. She knows nothing of him at all. But that is beside the point.' He shifted, taking her firmly round the hips and pushing her off his lap, though she derived some comfort from the fact that he placed her on the cushions beside him, rather than tossing her on to the floor, as she had half-expected he might wish to do at one point.

'It gets worse,' he said grimly, looking down at his boots, rather than at her. 'I made her the object of a wager. I bet Lensborough that I could get the prettiest débutante of the Season to grovel to me, though the very sight of me made her feel ill…' He ran his fingers through his hair, an expression of contempt on his face.

'I never cared for Susannah,' he confessed rawly. 'Not in the least. But because of that wager, Lampton set out in pursuit of her, thinking I was about to propose!' He laughed bitterly then, shaking his head at the absurdity of it all. 'I never had any intention of marrying her.'

He raised his head to look at her, as he said, 'The only woman I have ever wanted to marry is you.'

He got to his feet then, and paced away from her.

'God, what a mess.'

Deborah looked at the stiff set of his shoulders, the misery that had been a constant burden for so long lifting somewhat as she repeated, 'You wanted to marry me?' But she would not jump to conclusions. 'To get the money Miss Lampton had left you in her will. And to get revenge on Lampton for stealing Susannah from you....'

He whirled round, his expression so fierce it would have scared her had he looked at her like that earlier in the day, when she had still believed he was in love with Susannah.

'I did not consider he had stolen Susannah from me! It had nothing to do with her! Or, at least, very little. It was my past! My childhood. My God, Deborah, have you no idea how much I hate the Lamptons? Once I learned I could do him a bad turn, I did not care who I had to use, I wanted to hurt him! To avenge my mother, if nothing else! The Lamptons killed her, do you know that? Turning her out of her home, insinuating I was not my father's child, refusing to let her see Charles, who she thought of as a son...' His whole body was quivering with rage. 'And so I used you. I bullied you into marrying me, promising you a secure financial future, and children, without sparing one thought for what it would do to you.'

He marched back to the sofa, leaning on the back and gripping it tightly, his face a mask of grief as he said, 'And because of my selfishness, my desire for revenge, you got caught up in the feud, and those men took you, and hurt you...' With a hand that shook, he traced the fading bruises on her cheek, the scar on her lip.

'Raped you. And might have got you with child….'

She gasped. 'Nobody raped me!'

'But the bruises on your neck…your dress was torn…'

'You thought I had been raped?' she asked, shaking her head in disbelief. Instead of trying to comfort her, he had kept as far from her as possible. Had even decided to banish her to the country.

'You were wrong,' she informed him in a flat voice. 'My dress got torn when they hauled me out of the cab. They split my lip to teach me a lesson for trying to think I could escape. And my neck got bruised when they held me down to cut off a lock of my hair to send to you.'

'But Heloise said you burnt all your clothes. She said you would never feel clean again. I thought—'

'Yes, you have told me what you thought,' she said bitterly. 'I burnt my clothes because I was afraid I might have brought fleas into the house. And you would feel dirty if you had spent a couple of days sleeping in your clothes, in a filthy cell, with nothing but ale to wash in! I stank like a brewery!'

He came round the sofa then, intent on taking her hand. 'They did not rape you. Thank God….'

But she leapt to her feet, backing away from him. 'What kind of man are you? You can hold my hand now, when you know I have not been defiled, but when I needed you, when I woke in the night shivering with fear, where were you then, Robert?'

She was shaking with the force of her anger and disappointment. Every time she felt as though there might be a chance for them, he slammed the door on her hope yet again.

'I thought you would not want me near!' he protested. 'Not after that last time, when you ran out on me. Not that I blame you, but don't you think I noticed how you flinched every time I got anywhere near you, after that?'

She realised she was standing with her fists clenched at her sides, slightly crouching as though she was preparing to spring at him. She made herself straighten up, and uncurl her hands, before hissing, 'After you called me a slut, you mean?'

He took a deep breath. 'I was so angry with you, Deborah, after the picnic. I had been watching you all day, trying to see which of my so-called friends it was you were planning on cuckolding me with!'

Hope flickered and died. Wearily, she went to pick up her bonnet.

'You do not know me at all, do you, Robert? From the very first time you asked me to marry you, you have done nothing but insult me.'

'I know.' He drew himself upright, standing ramrod straight as she made her way towards the door. 'You deserve better. It is why I am letting you go.'

'Letting me go?' She let go of the door handle, and turned to him with renewed anger. 'You are sending me away. You have decided, for whatever reason, you can no longer bother with the pretence of wishing to be my husband, and so you hide behind all these pathetic excuses!'

She marched back to him, her eyes blazing with a fury that she no longer had any intention of trying to control.

'For once in your life, Robert, why don't you admit the truth!'

'The truth?' he said. 'The truth is that once you have left me, I shall feel as though my heart has been ripped out. I don't know how I will survive it, but for your sake, I know I must. It is the only thing I can do for you....'

His heart would be ripped out? Her own heart gave a lurch as one or two of the comments he had made earlier, which had so confused her, came to mind. He had spoken of threatening Lampton with a pistol, so that she would be safe from Hincksey. He had denied loving Susannah, vehemently, declaring she was the only woman he had ever wanted to marry. She remembered the almost defiant nature of that proposal, his certainty that any sane woman would refuse it. And suddenly, everything seemed to fall into place.

'You really are the stupidest, most self-absorbed man I have ever met,' she said rather shakily.

'Yes,' he admitted bleakly. 'I have done everything wrong where you are concerned.'

'I, too, have been remiss,' she said thoughtfully. She should have told him she loved him right from the start. And then shown him, day by day, that she meant it. It would have saved them both so much pain. 'In not telling you that I love you.'

'You cannot!'

'That is what I have been trying to tell myself, but, sadly, it is the truth.'

He made an angry, slashing gesture at himself. 'No woman could look at this and love this!'

'Do you know,' she said, placing her bonnet carefully on the table, 'the first time I saw you, at Mrs Moulton's card party, you never even noticed me? You walked in through the door, and immediately, all the other people there seemed to me like actors upon a stage. You were the only real person in the room. You were so vibrant, so alive, in your uniform, standing there, scanning the room like a man on a mission. I think I lost my heart to you in that moment.'

'Mrs Moulton's card party?' He looked bewildered.

She began to draw off her gloves, noting with feminine satisfaction that his eyes were riveted upon her actions, 'Your eyes slid straight over me as though I did not exist, but they snagged on Susannah, and stayed there. You looked at her the way all men do. Up and down her body, and then up to her face again, and then you sort of half-smiled.' She reached up to caress his face. 'Just a half-smile, the way you do. And that was when I noticed you had a few scars.'

'A few scars!' He flinched away from her hand. 'My face is a ruin!'

She nodded. 'A ruin of what it once was, perhaps. You must have been excessively handsome before you got burned. Probably too handsome for your own good.'

He stared at her as though she was out of her mind.

'I saw you on three more occasions before you spoke to me. At the theatre, at the Farringdons', and once, riding in the park, one morning, very early. It was not until you began to pursue Susannah, and got right up close, that I realised just how badly injured you were. And by then, all I could do was marvel at how well you concealed the fact.' She tilted her head to one side, running her eyes over his whole frame. 'When you wear your uniform, with those boots, it is almost impossible to tell that you have lost your left foot. You know, you are far more aware of your injuries than other people are. Certainly all I saw, in those days, whenever you came up to ask Susannah to dance, was the most attractive man I had ever met.'

'You…found me attractive?' He was leaning back against the arm of the sofa now, his breathing laboured. 'You lost your heart to me?' he said, as though her earlier declaration had finally sunk in.

'Why are you saying this?' His face flushed an angry red. He shook his head. 'You cannot have done. It is impossible.'

She shrugged. 'That was what I kept trying to tell myself. I knew a man as experienced, as sophisticated, as you would never look twice at a drab little provincial girl, scarcely out of the schoolroom, and that I must not let the infatuation grow any deeper. But I could not stop myself. And when you proposed…' her eyes were shining as she thought back to that day '…it was as though all my dreams had come true.'

'I am no woman's dream,' he persisted. 'More like a nightmare. Deborah, I do not understand why you persist in saying these things—?'

'Because it is the truth, you idiot,' she said rather sharply. 'Though heaven alone knows why I still love you. When you have been at such pains, right from the very first, to let me know how very little you think of me.'

'That is not true! At least, I may have led you to believe it, with the abominable way I have treated you, but it is not because I have no regard for you. I hold you in the very highest esteem. I have always known you are much too good for me, Deborah. You always looked so wholesome, so untouched, when my life has been tainted from the very start.'

'So you fought any tender feelings you began to have, and went out of your way to demonstrate you could do very well without me.'

'Yes,' he confessed, looking rather stunned. 'That is exactly what I did.'

'When did you…?' She cleared her throat, turned red, and looked down at her hands, which she clasped at her waist. 'When did you realise you loved me, Robert?'

Her voice was barely more than a whisper.

He pushed himself off the sofa, and gently took a lock of her hair in his fingers. 'When Linney opened that package Hincksey sent me, and your bloodstained glove tumbled out. I knew that then if I could not get you back, my life would no longer be worth living. I would gladly have given my entire fortune to ensure your release.'

She heaved a tremulous sigh of relief. It had been a gamble to try to goad him into confessing to a love she had still not been entirely convinced he felt. But he had confirmed it.

'So, why did you come and rescue me instead,' she asked, gazing up at him shyly, 'and make Lampton marry Susannah so he could pay himself?'

'Damn Lampton. It has nothing to do with Lampton. I just could not bear to think of you alone, afraid and possibly injured. I could not sit back and wait to receive a ransom note. I had to find you and bring you home. Deborah,' he breathed, pulling her into his arms at last,

'Deborah, do you really think you love me? Even after all I have done?'

She nodded, flinging her arms about his waist and hugging him back for all she was worth.

'I still do not understand how you can. It is not just the way I look. The man I am inside is as scarred and crippled as what the world can see of me.' He put her from him so that he could look down into her upraised face. 'I was weaned on hatred. I have drawn strength from bitterness for so long that it has made me cruel....'

'But you will not be cruel to me, ever again, will you? Not now you have finally let love into your heart.'

'You think my loving you will somehow make me a better man?' He smiled sadly. 'Deborah, you are so naïve, so innocent....'

'Not so innocent as when I first met you,' she declared. 'Loving you has changed me. And if love can change me, it can change you too.' She took his face between her hands and, looking deeply into his eyes, said, 'Robert, I am never going to back down again, or let your foolish pride stand between us. I am going to love you with every fibre of my being, until you believe you are worthy of being loved. And you are going to stop being afraid loving me will somehow make you weak. You will love me back, and the combined force of our love will wash clean all the bitterness that has eaten away at your soul—'

'Deborah,' he groaned, stopping her mouth with a kiss. 'If any woman could work such a miracle, that woman would be you. But what have I to give you, in return for all your self-sacrifice?'

'Children,' she replied without a moment's hesitation, deciding to ignore his reference to self-sacrifice. It would take time to rid his mind of such nonsensical notions, not arguments. With a determined expression on her face, she unbuttoned his jacket.

'I want your children,' she said, going to work on his waistcoat buttons. 'At least two boys and two girls.'

'I was thinking more in terms of jewels or carriages,' he riposted faintly, as she ruthlessly dealt with his neckcloth.

She shook her head. 'I want a tree house and a swing.'

'Tree house it is,' he gulped, as her hands descended to the fall of his breeches. 'For those sons you want so badly,' he groaned, a sheen of perspiration breaking out on his brow.

'For our daughters!' she protested, tipping him back on to the sofa. As he fell, he just managed to summon the presence of mind to pull her down with him.

'Ah, yes, for a minute I forgot.' And for another minute, no more was said, as they found another, and entirely more pleasurable, way of occupying their mouths.

'Their education,' he gasped, as Deborah reached down to tug her skirts out of the way, 'is to be of an exceedingly liberal nature, as I recall.'

'Equality,' she stated firmly, as he, too, reached down between their bodies. 'It is very important between the sexes. Females have as much right to…education and… tree houses…and… Oh…and…'

'Pleasure?' he groaned, as he finally slid into her.

'Oh, yes,' she agreed. 'Yes!' Though she had completely forgotten what they had been talking about. 'Oh,

Robert, I do love you so,' she cried, exulting in the freedom to be able to say it aloud at last. 'I love you!'

'I love you too,' he admitted, looking up into her gloriously flushed face. And discovered that surrendering was not an admission of weakness. Not in this case. This merging of two bodies, two hearts, two lives, was forging something stronger.

He was not alone any more, fighting for his place in the world.

As a couple, they would be strong enough to take on the whole world, should it prove necessary.

He had someone, at last, to whom he belonged as completely as she belonged to him.

His woman.

* * * * *

REGENCY

Collection

*Let these sparklingly seductive delights whirl
you away to the ballrooms—and
bedrooms—of Polite Society!*

Volume 1 – 4th February 2011
Regency Pleasures by Louise Allen

Volume 2 – 4th March 2011
Regency Secrets by Julia Justiss

Volume 3 – 1st April 2011
Regency Rumours by Juliet Landon

Volume 4 – 6th May 2011
Regency Redemption by Christine Merrill

Volume 5 – 3rd June 2011
Regency Debutantes by Margaret McPhee

Volume 6 – 1st July 2011
Regency Improprieties by Diane Gaston

12 volumes in all to collect!

www.millsandboon.co.uk

REGENCY
Collection

*Let these sparklingly seductive delights whirl
you away to the ballrooms—and
bedrooms—of Polite Society!*

Volume 7 – 5th August 2011
Regency Mistresses by Mary Brendan

Volume 8 – 2nd September 2011
Regency Rebels by Deb Marlowe

Volume 9 – 7th October 2011
Regency Scandals by Sophia James

Volume 10 – 4th November 2011
Regency Marriages by Elizabeth Rolls

Volume 11 – 2nd December 2011
Regency Innocents by Annie Burrows

Volume 12 – 6th January 2012
Regency Sins by Bronwyn Scott

12 volumes in all to collect!

MILLS
BOON

www.millsandboon.co.uk

"To say that I met Nicholas Brisbane over my husband's dead body is not entirely accurate. Edward, it should be noted, was still twitching upon the floor…"

London, 1886

For Lady Julia Grey, her husband's sudden death at a dinner party is extremely inconvenient. However, things worsen when inscrutable private investigator Nicholas Brisbane reveals that the death was not due to natural causes.

Drawn away from her comfortable, conventional life, Julia is exposed to threatening notes, secret societies and gypsy curses, not to mention Nicholas's charismatic unpredictability.

www.mirabooks.co.uk

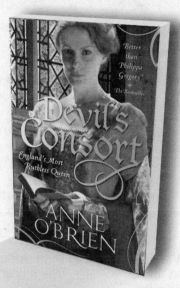